RT BOOK ... ...DAY
E...
CONSTANCE O'BANYON!

DESERT PRINCE

"In the hands of O'Banyon, ancient history comes alive in this fourth book set in Egypt during the rule of the powerful Roman Caesars."

DAUGHTER OF EGYPT

"The heroine is a smart, strong woman, a perfect match for the warrior hero. Their sexual tension permeates the novel, and the culmination of their love is hot and sweet."

SWORD OF ROME

"O'Banyon continues the tale she began in *Lord of the Nile* by introducing Adhaniá. The historical facts are intriguing, and the effort of the characters to foil the plot against Caesar is heartwarming. The sensual scenes are sparse but tender and hot."

LORD OF THE NILE

"Fans of Egyptian lore and facts will find O'Banyon's historical right up their alley. She sprinkles political intrigue and love throughout the pages of this enjoyable book."

HAWK'S PURSUIT

"O'Banyon's third book in her Hawk series is possibly the best yet, with a regular little spitfire heroine, great verbal sparring and some very emotional scenes."

THE DANCE

"You win, Brittany," he said in a voice of agony. "You have accomplished your purpose." He moved his hand up to tangle in her dark hair, and there was no softness in his eyes. "Your body promises—how did you put it—a thousand delights? I am ready to take pleasure with you."

Her eyes widened with innocence, and she had a ready answer for him. "But you have mistaken me, Captain. I wanted merely to dance for you. Did you not find the dance to your liking?"

His blue eyes seemed to burn into her. "You know I did. You deliberately tormented me." His hand moved to cup her face. "Let us be done with games of pretense. I only want what you have given Lord Simjin—and I intend to have you."

She tried to move away from him, but he held her tight. "You must go now, Captain. My dance was a gift to you. I have nothing more to offer you."

His hands slid up to caress her breast and she felt a warmth of pleasure spread throughout her whole body. "We both know this is what you want, Brittany. We have known it for a long time." His voice deepened. "I can no longer deny there is desire between us—why should you?"

"No, Captain, you misunderstand me. I only wanted to . . . to—"

He placed his finger over he lips to silence her. "You have given me your gift, now it is time for me to give you mine, little dancer."

He lowered his head and she knew he was going to kiss her.

"You have asked for this, Brittany, and by God you are going to get it . . ."

Constance O'Banyon

Enchantress

LEISURE BOOKS NEW YORK CITY

A LEISURE BOOK®

January 2010

Published by

Dorchester Publishing Co., Inc.
200 Madison Avenue
New York, NY 10016

ISBN 10: 0-8439-6373-5
ISBN 13: 978-0-8439-6373-1
E-ISBN: 978-1-4285-0796-8

Visit us online at www.dorchesterpub.com.

Rick, you have proven that with courage, climbing the highest mountains in life can be as simple as climbing the smallest hills. Keep climbing, my son, and I will try to keep up with you.

Enchantress

Part One

The English Rose

Daughter Of The English Rose

In the shadow of your smile, I see the whisper of another.

The image of the daughter, hence reflections of the mother.

So like a rose is the maiden fair, so like the sun is her golden hair.

So deep the hurt when betrayal is supposed.

So sweet are your dreams, lovely daughter of the English Rose.

—Constance O'Banyon

Chapter One

1790

The heavy pounding on her door caused Jillianna Sinclair to stir from a restless sleep.

"Madame, madame, it is the captain's orders that I speak to you at once!"

Jillianna slipped off the small bunk and pulled on her dressing robe, trying to shake off a sleep-drugged state. It took her a moment to remember that she was not in Philadelphia, but on board the American ship, *Scarborough*, and that the urgent voice she heard was that of the first mate.

With trepidation, she opened the cabin door and stared at Mr. Carver in confusion. "Yes, what is it you want, Mr. Carver?"

The man's eyes moved from her to Mrs. Franklin and her daughter, Linda, who had come into the companionway and were watching with open curiosity.

Mr. Carver motioned for the Franklin women to come forward to hear what he had to say. "Since you three are the only ladies on board, the captain has requested that you remain in your cabins. No matter what you hear, do not come out."

Mrs. Franklin, a woman who was accustomed to asking questions and receiving answers, was the first to speak. "My good man," she said haughtily, "my daughter and I could not possibly adhere to such an order without first knowing the reason for it. Why should Captain Stark make such an outrageous request?"

The first mate shifted his weight uncomfortably, as if he were unwilling to answer her question. After staring into the woman's determined brown eyes, he reluctantly decided to tell the truth.

"Late last night we sighted the sails of two ships. This morning the ships were spotted just off our starboard. They have now been identified. They belong to . . . an unsavory bunch of pirates. It is apparent they are making ready for battle."

Now Mrs. Franklin was not so vocal, and she retreated a step toward her cabin, as if she had been dealt a blow.

Jillianna's face whitened, for she had heard horrible tales of pirates and cutthroats who preyed upon unsuspecting vessels at sea. "What are you saying, Mr. Carver?" Jillianna asked, noting the disbelief in Linda's eyes.

Mr. Carver was not at all happy that the task of informing the ladies of the impending danger had fallen to him. "Well, ladies . . ." he began hesitantly, "I know no way to say it other than just to come out with it. You'll know soon enough anyway. The captain figures there is no way we can avoid a confrontation with the pirates. He wants to be assured of your safety, so you must promise to remain in your cabins until you are informed that it is safe to come out."

Linda Franklin, who was no more than fifteen years old, gasped, and moved closer to her mother. "What will happen to us?" she cried. "If the pirates have two ships, and we are but one, surely we cannot win."

The first mate tried to appear calm and assured. "I will not lie to you, for there will surely be an encounter. But feel confident, Miss Franklin, that every man on board this vessel will have your safety in mind when we go into battle. So I beg you to remain in your cabins, where you will be the least affected by what occurs."

Before Jillianna could voice the many questions that came to her mind, the first mate turned away and moved back down the corridor. She knew, as he did, that they would be outgunned and outmanned. Surely the *Scarborough* was doomed!

Mrs. Franklin pushed her daughter back into their cabin,

and turned to Jillianna. "If you know what's good for you, you will not allow the pirates to take you alive." Her eyes darkened. "I do not intend for them to get their hands on my daughter, if you know what I mean." She showed Jillianna a small derringer, which she quickly hid in her bodice. "You'd better think about the inevitable yourself," Mrs. Franklin warned. "Be prepared."

Jillianna shuddered, knowing very well that Mrs. Franklin intended to shoot her daughter rather than allow her to fall into the hands of the pirates.

The elder woman moved quickly into her cabin, and Jillianna watched as she closed the door. When Jillianna heard the bolt slide into place, she panicked, for she had never felt so alone and frightened. She wished that Mrs. Franklin had invited her to stay with her and her daughter. Now Jillianna would have to wait alone for the approaching battle.

She moved reluctantly into her cabin, wondering how she could have come to such a sad ending. At nineteen, she was a widow and was expecting her first child in four months. Fate had cast her upon this uncertain sea, and she could see no way for it to end but in tragedy.

Jillianna sank down upon her bunk, staring at the overhead beams, while a feeling of helplessness washed over her. The situation seemed almost dreamlike, with no place in her practical mind. Had she lived her whole life only to die alone, with no one to mourn her death?

All at once cannon fire erupted, and Jillianna jumped off the bunk to cringe in a corner as the sounds of battle heated up above deck.

She did not know how long she remained cowering in the shadows, jumping with fear each time she heard the roar of cannon and the splintering of wood. But, in the course of battle, the sun had risen high in the sky and was now dipping in the west. She clamped her hands over her ears to shut out the sound of agonizing screams of pain.

All at once there was a great explosion that rocked the

ship, and the force of the impact threw Jillianna to the floor. With fear ruling her movements, she ran to the door, fumbling with the latch before finally tearing it open. She stared in sick horror when she saw that the last explosion had ripped a gaping hole where the Franklin cabin had been!

Jillianna cried out in agony as she realized Mrs. Franklin did not have to worry about her daughter falling into enemy hands. They both had been victims of the cannon blast. There was no sign of them—nothing left. She covered her face with trembling hands, feeling grief for the two women she had hardly known.

Jillianna had no time to reflect on the grim fate of the others, because fire now engulfed the overhead timbers and was spreading quickly in her direction. She ran down the corridor, trying to escape the advancing inferno that by now had engulfed her own cabin.

Panic ruled her thinking when she approached the companionway and heard the sound of hand-to-hand combat on deck. She paused, weighing her chances above deck as opposed to the fire that crackled just behind her. Now the heat of the fire was closing in around her, and she could scarcely breathe because of the smoke. It took her only a moment to make her decision. Gathering up her skirt, Jillianna rushed onto the deck.

The sight that met her eyes was more horrible than she could have imagined. A yellow sulphur cloud hovered over the deck of the *Scarborough*, and the unmoving air was filled with the acrid smell of cannon smoke. The sounds of battle, metal clashing against metal, and men dying, filled her with horror. The American ship was listing and taking on water. It was apparent that the ship was sinking, but still her courageous captain and crew fought on against the constant stream of pirates that surged on board the crippled vessel.

The sight of so much blood made Jillianna's heart ache, and she had to fight against the nausea that tightened her stomach. The dead and dying were strewn like lifeless dolls among the debris of a broken mast and tangled ropes and canvas. Now the advancing flames leaped high into the air, hungrily devouring the *Scarborough*.

It occurred to Jillianna that today would be her last day on earth. Suddenly she thought of her unborn baby and felt a heavy hand of sorrow descending on her like a dark cloud. Her baby would die before ever having drawn the breath of life into its lungs.

Trapped between the raging fire that was growing in intensity, and the fierce battle that was taking place in front of her, Jillianna flattened her body against the steps leading to the foredeck, her whole body trembling with panic.

Her eyes moved hesitantly over the faces of the pirates. While the crew members of the American ship were dressed in sober blue, the pirates wore ostentatious colors of crimson, yellow, and purple. The enemy were dark-skinned and dirty, and most of them had mustaches and long, unkempt beards.

Jillianna did not hear the man who swooped out of the shadows toward her. She felt strong hands pull her forward, and she was immediately clasped to a smelly body.

A scream escaped her lips as she was tossed over the pirate's shoulder and carried away. She felt him leap from the deck of the *Scarborough*, to land with a thud on board the victorious vessel.

Jillianna had no time to ponder her fate, as she was thrust at a burly man who was issued orders in a guttural language she did not understand. She was pulled forward roughly, and she could see it was the pirate's intention to take her below deck. With one last glance at the *Scarborough*, Jillianna knew no one would be alive to rescue her. The crippled ship was now engulfed in flames, and it was uncertain whether it would first sink or be destroyed by the fire.

She was led down rickety steps to a darkness where she could scarcely breathe because of the repugnant odor of unwashed bodies and unmentionable filth that assaulted her nostrils.

Too frightened to disobey, she followed the man without

protest. When they had reached what she was sure had to be the bowels of the ship, the man unlocked a cell and roughly pushed her inside. Her whole body quaked with fear as he pointed a pudgy finger at her and uttered words she did not understand. She cringed in the corner while he locked the door, almost glad to be out of his frightening presence.

When her eyes became accustomed to the waning light, she was better able to see the cell. She trembled in fear when she saw the chains that were attached to the walls. At least she had been spared the indignity of being chained like an animal. There was straw strewn on floors, and several tattered straw mattresses were stacked in a corner. She shuddered, thinking the whole cell was probably bug infested.

Jillianna would not allow herself to think about what would happen to her, or she would lose the thin thread of sanity that she still clung to.

Now silence encroached, and it was even more ominous than the sounds of battle. The grief she felt for the passengers and crew of the *Scarborough* was almost unbearable. Slowly she sunk to the floor, wishing she had been allowed to perish with her companions. She feared a far worse fate than death awaited her and her unborn child at the hands of these loathsome pirates!

Jillianna had not intended to fall asleep, but the ordeal had exhausted her, and she sat down with her back to the wall and closed her eyes, soon drifting off into oblivion.

She had no way of knowing how long she had slept, but she quickly awoke, becoming alert when she heard the sounds of voices followed by the grating of a key in the lock.

She rose on shaky legs as several men approached her. One man caught her attention. From his cavalier manner and his voice of authority, she knew he was the captain. He wore a black, plumed hat and black trousers and shirt. He was not much taller than Jillianna, but he was wide of girth. Everything about him was dark: his complexion, his clothing, his eyes and hair.

While one of his companions held a torch, the captain's small black eyes ran the length of Jillianna's body. The man's lips tightened when he saw that his captive was with child. Turning to the man beside him, he growled something in anger before turning his attention back to Jillianna.

When he noted how lovely her features were, a wide smile eased the man's grim expression. Though heavily accented, his English was clipped and distinctive. "I am Captain Bijapur. Who are you?"

When she made no reply, he continued. "Forgive us, madame, for subjecting you to this cruel cell." He shook his head. "My men are fools to have placed a woman of your delicacy and beauty in this pigsty." He took in the cell with a wave of his hand. "I will see that you are immediately placed in a cabin where you will be offered every comfort."

Jillianna feared what he might have in mind for her and much preferred to remain in this cell. "I would as soon stay here, Captain," she said in a trembling voice. "I have no objections to this cell."

Captain Bijapur's eyes became hard. "No, you will not stay here, madame," he said harshly. "You are a very beautiful woman, and it would not be wise to leave you to the mercy of my men, for they seldom see a woman with your obvious charms." An evil smile did nothing to soften his dark features. "You will be under my protection."

Jillianna turned her face away in disgust. If this loathsome man had any plans for her, she would much prefer death.

Captain Bijapur snapped his fingers, bringing an immediate response from his men. One of them led Jillianna forward. So great was her fear that it was all she could do to bear her own weight. Once they were in the corridor, the men fell behind while the captain walked beside her.

She was led past several cells, and although she could not see the occupants, she could hear moaning and crying. Apparently, she was not the only prisoner who had been brought aboard.

She was led up the steps until the captain stopped before

a door. Once they were inside the cabin, the captain motioned for the others to leave. When Jillianna and Captain Bijapur were alone, his eyes moved over her from head to foot.

"Yes . . . you are a beauty," he said caressingly. His hands reached out and touched her golden hair. "An extraordinary beauty."

She pulled away from him and dared to ask the question that had been hammering at her mind. "What are you going to do with me?"

His eyes gleamed, as if he took pleasure in her anxiety. "You will be taken to Constantinople and placed on the block where you will be sold to whoever pays the highest price for you."

She gasped and backed away from him. "You are a monster," she whispered in fear and disgust. "How can you be so vile a creature?"

He shrugged. "Your opinion of me is of no importance. You are merely a beautiful woman who will bring me a good price at the slave market."

"What about the other prisoners?"

Again he shrugged sardonically. "You were the only survivor from the American ship."

"But I heard others in the cells."

"Merely two of my men who disobeyed orders." He fingered his beard. "I do not tolerate disobedience from anyone."

When he saw the color drain from her face, he laughed, and the sinister sound set her to trembling anew. "It is such a pity that you are no longer a virgin, or I could get twice the price for you."

Before she could protest, he pulled her to him and smiled, his rank breath fanning her face. "Still, you will delight the bed of a great man. Who knows—perhaps even the sultan will take a fancy to you."

She turned away from him and closed her eyes against the gleam of evil she saw in his eyes.

"Madame, if it were not for the child you carry, I myself would like to test the joys of your body. Perhaps even with the child, you would delight me."

For a long moment his words hung in the air as he waited for her reaction to his lewd suggestion. When she failed to react, he released her and moved to the door.

"Have no fear that you will be ravished by me, madame. A cold-blooded woman does not warm a man's bed. Look to your health, and do as you are bid, and you will be well treated. I want you looking healthy and beautiful when I place you on the slave block at Constantinople."

The hateful man moved quickly out the door, and when it had been secured behind him, Jillianna slid to the floor in a dead faint.

It was much later when Jillianna regained consciousness. The lantern had burned out and the cabin was in darkness. She felt around until she discovered the small bunk. Uncaring that it was filthy, she pulled herself up and fell forward, burying her head on the stiff mattress, where she lost herself in the misery of tears.

Through the endless night, she shed tears of grief. There was no hope for her—no one to come to her rescue and no one to care about what had happened to her.

At last her tears were spent, and she pondered this bizarre turn her life had taken. She had never had a happy life, but now she dared not even think about what awaited her and her unborn baby once they reached Constantinople!

Chapter Two

Constantinople

The queen of cities stood in multicolored splendor among her seven lofty hills, with a skyline dominated by spirals and domes of ancient mosques and palaces. Constantinople was the place where Europe met Asia, and it was considered by many to be the shining jewel of this ancient land. The city itself was sprawling, and flanked on one side by the Sea of Marmara, which was accessible only through The Golden Horn, an inlet some four miles long.

Mysterious women, with their features hidden behind thin veils, tread the twisting clay streets. Donkey carts stirred up dust which went unnoticed by the press of humanity that meandered through crowded shops and bazaars.

A donkey-drawn cart, transporting Jillianna and three other women, wound its way through the narrow streets. Two guards marched along beside the cart, while it rolled almost unnoticed through the crowded streets.

Jillianna took little interest in her surroundings because she was frightened, as well as humiliated by the sheerness of the costume she wore. She had been oiled, perfumed, and dressed in layers of lavender gauze, which did little to hide her nakedness. She was thankful for the veil that covered her face and hid her shame.

She stared at the city that was sprawled over the hills and spread down to the water's edge, trying not to dwell on what awaited her on the slave block. Her gaze shifted to the imposing Blue Mosque, which rose upward as if reaching for a piece of the blue sky. She caught a glimpse of a Gypsy in colorful dress, who prodded his dancing bear into action for the crowd's amusement. A dwarf was doing handsprings to draw attention to himself, while a blind beggar moved with amazing agility through the throng of humanity. A rug peddler displayed his handwoven rugs, while carts and peddlers moved slowly through the dusty streets.

Miraculously, Jillianna had not been ill-treated, either on the pirate ship or after the ship had docked. She had been taken by a stern-faced woman to a house near the Grand Bazaar, where she had been held captive for two weeks, seeing no one but the woman who brought her meals.

Then this morning two dark-skinned women had bathed and dressed her, taking great pains with her appearance. Jillianna had been frustrated because no one seemed to speak English, or else they had been instructed not to answer her questions. She had not known what was happening to her until she had been chained to the three other women in the donkey cart.

She glanced up at the burning sun overhead, gauging it to be near the noon hour. How strange it was that time had ceased to have any meaning for her. She had lived with fear for so long that she doubted anything would frighten her now—or so she thought.

The cart halted before enormous wooden gates, and one of the guards called out for admittance. As the gates swung open, Jillianna saw the colonnaded courtyard, which was flanked by several long chambers filled with women in chains. She did not have to be told that this was the slave market.

In shock, she watched the tall platform, where several black-skinned women were being led forward in chains. As they were poked and prodded and intimately examined, Jillianna felt their shame in the very depths of her heart, for she guessed it would soon be her turn to suffer the same indignities on the slave block.

Jillianna and her companions were herded into a long room by silent guards. A tall, slender man came forward, slapping the handle of a whip against the palm of his hand, his eyes moving over the four women who had just arrived. With a curt nod, he dismissed the men who had delivered Jillianna, then looked at her with interest. The slender man motioned with the tip of his whip to indicate that Jillianna was to be unchained from her three companions.

She was led into a small private chamber, where golden chains were clamped on her wrists. She was then led to an alcove and instructed to sit on one of the satin cushions, while a tall Nubian fanned her with a peacock feather.

Jillianna felt sick inside. What was to become of her? She clasped her hands together tightly, wishing she could still their trembling. Today she would be paraded before gawking heathens and sold like an animal.

A frightened gasp escaped her lips when a shadow fell across her face. Glancing up, she saw a woman with cruel, black eyes standing before her. She looked down her slender nose at Jillianna.

"You are the American?" she inquired.

"No, not American." A slight tremor shook Jillianna's voice. "I am English by birth."

"Ah, even better, madame. The Circassian girls go at a great price, but an English rose will bring even more." She shook her head. "Of course, there is your unborn child to consider. It may be that we shall have to rid you of that nuisance. Then perhaps the sultan himself will have an interest in you."

Jillianna cringed. "What do you mean? I will not give up my baby, and it will not be born for three more months."

"Do not worry, Englishwoman. I have ways to rid you of the child with little danger to yourself—and no scarring."

Tears swam in Jillianna's eyes, and her hand went down to rest on her rounded stomach. "You cannot force me to give up my child."

The woman's eyes hardened. "If it comes to that, you will have no say in the matter. Come," she said, pulling on Jillianna's chains. "Captain Bijapur wants you put on the block today. If we do not like the price that is offered for you, then he wants me to rid you of the baby."

Jillianna felt faint, and she clutched at the wall for support. When the woman yanked hard on the chain, Jillianna was forced to follow her.

She prayed that someone would pay a high price for her today. Then perhaps she would be allowed to keep her baby. It did not matter what degradation she had to suffer, but her baby must live.

Jillianna stood in the shade of the pavilion, watching a young dusky-skinned girl being poked and examined by a man who was using the same attention to detail as a horse-trader. Jillianna only hoped she could bear the degrading exhibition as regally as this girl when it was her turn. It suddenly became important to her that she rise above her surroundings. She would not let these people break her, or to humble her in the dust.

When she was led forward, it was with great fanfare. She was placed on a golden platform with silken veils waving above her head. While she could not understand what was being said about her, the people pressed closer and the crowd swelled to a great number.

She raised her head as one veil after another was removed. When the last veil was removed, a murmur rippled through the crowd. When she was approached by several men, who in their turn examined her, she was forced to endure their greedy, probing hands. One man ran his hands over her breasts, exposing them to a leering crowd. She did not blink when her mouth was forced open and her teeth examined. But she almost cried out when the outer layer of clothing was stripped away and she stood on display, covered only in a thin veil that was draped about her shoulders.

The more indignities Jillianna was forced to endure, the higher she raised her head. The only outward sign of what she was feeling was the trembling of her lips and the single tear that made its way down her cheek. She tried to pray, but how could one pray under such shameful circumstances?

* * *

The Grand Vizier, Lord Simijin Ibrahim, motioned for the litter bearers to lower his sedan chair. He had come to the slave market today with the hope of finding a cook to replace the one who had died two days before. It was a tiresome business, but a good cook was valued, and he would not leave the matter to one of his servants.

The Grand Vizier, like all the other men present, stared at the golden-haired woman on the platform, who was beautiful even though she was heavy with child.

It was obvious that the woman was terrified. She appeared so delicate and vulnerable that he was angered by the men putting their rough hands on her. Though his taste did not run to light-skinned women, he could not condone the callous manner in which she was being treated.

He admired her when she proudly raised her head as the indignities were practiced on her body. One of the tormentors ripped the veil from the woman's face, and a gasp of appreciation moved through the crowd. She was fair of face, and golden hair spilled down her back. Lord Simijin found his interest in her intensified.

He motioned to one of his guards, and the man stepped immediately to his master. Dropping a bag of gold into the guard's hand, he nodded at the golden-haired woman. "Buy the female and cover her with this," he ordered, shoving his own cloak at the man. "Bring her to me at once."

Jillianna was surprised when a cloak was folded around her and gentle hands led her down from the platform. She did not stop to ponder her fate; she was too grateful that the loathsome exhibition was at last at an end.

The throng of people moved aside to allow her passage, and she realized that whoever had paid her purchase price must wield a great deal of power and respect. She had little time to reflect on her owner as she approached the litter.

The shimmering gold curtains were pulled aside. A jeweled hand reached out to assist her into the litter, and the strength of the man astounded her. She stared into dark-brown eyes, and she shrank from him, suddenly averting her gaze, too afraid to meet those probing eyes.

Her body trembled uncontrollably. Ever since she had been taken prisoner, she had been under an illusion of unreality. Now it was difficult to believe that she had been bought and sold, the same as one would buy cattle.

Jillianna was startled when a deep voice spoke to her in perfect English. "I trust you have not been made to suffer unduly from your ordeal?"

She raised her eyes to the man, and found what appeared to be an expression of compassion on his face. But surely she was mistaken.

He was much younger than she had thought at first, but it was hard to tell much about him since he was in the shadows. She supposed one might call him handsome if one did not mind dark-complected men. His brow was high and noble; his expression was one of authority. His hair was black, as was his immaculately clipped beard. Yes, his features were arresting, and he was a man one would notice even in a crowded room.

"Who are you?" she asked, grateful that she could at least converse with the man.

"You may refer to me as Lord Simijin," he answered, his eyes sweeping her face and taking in the bright tinge to her cheeks. He had never seen a woman with eyes the color of rare green turquoise, and he suddenly found her most intriguing. He was beginning to believe he had made a fair bargain today, for she was a rare beauty indeed.

Jillianna raised her head and gave him a scathing glance. "You may as well know right now that if you do anything to harm my baby, I shall find a way to escape from you, and you will have naught for the money you expended."

His eyes moved to her swollen stomach. "Why should I want to harm your baby? As I see it, I made a good bargain today, buying two slaves for the price of one."

A new and unsettling thought struck Jillianna. Dear

Lord, her baby would be born into slavery! No longer able to hold her head up with pride, she felt ready to collapse. "Why have you done this?" she asked, feeling defeated at last.

"If you are asking why I purchased you today, I am not certain myself. In a moment of weakness, I felt your suffering and wanted to alleviate it."

She looked at the man in disbelief. "I cannot credit that was your reason."

"Nonetheless, it is true."

Jillianna studied him critically. Even though he was seated, it was easy to see that he was a tall man. She looked into his dark eyes, wishing she could read the truth in their depths.

"I am certain that you will not like me, my lord," she said at last. "My husband often told me, before he died, that I was too fanciful and forward for a woman. And my husband's mother found me not at all to her liking. On numerous occasions she accused me of being headstrong and ungrateful—which, if the truth were told—I am sure I am."

Warm laughter came from the man as he observed the willfulness in Jillianna's eyes. "I am an admirer of honesty, and I abhor deceitfulness of any kind; therefore, already I admire you. What is your name?"

"You may call me Mrs. Sinclair," she said with a defiant spark in her eyes.

His lips curved into an almost smile. "I was referring to your first name."

"J-Jillianna."

"Well, Jillianna, I am beginning to realize how fortunate I am that chance allowed our paths to cross today."

Feeling tense and uncertain, she moved back against the red satin cushions. The litter swayed from side to side, and she could hear the jingle of the golden bells that were attached to the curtains.

"My lord, I believe it is my duty to convince you that you will not have such a high opinion of me once you come to know me," she stated almost airily. "I can assure you that my shortcomings are many."

Again the Grand Vizier's laughter was warm with delight. "Jillianna, Jillianna, you try so hard to make me dissatisfied with you, but with each try, you only intrigue me more."

She felt a shiver of fear touch her spine. "Do not like me, my lord, for I have no intentions of liking you—not ever!"

He reached out and tilted her chin up, bringing it into the light so he could study her closely. "Forever is a long time, Jillianna."

"I have an intolerable temper," she told him, with a rush of feeling.

"I will allow you that since you are lovely beyond reason." His voice softened. "Yes, I have made a good bargain in you, Jillianna."

She resented being referred to as a bargain, but she was too weary to protest. She had lived with fear for so many weeks that it had somewhat dulled her senses. Now all she could think of was a place to lay her weary body. She huddled in the corner, too fatigued to wonder at the fate of herself or her unborn child. Until a few weeks ago, Turkey had been only a name of some obscure corner of the world—now it would surely be her home until the end of her days.

Jillianna fell forward when the litter was suddenly set down with a thud, but Simijin reached out to steady her. "It requires practice to ride the litter. You will learn in time," he told her.

The Grand Vizier helped Jillianna out of the litter. She was surprised to find that they were inside a huge courtyard. She was immediately struck by the beauty of the magnificent palace that was within the confines of a twelve-foot-high wall. Great wealth was displayed by the intricate designs that were cut into the marble pillars of the palace and the delicate workmanship of the outer walls that sparkled with precious jewels. High domes were interwoven with the purest gold, and Jillianna felt awed in spite of herself.

"I trust you will like it here, Jillianna," Simijin remarked.

Before Jillianna could answer, he left her. Immediately, a veiled woman appeared from out of nowhere to lead Jillianna into the palace by a side door.

They walked down a long corridor, through arched doorways and past beautiful gardens, approaching a high door where a man in cossack trousers and a beaded tunic stood guard. The man was huge and had the blackest skin Jillianna had ever seen.

He moved aside to let them pass only after the woman spoke to him. Looking fierce, he took in Jillianna's appearance with one sweeping glance. Suddenly his laughter boomed out, and he said in broken English, "The master has asked that you be accorded special treatment, madame." His laughter was amused when he saw her color heighten. "The blush is on the English Rose. Yes, we shall call you the English Rose."

Jillianna was led through the door, and when she heard it close behind her, she had the feeling she would never again draw a breath of freedom.

In a nearby pool, she could see several scantily dressed women splashing and playing, and she wondered if she were expected to join their numbers.

Jillianna balked at the notion of being any man's slave, and she would never be content to live in this alien world where men seemed to dominate and women were meant to serve.

She paused at the arched doorway, where she could hear the sound of tittering laughter. Her worst fear had now been realized. She was in a harem!

Chapter Three

Jillianna walked through the splendid walled garden. She paused near a shimmering ornamental pool, where she stared down at her reflection, trying to find the woman she had once been behind the strange clothing she wore. Draped in gauzelike robes, she longed for her own clothing that had gone down with the *Scarborough*.

In the two weeks Jillianna had been in the harem, she had come to understand that the Grand Vizier was one of the most powerful men in Turkey, second only to Sultan Abdul Hamid I.

Her eyes moved over the gardens, which were spacious, and filled with tall, dark cypress trees, grassy terraces, and numerous ponds. The tinkling sound of water splashing from ornamental fountains seemed to be the dominant sound in this obscure section of the garden. She had come to this spot because it was the farthest point from the harem, and she could be alone.

Jillianna had not seen Lord Simijin since that first day when she had been delivered into the hands of his head eunuch. In the past days and nights, she had pondered her fate. What the Grand Vizier's plans were for her, she could not guess, for he had many women more beautiful than herself.

She had discovered that the other women in the harem were as varied in their nationalities as they were in the colors of their skin. Jillianna had been told by one of the women that the Grand Vizier's head wife had died in childbirth, and that he had neither replaced her in his affections nor elevated anyone to her station. There was much speculation as to who would have that honor, and Jillianna hoped she would not be considered; indeed she hoped the vizier would forget about her altogether.

Jillianna was not certain of the exact number of women in the harem, but it was soon apparent to her that they were all trained in the art of pleasing their lord. All day they would be pampered and preened in hopes that their master would cast eyes in their direction and choose one of them to share his bed for the night.

In this private world, that was located far away from prying eyes, the women appeared to pass their days in frivolous activities, some preferring to merely recline on silk couches with no purpose to their lives, or so it seemed to Jillianna.

She had learned that this was in impregnable fortress, a city within a city. Closely guarded by the head eunuch and his underlings, the doors were closed to all but the Grand Vizier and the serving women.

The harem itself was made up of nine pavilions. The lesser women lived together in several rooms, while the most important woman dwelled in the center apartment, which at this time was unoccupied.

Hearing the sweet sound of some exotic bird, Jillianna glanced up to see a brightly plumed bird in the nearby cypress tree. Scattered throughout the gardens were different varieties of birds in golden cages.

Although Jillianna had not seen her or been summoned into her presence as of yet, she was told that the mother of the Grand Vizier lived behind the palace walls. She was extremely powerful and extracted an oath of obedience from the women in her son's harem. None dared visit her without her permission, and never without being formally dressed.

Even though Jillianna had only been in the harem for a short time, already she had encountered the jealousies between the women, which were like sores ready to canker. She found the whole situation demeaning to womanhood, and she had no intention of joining in their way of life. Her one fear was that Lord Simijin would single her out, while she preferred to remain one of many.

Accustomed to a cooler climate, she was feeling the heat more than ever, because she was heavy with child. She sighed, thinking England was so far away. She doubted she would ever see her family again.

Suddenly, a shadow fell across Jillianna's face, and she looked up to see the pot-bellied eunuch, who was master of this domain. He motioned for Jillianna to follow him. Until today the man had paid not attention to her. Most probably he had not considered her important. As she fell into step beside him, she wondered what he wanted with her now.

She was learning that this black eunuch was a man of immense power and wealth and even owned his own slaves. He was also the only link the harem had with the outside world.

She glanced sideways at him. He wore a silken robe and a broad sash. A sable-trimmed pelisse reached almost to the ground, and a pointed headdress sat atop his bald head.

Jillianna paused at the door when he entered the bath, following only when he called her forward. There were white marble floors and several marble tubs inside. The water was heated in copper boilers and gushed into the tubs through delicately carved fountains.

It seemed the vizier was a fastidious man, who insisted the women of his harem not only bathe daily, but also wash their hands before each meal. This was the first time Jillianna had been brought to the bath, and she cringed inside, fearing it meant that the Grand Vizier had summoned her.

The eunuch nodded toward the tub. "It is time for you to bathe, English Rose." He bowed to her and quickly departed, leaving her confused.

Not knowing what was expected of her, she looked at the walls, which were inlaid with semiprecious stones of remarkable color and designs. In a ponderous mood, she sank down on a crimson cushion, knowing that she did not belong here. She was shocked by how frivolous the women were. And she would never grow accustomed to how little clothing they wore.

She glanced up as a woman draped all in black entered the room, followed by six slave girls. The woman in black bowed to Jillianna and spoke to her in heavily accented English. "I am Lord Simijin's mother, Lady Bija. I am here to see that you are prepared for my son." Her eyes swept over Jillianna, and she nodded approvingly. "Yes, you may be the one who can make my son smile again. Many have tried, but none have succeeded."

Jillianna came to her feet quickly, as fear pounded in her heart. "Surely you must be mistaken. I was told that women linger for years without seeing Lord Simijin. I have been told that some of them never see him. Why should he want to see me now?"

His mother shrugged. "It is not for you to question. Lord Simijin has asked for you, and you must be prepared to receive him."

Jillianna knew the moment she dreaded had come. But why would the Grand Vizier want her, when he had so many beautiful women in his harem? Surely he could not want a woman who was heavy with child. Her mind was in a quandary as she tried to think how she could save herself from this situation.

Jillianna realized that she had no choice but to give in to the inevitable. Her body was shaved, and she was scrubbed and bathed, then wrapped in rice flour and oil to soften her skin. She was perfumed, and her long lashes were painted with kohl and her fingernails dyed a deep crimson. She was draped in a cloth of the finest gold, and shimmering jewels were placed about her neck and wrists.

At last the women stood back, studying their handiwork, and Lady Bija spoke words that struck fear in Jillianna's heart.

"You are very beautiful, even swollen with child. It is easy to see why my son desires you." Then the Grand Vizier's mother withdrew, motioning for the other women to follow her.

Jillianna was alone for only a moment before the head

eunuch reentered the bath. When he motioned for her to follow him, she had no choice but to comply.

He led her down twisting walkways, past colorful gardens, and finally into a brilliant, domed pavilion. Her golden sandals were noiseless as she walked across the colorful mosaic floor.

A magnificent door, which reached to the height of the building, was pushed open, and the eunuch motioned for her to enter.

After Jillianna reluctantly stepped inside, the door was closed behind her, and she found herself in an astonishing round room. The walls and floor were crafted from white marble, and priceless Persian carpets were scattered about the room. On the western wall, there were twelve windows decorated with delicately carved woodwork. The furnishings consisted of a desk, several divans, and a table laden with food.

She could see another room beyond a carved archway, and her eyes moved quickly away from the white, satin-draped bed with its scarlet tassels.

She had not seen him there at first, but the Grand Vizier himself stood before one of the windows, his hands clasped behind his back, his dark eyes closely observing Jillianna.

Simijin was dressed in a black flowing robe without benefit of ornaments, and his head was uncovered. When he spoke, his voice was deep. "I am delighted to see you, Jillianna. I had feared your many adventures might have proved detrimental to your well-being. I am glad that is not the case. You look lovely."

She stood like a statue, her spine straight, her head high, but still she clung to the doorknob, unwilling to venture farther into the room.

"My lord, how can you speak of my well-being, when you hold me here against my will?"

She thought he smiled, but she could not be certain. "I trust you are enjoying good health?" he inquired.

"Yes. My health has always been good."

"Then you are most fortunate. I can assure you that good health is a gift from God."

She met his eyes. "Which God, yours or mine?"

He inclined his head. "I believe your God and mine are one and the same, as you will soon learn."

She looked skeptical, but decided not to pursue the subject. "You may as well know right now that I do not want to come to you tonight, my lord."

She had expected anger, but his expression was composed. "I am aware of that. But allow me to assure you that you have nothing to fear from me." He held his hand out to her. "Will you not be seated with me at the table? I have had my cook prepare many delectable dishes just to please you."

Jillianna ignored his hand, and glanced at the food—succulent lamb, calf, lobster, swordfish, stuffed pheasant and venison, not to mention delicacies she had never seen before. Surely there was enough there to feed the whole harem. The air was thick with the scent of the onions and garlic that flavored the meats. There were dates and plums dipped in honey for sweetening. She saw a large variety of fruits and sherbets, iced in snow, and she was tempted by the sight of the thick almond cream sweetened with honey and sprinkled with ginger.

She took one hesitant step away from the door to stand on the edge of a yellow-and-blue carpet. "There is much you do not know about me, Lord Simijin."

He drew near. "Such as?"

"Such as, unlike the women in your harem, I do not desire your company."

He seated himself at a table and motioned for her to come forward. "I wonder why you should feel thus, Jillianna. Have you not been shown every kindness since I brought you to my home? I would think you would want to come here tonight, if for no other reason than curiosity about your benefactor."

"You do not have to remind me that I owe you, my lord. I am not ungrateful that you saved me from the slave market."

"I was not reminding you, Jillianna."

She took a timid step toward him. "I have been treated kindly, and I must confess to a certain amount of curiosity concerning you," she admitted. "But I have no wish to know you better, my lord."

"I see. It was by my orders that you were left alone until you felt comfortable with your surroundings. Unlike you, I have anticipated this night because *I* want to know *you* . . . much better."

Reluctantly, she moved across the room toward him, her fear lessened by her need to make him understand her feelings. As she stood before him, she looked into his eyes, thinking how dark and foreign he looked.

"I do want to talk to you, my lord," she said, in a voice that came out in a painful whisper. "Will you hear what I have to say?"

"Please be seated, Jillianna, and then we can converse much more easily. I find it very difficult to talk to you when I am looking up at you."

She dropped down on a cushion, glancing at the food with interest. "I could not eat a bite until I have had my say, my lord."

He smiled. "I can see why your husband accused you of being a strong-willed woman."

Her green eyes sparkled with feigned innocence. "Oh, I am most dreadfully strong-willed, Lord Simijin. You should be rid of me without delay. Most probably I shall soon disrupt your whole harem. I am not in the least humble. I could never be subservient to a man, and trouble seems to follow me wherever I go."

Simijin picked up a golden plate and piled it high with food before handing it to Jillianna. "You must eat, for the health of your baby. I am told you take very little nourishment. Do you not find my food to your liking?"

Without thinking, she shoved the plate aside. "I suppose the food is all right. But, I find it difficult to accustom myself to eating without the aid of a knife and fork. I have not been taught to eat with my fingers, like some . . . barbarian."

His laughter was soft. "It is a good thing that I do not take offense at being called a barbarian, Jillianna."

Her face reddened. "Oh, my lord, I did not mean to imply that you are . . . that you—"

He held up his hand to silence her. "I have long admired the English and many of their customs. I shall see to it that you are furnished with whatever it takes to make you feel at home here."

Her eyes met his. "My lord, I could never feel at home here. Will you not send me to England? Be rid of me with all haste, and save yourself grief later."

He leaned forward and pressed a date between her teeth. When she shook her head, he persisted until she took it in her mouth. "Tell me about your home, Jillianna."

She swallowed the date without tasting it. "There isn't much to tell. I grew up in London, since my father, an impoverished nobleman, had lost his lands and holdings. I am certain my father despaired of ever being rid of me. So, when an offer of marriage came from a distant cousin from Philadelphia, my father quickly accepted the proposal on my behalf and sent me to America. There I was married and lived for four years."

"I was certain that you were from the nobility, Jillianna. It shows in the proud way you carry yourself, and in your delicate features."

He picked up a thin slice of lamb and offered it to her. This time Jillianna took it in her mouth and found it delicious.

"So you went to America to marry a distant cousin?"

"Yes. I was but fifteen, and Matthew was thirty-five. He and his mother were successful silversmiths, and they were wealthy, though miserly."

She was only nineteen. He could see that she was losing some of her fear of him and it gladdened his heart. She was a rare and beautiful flower, and though he wanted to keep her, he knew that if she did not find happiness here, he would send her to England.

"Did you like America, Jillianna?"

"No, I was not happy there," she admitted. "You see, I was always in a predicament. I have come to believe that the devil was always knocking me down and then kicking me for falling."

His lips twitched, and his eyes danced with mirth. "So you were always in trouble?"

"Yes." Her eyes sparkled with a determined light. "I tried to be obedient, but I was always doing things like singing an Irish ballad in the church to the embarrassment of my husband and his mother. Then there was the time I caught my slipper on my mother-in-law's finest shawl, and most of it unraveled before I discovered what I had done. I once spilled a plate of corn in the minister's lap. And that's just the start. I am guilty of much worse. My mother-in-law would tell you that I am most disruptive."

Simijin found her confession so endearing that a strong urge to protect her took hold of him. "You will not find us so critical of you here, Jillianna."

"I am certain that my husband had great forbearance, but he had much to contend with in me."

"And did you come to love your husband?"

She looked at Simijin, not knowing how anxiously he awaited her answer. She had never considered love to be a part of her relation with Matthew Sinclair. "I never really got to know Matthew. We lived in the same house with his widowed mother, and he spent most of his time with her. You see, his mother was a very religious woman, and I fear I was often a great disappointment to her . . . and to Matthew as well."

Simijin could read much of what she had suffered in her eyes. It was apparent that she had known little kindness or happiness with her husband. He found himself wanting to see that she had both kindness and happiness from now on.

"So, your husband died, leaving you to bear his child alone?"

"You make it sound like he died intentionally. Matthew had a fever, and he just wasted away to nothing in a matter of two weeks. I was sorry that he died, and I was grievously sorry that his mother had lost her only reason for living. She is a very sad old woman."

"What made you decide to leave America and return to England? Surely your mother-in-law would have rather you stayed with her since you were having her grandchild?"

Jillianna absentmindedly picked up a ripened pear and bit into it. "Mrs. Sinclair was still grieving for her son when she learned that I was . . . with child, and I feared she might force me to stay with her. But poor Mrs. Sinclair was wishing for death at the time, and when I suggested that I return to England to live with my father, she readily agreed. She provided me with passage money, and was probably glad to see the last of me. I believe she thought of my unborn child as belonging to me more than to Matthew."

"Why do you think she was displeased with you?"

Jillianna took another bite of the pear and savored its sweet taste. "I often wondered that myself. Since I am English, I was raised in the Church of England, while my husband and his mother were Quakers. I am certain they found me sadly lacking in humility and what they considered proper Christian spirit." She took another bite of the pear and smiled at Simijin. "I fear you will soon see those qualities lacking in me as well."

He reached out and took her hand, studying the delicate bone structure. "I believe your husband was undeserving of you, and his mother was a fool for letting you go." He rubbed his thumb over her wrist. "Shall I tell you something else, Jillianna?"

She wanted to drag her hand from his grasp, but she dared not. "If you like."

"I have been unable to get you out of my mind. I had to see you again, just to know if you were as beautiful as I remembered. I fear I shall never be able to let you go."

Now she did jerk her hand away. "Beauty can be an evil thing, Lord Simijin. You would be wise to be done with me. I have been told that my heart is black with sin."

He laughed at the thought of this angelic and innocent beauty being sinful. "That is a risk I am willing to take, Jillianna."

Now her eyes took on a haunted look. "Will you allow me to keep my baby?"

He sat back and gave her a long, searching look. "Not only shall I allow you to keep your child, but on the day it is born, I shall rejoice with you."

Relief washed over her. She had not expected him to be so kind and agreeable. The only men she had known had been her father and Matthew. Neither of them had ever said a kind word to her. She was suspicious of this man's motives.

"What will you want from me in return, Lord Simijin?"

"You will learn at a later time. For now, I want no more than to see you smile."

"If I smile, may I return to the women's quarters?"

His amused laughter filled the room. "Careful that you do not wound my pride past mending."

She blessed him with a smile. "Now may I leave?" she asked.

His eyes moved over her face. "Only if you will promise to return tomorrow."

"If it is your command."

"It is my hope."

"Very . . . well," she agreed reluctantly. "I shall return tomorrow."

Simijin stood up and moved so his face was half in shadow. "Go now, Jillianna. You will find a servant waiting outside the door to return you to your quarters."

As if he had lost interest in her, he turned away and moved back to the window.

Jillianna rose to her feet and stood there for a long moment, wondering what kind of man Lord Simijin was. She had come here not knowing what to expect, but he had shown her only kindness and had agreed that she could keep her baby.

Even so, her footsteps quickened as she moved across the marble floor, least the Grand Vizier should change his mind and force her to remain.

When Jillianna returned to the women's quarters, she lay down on her couch and stared into the night long after silence fell across the harem. How strange was this man who tugged at her heart. She was frightened of her feelings for him, although she dared not examine those feelings too closely.

When she at last fell asleep, she dreamed of soft brown eyes that seemed to look into her very soul.

Chapter Four

The carefully manicured gardens that Jillianna walked through were Lord Simijin's private gardens, where the women of the harem were seldom allowed. The grounds were magnificent. There were seven terraces with a reflecting pool that flowed down through all seven levels. But Jillianna knew the palace was more than a place of beauty: it was a fortress where none could enter or leave without permission from the Grand Vizier himself.

She looked at the marble-domed buildings decorated with art work cut deeply into the stone. The arched doorways that led to the interior of the palace were layered in the purest gold. This might be a dream palace, dazzling in its splendor, but to Jillianna, it was no more than a prison.

It had been over a week since Jillianna was first summoned before the Grand Vizier, and since then, she had dined with him every night. She had long since lost much of her distrust of him, but she was still unsure of what he expected of her. Their conversations were lengthy, and he questioned her extensively about her home in England.

The sun was setting, and her footsteps hurried toward the bath, for it was time to prepare to be received by Lord Simijin. She hurried along, wondering what there was about her that attracted the Grand Vizier. Would he soon tire of her and cast her aside? She had seen the envious glances the other women cast her way, and she wondered if each of them had also received this special notice from their lord at one time. Did he so easily tire of women that he needed so many of them to entertain him?

* * *

Jillianna reclined on a soft yellow divan, and Lord Simijin was seated next to her. "My lord," she began almost hesitantly, "why do you insist that I come to you each evening? It is causing great distress to the women in your harem. I fear they do not like me very well. I believe they suspect my motives are devious, which of course they are not."

His eyes were alert. "None of them have dared to reproach you or have threatened you in any way, have they?"

"No. The women have kept their distance, but all the same, I can feel their hostility in every glance they cast in my direction. Would it not be better, my lord, if you dined with one of them instead of me?"

"I thought you were beginning to enjoy our time together. Was I mistaken, Jillianna?"

"I . . . find you most informative. You are the first man who has ever treated me as if I had a serious thought in my head." She smiled mischievously. "I have even learned to eat with my fingers."

"But it does not come easy to you," he said seriously. "I have sent for all that you will require to make you feel at home here."

She felt a warmth spread throughout her body. "You have shown me such kindness. How can I ever repay you?"

His smile was sad. "I will think of a way, my English Rose. I wonder if you will bloom in my garden of flowers."

She avoided his probing glance and chose to move on to another subject. "My lord, I will never like living in a harem. And if my child is a daughter, I do not want her growing up in that kind of environment. My husband would have been horrified to think of his child growing up in such a manner."

Simijin took her hand, and this time she did not pull away when he raised it to his lips. "I know you feel that way, and I doubt that you will ever change your mind. Soon you will never have to enter the harem again unless it is your desire."

Jillianna could not believe what he was telling her. "Are you going to let me go?" she asked hopefully.

"No, Jillianna," he told her simply. "But you shall have your own quarters, as well as your own slaves, and anything else that will make you happy. But do not ever ask me to allow you to leave."

She felt an unknown sensation tighten the muscles in her stomach as Simijin's lips brushed against the palm of her hand. "Why would you allow me to live apart from the harem?" she wanted to know, still suspecting his motives.

He released her hand and picked up an almond sweetened with honey and placed it in her mouth. "One day I shall tell you why. For now, let us say I enjoy being with you."

She shook her head with disbelief. "You do not want me to . . . to . . ."

"To share my bed?" he offered. "No. I have an aversion to reaping a field that has already been sown by another man."

Jillianna was shocked by his words, but at the same time she was disappointed, which shocked her even more. "You do not desire me, my lord, because I have been with my husband?"

"That is not what I meant, Jillianna. I merely stated that I would not touch you while you carried a child within your body."

"I know that I am very clumsy and ugly now," she said, wondering why it should matter to her how he perceived her.

Simijin stood up and helped her to her feet. Taking her arm, he steered her out into the garden before he answered.

"I find you the most beautiful woman I have ever known. More than that, my desire for you is great, but it is of the lasting kind. When you come to me, I want no man's child between us, and I want it to be because you also desire me."

"I do not understand you, my lord. Why would you want me when you have so many beautiful women who would be happy to please you?"

He merely smiled. "I wonder if *you* would be willing to do something to please me, Jillianna?"

Suspicion lit her eyes. "You will have to tell me what you want before I decide."

"Fair enough. It is a very simple request really. All I ask is that you willingly come to me as you have been. We shall talk, and you will tell me many things about your world."

"Is that all you require of me?"

His eyelashes lowered, masking his eyes. "That is all for now."

"I will be glad to visit with you, my lord . . . provided you do as you have promised and give me my own quarters."

"Agreed. Later perhaps you will grow to trust me a little more. There are many things I want to teach you, and I would like to learn many things from you."

She smiled reluctantly, not really comprehending his meaning. "I fear I have little to teach you, my lord."

For the first time since Simijin's beloved wife had died, he felt alive again. Even though he had taken many women to his bed to ease the pain of his loss, his heart had never been involved. Now he found himself unable to curb his impatience to take this English beauty to his body. She must never know the power she had over him.

"You will be happy in your new life, Jillianna."

"I am not certain I know what happiness is. My husband often reminded me that happiness was sin's companion."

Simijin's words came out in a harsh whisper. "After this day, you will no longer mention the man you were once married to." His eyes darkened with hidden passion. Although Jillianna had been married, Simijin could tell she knew nothing about lovemaking. He would be the one to spark fire in her eyes and to melt her untouched English heart.

He pulled her stiff body into his arms, and was encouraged when she did not pull away. "Jillianna, my Jillianna, the day will come when you will desire me, this I promise you."

She felt the warmth of his breath on her cheek as he laid his face against hers. "Oh, yes, my little English Rose, I will light a fire inside you that will consume us both."

She twisted away from him, and shook her head. "I will never allow that to happen. S-stay away from me."

His eyes took on a sadness. "There is no need for distress, Jillianna. I will bide my time and not rush you. Have I not given you my word?"

She turned away and fled, fearing he would try to stop her retreat, but he did not. When she returned to her quarters, she found her heart was racing, and she lay on the bed until it quieted.

It was but three days later that Simijin kept his promise, and Jillianna was moved into the main part of the palace. She had five slaves to tend her needs, and a eunuch named Achmed to stand guard at her door.

Since the night Jillianna had ran away from Simijin, he had not asked her to come to him again. She was surprised to find that she missed the visits desperately. At first she blamed herself for being so suspicious of his motives. Then she moped about, fearing she would never see him again.

Jillianna missed Simijin's stimulating conversation, and he had treated her as a valued friend, rather than as a mere woman. She had been love-starved all her life: first ignored by her father, and later by her husband. Now she found herself wrapped in the warmth of Simijin's kindness, and though she did not know it, she was beginning to fall in love with the man who held her captive.

December

The cold wind blowing off the Sea of Marmora stung the face of the slave as he rushed down the pathway that led to the great pavilion where the Grand Vizier was closeted with none other than the Sultan himself. The man hoped he would not come to grief for disturbing his master. But had not Lord Simijin's mother, herself, sent him to deliver the news that the English Rose would soon give birth?

* * *

Jillianna twisted in agony as pain ripped through her body. She was seated in a birth-chair with three midwives attending her. There would be no physician in attendance since no man but the Grand Vizier himself was allowed near any of his women.

Simijin's mother, Lady Bija, stood beside Jillianna, speaking words of encouragement and bathing the beads of perspiration from her forehead.

"Jillianna, the pain will soon pass, but the joy you experience in your child will remain with you throughout your life."

Ever since Jillianna and the Grand Vizier had become good friends, his mother had been kind and generous toward her. Now Jillianna was soothed by the older woman's words.

"Your time of travail will be long," Lady Bija remarked, with a worried frown on her face. "This baby takes its time being born."

As another pain stabbed Jillianna's body, she dug her fingernails into the arm of the chair. No one had told her that bringing a baby into the world would be so painful.

Hour after hour she labored. The day passed into night, and still the child would not be born. Unknown to Jillianna, Simijin waited in the outer room, pacing the floor, fearful that his English Rose might die.

At last, just as the sun was painting the eastern sky with rosy glow, Jillianna's daughter was born.

As the infant let out its first lusty cry, Lady Bija smiled and held it up for Jillianna's inspection. "Allah be praised, you have a daughter," she proclaimed.

Jillianna was exhausted. All she cared about was that the pain was over and she could sleep. The midwives moved her to her bed, and silken covers were placed over her. She drifted off to sleep with the sound of her newborn daughter's cries echoing in her ears.

March

The day was cold, and dark snow clouds hung in the western sky. Jillianna had wandered out, into the garden that was devoid of color. The bleak and dismal atmosphere suited her mood, for she was overcome with a strange feeling of melancholy. She had not seen Lord Simijin for such a long time. He had not even come to see her baby daughter, and there had been no word from him. She felt abandoned and alone.

As she walked along the path, she pulled her cloak tightly about her neck to ward off the chilling wind. She had to admit to herself that she was jealous. She was in torment, thinking of Simijin visiting his harem and selecting one of the beautiful women there to share his nights. Her days were filled with playing with her lovely daughter, but she did so miss her talks with Simijin.

When had she come to love him? She could not pinpoint the exact moment, but she did love him most desperately.

Hearing footsteps, she turned to see Achmed, the eunuch who guarded her quarters, walking toward her. He smiled widely as he stopped at her side.

"Mistress, you are to be made ready to go to Lord Simijin. Is that not a great honor?"

She blinked her eyes when they filled with tears. "Yes, a great honor."

Jillianna's heart was pounding when she entered Lord Simijin's private apartment, but this time it was not from fear. When he walked toward her, she was warmed by the glow in his dark eyes. When he took her hand and raised it to his lips, she wanted to throw herself into his arms, but she held herself erect, afraid to let him see how much she cared.

His dark eyes traveled over her face, then down the transparent gown she wore, and she saw admiration in his eyes. "You are the most beautiful woman I have ever seen, and

I have seen many, Jillianna." His eyes moved across her breasts that were filled with milk to feed her infant daughter. "Even more beautiful now that the child has been delivered."

She quivered with delight as his hand trailed down her cheek. "I am told you are now completely recovered from the birth of your daughter."

"I am well," she agreed in a whispered voice.

He raised her chin and stared into her misty green eyes. "Even though I sent for you tonight, Jillianna, did you come to me of your own accord?"

She took his hand and raised it to her lips. "I came willingly. How can I repay you for your many kindnesses?"

He led her to the satin-draped bed, and she followed willingly. "I will think of a way. Tell me, Jillianna, do you still wish to return to England?"

"No," she answered truthfully.

His eyes burned into hers. "Then you will stay with me of your own free will?"

"Yes."

He closed his eyes to hide the hope that shone there. When he held out his arms to her, she came to him eagerly.

"Your prediction has come true," she admitted, pressing her cheek against his shoulder.

"What prediction is that?" he asked in a voice that trembled with feeling.

"You said you would melt my cold English heart, and indeed you have."

Gently he lifted her into his arms and placed her on the satin bed. Her body was on fire for his touch, and when he removed his robe and joined her, she went eagerly into his arms. Softly at first his lips touched hers, and she moved closer to him, seeking his warmth.

Jillianna had never known a man could be so gentle and bring such pleasure. All she had ever known was Matthew's awkward lovemaking, and she had suffered his touch because it was expected of her as his wife. Matthew had always insisted when they had made love that it be in a darkened room, and, afterward, he had turned away from her as if he found her repulsive. With Simijin, she felt beautiful and cherished.

"Jillianna," he whispered against her arched neck. "I have dreamed of this moment, and now that you are mine, I want you always to remember this night."

"Yes," she murmured, her trembling fingers brushing against the hair on his chest. "I will always remember."

His lips brushed against her mouth, circling, tasting, and then they captured hers in a searing kiss that took her breath away. A thousand unanswered questions were ripped from her mind as his wonderful hands moved over her soft curves, undressing and caressing at the same time.

Jillianna was mindless with desire when Simijin finally pulled her naked flesh against his.

His voice was deep with emotion. "Now, Jillianna, the ultimate moment. The moment when your flesh becomes as one with mine."

A whimper escaped her mouth when he poised above her. She waited for what seemed like an eternity until his hard shaft entered her body, giving pleasure beyond anything she could ever have imagined. She clung to him as his sensual movements stirred her body into a burning inferno.

Her body obeyed his every command, straining against his muscled hardness. She ground her body against his, wanting to get ever closer to the throbbing instrument that gave her so much pleasure. He was truly the master, and she his slave.

"Jillianna," he cried out in a passionate voice. "You are mine at last."

"I am yours," she agreed without hesitation.

In a world filled with strange incense, and with snow falling in the garden beyond, Simijin taught Jillianna the meaning of love. His lovemaking was gentle and tempered with patience. He introduced her to feelings she had never dreamed existed, and she fell more in love with him.

After their passions had cooled, Simijin still held her in

his arms. When she would have voiced her feelings, he placed his finger over her lips. "No, do not say what you are feeling tonight. I have taken advantage of your innocence, and you may not know your true feelings. Tomorrow we shall talk."

She was hurt that he did not want to hear her confession of love. But when he pulled her into his arms, she sighed contentedly, loving the feel of his chest rising and falling against her breasts.

Long after he had fallen asleep, she lay there in the half-light from a single candle, studying his face. She loved him so desperately that the thought of him loving another woman was unbearable. How would she be able to share him with the women of his harem, she wondered frantically? Pushing her troubled thoughts aside, she decided she would have to take what happiness she could, and not expect too much.

Suddenly she sat up in bed, as motherly instinct pushed every other thought from her mind. She had insisted on nursing her baby herself, refusing the wet nurse that had been sent to her. Instinctively she knew it was the baby's feeding time.

"Why are you frowning, dear love?" Simijin asked, rousing up and turning her to face him.

"My daughter will be hungry."

"Ah, I had not thought about that." He stood up and pulled on a flowing silk robe. "I will return shortly," he told her, moving out of the room.

The guards in the hall were shocked to see their master venture out into the snow, making his way across the garden to the English Rose's quarters. They were further shocked when he returned a short time later carrying Jillianna's infant daughter in his arms.

When Simijin entered his bedchamber, he laid the baby in Jillianna's arms, and she gave him a grateful smile. He watched with his heart in his eyes as the tiny rosebud mouth suckled at Jillianna's full breasts.

Suddenly Simijin felt love for this daughter of the woman he loved. She would be his daughter as well.

He touched the soft golden hair that covered the child's head, wishing that she was of his body. "Have you named the child?" he asked.

"I call her Brittany, after my beloved England."

"It is a good name."

"Simijin?"

It was the first time she had called him by his name, and he liked the sound of it. "Yes, beloved?"

"How can I thank you for all you have done for me and my daughter?"

"Will you allow me to feel a part of this child's life? My great sadness has always been that I have never had children of my own flesh. Will you allow me to feel that this child belongs to me?"

"Oh, yes, Simijin. You are such a gentle, loving man, and I believe she will grow up to love you as a father."

His eyes darkened as he looked at Jillianna. "I want to believe that. I shall become her guardian, if not her father. I shall engage only the best tutors for her. She will be well educated, and she will want for nothing."

Tears brightened Jillianna's eyes. "I love you," she admitted, laying her head over on his shoulder.

He closed his eyes, grateful that at last he had won the heart of the beautiful English Rose. "Will you consent to becoming my wife?" he asked, tensely watching her expression. He, who had been with many women, knew that his future happiness rested with this one alone.

She looked up at him, overwhelmed by the honor he paid her. "I belong to you, and you have no need to ask my permission about anything, and you do not have to marry me. . . ."

"I want you to be mine without reservation. I want you to desire me as much as I desire you. I believe you did tonight, but will you love me when the sun is high in the sky?"

She laid her sleeping baby down and threw her arms about his neck. "Oh, Simijin, I shall always love you. I will be honored to be your wife."

"Jillianna," he said, pulling her tightly against him. "With you I have found true happiness. I will see that you never know one day of sadness."

Jillianna glanced down at her sleeping daughter, wondering what the child's life would be like. She was determined that her daughter would not be affected by growing up in the shadows of a harem. She wanted Brittany to always know who she was, and that she was loved.

Simijin must have read her thoughts. He gently touched the cheek of the sleeping child. "Because you love her, I shall love her also. She will be the daughter of my heart."

Part Two

Daughter of the English Rose

Chapter Five

1807

"Brittany, where are you, girl? Come out of hiding at once!" Mrs. Potter called out in an irritated voice. "You are much too old to be playing such childish pranks. If you don't come here now, I will report your behavior to Lord Simijin."

The mischievous beauty raked her golden hair out of her face and sank lower behind the box hedge just as the stern-faced, chubby little woman came charging past her hiding place. Brittany was not intimidated by her governess's threat to go to Lord Simijin. For he was never cross with Brittany, and was more inclined to indulge her than punish her.

Mrs. Potter also knew that Lord Simijin would never deny Brittany anything, and he would certainly not take the governess's side against the stepdaughter he adored.

At seventeen, Brittany considered herself too old for a governess who persisted in curtailing her movements. But she admitted to herself that poor Mrs. Potter did not have an easy time trying to make a proper lady of her.

As the governess moved on down the path and out of sight, Brittany stood up, happy that she had once more escaped the woman. She was weary of the strict discipline that had been laid down for her; she was young and longed for adventure.

All of her young life, Brittany had lived behind the high walls of Simijin's palace, and she longed to walk free as her mother had in her girlhood in England.

As often as possible, Brittany would sneak away to the harem, although it was forbidden to her because her mother disapproved of the women there. But Brittany had formed friendships with the seven concubines who remained in Simijin's harem. There was Adrianna, from Russia; Milo, the Egyptian; Asha, from India; Juanita, the Spaniard; and three others who were born in Turkey. If only her mother would understand that the women of the harem had befriended her and she had learned so many fascinating and interesting things from them.

Most of all, Brittany liked the kindly eunuch, Achmed, who always managed to turn a blind eye when she wanted to enter the women's pavilion. He was her friend, and she knew he would never inform her mother of her visits to the harem.

Achmed had told her that Lord Simijin had once been master to over one hundred concubines, but that since he had taken the English Rose as his wife, he no longer frequented his harem. Most of the concubines had been allowed to leave to seek husbands, taking with them large dowries, while the ones who chose to remain had stayed with the knowledge that Lord Simijin would no longer seek them out. Twenty had remained, but only seven were still alive today, and they were no longer young.

Since Simijin had never fathered children of his own, Brittany was the only child who had grown up in the shadows of the palace walls, and the women had adored and indulged her on those times she had secretly made her way to their quarters.

It was in the harem where Brittany had learned to dance exotic dances. She had also been instructed in several different languages. She had even been trained in the ways to please a man. She was well versed in the art of love, and Brittany found it all intriguing, but she doubted she would ever put it into practice. After all, the only men she knew were Simijin and the eunuchs!

With deliberate steps, she raced past the purple cloud of hanging wisteria on her way toward the forbidden harem.

When she approached the tall double doors, they swung inward as if by magic, to offer her admittance. Achmed stood with arms folded over his broad black chest, his dark eyes challenging, yet shining with hidden mirth.

"Who dares seek entrance to Lord Simijin's harem?"

"Hide me, Achmed," Brittany said frantically. "Mrs. Potter is searching for me."

Suddenly Achmed smiled at the lovely vision, who looked strangely out of place, dressed in the French-style, high-waisted gown, rather than in garments like the harem women wore. Her golden hair made a halo around her face, her green eyes danced with impishness, and her rosy cheeks proclaimed her good health.

He stepped aside with an exaggerated bow, allowing her to enter. "So, little mistress, again you have escaped the sour persimmon who is your governess."

"Poor Mrs. Potter, I fear I am a real trial to her, Achmed. She deserves much better than she gets from me."

The eunuch winked. "Let us hope she gets all that she deserves . . . in England or some other remote corner of the world, hmm, little mistress?"

Brittany frowned. "Mama will never send Mrs. Potter away, Achmed. She hopes the poor woman will be able to teach me to be a lady—but I have my doubts." She sighed. "Hers is a thankless task."

The black man chuckled at the charming little imp. The little beauty was a favorite with everyone with her winsome ways and her compassionate nature, and he was always glad when she could escape the dour governess to pay the harem a visit.

"You should hurry along, little mistress. Already the women have started dancing."

Brittany heard the music coming from the garden room, and she rushed in that direction. When she approached the pavilion, several of the women rushed forward to greet her.

Brittany was soon dressed in a transparent dancing costume with golden bells on her wrists and ankles that made a tinkling sound with each step she took. While the music played, she joined the other dancers, feeling a prickle of remorse because her mother would disapprove of both her dancing and the revealing costume she wore.

But, as the tempo of the music built up, she soon forgot everything but her dancing feet. Her fingers snapped, and her hips swayed to the rhythm of the music. The other dancers paused to watch her perform. Though she did not know it, her movements were seductive and enticing, for she had learned well from the dancers of the harem.

The women laughed and clapped their hands. The little English miss had a great talent; the shame was that she would never be allowed to use it. Brittany was apart from the harem, and it was rumored that she would soon be sent to England to complete her education.

Brittany whirled, her flimsy costume making a wide circle about her body, her feet moving faster and faster as the music intensified. With a final whirl, she dipped to the floor in a wide curtsy while the women murmured their approval.

A stern voice cut through the merriment. "Brittany, come with me at once!"

Brittany glanced up to see Mrs. Potter glaring at her, hands on hips and eyes snapping with anger.

"I said come with me at once! This time you have gone too far, and your mother will hear of your doings. You are a hellion, and it is useless to try and instruct you in gentility. Wait until your mother sees you dressed in such a disgusting manner. Then she will do something about you, miss."

Brittany received many sympathetic glances from the women as she scooped up her gown and meekly followed the governess, not daring to take the time to change her clothing. For the first time, Brittany felt ashamed of her actions, knowing her mother would be disappointed in her. She wanted to be a dutiful daughter, but she always managed to do the wrong thing.

As she left the harem, Achmed cast Brittany a sorrowful glance before stepping aside to let them pass. He said, in Turkish, so Mrs. Potter would not understand, "The old dragon found me away from the door and crept inside. I blame myself for your sorrow, little mistress."

"It is not your fault," Brittany assured him in the same language.

"Stop speaking that heathen language," Mrs. Potter snapped as she gripped Brittany's wrist and pulled her across the garden to the palace. To Mrs. Potter, any language that was not Enlgish was heathen.

The governess's mouth was set in a severe line of disapproval. As they approached her mother's quarters, Brittany found herself wishing she had taken the time to change her clothing, for each time she took a step, the golden bells around her ankles jingled, reminding her of her transgression.

Jillianna was seated before the window where a brilliant light fell across the tapestry on which she was working. Hearing the door open, she glanced up to see Mrs. Potter storming toward her, with Brittany following forlornly.

Jillianna's bow creased into a frown when she saw the reason for Mrs. Potter's outrage. She did not have to be told that Brittany had been to the harem again.

"My lady, you cannot guess where I found your daughter."

Noting Brittany's dancing costume Jillianna nodded. "I can guess, Mrs. Potter."

"This time I was forced to go into that vile place where the women were half naked, to bring your daughter out."

Jillianna looked at Brittany in disbelief. "Is this true, Brittany?"

The young girl could not meet her mother's eyes. "Yes, Mama."

Jillianna stood up and walked to her daughter. "Have you not been forbidden to enter the harem, Brittany?"

Brittany raised her head to look into green eyes not unlike her own. "Yes, Mama."

Mrs. Potter puffed up her bosom and gave the young girl a disapproving look. "I find it impossible to control your daughter, Lady Jillianna; therefore, I am forced to leave your service and seek employment elsewhere. Your daughter is a hellion and will never be a proper young lady."

Jillianna's lovely face paled, and she pulled Brittany away from the hateful woman. "You will not speak of my daughter in those terms, Mrs. Potter. Kindly remove yourself from my presence at once. Consider yourself dismissed!"

Mrs. Potter's eyes narrowed with spite. "I am going, and gladly. But if you want my opinion, your daughter will never be any better than those women in the harem."

Jillianna raised her head and said in a commanding voice, "You will gather your belongings and leave the palace at once."

"Most gladly," the governess stated. She turned on her heels and left in a huff, her head held high, and her shoes clicking on the marble floor.

Brittany was sorry that her actions had hurt her mother, but she was not sorry that horrid woman was gone from her life forever.

"Mama, I suppose Mrs. Potter spoke the truth when she said I will never be a lady. I try to be like you, but I always do the wrong thing. I am impossible."

Jillianna saw much of herself in her daughter, and it wrenched at her heart. When she had been Brittany's age, she, too, had always been in trouble. "Dearest one, you are just adventuresome and easily bored. You are already a young lady. It's not your fault that you do not fit into your life here. I know that you have found friendships in the harem, but you must resist going there. Will you give me your word that you will not go there again?"

To give up her friends would be painful indeed, but she would do this for her mother. "Yes, Mama, I promise. I will never go there again."

Jillianna's heart broke for her daughter. Already Brittany was a beauty. Her golden hair enhanced her creamy skin. Her eyes were jade-green and fringed with long golden lashes which were black at the tips. Jillianna saw through the thin costume that Brittany's body was softly curved and mature.

She had not realized that her daughter had grown into a woman. She shuddered, thinking what Brittany's life would be like if she remained in Constantinople.

Jillianna realized that the time had come to make a decision about Brittany's future. She must be sent to London as soon as it could be arranged, even though it would not be easy to let her go when the time came. But it was time that Brittany learned about her own heritage. Jillianna would write a letter to her brother this very evening asking him to take Brittany into his household.

"Are you very disappointed in me, Mama?"

Jillianna drew Brittany into her arms. "None of this is your fault, my love. It is very difficult for you to live on the edge of two worlds. Here in the palace you are taught as any proper young English girl would be taught. But when you slip behind the harem walls, you walk into a world apart. I have forbidden you to go there, thinking to spare you the unsettling reality of those poor women and the useless lives they lead, but I have failed."

"You have not failed, Mama. Most of the women are my friends. They have taught me many wonderful things. If you knew them, you would know their worthiness."

Her mother arched her brow. "Many things you have learned from them would be better left unlearned. That kind of an education will not help you in England, Brittany."

"They have taught me to speak many languages, Mama. I can read and write in at least eleven languages."

Jillianna smiled. "Yes, there is always that." Her eyes ran over the scanty costume Brittany was wearing. "You had better change before dinner. Simijin will be wanting to see you. We have to discuss your future."

Brittany's eyes were bright with tears. "Do not send me away from you, Mama. I could not bear it. I promise I will never disobey you again. If it will make you happy, I will go to Mrs. Potter and apologize."

"Oh, my love, do not torture yourself so. If only . . . if only you could have grown up in different surroundings."

"But many young girls grow up in harems, Mama. Why should I be any different?"

"You *are* different, Brittany. I am English, and your father was American. Don't you see that you do not belong here?"

"I think of Simijin as my father."

Jillianna rolled her eyes toward the ceiling. "When the time comes for you to marry, I want you to have an English husband. You don't even know how to behave around a young man, and you never will learn here."

Brittany shook her head. "I know about men, Mama. A man is master, and it is a woman's place to serve him."

Jillianna shook her head. "That is exactly what I mean. You are repeating what you have learned in the harem, I want you to live in a world where a woman is a helpmate to her husband and not his slave."

"You are not a slave to Simijin."

"Simijin is different from his contemporaries. He allows me the freedom to be both myself and his wife. Simijin has also made certain that you are well protected. But make no mistake about it, Brittany, this is a barbaric country, and you do not belong here."

"*You* belong here, Mama."

"Only because this is the country of the man I love. I belong with Simijin, just as you will one day belong with the man you will love."

If Brittany did not fit into the world of the two people she loved most, where did she belong?

Jillianna gave her daughter a hug. "Go and change now, Brittany. We will talk more on this later."

Jillianna stood silently watching her daughter's departure. Until now, she had been selfish in keeping Brittany with her. Although it would tear her heart out, she would have to let her go.

Brittany had dressed carefully in an ivory silk gown which had just arrived from Paris the day before. It was a lovely creation with pink and green lace intertwined across the high-waisted bodice and sleeves. Her hair was pulled back from her face and laced with pink and green ribbons. She hoped the style made her appear older.

When Brittany entered the formal sitting room, she found Simijin and her mother deep in conversation. She realized they were discussing her, because they fell silent as she approached them.

Simijin, in his regal manner, motioned her forward, but the smile he gave her was warm and encouraging. She dipped down beside him, and he pulled her into a warm embrace. "I hear you have been in trouble again," he whispered in her ear so her mother could not hear. Aloud he said, "How lovely you look tonight, Brittany. Is that a new gown?"

"Yes, Simijin, it only arrived yesterday."

She glanced at her mother to see if she was still displeased with her, but her mother smiled and kissed her cheek. "We have been discussing your future, Brittany, and we have made a decision that we hope will please you."

The young girl's eyes held a hint of fear. "I do not want to leave you and Simijin. Do not send me away, Mama—please don't."

Simijin held up his hand. "We will not discuss this until after—"

Simijin was interrupted by a man's voice coming from the hallway. They could hear a servant's voice, and a commotion at the door, and suddenly a man stepped into the room.

Sultan Selim III had been to Simijin's palace before, but never in the Grand Vizier's private quarters. Brittany had often watched the sultan conversing with Simijin on state affairs, from her hidden place behind the wooden latticework at the top of the stairs. She was shocked, however, that he would enter Simijin's private quarters, which were forbidden to all outsiders. No man had ever been invited to see Jillianna unveiled, not even the sultan himself.

Selim III had vellum-toned features which were so delicate they were almost feminine. His face was thin, and his chin weak. His eager glance swept over Jillianna's face, and then his almond-shaped eyes stared at Brittany so long that she squirmed uncomfortably.

When Simijin got over the shock of the situation, he came to his feet, quickly motioning Jillianna and Brittany to withdraw into the other room. "Your Majesty," he said in a cold voice, "what an unexpected pleasure."

"Forgive me for barging in on you, Lord Simijin. But I have urgent matters to discuss with you."

Simijin was not pleased that the sultan had come into his private quarters, and his irritation showed on his face. "Had you sent for me, I would have come at once," he said with the merest reprimand in his tone.

The sultan watched the beautiful young girl slip through the curtains in the back of the room. "Who is that exquisite creature?" he asked.

"She is daughter to my wife," Simijin replied, not wanting to discuss Jillianna or Brittany.

"Ah, yes, I have heard of your stepdaughter. The rumors that she is beautiful are understated. She is an enchanting creature."

"You said you came on urgent business?" Simijin reminded him.

"What is the girl's age?"

Simijin was beginning to feel a sense of dread. Selim was showing far too much interest in Brittany. Simijin had never liked him, and now he liked him even less.

The sultan had only recently come to power after the death of his uncle, the great Abdul Hamid. Head of the Ottoman Empire was a task he was ill-suited for and ill-equipped to handle.

"Should we not be discussing your pressing matters, Your Majesty?"

Sultan Selim ignored Simijin's subtle hint. "It is well known that you gave up your harem for the English Rose. After seeing her today, I know why. She is a rare beauty. It is easy to see that daughter of the English Rose will one day match her mother in beauty."

With a heavy feeling in his heart, Simijin now realized that the sultan had purposely intruded into his quarters with the express hope of seeing Brittany. He was an evil man, and Simijin saw the way his mind was working—he wanted Brittany!

"I am certain you would not expect me to discuss anything so personal as my family with you, Your Majesty."

Selim's eyes narrowed in thoughtfulness. He knew what he was doing was unacceptable, but was he not the sultan? "Call the girl back so I talk to her," he demanded.

"You know what you ask is impossible," Simijin replied in a cold voice.

The sultan stroked his thin beard. "I have to confess to you that I have heard many rumors that the girl was lovely beyond reason, and that is why I came here tonight unannounced," he admitted, confirming Simijin's suspicions.

"I cannot imagine how you would hear about my stepdaughter."

"Come, Lord Simijin, you are too modest. Everyone knows of the beauty of your wife. Now the rumors run hot that her daughter is also a beauty. Did you not think this word would reach my ears?" The sultan studied his hands. "I appreciate beautiful women, and I will stop at nothing to possess one who interests me."

"My stepdaughter can be of no interest to you."

"I would like to honor the girl by adding her to my harem."

"I cannot allow you to do that, Your Majesty. I made my wife a promise that her daughter would never be subjected to harem life. Only this evening we were discussing sending her to England to further her education."

"I am told she is already very well educated for a woman. I would consider it a favor if you would make me a gift of her. I am in a position to reward you for your generosity."

Simijin's face darkened in anger. "She is not mine to give. If she were my own flesh, I would gladly give her to you, but the promise I made her mother prevents me from doing so. You know, Your Majesty, that I am a man of my word."

The sultan's features hardened, and his voice was threatening. "You will not change your mind?"

"Alas, I cannot."

Sultan Selim's eyes narrowed. "I will give you seven days to reconsider." Without another word, he turned away and strolled leisurely out of the room.

Simijin sank down on the couch, knowing he must tell Jillianna about the reason for the sultan's visit. He knew the sultan well enough to realize that Brittany was in real danger. Simijin would sooner see Brittany dead than in that madman's hands. Something had to be done, and soon. Brittany would have to be sent away at once!

Brittany and her mother sat quietly on the sofa, waiting for Simijin to join them. They both knew that the sultan had committed a great breach of etiquette by coming to their private quarters, but they did not know what the consequences would be.

Jillianna shook her head. "They are talking for a long time," she said anxiously. "I wonder what has happened."

"Simijin was not pleased, was he, Mama."

"No. And he had every reason not to be." Her brow knitted in a frown. "Simijin is a powerful man and will not take this insult lightly. I only hope . . ."

At that moment the door opened, and a grave-faced Simijin entered. "Come," he said, extending one arm to his wife and the other to Brittany. "Let us dine. Later we will talk about the sultan's visit."

Jillianna could tell something was bothering Simijin, but wisely, she did not question him. She watched him during dinner, and it was obvious that he was distracted. Once she found him watching Brittany with a sadness in his eyes, and it frightened her.

That night after Jillianna had gone to bed, Simijin came to her, gathering her into his arms.

"You are troubled," she said, laying her cheek against his. "Do you want to talk about it?"

"Jillianna, we have to decide quickly what is to be done about Brittany. The sultan wants her, and we have to be very clever and keep her out of his reach!"

Chapter Six

Captain Thorn Stoddard stood on the deck of the *Victorious* overseeing the loading of cargo. Even though it was early morning, a punishing heat beat down on him.

He rolled up his sleeves and blotted the perspiration from his face. He was pressed to finish taking on supplies today because he intended to catch the morning tide and sail for home.

Tall and bronzed, there was a proud and haughty look in Thorn Stoddard's blue eyes that reflected the mirror-bright water. His black hair lay damply against his handsome brow. There was an air of authority about him, as with all men who commanded their own ships.

"Looks like we got company, Captain," Cappy Hamish, his second-in-command observed, with a nod at the gangplank. "And a strange one he is, too, from the looks of his appearance."

Annoyed by the interruption, Thorn glanced at the tall black man who stood on deck, his legs spread wide to keep his balance.

Although Thorn had never seen a eunuch, his instincts told him that this man was one, because of his soft features and flamboyant manner of dress.

"Find out what he wants, Cappy," Thorn commanded, "and then see that he goes ashore. If he's selling something, I'm not buying."

At that moment, one of the pulley ropes snapped, requiring all Thorn's attention. Men scattered in every direction to keep from being crushed by the wooden crate that smashed onto the deck. Thorn's lips tightened in annoyance that a whole crate of sugared figs was ruined. He was not in the best of moods when the black man approached him.

"Excuse me, Captain, sir." The man spoke excellent English. "If I could but have a moment of your time, it is most important."

"I have no time to talk now. Stand out of the way." Thorn shoved the man aside as he unwound a new rope and cast it upward to be threaded through the pulley.

The eunuch was persistent. "Please hear me out, Captain Stoddard. It is imperative that my master speak to you as soon as possible."

"Not now," Thorn barked. "Can't you see we are busy? Move out of the way, before you get hurt!"

"My name is Achmed, and I am Head Eunuch for the Grand Vizier, Lord Simijin. It is his wish to have an audience with you right away."

Now the man had Thorn's attention. Certainly he had heard about Lord Simijin. "Tell your lord that if he can attend me here, I will talk to him. Otherwise, I am much too busy, and I sail in the morning."

Still Achmed lingered. "Sir, I am to mention to you that if you will take a certain cargo with you, my master is willing that you should name your own price."

Thorn looked at the eunuch skeptically. He did not believe that anyone as important as the Grand Vizier would wish to ship goods on an American ship, since he would have the whole Turkish fleet at his disposal.

"Why should your master wish to ship his cargo on the *Victorious?*"

"I am but a humble servant, and he does not confide in me," the eunuch said, looking anything but humble.

Thorn tossed the rope to his first mate. "See that this is mended. I shall be going to the Grand Vizier's palace." He glanced at Achmed. "But this had better be important."

Achmed smiled. "Only my master can answer that for you." He bowed respectfully. "If you will come with me, I have a carriage waiting to transport you, Captain Stoddard."

Brittany knew that something was amiss, but she could not imagine what it was. Since the night of the sultan's unannounced intrusion, a disturbing quietness had settled over the palace. She was aware that her movements had been curtailed, and she was never left alone for a moment. When she asked her mother what was the matter, Jillianna had been vague, and decidedly distressed.

Brittany moved down the corridor with her maid, Ikaia, just behind her. She paused at the wide staircase that led to Simijin's private audience chamber. She was hoping to find him alone so she could ask him why her mother was so upset. She paused on the upper landing where the stairs descended into the main hallway to make certain Simijin was alone, for she would not be allowed to go to him if he was with other men.

The latticework across the balcony was a perfect place to view the chamber without being seen. Many times Brittany had come here to watch dignitaries from all over the world who had come to confer with Simijin.

She loved to observe the flashing jewels, ostrich plumes, elaborately embroidered robes, and sable-lined pelisses worn by many of the foreigners. Envoys from vassal states often gathered here to pay their respects and to present Simijin with gifts. Ambassadors robed in scarlet and gold often arrived to ask Simijin's wise counsel.

Long ago Brittany had learned to recognize the importance of guests by their manner of dress. The law governed the color and shape of their turbans. The lesser viziers wore green, the priests white, the court chamberlain scarlet, the sheiks blue. The huntsman wore a gold-colored, horn-shaped cap, while the chief cook wore a pointed cap.

Today, however, the chamber appeared to be empty, or so Brittany thought. Her foot was on the top step when she heard the sound of voices. She moved quickly into the shadows because Simijin was talking to a man who was just out of her view. She pressed her forehead against the carved woodwork so she could observe Simijin's guest.

Ikaia, who had joined her mistress, sucked in her breath and exclaimed, "Look at the handsome man, mistress. Surely he is the most beautiful man I have ever seen. I cannot tell for certain, but it appears that his eyes are as blue as the skies. Can that be?"

"Shh. I am trying to hear what is being said," Brittany scolded her maid. "They are speaking English," she said in amazement.

"Pity I do not understand the English," Ikaia said wistfully. "I would know what this handsome man wants with Lord Simijin."

Brittany looked at the dark-haired man. She wasn't certain, but she thought he might be American because of the way he spoke English. Her interest intensified since she knew her own father had been American. All the men Brittany had seen, besides Simijin and the eunuchs, had been viewed at a distance, so she was not one to judge if the man was handsome; but yes, she would certainly call this man interesting.

She heard Simijin's voice drift up to her.

"Thank you for coming, Captain Stoddard. I am sure you question my motives for asking you here today."

"I admit I am curious."

"I have a great favor to ask of you, and even though you will be well paid, I want to impress upon you the gravity of my request."

Thorn nodded. "I am listening."

"I did not just pick you at random, Captain Stoddard. I made inquiries about you, and I found that you are highly esteemed by other captains. I have been told that you are honorable and trustworthy."

Thorn smiled. "I would say that would depend on who you ask. And I believe I should point out to you that my cargo hold is full now. If you have goods you wish to ship, you will have to wait until my next voyage."

Brittany knew Simijin well enough to realize there was a tenseness about him. "You do not understand what I want of you, Captain Stoddard. But before I speak, can I count on your discretion?"

Thorn could hardly conceal his bafflement. "Yes, of course you may."

Simijin lowered his voice, so Brittany could barely hear what he was saying. "The cargo that I wish you to transport, is . . . one of the women from my . . . harem. Will you agree to take her on board the *Victorious* and transport her to England?"

Thorn shook his head. So the important matter Lord Simijin had wanted to discuss concerned a woman from his harem, Thorn thought in disgust. "My destination is America, Lord Simijin," he snapped. "You will have to find another ship to transport your lady to England. I happen to know that there are three ships in harbor at this time that are headed for that destination."

"That is so, Captain. But the English ships will not be sailing for at least a fortnight. Out of desperation, I was forced to seek you out. If money will change your mind, I am willing to pay whatever you ask."

From her vantage point, Brittany was mystified as to which lady from Simijin's harem he would be sending to England. With heightened interest, she listened to the American captain as he spoke.

"*If* my destination were England, and *if* I took passengers on board, Lord Simijin, your lady would pay the same passage as anyone else—for I have never yet taken advantage of any man. But as I said, my destination is America, and that will not change. Even if you wanted to send your lady to America, I would have to refuse, for the *Victorious* is not equipped to accommodate a woman passenger."

Simijin looked into steely blue eyes and knew this man could not be bought for any price. "Very well, Captain Stoddard, I see that I cannot change your mind. But I am grateful to you for coming all the same."

Brittany's eyes followed the tall American as he moved across the room. She thought it would be wonderful if she could talk to him about the land of her father. After the captain had disappeared, she watched Simijin nervously pacing, and she was more certain than ever that he was distressed about something. She was still mystified as to which woman from the harem he wanted to send to England. She would ask her mother if she knew anything about the strange incident.

She turned to her maid. "Let us leave, Ikaia. I do not believe we should disturb Lord Simijin at this time."

Achmed was out of breath because he had been running. He drew air into his lungs and paused before his master's door, saying to the guard: "Open the door. I must see Lord Simijin at once."

The guard stepped aside respectfully and immediately admitted the eunuch.

"Lord Simijin," Achmed blurted out, "I have just come from the market, where I spoke with Cridia, the head eunuch from the Grand Seraglio. He told me that they are making ready for a new woman of great importance." He paused to take a deep breath. "He said that the woman is the daughter of your English Rose. It is the young mistress he was referring to, my lord."

Simijin, a man who was always calm in the face of adversity, now paled. "Did the man say just how this was to be accomplished?"

"Yes, my lord. Since Cridia knows how fond I am of the little mistress, he warned me, at great risk to himself, that a troop from the Janissaries will come and take her away this very afternoon! He could tell me nothing more, but he warned that we should get her to safety with all dispatch."

Simijin nodded at the eunuch. "Thank you, Achmed. We shall make haste before it is too late."

* * *

Brittany had been unable to find her mother, but as she was dressing for dinner, Jillianna came rushing into the bedroom, her face pale, her eyes wide with fear.

"Brittany, you must come with me at once; there is not a moment to lose!"

"But, Mama, what—"

Jillianna took her daughter's hand and pulled her toward the door. "There is no time to talk. We must hurry to the harem before it is too late!"

Brittany was mystified. Why was her mother so afraid? And why was she taking her to the harem when she hated it so much?

As they moved quickly across the garden, they were joined by Simijin. Brittany could feel the tension between her mother and stepfather and she saw that her mother was trembling with fear. Something was terribly wrong.

When they reached the pavilion, the door of the harem swung wide, and she was immediately surrounded by Simijin's women. Gentle hands pulled her into a secluded room behind the bath.

Before she could ask questions, she was stripped of her gown and then her thin chemise. Juanita and Asha began rubbing a dark walnut oil into her naked body.

Brittany's eyes sought her mother's. "What is happening? What are they doing to me?"

Jillianna took a deep breath, knowing it was time to tell Brittany the truth. "Do you recall the night the sultan came into our quarters?"

"Yes, but—"

"He came that night with the express purpose of seeing you. He is a devious and evil man, and he has decided he will stop at nothing to have you. That is why you must be disguised, and we must sneak you out of the city and away from Constantinople. Once the sultan finds out you are missing, he will have his Janissaries searching for you everywhere."

Brittany trembled in fear, cringing at the thought of that odious man touching her. "I will not go with him, Mama."

"No, you shall not. Simijin has a plan, and you must trust him."

By this time, Brittany's whole body was covered with the oil that stained her skin dark. Now she understood the reason for Simijin's conversation with the American sea captain. He had been bargaining with Captain Stoddard to take her to safety.

"But where will I go, Mama?"

"You are not to worry, my dearest. Simijin will see that you are safe."

Brittany stood trembling as her golden hair was covered with ebony dye, and her eyebrows were darkened with kohl. After this was done, she was dressed in a heavy black robe.

"Mama, I am so frightened. Will you come with me, please?"

Jillianna blinked back her tears. "No, my dearest, I cannot come with you, for I would endanger you. You are going to America, where you will be with your father's people for a while. I do not know if your grandmother is still alive, but your father's family will surely take you in until it is safe for you to return to me."

Brittany knew that she must be brave for her mother's sake. "I will be all right, Mama. Do not concern yourself about me."

Jillianna's eyes filled with tears. "You must remember to keep the dark oils on your skin and the dyes on your hair until you are safely with your grandmother. Simijin and I have discussed this at great length, and we have decided that you are to tell no one who you are until you reach Philadelphia, because you do not know who you can trust. Swear this oath to me, Brittany, that you will keep your identity a secret. Let those you meet believe that you are merely a woman from Simijin's harem so that you will be left alone."

"I give my oath, Mama . . . but I do not understand the reason for it."

Everything was happening so quickly that Brittany was being swept along in a tide of unreality. The thought of becoming one of the sultan's women brought a shudder of horror to her, but to be parted from her mother and Simijin would be so painful.

A dreadful thought tugged at Brittany's mind. "Mama, will you or Simijin be in any danger from the sultan because you helped me escape?"

"Of course not. The sultan would not dare harm me or Simijin, for fear the people would rise up in revolt since they love Simijin well. Our concern is getting you safely out of that evil man's clutches. You will have to be very careful and do exactly as you are told, Brittany. Remember, you must pretend to be a woman of the harem."

Brittany stood before the mirror, staring at the image of a stranger. Her skin was dark, her hair black, and she did indeed look like a woman of the harem. Her slight body shook with fear, and she turned worried eyes to her mother.

"What will I do without you and Simijin?" She looked at the dear faces of the women in the harem and saw that they were all crying. "I shall miss you all."

Brittany's mother embraced her, trying hard not to cry. Several of the women came forward and hugged Brittany, their silent glances telling her they feared for her. One of them placed a heavy veil across Brittany's face so that only her green eyes were visible.

Jillianna looked about the harem at the faces of the women who had befriended her daughter. She could see from their expressions that they, too, were worried about Brittany. There were none here who would betray Brittany to the sultan. Jillianna felt ashamed because she had always shunned these women.

Jillianna took her daughter's hands, wondering if they would ever see each other again. Brittany's tears ran down her face and she wanted to cling to her mother. It was frightening being cast into a world she knew nothing about.

Jillianna smiled sadly. "I have written a letter to your grandmother in America, hoping that she still lives. You must communicate with me as soon as you are able." Again she hugged her daughter to her, then quickly released her, fearing she would lose courage and not be able to let Brittany go.

Simijin quickly entered the room, and he looked startled when he saw the transformation that had come over Brittany. He took her hand and spoke to her lovingly. "Take courage, daughter of my heart; you will be in good hands. One day we shall all be reunited."

Brittany embraced the man whom she thought of as her father. "How can I leave you and Mama? I will miss you both so dreadfully."

He gazed into her eyes. "It is but temporary. Always remember that you are the daughter of the English Rose, and be proud."

Simijin was leading her out of the room. Brittany turned back for a last glance at her mother, and found she was being comforted by the women of the harem. Simijin led her to a donkey cart that had been driven up to the harem door. Ikaia handed Achmed a leather satchel in which she had packed Brittany's clothing and toilette items.

"Brittany, you will not be alone," Simijin assured her. "Put your faith in Achmed, for he will be with you and has sworn to protect you with his life."

Before Brittany could ask questions, she was hoisted onto a cart and Achmed whipped the donkeys into motion.

Too frightened to think clearly, Brittany wanted to jump down and run back to all that was familiar. She was about to enter a world that was foreign to her.

The gates of the palace loomed ahead. In her whole life she had never been on the other side of those gates, and she could only imagine what she would find there.

When the cart lumbered up to the main gates, Achmed halted and turned to Brittany, pointing to the satin-padded crate he had placed there earlier.

"You must get in and lie down among the cushions and let me close the lid. It is Lord Simijin's wish that we take no chances on you being discovered."

Brittany shook her head when she gazed at the small crate. "I cannot fit in that. How will I breathe? It frightens me, Achmed."

"See . . ." he said encouragingly, "I have cut these holes in the wood. You will be able to see where we are going, and you can breathe quite well."

Trusting Achmed, she gathered her courage and climbed into the crate.

For a moment, she was certain that she would suffocate. But she found she could breathe and the thought of being discovered by the sultan's men gave her the courage she needed.

She closed her eyes, wondering if this horrible ordeal would ever be over. Why had the hateful sultan come into her life? How would she ever find her way home?

Chapter Seven

The streets of Constantinople hummed with life, so the donkey-drawn cart driven by Achmed attracted very little notice as it moved slowly along, stirring up the red-colored dust in its wake.

Achmed guided the donkeys past covered markets where spices, ivory, and silk were displayed to catch the buyer's eye. There were shops where rare pearls, gold, and precious stones were sold. When they moved past the Grand Market, the air was filled with the delicious smell of hot bread baking.

As the shaggy animals plodded along at their leisure, Achmed glanced back over his shoulder at the wooden crate, knowing how uncomfortable Brittany must be in the limited space. Even though he had cut holes for her to breathe, she would be feeling the intense heat. He noticed that the sun was going down and felt the need for haste, but the mass of humanity that surged about the streets slowed his progress to a crawl.

When a troop of Janissaries rode past, heading in the direction of the Grand Vizier's palace, Achmed cast his eyes downward and hunched his shoulders, hoping he would not be recognized.

Soon, the hue and cry would go out that Brittany had escaped, and the sultan's guards would be scouring the city for her. Achmed was determined to get Brittany safely on board the *Victorious* before that occurred.

Thorn Stoddard placed his signature on the document that had been handed him by Sydak, the harbormaster. "I am sailing with a full load this time," he told the man. "So, we are riding low in the water."

Sydak, who had been harbormaster for over forty years, shook hands with the captain, as was his habit when he encountered an American. They seemed to expect it! "It is good that you are soon sailing, for there is trouble in the city tonight, Captain Stoddard."

"I had not heard. Of what nature is this trouble?" Thorn asked, not really interested, but sensing the old man wanted to talk about it.

"The sultan's Janissaries are out tonight on a nasty mission, I am told. It may even be that they will close the harbor. Perhaps you should leave as soon as possible."

"I have heard no good of the Janissaries. They are a ruthless lot, are they not?"

The harbormaster looked around furtively, and when he saw that no one would overhear, he answered. "At one time they were the elite guard, but that has not been for many years."

"What are they about tonight?" Thorn inquired.

"It is said that they seek a woman of rare beauty whom the sultan desires. She is a woman from the house of the Grand Vizier, and there will be trouble and woes before this is brought to a conclusion."

Thorn's interest was aroused. "Like everyone else who comes to your shores, I have heard that the Grand Vizier has a wife of great beauty. I believe she is referred to as the English Rose."

"Yes, this is what they say, but of course none has ever seen the English Rose."

"Could it be her whom the sultan seeks?" Thorn wanted to know.

Sydak shook his head. "No, never her! The streets would run with blood if anyone, even the sultan, tried to take the English Rose from Lord Simijin." Sydak leaned in closer and whispered, as if he were afraid of being overheard. "I do not know who this woman is," he shrugged his shoulders, "but to think a mere woman would cause such a commotion. She must indeed be beautiful. Pity her if the sultan does find her, for it is said that he is touched by madness. Many of us wish for the days before his uncle, Abdul Hamid, died and Selim came to power."

Thorn recalled his audience with the Grand Vizier. He was grateful that he had rejected Lord Simijin's offer to take his woman to safety; she must be the one the sultan was searching for tonight. All he needed was to become embroiled in the politics of Turkey!

Sydak saw the impatience in the captain's eyes and bowed low to him, taking his leave. What did an American care about the fate of one woman, he thought regretfully, or the problems of Turkey and the ruthless Sultan Selim?

Thorn watched the old man depart before he went below deck to his cabin. He had to make ready to sail before dawn. If there was going to be trouble between the sultan and his Grand Vizier, he wanted to be out of the harbor when it happened.

Cappy Hamish, the first mate of the *Victorious*, watched the big black man lumber up the gangplank carrying a bulky crate with obvious ease.

Gently the eunuch sat the crate down, and smiled at the first mate. "You will remember that I was here this afternoon. My name is Achmed, and I come from the Grand Vizier with a gift for your Captain Stoddard."

"The captain has left orders that he is not to be disturbed. I will have to stow the crate in the cargo hold for now. The gift will be given to Captain Stoddard after we have sailed."

Achmed smiled. He had purposely waited until the hour was late in hopes that the captain would be too occupied with charting his maps to be disturbed.

Cappy called two of the crew. "Here . . . look lively, men. Stow this crate in the hold."

When the men tilted the crate on its side, Achmed

protested. "The gift within is of a great value, so I would caution you to have the greatest care and carry it upright."

Cappy instructed the men to do as the eunuch requested. He also gave his consent when Achmed begged to be allowed to accompany the crew below deck to make certain the crate was properly stowed.

It was but a short time later when Achmed returned and bowed before Cappy. "Sir, it is my wish to take passage on your ship. I have always desired to see your America."

Cappy looked surprised. "Are you aware that this ship is bound for Charleston, South Carolina?"

"It does not matter the destination. Here I am a slave; there I will be a free man."

Cappy looked astounded. "Do you know anything about America—in particular, the South?"

"No, but I am willing to learn."

Cappy shook his head. "You may be trading one master for another. I have never heard of a time when a man of black skin asked to be transported to the South. Sounds like Daniel asking to be put in the lions' den to me."

Achmed did not understand the first mate's meaning. Taking a purse from his belt, he held out a gold nugget. "Will this pay my passage to America?"

Cappy nodded. "Yes, and you will have money left over. But you should know that there are no cabins available, so you will have to be contented with sleeping on deck."

"If it is all the same to you, I will remain below with Lord Simijin's gift. I will be quite comfortable there."

Cappy found the request strange, but he had other matters on his mind and he readily agreed. He could not understand why the eunuch wanted to watch over the Grand Vizier's gift, when he was running away from him. He shrugged his shoulders. Turkey was filled with strange people with even stranger customs.

Jillianna stood behind the latticework, watching Simijin greet the sultan. Fear caught at her heart as the sultan glanced in her direction, and she had the feeling his evil black eyes were staring right at her. She stepped back a pace until she could compose herself. Even though she was still uncertain about her daughter's future, she was thankful that Brittany was well out of that evil man's hands.

The sultan's voice was silky. "So, Lord Simijin, I come to seek my little bird and find only an empty nest." His eyes narrowed to slits. "Where is she?"

Simijin merely shrugged in an offhand manner. "Are you referring to my stepdaughter?"

"You know very well I am. Where is she?"

"Do you not recall that I told you she would be going to England?"

A look of triumph gleamed in Selim's eyes. "You would like me to think she is on her way to England, but I know better. I know she sailed on the American ship, *Victorious*. Several of my swiftest ships will put to sea within the hour, and I am sure they will easily overtake the merchant ship. And when they do, all aboard will be put to death, except, of course, the daughter of the English Rose."

A cry escaped Jillianna's lips, and she trembled with loathing and fear. With hands clasped, she dropped to her knees and prayed that her daughter would not fall into the evil sultan's hands.

Simijin's voice was calm. "I would not advise Your Majesty to touch my stepdaughter."

Selim smiled. "Do you threaten me, Lord Simijin?"

"No, not I. But you are the leader of a great country. As you know, Turkey is important to many of the world powers because of her location. England will protect us because she craves this route to India, while France and Italy want to protect their rights to the Mediterranean. It might be well advised for you to remember that my stepdaughter is half English by birth."

"That is one of the thing that intrigues me about her."

"But, Your Majesty, with the rest of the world watching, and comparing you with your uncle, you need to be a strong leader, and one the European countries will respect. It must not look like any woman is too important to you. It must appear that you are buried in matters of state."

For a moment the sultan's eyes gleamed with the feeling of power, then he smiled. "You are very clever, Lord Simijin. But take care that you are not too clever. There are many worthy men who covet the title of Grand Vizier. Before he died, my uncle told me to put my trust in you and heed your advice. I will listen to you in all matters of state, but I will also have this girl. Have a care that I do not strip you of your office," he threatened with a gleam in his eyes. "You could be replaced with a more . . . loyal subject, shall we say."

Simijin bowed from the waist. "That is Your Majesty's right."

Selim moved across the room and turned at the door with a menacing snarl on his thick lips. "I will have the daughter of the English Rose, Lord Simijin, for I have my heart set on her."

After the sultan had gone, Simijin rushed to Jillianna, because he knew she had been listening to his confrontation with the sultan. He was worried about her. She was going to need his strength in the weeks ahead until they learned Brittany's fate.

Brittany felt the heat pressing in on her, and she was having difficulty breathing. She was in total darkness, and she was frightened. She had always been pampered and protected, and had never known the word fear until today. Now she was on board a ship that was headed to a country she had only read about in books.

"Little mistress," the dear, familiar voice of Achmed cut through her fears, "I am going to help you out of the crate now, but you must be very quiet."

When the lid was ripped open, she drew in a deep breath and blinked her eyes until they became accustomed to the dim light. Achmed helped Brittany to her feet, but she had to lean on him for support since her legs felt as they would not hold her upright.

Brittany glanced about her. There were crates, barrels, and boxes, as well as coils of rope and extra canvas for sails. It was damp here, and she shivered.

"I am hungry, Achmed. I hope you have brought me something to eat."

"I will return shortly with food. I first wanted to get you out of the crate." He led her over to the steps and guided her into the shadows. "Stay hidden until I return," he warned. "Do not come out unless you know I have returned."

The ship swayed and rocked, and she leaned back against a barrel, trying to keep her balance. "Are we underway, Achmed?"

"Yes, mistress." He moved up the steps and called over his shoulder. "I will return quickly."

Brittany sank to her knees, too weary to stand. This had been the worst day of her life, and she shuddered to think what lay ahead of her. Each swaying of the ship took her farther away from her mother and Simijin.

True to his word, it was but a short time later when Achmed reappeared. "I have brought you food, little mistress, and it looks edible. I am sure it is not pheasant, but it appears to be some kind of fowl." He smiled. "It will surely fill an empty stomach."

He dusted off a barrel for her to sit on, and watched as she picked up a slice of the meat and tasted it. Wrinkling her nose with loathing, Brittany said, "Achmed, perhaps I am not so hungry after all. This does not have a pleasant taste."

"You will find that ship food does not compare with the diet you are accustomed to eating. Whatever it is, you must eat, mistress, for we do not know what is ahead of us."

Nodding her head in understanding, she managed to take several mouthfuls before she handed it back to Achmed. "I suppose I am too miserable to eat. I am worried about my mother."

Suddenly Achmed tensed. "Shh," he whispered, waving her back into the shadows. She ducked behind a wooden crate just as heavy footsteps dropped down from the rope ladder. She hugged the darkness as Achmed blew out the candle, and they were enveloped in total darkness.

A crewman appeared, carrying a lantern which flickered eerily across the walls and danced drunkenly to lighten darkened corners. From their hiding place, Achmed and Brittany watched the man stow a small crate and then move back up the steps. When his footsteps faded away, Brittany breathed in a sigh of relief.

"How long must I remain in this place and hide from the captain and crew?" she asked wearily.

"A few more days. Once we are far enough out to sea so it will be impractical for the captain to return, only then shall we reveal your presence."

Thorn stood at the wheel, expertly maneuvering the *Victorious* through the treacherous waters of the Golden Horn.

For some reason he had grown weary of the sea, and more and more he was becoming dissatisfied with his life. Lately his thoughts were often of his father, and Thorn wondered if he ever regretted the harsh words that had passed between them the night Thorn had left the family plantation, Stoddard Hill.

His mother had died when Thorn was just a young boy, so he and his father had become very close—at least until trouble had torn them apart—trouble in the guise of a woman. His mind traveled backward to the night it had all begun . . .

The ball had been held at the Burke mansion, and everyone in the county was in attendance. Thorn had just returned from a grand tour of Europe. He was basking in the attention of every available female, dancing with them all, old and young, while his father looked proudly upon his only son's popularity.

Thorn had paused to catch his breath, when he looked up

winding stairs to see a beautiful woman smiling down at him. Her name was Wilhelmina; her hair was black, and her skin soft and white. Even to this day, Thorn could not recall the color of her eyes, but she had the face of an angel.

Like a man in a trance, he gravitated toward her. As she came into his arms, he danced her across the room, discovering that she was a distant relation to the Burkes. They danced the rest of the evening, and later she walked with him in the garden. She had seemed shy and innocent, and that night he fell in love for the first time.

After that night, Thorn and Wilhelmina were together every day, and he was beginning to think of marriage and even children. Then one night they had walked in the garden, and she had allowed Thorn to kiss her. He remembered fearing he would frighten her with his unleashed passion.

How could he have known that Wilhelmina was not the innocent she pretended to be? That night she had taken his hand and led him to a distant part of the garden. With her breath coming out in short gasps and her eyes gleaming with desire, she lifted her gown and took his hand, placing it on her thigh.

He remembered being shocked by her boldness, but he had been too swept along by his desire to care. All he knew was that he had to have her.

She unfastened his trousers, and handled his throbbing manhood until he was almost mindless. She pulled him down to the ground, lifted her skirt, and straddled him. He slipped easily inside her, for she was no virgin, as he had thought . . .

Thorn balled his hands into fists. How little he had known about a woman's deceitfulness at that time. He could still see the moonlight shining on Wilhelmina's face, while her eyes were glazed and half-closed . . .

"Faster, faster," she had breathed in his ear. "Go deeper. I want to feel all of you."

Suddenly his passion had cooled, to be replaced with a feeling of repugnance. All he wanted was to get away from her. There was something base and wicked about Wilhelmina, he could feel it. He was not to know just how evil she was until a year later.

Wilhelmina had felt him withdrawing from her, and she protested. "What are you doing? You have not satisfied me yet. I thought you were a man, but perhaps I was mistaken."

His pride was wounded, and his prowess challenged. "Perhaps I am not versed enough in the ways of the world to suit you," he replied, moving her aside and standing up.

"I could teach you," she purred. "You excite me as no man ever has." She reached up and touched him intimately. "I could show you how to please me."

He had helped her to her feet. "Yes, I daresay you could. But I'm just not interested."

Her eyes took on a cruel glint. "I was under the impression you wanted to marry me; was I mistaken?"

He shook his head. "I do not believe we are right for one another."

"I have told all my friends that we are to be married. Will you make a laughingstock of me?"

"I do not recall that we discussed marriage."

She was quiet for a long moment. "You are angry because I have been with other men." Her laughter rang out. "I have been with more men than you can count. You were such an innocent, you could not guess that I wanted you to make love to me that first night we met. You cannot know what torment I have been in, wanting you to make love to me."

He tried to shake off his disgust. "Perhaps we should both forget that tonight happened. I know I intend to."

"You men are all alike," she whispered through stiff lips. "You blame a woman for doing what you do and call her a whore, while you are proud of your accomplishments with the very women you condemn."

He stepped away from her, wanting to put some distance between them. "I do not think—"

She held up her hand to silence him. "No, men never do think."

"I am sorry this had to happen," he said, regretfully.

Suddenly she surprised him with a smile. "Do not reproach yourself, Thorn. I always get what I want in the end—you will see."

She straightened her gown and patted her hair into place. "I was leaving for Savannah in the morning anyway, and this was to be my little going away gift to you." Her eyes became hard and cold. "Can I assume you are a gentleman and will not mention what happened between us tonight?"

"Yes, you can assume that."

Thorn was numb, but also relieved that she would be leaving Charleston. He hoped he would never have to see her again, but he had not reasoned with Wilhelmina's strong drive for vengeance.

How could he guess that Wilhelmina would one day come back into his life. It was but one year from the day she left Charleston that she married Thorn's father. It did not matter that she was twenty years younger than his father; all she cared about was getting even with Thorn.

Thorn's world had been shattered the day his father brought Wilhelmina to Stoddard Hill as his wife. "I know you were fond of her at one time, Son. Now she will be your stepmother, and we will have her in our family."

Thorn was sick inside, knowing that she was making a fool of his father. Wilhelmina knew that Thorn could never tell his father that his new bride was not the innocent she pretended to be.

As the weeks passed, Wilhelmina took pleasure in flaunting her indiscretions in Thorn's face, as if daring him to tell his father. She was a brazen creature, but Thorn managed to avoid her whenever possible. And he made sure he never saw her without his father being present.

One night when his father had been away from home, Wilhelmina came to Thorn's bedroom. In a cold voice, he ordered her to leave, but she merely laughed at him.

She slipped out of her dressing gown and stood naked before him. Anger burned inside him as she walked toward him slowly.

"I told you I always get what I want, Thorn. Are your dreams haunted by the thought of me lying in your father's arms? Do you desire me?" she taunted.

He scooped up her dressing gown and threw it at her. "I am merely disgusted by you, Wilhelmina. Have you no feelings of regret for what you have done?"

Her eyes sparkled with the light of madness. "No, no regrets . . . save one. I still desire you." She crept across the room, moving her hips sensuously, and his eyes fastened on her creamy breasts. He hated himself because she still sparked desire within his body.

"Get out," he growled as she slid her arms about his neck.

It was at that moment that the bedroom door was torn open and Thorn looked up to see his father standing there. He would never forget the stricken look on his face.

He could still remember the anger in his father's voice as he had accused him of seducing his innocent wife. Thorn had not told his father that Wilhelmina had come to his room, nor had he told him that she had been with every man at Stoddard Hill from the stable boy to the overseer. By his silence that night, Thorn had taken the blame for Wilhelmina.

His father had ordered him to leave Stoddard Hill that night, and Thorn had not been back since . . .

Sometimes, even now, if Thorn closed his eyes, he could smell the freshly harvested hay, and hear the wind in the pine trees outside his bedroom window at Stoddard Hill. He had been only twenty when he left his home. How foolish he had been to allow lies and pride to come between him and his father.

Lately, Thorn had been overcome with a strange loneliness. He wanted to gaze upon the land where he was born, the land where his mother had been buried. He had come to realize that his real love was for the land. He was no longer content with a seafaring life.

Thorn had made up his mind that when the *Victorious* docked once more in Charleston Harbor, he was going home. His father might order him out of the house, but not before they cleared the air between them.

Chapter Eight

Brittany lay on the cushions that Achmed had arranged for her on the floor. Closing her eyes, she wished she was back home in her own bed at the palace. She missed her mother and ached for that which was familiar to her. She turned her face to watch the faithful Achmed, who was lying nearby, his eyes ever watchful in the event there should be any danger.

"Achmed, are you sure the sultan will not take revenge on Mama and Simijin?"

"The sultan may be a mad man, but he is not witless. He knows he would lose his head if he harmed Lord Simijin. The Janissaries, as well as the people of Constantinople, would rise up against him."

"How long do you think I will have to stay away before I can return home?"

"I do not know, young mistress. When we get to America and we inform Lady Jillianna that you are safe, then she and Lord Simijin will inform us what to do."

"Achmed?"

"Yes, little mistress."

"Thank you for accompanying me. I do not know what I would do without you."

"There is no place I would rather be, little mistress. Just know that you are safe while I am watching over you. Now, go to sleep, for nothing will harm you tonight."

Strangely enough, Brittany did fall asleep. She was rocked by the gentle swaying of the *Victorious* as the vessel made its way to open sea.

* * *

The *Victorious* was a large frigate that had been in Thorn's mother's family for three generations. She had once been a warship and had seen many battles. Thorn's uncle David, the previous captain, had joined the French Navy and quickly worked up to the rank of admiral. He had been a hero after sinking seven English ships.

After the end of the war, Admiral Stone had rebuilt the *Victorious* for peacetime, and made her a merchant ship. Her forecastle deck had been removed to add cargo space, and she was enlisted in trade.

Even so, the *Victorious* was still well equipped for combat. She had fourteen gun-ports on her main deck, and she supported three twenty-four-pounders, so if the need arose, she was able to do battle.

Thorn would always be grateful to his uncle David for helping him through a very difficult time and helping him regain his self-respect. After leaving Stoddard Hill, Thorn had gone with his uncle David on his next voyage to France, and he took readily to the sea.

Thorn had been devastated when his uncle died three years later. Having no sons of his own, David Stone had left a house in Charleston and the *Victorious* to Thorn, along with vast debts to pay, for David had lived a flamboyant life.

For the past seven years, Thorn had struggled to keep the ship afloat. Perhaps after this voyage, he would have enough money to pay off the last of his uncle's debts, and he would have a clear title to the *Victorious*.

It had been a long, hard struggle for Thorn to pay his uncle's obligations; but he did it gladly, for he owed his uncle a debt that mere money could never repay.

Thorn Stoddard had learned well from Admiral David Stone. Now his ability as a captain was legendary, and any would-be enemies had always given the *Victorious* a wide lane.

Thorn stood on deck, keeping a trained eye on the heavy clouds gathering in the east. His instincts alerted him that there would be a storm sometime after nightfall. He wanted to be out of the Golden Horn and on the Sea of Marmora before the storm hit, to lessen the danger of being blown aground.

Thorn glanced to his starboard side with little interest when the watch called down that three Turkish ships were closing in on the *Victorious*. The Golden Horn was the gateway to Constantinople; therefore, the lanes were always crowded with ships and he paid them little heed.

By midday, a heavy wind was blowing out of the north, churning up the waves which reached for the sky and splashed over the sides of the *Victorious*.

That was when Thorn realized that the three Turkish ships were heading their way—two of them were man-of-wars, while the third was a thirty-six-gun frigate.

Because of the wind shift, Thorn changed directions, and it soon became apparent that the three ships also changed directions and were gaining on him.

The *Victorious* neared the end of the Golden Horn, where the Turkish shoreline loomed just ahead, and a heavily armed fortress was perched on the highest cliff. Thorn knew he must pass within range of the shore batteries to reach open sea. Training his spyglass on the vessel that was immediately behind him, he saw that she carried the banner of the Turkish Navy.

Again he changed directions and saw that the three ships did likewise.

Thorn was beginning to have the uneasy feeling that he was being pursued, though he could not think why. It was at that point that one of the vessels fired a cannon shot over the bow of the *Victorious*, confirming his suspicions.

Cappy had rushed on deck and stood beside Thorn, while the crew tensely waited for orders from their captain.

Thorn spoke to his first mate. "What in the hell is going on, Cappy? To my knowledge, we have done nothing to provoke the Turkish Navy."

"I don't know, Captain, but look—they are beginning to form a line of battle!"

It was true—the Turkish ships were sailing three abreast, and had been joined by a fourth, larger ship, a seventy-four gun man-of-war.

"If it's to be a fight," Cappy observed, "we are badly outnumbered, but we have the best gunners. Each man's been trained by a master, and they all know their assignments. The Turkish Navy is notorious for their inferior gunners."

Thorn's face was grim as he stared straight ahead. "Even if they are inferior, with all their firepower they are likely to land a fortuitous shot. Our only hope is to make it into open water. There we have a chance—slim though it may be."

Quickly Thorn signaled to have all sails set, gambling that the Turkish ships would not dare carry a full sail in the wind that was quickly becoming gale force.

In the belly of the ship, Brittany heard the sound of an explosion, and she looked at Achmed, her eyes wide with terror. "What was that? What can be happening?"

The black giant shook his head. "I do not know. It sounded like cannon fire. Stay hidden while I go topside and inquire into the matter."

Brittany blinked her eyes and nodded. She was terrified to be left alone. She was in a hostile world which she did not understand, and she had no one to cling to except her steadfast Achmed.

Thorn saw the huge black man the moment he stepped onto deck. Turning to Cappy, the captain's eyes snapped with anger. "What in the hell is going on, Mr. Hamish? What is that man doing on board the *Victorious?*"

"Sir, you were occupied with other matters when he came on board. I forgot to tell you about him. You will remember him. His name is Achmed, and he has booked passage for America."

Thorn's eyes narrowed. "Of course. I didn't recognize him at first because of his plain garments. There can be no mistake he is the Grand Vizier's servant." Thorn looked past his first mate to the oncoming warships. "It just might be that I know why we are being pursued by the Turkish Navy, Cappy. Did the man bring a woman on board with him, Cappy?"

"No, Captain. He was alone."

Thorn glanced back to see the frigate gaining on him. He turned to the starboard so quickly, his top mast almost touched the plunging waves. "Something is not right here, Cappy. Unless I am mistaken, that eunuch smuggled a woman on board while you weren't looking," Thorn said grimly.

"Nay, Captain. All he brought was a leather satchel with his belongings and a large crate containing a gift to you from the Grand Vizier."

Thorn's blue eyes darkened, and he stared at his first mate in irritation. "Could the crate be large enough to hold a woman?"

Cappy looked bemused. "I . . . suppose so, but— Yes, it would have been a tight fit, but it would have been large enough."

There was no time for Thorn to act on his suspicions, for at that moment, the Turkish frigate fired a succession of volleys which came dangerously close to hitting the *Victorious*. Thorn would need all his skills if he was to avoid disaster. Later, he would deal with the eunuch.

Cappy was feeling like a fool for his lack of perception. By allowing the eunuch to take passage on the *Victorious*, he had probably brought the whole of the Turkish Navy down on his captain's head.

The captain yelled out his orders so as to be heard above the howling winds. A heavy gust caught the *Victorious's* sails, and she was moving out of the Golden Horn and into the Sea of Marmora, but still the fortress loomed ahead.

Admiral Kainardji stood on deck of the Turkish frigate, believing he had his prey caught between him and the shore batteries. What he did not realize was that his prey did not know the word "defeat."

Thorn realized he could not outdistance the Turkish vessels since he was running with a full cargo which was slowing him down. He could only hope to outmaneuver the enemy—a slim chance, but his only one.

Hope sprung to life within the crew of the American ship when they watched the command frigate leave her sister ships behind in her pursuit of the *Victorious*. This gave their captain the chance to pit all his skills against the one ship, instead of four. The crew felt Captain Stoddard was worth any dozen Turks when it came to matching of wits.

The crew was startled when their captain maneuvered close to shore, ordered them to let down the canvases, and then turned to the lee side.

"If the enemy follows true to form," he called out to Cappy, "they will swing into the wind. And when they do, they will be vulnerable to our cannons," Thorn shouted to be heard against the wailing wind. "This will be our chance to do the most damage. Have the guns primed and ready to fire as she passes."

Just as Thorn had predicted, the frigate turned sharply, and when she did, he gave the signal to fire.

Seven cannons spit fire, hitting their target and fatally damaging her hull. The enemy ship foundered, and her gun-ports had not fired but were open and taking in water from the rough sea. Thorn ordered a broadside that ripped the enemy ship open from the wind and water.

A loud cheer went up from the crew of the *Victorious*. They had taken first victory, for one enemy ship was badly crippled. Of course, there was always the danger that she might still use her guns, so they could not yet claim victory—and now the other three ships were bearing down on them. But the *Victorious* had struck so quickly it had left the enemy dazed and unprepared.

Thorn Stoddard's code of honor and bravery compelled his crew to fight beside him. Even against impossible odds, it never occurred to them that he would not win. As the day progressed, and with each successful encounter, their belief in their captain's ability intensified.

While the crew of the *Victorious* cheered, their captain

turned the ship and brought her alongside the enemy, passing so closely that their riggings touched.

Thorn then ordered another firing of cannon, and the enemy frigate exploded into splinters.

Turning the *Victorious* to catch the wind, Thorn knew they still faced insurmountable odds that had only been lessened by one. There were still the fortress guns and the other three ships to deal with.

Going with the wind behind him, Thorn noticed that the enemy ships had piled on more canvas. No, his troubles were not over; they had just begun.

"Hoist the signal to prepare for action," Thorn ordered. "Reload and make ready all cannon!"

Thorn concluded that he had only two choices. He could either try to outdistance the enemy by dumping his cargo overboard, or he could try for a fight.

By now the sky was dark and a heavy rain had begun to fall.

Thorn saw that the enemy had turned and was headed for shore, where a heavy barrage of cannon fire from the cliff stronghold spit out a continuous bombardment.

Cappy seemed to read his captain's mind. "They have the supremacy of numbers, but we have the skill. Do we fight or run, Captain?"

"We fight," Thorn stated with conviction. "Because we are of a lesser strength, we shall have to hit—sail away— and hit again. We will bother them with the persistence of a stinging wasp. We shall wound the enemy little by little, until he bleeds. Then we shall finish him off. Pray he does not send for reinforcements."

"But we don't know these waters, and the storm will not be in our favor. It looks like the Turks have decided to anchor and ride the storm out. Should we not take our advantage and flee?"

"Not at all, Cappy. If the enemy can anchor, so shall we." Thorn's eyes brightened with the challenge of battle. "Or . . . we could make them think we have anchored."

Cappy's eyes sparkled. "So, we are to fool them into thinking the storm deterred our movements?"

"It seems to be to the likely thing to do under the circumstances."

Thorn motioned for his first mate to take the wheel while he adjusted his spyglass so he could study the enemy. His jaw locked in a grim line, and he slammed the spyglass against his palm. "Damn, they have raised the Blood Flag, signifying that there will be no quarter."

"Whatever have we done to provoke such action, Captain?"

"Past sinking their frigate, I can only guess. I would wager we have that woman the sultan is looking for on board, and apparently the Turks are willing to go to great lengths to get her back."

"But, Captain, to offer no quarter and no mercy when our two countries are not at war—this is barbaric."

"They don't seem to be as concerned about that as you are. Inform the men that we must fight, because surrender is not a possibility for us. We must win or die trying. Tell them of the gravity of our situation, and warn them what will happen if we should be taken."

Brittany buried her face in her hands as her body trembled with fear.

Achmed tried to soothe her anxiety with words of optimism. "I talked with one of the crewmen, and he told me that Captain Stoddard's courage is legendary, and it is said that he is a tactical genius. He enjoys danger and scoffs at death. I have never seen such devotion in a ship's crew."

Brittany knew that Achmed was merely trying to make conversation to take her mind off her fears. "Why are the men so devoted to him?" she asked, but did not really wish to know.

"I was told that he cares about them, and that if asked, he could tell you the names of each of their wives and children. Hard-bitten sailors of every rank would follow him into hell if he asked it of them. On the other hand, with the ladies, I was assured he has an irresistible charm."

Brittany remembered seeing Captain Stoddard when he had been with Simijin. Of course, he had been too far away for her to make out any detail of his face, but he had seemed handsome. "I hope he is as good as his men believe, Achmed, for it will take a miracle if the American captain is to win against the Turkish Navy."

"Stranger events have happened," the big man said cheerfully. "I find this all very exciting."

She shivered. "Tell me more about this American captain."

"I know nothing more of him. But I could tell you a tale I was once told about another sea captain."

Knowing Achmed as she did, Brittany realized he was again trying to keep her mind off what was happening above deck. "Tell me," she urged.

"This captain in my story was French, and this event I am about to relate to you took place during a battle with the English. The captain had his right arm shot off, then his left arm, then one of his legs. He had himself put in a tub of bran to slow the bleeding, and he continued to give orders until he died from loss of blood. Is that not marvelous?"

Brittany leaned her head back, feeling sick inside. "Do not tell me anymore. I do not want to hear about blood and dying."

Achmed felt sorrow in his heart that he had upset her when he had merely wanted to make her feel better. She knew the seriousness of the battle that raged around her; she also understood that none of them might live past the night.

The eunuch vowed that if it came to going down in this ship, or being taken by the sultan's men, he intended that Brittany would go down with the ship. The English Rose would not want her daughter turned over to the sultan.

Like a phantom ship, the *Victorious* rose up out of the darkness, came up on the lee side of her enemy, and fired all port cannonade before disappearing in a cloud of gunsmoke. The enemies' masts came crashing down onto her deck, and she was listing badly, and fatally crippled.

Thorn then turned into the wind to take on the man-of-war. Again he came out of the darkness to unexpectedly surprise the enemy who was anchored near the cliffs.

With a quickness of mind, Thorn ordered his gunman to fire at the enemy ship's unprotected stern, which splintered with such a force that it sent debris flying into the air. Thorn then had his cannoneer blast the ship with a heavy, concentrated fire.

As darkness fell, the wind intensified and still the *Victorious* was not out of danger. Across her stern, Thorn faced two enemy ships, and the night battle was lit by flames of the burning man-of-war.

The cannonading from the fort went on all night, but with the benefit of the storm, and the enemies' inability to see their target, they never came close to the *Victorious*.

Brittany clamped her hands over her ears as flashes of light and the thunder of guns jarred the ship. She wondered if it would not have been far better to have faced the sultan than to die here in hostile darkness.

The storm played out during the night, and the daylight revealed the tragic sight of the battle that had taken place through the hours of darkness.

Of the four enemy ships, one was burning with her rigging crumpled and plunging into the rough seas, two had sunk, and the last was crippled, though still intact, and she drifted away, unable to control her direction.

Well out of reach of the stronghold's guns, the *Victorious* was battered but triumphant! She sailed away with every sail hoisted to the yard and the cheer of her crew filling the morning air.

Chapter Nine

The calm blue waters of the Mediterranean stretched before the *Victorious* in a wide, seemingly unending, shimmering expanse. Thorn, looking tired and haggard after the long battle, turned the wheel over to his third in command. Even though his muscles ached and his body cried out for sleep, there was something to do before he could rest.

His blue eyes were burning with anger as he called out to Cappy: "Have the watch keep a keen eye out for Turkish vessels. I doubt that they will pursue us this far, but one can never be certain what they might do." His expression was grim. "Find our passenger, Cappy, and bring him to my cabin at once. And have the hold thoroughly searched. I suspect you will find a woman hiding there."

Thorn turned away, moving into his cabin. His bed looked inviting, but it would be in the late afternoon before he could sleep. Dropping down at his desk, he stared at a map of the Mediterranean without really seeing it. His mind was on the battle they had just come through, and the audacity of the Sultan of Turkey to attack an American vessel without just cause.

Hell, if the sultan had contacted him, he would have immediately turned the woman over to him. The affair of two men fighting over some woman would have been of no interest to him, except that he had been used by the Grand Vizier. The last thing he wanted was complication in his life. But like it or not, he was now at odds with the Turkish government.

He picked up a quill and twirled it between his fingers.

After the battle last night, the *Victorious* would never be allowed to sail in Turkish waters again. But what did it matter to him, since this would probably be his last voyage?

A heavy rap sounded on the door, and Thorn admitted Cappy and the big eunuch to his cabin.

Achmed smiled, flashing a mouthful of white teeth, and his voice boomed out with enthusiasm. "The battle was magnificent, Captain Stoddard. I am glad I was here to witness your glorious triumph."

Thorn stared at the man in silence for a long moment. Achmed wore a heavy headdress and brown cossack trousers, brown boots, and blue collar buttoned to the chin. Thorn wondered with distaste what would ever induce a man such as this one to give up his manhood to look after another man's harem.

"I am told that you want to go to America, Achmed."

"That is so, Captain Stoddard."

"I was also told that you insisted on remaining in the hold, rather than above deck."

"It was not that I insisted, Captain. It was that I preferred to be in the hold rather than sleeping on deck."

Thorn's eyes glinted. "And I insist that you wanted to remain where you could keep watch over the woman."

Achmed met the captain's eyes, and he knew there was no reason to deny the truth. "Yes, Captain Stoddard, I have deceived you—but it was for a good reason." He raised his head, looking proud and haughty. "It is my sworn duty to watch over this woman for Lord Simijin."

At that moment, there was a commotion outside the door, and two of Thorn's men entered, leading a veiled woman who was twisting and kicking, trying to free herself from their grip. Achmed reached out to her, and when the two men saw the look in his dark eyes, they relinquished her into his care.

Brittany stared through her transparent veil at the man who was captain of the *Victorious*. On seeing him up close, she was struck by his rugged handsomeness. She could not judge his height since he was seated at his desk, but his blue coat fit snugly across his broad shoulders. His white cravat was untied and disheveled.

She raised her eyes almost reluctantly to his face. He was tanned, and his face was covered with a dark stubble because he had not shaved since the battle. Tired lines fanned out about his deep blue eyes, and she had the strongest urge to take that head and rest it against her shoulder. That feeling did not last long, however, for he stood up to his full six-foot height and his eyes became piercing and accusing.

Brittany shrank back against Achmed, grim and silent, waiting for Captain Stoddard to announce her punishment. His voice was deep and authoritative when he spoke.

"Can I assume that this is the woman who brought all hell down on our head yesterday and last night?" Thorn directed his question to Achmed.

Lord Simijin had told Achmed that Brittany was to be presented as a woman of his harem so her privacy might be respected and so she could hide behind her veils. "This is the woman who is sought after by the Sultan Selim, Honored Captain. Lord Simijin will be most appreciative, and will reward you handsomely, when he learns of your courage in keeping her out of the sultan's hands."

Thorn looked with distaste on the woman shrouded in blue veils. He suddenly felt repulsed by her. The thought of a woman allowing herself to be used so harshly by a man was beyond his understanding. It did not speak well of the woman's character.

Anger made Thorn's eyes a deeper blue. "I can assure you the battle we fought last night was not to save the Grand Vizier's woman, Achmed, but rather to save my men and this ship. Your lord has a lot to answer for. He had no right to place this woman on my ship without my permission."

Achmed blinked his eyes. "But, Captain Stoddard, I have heard that there were no casualties among your crew, and there is only minor damage to your ship, so I do not understand why you are so angry."

Thorn glared at the big man, while he avoided looking at the shapeless woman who stood silently before him. "My first mate will show you and the woman to your cabins, which I might add, had to be vacated by members of my crew. I have not yet decided what is to be done with you. You will keep this woman away from my crew. Is that understood, Achmed?"

Achmed bowed low, while he backed toward the door, taking Brittany with him. "It will be as you say, Captain Stoddard. We have no desire to socialize with your crew."

Thorn now glanced at the woman. He could not see her features through the blue veil, but he sensed her uneasiness. "This is the only warning you will have to keep the woman out of my way."

Brittany was furious with the captain's high-handed manner. Why did he treat her as if she did not exist? Did he believe her an imbecile with neither understanding nor feelings? She allowed Achmed to lead her out of the cabin, deciding she did not like the captain in the least.

For two days Brittany had occupied a cramped cabin. At home in Simijin's palace, she had been accustomed to silken bed coverings and rich carpets on the floor, and she was appalled at the roughness of this sparsely furnished cabin.

She was seated in the middle of the small bunk that served as her bed, her anger hanging by a slim thread and barely under control. She had never expected a man to be as stubborn and unfeeling as this Captain Thorn Stoddard. She was not allowed out of the cabin other than for a brief walk on deck at sundown. At all other times, she was forced to endure this small place. She was accustomed to being active, so she was bored with nothing to do. She was young and high-spirited, and did not take well to a life of idleness.

Brittany did not know anything about men, except Simijin—who had always indulged her every whim—and Achmed and the three eunuchs at Simijin's palace, but they were not like other men, and they had always treated her with the greatest respect. Now she had met a man who ignored and humiliated her.

Of course, she and Achmed had tricked their way on board the ship, but they had paid for their passage. Surely the captain could treat her with the same respect he would give to any other passenger.

She looked at herself in the hand mirror, still unaccustomed to the stranger that stared back at her. Each day, she had to rub her skin with the dark stain which had been made of black walnut oil. She also had to apply the henna rinse to her hair.

While in the cabin, she refused to wear the veils because they were too restricting and the heat was so oppressive. She glanced at the leather satchel, knowing it held some of her own gowns. She was weary of this deception and wished she could throw off this disguise and be herself. But no, she had promised her mother that she would pretend to be a woman of the harem, and she would keep her promise.

When the light knock fell on her door, Brittany scrambled to pull on her veil. She opened the door to find Achmed beaming at her.

"Did you have a nice afternoon sleep, little mistress?" he inquired, with the same concern as a protective mother. "I fear you will suffer from the heat."

"Yes, it was too hot to sleep." She looked wistfully out the porthole. "I wish I could go on deck and walk in the cool breeze. I do not like it here."

"Oh, no, little mistress, you cannot do that. The captain has forbidden it, and I would not advise that you go against his orders."

"I do not care if he objects or not. I will not stay in here like a prisoner." She wrapped her blue veil about her face so nothing but her eyes showed. "I *am* going on deck; you can come or stay, just as you please."

Achmed smiled at her. "I will come with you, mistress, but do not blame me if the captain throws you in the brig. He is not at all happy that you are on board his ship. He would welcome the chance to be rid of you."

"I am . . . not frightened of that man." Her voice did not sound convincing, and Achmed smiled.

"Very well, mistress, shall we go topside?"

She hesitated at the door, but when Achmed's laughter rang out, she straightened her spine and moved purposefully down the companionway. With a show of bravado, she stepped out into the sunshine and moved quickly to the railing, fearing she would lose her nerve. She avoided looking up at the helm, lest the captain was there. She was aware of the curious stares the crew members cast in her direction, but she paid them no heed.

The sight that met Brittany's eyes left her speechless. The waters of the Mediterranean were so shimmering and motionless that the surface looked like a bottomless mirror. The sky was blue and the air was clean. In the distance, she could see high cliffs, which she pointed out to Achmed.

"What country do you suppose that could be?" she asked eagerly.

"I am uncertain, but I shall ask," he said, moving away before she could stop him.

Brittany breathed a sigh of relief when she saw Achmed approach not the infamous Captain Stoddard, but his first mate. After conversing with Mr. Hamish for a time, they both walked toward Brittany.

Smiling, Cappy Hamish approached the veiled woman. "Tell your mistress . . ." Cappy began, "that what she is seeing is the southern coast of Spain. Tonight we shall go through the Strait of Gibraltar, and tomorrow we shall reach the Atlantic Ocean."

Pretending that Brittany did not speak English, Achmed translated for her, although she understood Mr. Hamish very well.

"Ask Mr. Hamish if we are going to put in anywhere, or if we are going to sail straight for America," she said in the Turkish language.

While Achmed translated, Cappy nodded. "Tell your mistress that we will be putting in at the Canary Islands for some needed repairs."

Brittany liked the first mate—he was nothing like his overbearing captain. She judged him to be near Simijin's age. He was stocky and had soft gray eyes and graying hair. He had a ready smile, and he did not try to make her feel like an inferior, as his captain had.

A loud voice called out in anger, and Brittany moved closer to the railing as Captain Stoddard approached. "Achmed, I thought I told you to keep this woman below deck except at the hour I specified."

"My mistress is unaccustomed to being shut in such a limited space. She needed air."

Thorn's eyes settled on the veiled figure. "Tell your mistress she will do as I command. If she finds her quarters too cramped, she might want to consider going ashore at the Canary Islands and finding another ship to take her to her destination. Perhaps she will fare better with a ship that is headed for England. That was her original destination, was it not?"

Achmed smiled. "That was the first destination. Since then, it was decided that she will go to Philadelphia."

Thorn looked dumbfounded. "What can either of you know about Philadelphia? Have you ever been there?"

Achmed's eyes suddenly became secretive. "I have not been there myself, but it is my master's wish that my mistress be taken there."

Thorn glanced out to sea. "If you obey me, I may consider taking you as far as Charleston, South Carolina, but you will have to find your own transportation to Philadelphia. Until then, keep this woman where she belongs. I am sure she is accustomed to always getting her own way, but I will not tolerate my orders being disobeyed. Tell her that."

Brittany stared at Thorn Stoddard through her misty veil. Surely the blue of the sea was reflected in this American's eyes. She found herself wanting to reach out and touch his clean-shaven face. Instead, she turned away, moving across the deck. She felt lost and alone. She had never known unkindness, and she found it unsettling.

The heat intensified as the day progressed. Since she was accustomed to bathing each day, Brittany could no longer tolerate washing herself out of the pail of water that was allotted her. She had sent Achmed to the captain to deliver her demands for a tub and enough water for a bath.

Achmed now stood before the captain, his legs widespread, his arms crossed over his chest, mustering as much dignity as he could summon.

"My mistress has asked if it would be possible for her to have a tub bath. She is unaccustomed to this heat, and has always taken a daily bath."

Thorn glared at the man. "Is there anything else that she would like?" he asked ironically.

"Yes," Achmed answered, choosing to ignore the captain's ill humor. "Since we will be stopping at the islands, I wonder if it would be possible to acquire silk bedding for my mistress. Her skin is so delicate that the rough sheets on her bed make her uncomfortable."

Thorn looked at the man with little understanding of his devotion to such a spoiled and pampered woman. "Tell your mistress she will have to make do with what she has. As for a tub bath, that will be impossible until we take on fresh water."

"My mistress will not like that. Cleanliness is important to her."

"Do you never tire of catering to that woman's slightest whim?"

"I do not find her unreasonable. She is unaccustomed to rough ways."

"Need I remind you that I am captain of this ship," Thorn drawled. "Your mistress should have thought of the discomfort she would encounter before she snuck on board. In the palace of the Grand Vizier, she may have been treated like a princess," Thorn continued, "but on board my ship, she is just a passenger, and not even a welcome one. Tell your mistress that for me."

"I shall not tell her that, Captain. She is here through no fault of her own." Achmed bowed. "I will inform my mistress of your decision."

After Achmed returned with the captain's message, Brittany was so angry that she did not stop to consider her actions but stormed out of her cabin and up one deck to the captain's quarters. She did not wait for an answer to her knock, but pushed the door open to find Thorn Stoddard seated at his desk. When he glanced up at her, there was shock on his face, but it was quickly masked by a look of anger.

Brittany moved quickly over to Thorn and stood with her hands on her hips. "Captain Stoddard, I am told that I cannot have a bath. I have given up much to be on this ship, but I will not give up cleanliness."

He was not only startled that she spoke English, but that she spoke it with the same clear distinction of the upper class British. Thorn stared at the veil, unable to see the face behind it.

"I do not see that you have any choice, madame. You will find that the rules here on this ship are not so much governed for your comfort as for your safety and the safety of my men."

"All I ask of you is common courtesy. I would not keep an animal cooped up as you have kept me. I will have my bath if I have to go swimming in the ocean."

A slight smile tugged at his lips. "It's a long swim back to Turkey, madame."

"You are a hateful man, and I do not like you at all well."

"And you, madame, are spoiled and pampered. In the past, I am sure you always had your own way. That will not be the case on board the *Victorious*."

She leaned against the desk, propping the palm of her hands on the smooth surface. "You are arrogant and impossible, Captain Stoddard. I suppose you blame me for the battle with the Turkish Navy."

The daintiness of her hands drew his attention, and he took notice of how dark her skin was. He realized she was much younger than he had supposed. Although he could not see her expression, he could feel her glaring at him from behind her veil of secrecy.

His eyes narrowed. "You *are* the reason for the battle, and you know it. I have known women like you, who only consider their own needs and not what consequences their actions might have on other lives. I should think you would appreciate the battle that was fought on your behalf."

"I do appreciate what you did that night, Captain. But I do not appreciate that even though we are not acquainted, you have formed an opinion about me."

"I have seen enough of you to know what you are like, madame."

"Oh—are you such an expert on my kind of women, Captain Stoddard?"

"Yes, I know your kind of woman," he ground out. Then his gaze suddenly clouded. "I have often met your kind."

She straightened and moved back a pace, not understanding the anger in his voice. But he was not looking at her—he was looking through her. "Will . . . you allow me to have a bath?" she dared to ask again.

He stood up towering above her, his eyes closed. "Say please."

"Never!"

"Is please such a difficult a word to say? Have you never said it before?"

"I will see you in hell before I beg anything of you, Captain."

His laughter was filled with amusement and his eyes sparkled. "Very likely, madame, very likely. On thinking it over, I have decided to be generous and allow you to have your bath. Go to your cabin and send your slave to me. I will give him all you require."

She moved to the door and turned back to him. They were both aware that she had not won a victory over this man just because he was allowing her to have her bath. "Achmed is not my slave," she said in a heated voice.

"Your lap dog then?"

"You are a hateful man, Captain. I do not like you at all."

"So you have already pointed out to me. But be assured that I will not wither away and die from your lack of regard for me."

She turned away and rushed through the door, not wanting to be near that man one moment longer than necessary. He was the most arrogant, self-assured, and hateful man she had known. Of course she had not known many men, but she doubted that anyone could be worse than Captain Thorn Stoddard.

On returning to her cabin, Brittany unpacked her satchel and surveyed her meager belongings. There were several robes and veils, and a dancing costume that must have been placed in the satchel by one of the harem women, as well as three of her own gowns and undergarments and three pairs of shoes.

Brittany picked up the wooden chest that had been her mother's. She opened the lid and fingered the jewels and gold that filled the chest to the brim, knowing her mother had given her the jewels. Suddenly she saw the edge of a paper and discovered the letter at the bottom of the chest. She recognized the handwriting as her mother's.

> "My dearest Daughter,
> Please know that my prayers are with you, even as you read this note. I pray that God, in his infinite mercy, will see you land on safe shores. Know that it breaks my heart to send you away from my protective arms, but I can no longer keep you safe. Take care of yourself and rely on Achmed as I have all these years, and as soon as conditions permit, we shall be reunited. God bless and keep you, my dearest."

For a long moment Brittany held the letter to her breasts, while tears of despair washed down her cheeks. "Oh, Mama. I am so confused and alone. I wish you were here."

The halls of the Grand Seraglio rang with the sultan's angry voice. He ranted at the poor, unfortunate Admiral Kainardji who had brought him news of defeat at the hands of the American captain.

"Am I surrounded by addle-brained imbeciles? How can you, Admiral Kainardji, allow one ship to out-maneuver and outfight the best of my navy?"

Admiral Kainardji lowered his eyes. "The weather was against us throughout the battle, and this Captain Stoddard struck at us at night. Like all Americans, this one did not fight by any rules."

Selim's eyes became dark pools of rage. "I want this man's head brought back to me. No—better still, bring him back to me in one piece. I do not care how this is accomplished, just do it!"

Admiral Kainardji's eyes closed against the fury he saw etched on the sultan's face; he trembled because that rage was directed at him.

"But, Majesty, the American, Captain Stoddard, will by now be out of our territorial waters. How can I pursue him in open sea?"

"Fool! Find him wherever he goes, and bring him to me. We will see how strong he is when he is confronted with a real man, like myself."

"And the daughter of the English Rose?"

"She is not to be harmed—is that understood? Bring her to me, and do it as quickly as possible. But if you have to subdue her, take care that you leave no lasting scars. It will go hard with you if my orders are disobeyed this time."

Admiral Kainardji bowed low. "Yes, Your Majesty, it will be as you command."

Chapter Ten

"Sails in the distance, Captain," the watch called down from his lofty perch. "Looks like it's a Turkish vessel, and she's closing on us fast."

"Damn," Thorn muttered under his breath. "Look sharp and man all positions," he called out as he ran across the deck to take the helm. "Get Cappy up here on the double, and have all cannon made ready."

"Aye, aye," the watch called out, sliding down the rope and landing with both feet upon the deck.

The afternoon was tense as the Turkish ship matched the course of the *Victorious*. Thorn kept a wary eye on the distant sails, while his men stood by the cannons, ready for their captain's command.

By sunset, the enemy had closed the gap between them, and the crew of the *Victorious* were primed and ready for battle. Just as the enemy vessel came near enough to fire her port cannon, she lowered her sails and turned back to sea.

Thorn called down to his men. "We are within sight of the Canary Islands, so the Turks dare not engage us in warfare. Rest easy men, they are sailing away. Make ready to come into port by sunrise."

"Looks like we bested those devils again, Captain," Cappy observed with a grin. "The bastards have turned tail and run. We've seen the last of them."

Thorn turned the wheel against the wind. "Don't be too sure, Cappy. They wanted the woman bad enough to send their fleet against us; it isn't likely they will give up without another go at us."

"We can't let them get their hands on the woman, Captain."

Thorn looked long and hard at his first mate. "How do the other men feel about this?"

"They think it's a matter of pride, Captain. We didn't run from them before, and we won't run now. They hope the Turks will give us another chance to fight."

Thorn chuckled. "What kind of bloodthirsty crew have I here?"

"The best damned crew that ever sailed, Captain," Cappy announced with pride.

"Aye, Cappy, that they are." Thorn glanced at the sky and saw the high, fleecy clouds. "Go below and get some sleep, Cappy. I'll take the first watch. I don't anticipate any trouble tonight."

"Aye, Captain."

The view of the Canary Islands was shrouded by the morning mist that had closed in around the *Victorious* just before sunrise.

But by noon, a strong trade wind had blown the mist away and the tall mountainous peaks and volcanic cliffs of the island of La Palma appeared to rise up from the ocean floor like dark phantoms.

A fresh breeze touched Thorn's cheek as he brought the *Victorious* windward. It was a bright afternoon without a cloud in the sky as Thorn rounded a wide cove and the village of Santa Cruz de la Palma came into view.

Thorn called his crew together and informed them that they would be on the island for a week since the ship needed several repairs. Here they would also unload crates of dates, almonds, and olives, then take on a cargo of bananas, oranges, and coffee to transport to America.

Thorn skillfully maneuvered the *Victorious* with the tide and anchored her in four fathoms of water so his crew could easily perform the needed repairs.

His eyes ran up the tall mast, where he observed that new

canvas would have to be stretched; that would keep the sail-master occupied for several days. One of the masts had splintered, and the railing and part of the deck on the lee side needed to be replaced.

The clinking of the anchor sliding into place blended with the cry of noisy sea gulls that hovered above the ship. Thorn tied off the wheel, and the *Victorious* danced on the surface like a cork bobbing in water.

Thorn glanced down at the main deck to see Achmed lumbering up the steps toward him. In a strange way, Thorn had begun to admire the big eunuch. He had certainly never seen anyone with the black man's capacity for devotion to such an unworthy individual as the Grand Vizier's woman. Thorn could only imagine what hell Achmed must live through, trying to cater to the demands and whims of that spoiled female he served.

"Captain Stoddard," Achmed said, smiling, "will it be possible for my mistress and myself to go ashore today? I believe it would be good for her."

Thorn sighed. The woman's demands had already started. Against his will, Thorn was beginning to be intrigued by the mystery that clung to the woman. He resented the fact that she was often on his mind.

Thorn quickly nodded in agreement. Perhaps the woman could use a respite from her cramped quarters, he thought, and, besides, it would be good to be rid of her for a while.

"The *Victorious* will be under repair for several days. Perhaps the noise will disturb your mistress, and she might find it more pleasant staying in the village. I can recommend the Casa del Oro, an inn where I have stayed on occasion."

"I am certain my mistress will agree to this. She will not want to be a burden to you and your crew while the vessel is being repaired."

Thorn gave the man a doubtful glance. "Tell your mistress to make ready at once. I will be going ashore in exactly twenty minutes, and I do not intend to wait for her."

"She will be ready, Captain Stoddard, you have my word on this."

"Very well, but I want it understood that I will not be responsible for the woman's safety while she is off my ship. And when I am ready to sail, she had better be back on board, for I will not be delayed because of her."

"You will not have to worry about her, Captain. She will do what is expected of her."

Thorn's deep-blue eyes clouded with skepticism. "Just keep her close to you, and see that she doesn't come to any harm. I have enough to worry about without indulging your temperamental mistress."

"You will have no trouble from her, Captain." Achmed knew that Thorn Stoddard had completely misjudged Brittany, but there was no reason to enlighten him. Perhaps it would be best that no one knew how young and unspoiled Brittany was—especially not the handsome young captain.

Brittany was seated in the longboat, her veil in place, making her anonymous, or so she thought until she caught the four men who were rowing the longboat casting inquisitive glances her way. They apparently thought her something of an oddity. However, their captain, who was seated directly across from her, did not even look in her direction.

She studied Thorn Stoddard's profile. She liked the clean sweep of his brow, and the manner in which his dark hair fell across his forehead. She was not certain if she approved of the arrogant tilt of his chin that suggested impatience and a ready temper—but of course she already knew that about him. He was insufferable, yet intriguing.

Suddenly Thorn raised his eyes to her, and her heart skipped a beat. Brittany found it was hard to breathe, for it felt as if his piercing gaze could see past the thick gauze of her veil—but she knew that was impossible.

When she could bear his scrutiny no longer, she turned

away and refused to look in the captain's direction, although she could still feel his glance on her.

Thorn watched the delicate hand that pulled the veil into place, and cursed his growing fascination with this woman. She was mysterious, and he found himself wanting to rip the veil from her head and look upon the face that made the sultan want to possess her and had driven the Grand Vizier to desperate means to keep her from him.

The rising tide propelled the longboat forward on swift frothy waves, and with the help of the four able seamen who plied the oars, the boat soon reached shore. One of the men leaped onto the pier and secured the boat.

When Achmed swung Brittany onto the pier, her legs felt as if they had no substance, and he laughed as he aided her up the steep slope. As they moved away, she could hear Captain Stoddard issuing orders to his men, and she urged Achmed to hurry to the carriages that were waiting to transport passengers into Santa Cruz de la Palma.

As Achmed assisted Brittany into the carriage, many of the local inhabitants cast inquisitive glances their way. Apparently they were curious about a woman who covered her face, and was accompanied by a big colorfully dressed eunuch.

Brittany longed to rip the veil away so she could feel the sun on her face. Glancing back over her shoulder, she was glad to see that Captain Stoddard and his men had moved in the direction of the warehouses on the other side of the pier. Although she told herself she was glad to be away from the captain's searing glance, her eyes followed his movements until he was out of her view.

As the horse-drawn carriage moved forward with a sudden lurch, Brittany soon became interested in her surroundings. This was a land of vibrant colors. The carriage moved past orange groves, where the trees were so ripened with fruit that the branches dipped toward the ground. Banana trees displayed their golden bounty beneath a clear blue sky. The houses were whitewashed, with red tiled roofs. Beautiful multicolored birds sang from treetops, and a gentle breeze brought with it the smell of the sea. Barefoot children played in the narrow streets with joyous laughter. The people were very dark-skinned, and Brittany felt certain that with her darkened skin and hair, she could easily be mistaken for one of them.

Achmed appeared to be taking in the scene with equal interest.

"I have never seen anything so lovely, Achmed," Brittany told him. "Surely this is a paradise."

"You say that only because you have seen so little of the world." He drew himself up with proud dignity. "I once traveled to Paris, France, with Lord Simijin, and that city was indeed wondrous to behold. But this is indeed a lovely village, little mistress. It might be pleasant to live here."

"One would have to be a Spanish citizen, Achmed, for the Canary Islands belong to Spain."

"Then it might not be so pleasant after all." He smiled broadly. "Much better to go to America, where you may have a grandmother to welcome you with love."

"A woman I do not know. I believe she was never kind to my mother, although my mother has not said so. It is just a feeling I have. Mama once told me she wrote my grandmother and her father in England about my birth, and yet, she heard from neither of them."

Achmed looked at her gravely. "If your grandmother is not kind to you, do not fear, for I shall take you somewhere else."

Her eyes clouded with distress. "I wonder what America will be like. I know that it was once at war with England but that the two countries are at peace now."

"I do not know about such things, although I have heard it said that there is much to admire in America."

"I hope so, but it sounds like the end of the earth to me, Achmed."

"It will not be so bad, little mistress, and I will be with you."

She laid her hand on his. "That is the only thing that makes this all bearable, my dear friend."

The Turkish man-of-war sailed into a secluded cove. With a satisfied smile, Admiral Kainardji adjusted his spyglass. Yes, there was the *Victorious*. Her crew was unsuspecting that they were being watched.

He slammed his spyglass down, and laughter filled the air. To capture Thorn Stoddard might prove to be easier than he had hoped. He could not attack the *Victorious* outright, for they were both in Spanish waters. No, he would wait and find the captain alone at sea.

First, he had to locate the daughter of the English Rose. It was unlikely she was on board the ship since it was under repair. Most probably she had moved into the village—or so he hoped. It would be easy enough to find out.

Kainardji aimed his spyglass at the shore and saw a carriage making its way to the village. Excitement throbbed through his body. Yes, there could be no mistaking the woman draped in veils and accompanied by the eunuch. It must be the woman he had been sent to find.

Satisfaction gleamed in his dark eyes when he saw she was not guarded. He would soon have her in his custody. Captain Stoddard might be harder to capture, but Kainardji would have the advantage of surprise on his side.

The night was dark. Brittany stood at the window of her small bedroom, looking down on the square below, hoping to catch a glimpse of Achmed. He had insisted that she remain in the room while he purchased food for them both.

The air was suddenly filled with music, and the small square across the way was alive with flickering candles. People were beginning to gather, so Brittany leaned out, trying to see what was happening.

Brittany was not aware that dark, hostile eyes watched her from the shadows below. Admiral Kainardji slipped behind a flowering bush and motioned for his four companions to join him there.

"See the woman there at the window? You must bring her to me at once, but do not harm her in any way or the sultan will see you punished. Go now to capture her before her eunuch returns!"

Admiral Kainardji's men moved swiftly toward the Casa del Oro. Unnoticed, they slipped inside the inn and silently climbed the stairs.

Brittany tapped her foot, keeping time with the music. It appeared the island people were fond of music, for a crowd had gathered in the square to dance and join in the merry-making.

Unconsciously, she swung her hips in rhythm with the music, for she had been taught by Juanita to dance to Spanish folk songs.

Because of the heat, Brittany had removed her veil and was now dressed in her own pale-pink muslin gown. She hummed to herself and tapped her heels, then whirled around the room with wild abandonment, the tempo filling her senses and her feet tapping out the rhythm.

When the knock fell on her door, Brittany laughingly opened it, expecting to see Achmed standing there. "I have just been dancing, Ac—" She broke off in horror when she saw the four Turkish sailors, and knew they had been sent by the sultan.

Rough hands pulled her into the hallway, and she would have screamed but for the hand that clamped painfully over her mouth.

Brittany kicked and fought against her assailants, but she soon realized she could not win against them. Twisting and turning, a silent whimper caught in her throat, and she felt tears sting her eyes.

"Be still," a voice warned as one of the men spoke to her in the Turkish language. "You will not be harmed if you come with us without a struggle."

Dear God, she thought frantically, she would be taken to Sultan Selim. What would become of her then? She had not thought that the sultan would have her followed this far. What was she to do?

She thought of her mother and wondered what she would do if she found herself in these circumstances. *Oh, Mama,* she cried silently. *I am so frightened. I wish you were here to tell me what to do.*

The sound of music and dancing in the square drew everyone out of the inn to witness the spectacle. Achmed had stopped to watch for a moment. With a lightness of heart, he entered the Casa del Oro. The little mistress would like the lively music. It would cheer her, for she had known much sadness lately.

The eunuch heard the commotion at the top of the stairs, and he rushed upward, fearing the horrible truth. When he reached the landing, his heart froze with fear for his young mistress, who was struggling with three men. With anger burning in his breast, Achmed removed the knife from his belt and advanced swiftly on her abductors.

Achmed did not know that Admiral Kainardji had followed him up the stairs. He was so intent on rescuing Brittany that he was taken by surprise when Kainardji's sharp blade slipped between his shoulders. The sudden pain made the big eunuch drop his knife, and it clattered to the floor just out of his reach.

Achmed fought on in a rage; his one thought was to save Brittany. Like a dying stag, he lashed out at everything around him. He lifted one of the men over his head, tossing him over the railing so he landed below with a thud.

Achmed charged the second man, trying to ignore the weakness that washed over him. His hands closed around the man's neck, and he squeezed with his last bit of strength. But Admiral Kainardji struck again and again, until his knife finally broke off in the big eunuch's back!

Fighting against the darkness that blurred his sight,

Achmed fell to his knees, a sorrowful look in his eyes as he glanced at Brittany. He could not help her. With one last tremendous effort, he struggled to get to his knees but fell forward, face down, to lie in a pool of his own blood.

Brittany frantically reached out to Achmed, but she was forcibly drawn away. A heavy hand came down on her jaw, and her head seemed to be spinning around and around in a dark cloud of unconsciousness.

"Fool," Admiral Kainardji cried. "If you have bruised the girl—" His voice trailed off in confusion. "I had not thought the English Rose's daughter would have dark skin. No, it is not possible. I was told her hair was golden and her skin white."

One of the men touched Brittany's dark hair. "Perhaps we have the wrong girl?"

Kainardji's eyes narrowed. "Perhaps we have. I cannot take this girl back until I learn if she is the daughter of the English Rose."

By now there were loud voices coming from below the stairs, so Admiral Kainardji motioned for the men to pick up the girl and follow him as he led them down the back stairway and into the night.

The admiral was troubled as he led the way to the waiting carriage. In his heart he hoped he had not made a mistake in capturing the wrong girl.

"Take her on board the ship until I can determine if she is the one we seek. Secure her below deck, and keep seven men on deck to guard her."

"Where will you be, Admiral?" one of the men asked.

"I will be searching for the American captain. We cannot leave without him, imbecile. Captain Stoddard will regret the day he challenged me. He will not only lose his life, but his ship will be put to the torch."

Chapter Eleven

Thorn heard the sound of music and laughter when he approached the village square. With quick steps, he made his way toward the Casa del Oro feeling somewhat foolish about his misgivings. It was perfectly natural that a Turkish ship had been spotted this afternoon by one of his crew members, since they must frequent these waters.

Still, he could not easily dismiss the danger it might present to the woman. After all, the Turks had fought a battle for her, so perhaps they had not given up. He would just make certain that she was safe in her room before returning to the *Victorious*.

When he entered the inn, he found the main room empty. The serving girl told him that most of the townspeople had gone to the fiesta in the square. Perhaps the girl and the eunuch had gone there also.

Now that he was here, Thorn reproached himself for being overcautious. The Grand Vizier's woman had caused him enough trouble already. Why could he not just put her out of his mind? He was not her protector. Thus far she had been more trouble than a dozen females, and she would apparently go on causing him woes as long as he felt responsible for her.

When Thorn moved up the stairs, he saw that several men were gathered in a circle, murmuring excitedly. Pushing his way through the crowd, he saw Achmed sprawled on the floor in a pool of blood. He quickly bent over the big man. "Has anyone called a physician?" he demanded.

"*Sí, señor*, but the man has lost much blood, and it is doubtful that he will live."

Thorn's face was grim. "Did anyone see what happened here?"

"I saw it, señor," one of the men admitted. "I am the proprietor of the Casa del Oro, and I saw this poor man fall. The unfortunate girl fought like a demon, but the Turks took her anyway."

With a feeling of dread, Thorn grabbed the man by his shirtfront and pulled them forward. "Describe the girl to me. What did she look like?"

"I do not know, señor. It was too dark, and I was afraid, so I ran away."

Thorn shoved the man away. "How long ago did this happen?"

"It was not long ago, señor. I did not interfere, because I thought one of the men might be the woman's husband or even her father."

"I do not think so," another disagreed, "because the big man with the strange clothing was trying to protect her. He fought until he could no longer get up. If he is not dead, he soon will be."

Thorn stared at the innkeeper. "In which direction did they go?"

The man pointed westward. "They went that way, señor. I felt that they were men of the sea." He looked at Thorn. "Like yourself."

Thorn dropped several coins into the landlord's hand. "I am Captain Thorn Stoddard. See that the big man has the best of care, and send someone to the ship *Victorious*. Inform my men what has happened here, and tell them I am trying to locate the woman."

"Those men were very dangerous, señor," the man warned. "Would it not be better to allow the authorities to find the woman?"

Thorn's eyes took on a dangerous glint. The woman had

been under his protection. He knew this could happen; he should have been prepared for it. With long strides, he hurried to the back stairs. He was duty-bound to get her back.

The music faded in the distance as Thorn rushed away from the village square. He cursed himself for a fool. What in the hell was he doing, chasing after men that had rid him of a woman who had been nothing but a nuisance to him? Hell, he did not even know her name.

But deep inside, he knew he had to find her. With or without his consent, she had come under his protection, and he would be damned if anyone was going to take her back to Turkey and place her in the hands of that madman, Selim, if he could prevent it.

He felt in his breast pocket and realized he did not even have his pistol with him. Ill-prepared as he was, he wondered how he would rescue her if he came upon her abductors.

His jawline tightened with determination as he raced into the darkened night. He would find out if she had been taken to the Turkish ship. If he located her, he would enlist several of the men to aid him in releasing her.

Thorn stopped short when he spotted a flickering light just ahead on the docks. He proceeded with caution, and before he realized what was happening, he was surrounded by Turks, their lanterns blinding him for the moment. Thorn never saw the man who struck him from behind, but he felt pain explode in his head and he fell forward into a world of oblivion.

The darkness was oppressive within the small cell where Brittany had been placed by her abductors. The swaying of the ship made her nauseated, and she had no concept of the passing of time. She had cried until there were no more tears left. Now all she could do was tremble with cold and fear, hoping it was not rats she heard scurrying across the floor.

When she heard the cell door open and saw the flicker of

a lantern, she pressed her back against the damp wall, fearful that the men were coming for her.

She heard a muffled sound and watched as two men tossed someone onto the floor. Before her eyes could adjust to the light, the men left, carrying the lantern with them, and the cell was once more in total darkness. She waited until she heard the door lock before she crawled forward to investigate, fearing it was Achmed who shared her dismal fate.

In the pitch-black, she felt cautiously in front of her, fearful of what she might find. It appeared that the man was unconscious. She touched a man's rough face, and drew back quickly. It was not Achmed—but who could it be? Achmed must have been badly injured or else he would surely be locked in here with her.

Brittany moved back against the wall and closed her eyes, fearful of what would happen to her. If only she had not been so determined to go ashore, she would still be safely on board the *Victorious*.

She hugged her arms around herself for warmth. Strange, she thought, that it was so cold inside the bowels of this ship when the day had been unusually hot.

There was a soft groan, and Brittany tensed. The other prisoner was regaining consciousness!

"Where the hell am I?" came the unmistakable voice of Captain Thorn Stoddard.

Brittany did not stop to wonder how he had come to be a prisoner with her, but hurried to him, fumbling in the dark until she found his hand.

"You have come to help me," she said in a relieved voice. Then she began speaking more rapidly. "I have been utterly frightened and so certain that no one would ever find me. It is cold and dark in here, and I think there are rats."

Thorn sat up and touched his head, only to groan when he found a painful lump there. "I hardly think I could be credited with rescuing you, madame. At the moment, I am as much a prisoner as yourself."

"Yes," she sighed. "I fear we have fallen into the hands of Sultan Selim's Admiral Kainardji."

"Yes, that is what I suspect."

"I am sorry that you have been drawn into this because of me, Captain Stoddard."

He winced in pain as he tried to straighten up. "Are you sorry?"

"Of course." She reached out her hand to him. "Are you hurt?"

"Most of my injury comes from my wounded pride," he admitted. "I came into those devil's hands like a lamb being led to the slaughter. I doubt they have ever had their prey come more willingly to them."

Brittany shivered. "What is to become of us, Captain Stoddard?"

He reached out and awkwardly patted her shoulder. "Worrying won't help. I don't suppose there are any windows in this cell?"

"No, only the one door," she said in a distracted manner, for never before had she felt a man's touch, and it unsettled her.

He stood up and pulled her up with him. "At the moment we can do nothing but wait."

When he felt her tremble, he spoke encouragingly. "We will come out of this. I have survived worse predicaments."

"It seems that to do nothing would be to admit defeat," she stated. "Knowing what a stubborn nature you have, I cannot see you going down in defeat without a fight."

He smiled at her assessment of his character. "I would admit that our chance of escape would lessen if this ship were to put out to sea," he replied. "Whatever we do will have to be accomplished soon."

Brittany wanted to believe that they would escape. Captain Thorn Stoddard was so commanding and self-assured that he instilled confidence in her and made her believe that there was reason to hope.

Again Thorn felt the woman shiver. "You are cold."

Brittany felt warmth spread through her body when he placed his coat around her shoulders, for it was still warm from his body heat.

Thorn sank down to the floor, bracing his back against the wall. "I am going to have one hell of a headache in the morning," he acknowledged, testing his head once more.

Brittany sat down close to him, and bravely reaching up to touch his brow, found it sticky with blood. "You have been wounded."

"It's nothing—don't make a fuss," he replied, pushing her hand away.

With a stiff determination, Brittany ripped a strip from her petticoat and bound it around his head. Then for a long moment they sat listening to the timbers creak and feeling the swaying of the ship as it rode the restless waves.

At last Thorn spoke, knowing he must prepare her for whatever lay ahead. "Madame, you are going to have to be very brave. Do you think you can manage that?"

"Yes . . . I will try."

"And you will do exactly as I tell you?"

"Yes, I shall."

"Good. For the time being, it will be best if you get some rest. I would not be surprised in the least if my crew came to our rescue before daylight."

"Do you truly believe that, Captain?"

He didn't, but he had to keep her hopes up. "Certainly. They will have missed me by now. You know what an ingenious fellow Cappy is."

"Shouldn't we do something now?"

"I doubt if any opportunity for escape will present itself until morning."

"Suppose the admiral should set sail?"

"He would not chance it in these waters at night because they are too treacherous to navigate." Thorn pulled her head against his shoulder. "Get some rest."

"I suppose you are right, but I am not sleepy."

He thought she sounded more like a little girl than a woman. "You promised to obey me."

"Yes, and I will."

"I don't suppose you swim."

"Yes, I swim very well, Captain Stoddard."

He felt her move closer to him, and he realized she was trembling with fear. Protectively, his arms went around her, and he pulled her close. "I'll say one thing in your favor."

"A compliment, Captain Stoddard?"

He laughed softly, thinking she no longer wore her veil and if it were light he could see her face. "Merely an observation."

"I cannot wait to hear this."

"You haven't cried and carried on like most women I know would have."

"That does not say much for the women of your acquaintance, Captain."

"Sharper than a serpent's fang is a woman's tongue," he quoted glibly.

She sighed wearily, refusing to be baited by him. If anything, she felt comforted by his attempt to distract her. Now she understood why he instilled confidence in his crew, for she felt it, too. He was such a strong presence, and she felt there was nothing he could not accomplish. Had he not won the sea battle when the odds had been four to one?

Her eyes fluttered shut, and she yawned. "I can swim, and I can also use a scimitar with deadly accuracy."

He smiled, trying to picture the delicate brown hands swinging the big sword. "That's good to know. If only we had a scimitar."

"It amused Simijin to instruct me in swordplay. He was proud of my accomplishment."

Thorn moved a little away from her when she mentioned her lover, Lord Simijin. "We may both need all our skills to come out of this."

"So tired," she murmured.

He pulled her back into his arms, smelling the sweet scent

of her hair. "You have had an extraordinary day. Sleep now, and I shall keep watch."

"Yes," she said, her head falling forward. "I will sleep if you do not mind—"

Thorn held the woman in his arms, feeling as if he had somehow misjudged her. She was being uncommonly brave, although she must be terrified of the sultan if she had taken such drastic measures to flee Turkey.

He heard her soft breathing and suddenly felt an overwhelming urge to protect her. He smiled ironically. Here was a woman whose face he had never looked upon—and one he knew so little about—yet their lives had become hopelessly intertwined. That he faced death at the hands of the Turks was a certainty, but what this woman faced could be far worse. They would encounter impossible odds, but then, he told himself, the faint at heart never won a battle.

Without his being aware of it, he reached for, and found, her hand. Her long, slender fingers were cold, and he clasped them to bring warmth to her. Finally, he shifted her weight so she was lying across his lap. She stirred, and he spoke softly to her.

"Go back to sleep. You are safe in my arms."

She turned her head against his wide chest, feeling warmth penetrate her whole body. Yes, she was safe with this man holding her.

Thorn had not intended to fall asleep, but he had. Being a light sleeper, he was suddenly jarred awake by the sound of a bloodthirsty yell that he recognized right away as that of Cappy Hamish. Help had come sooner than he had expected. He shook the woman, speaking to her quickly.

"Awaken, madame!"

At first Brittany could not shake off the sleep-drugged state that held her in its thrall. She shook her head to clear it, while Thorn raised her to her feet. It was still dark in the cell, and she clung to his arm.

"What is wrong, Captain? Are we underway?"

"Shh, listen."

She could only hear the creaking of the ship, but then she became aware of the sounds of a battle on deck. There was no mistaking the sound of clashing swords which was followed by cries of surprise and then pain.

Soon dancing flames of a lantern lit the darkened shadows, and there was the jingle of keys and the door was shoved open.

Brittany gasped when she saw what looked like an avenging angel, his pistol trained on the Turk he had in a viselike grip. Cappy smiled at his captain and Brittany.

"It's like this, sir; when you didn't come back, we decided you was in trouble, so me and several of the men thought we'd come and give you a hand."

"Cappy, you old sea dog!" Thorn exclaimed, pulling Brittany forward. "I never thought I'd see the day I would be glad to see that face of yours."

Three other men from the *Victorious* appeared just behind Cappy, each smiling at the sight of the captain.

"We'd best be off, Captain," Cappy urged. "The Turks only left a skeleton crew on board, but I'm betting the others will be arriving soon, since it'll be light within the hour."

"Yes, let's be away," Thorn concurred.

"Excuse me just a moment, Captain," Cappy said, turning to his prisoner and bringing the butt of his gun down hard on the man's head. When the man crumpled to the floor, he smiled his lopsided grin. "Shall we go? The boat is waiting."

Thorn pulled Brittany out into the dimly lit corridor, and they all moved quickly up on deck. They had to step over several prone bodies, but none of them were men from the *Victorious*. Apparently the Turks had once more underestimated them.

Thorn was glad there was no moon so they could make their departure under cloak of darkness.

When they reached the railing, he picked Brittany up in his arms and agilely climbed over the side, dropping with a thud into the swaying boat below. They were soon joined by the others, and the small craft was propelled forward as the crew swiftly rowed away.

To Brittany, all the events of the evening had happened so quickly that they had taken on a sense of unreality. She sat shivering in the aft of the boat, still clinging to Captain Stoddard's coat for warmth.

"How is Achmed?" she asked in an urgent voice. "Has anyone seen him?"

Some of the men were surprised that the Turkish woman spoke English.

"Yes, madame." Cappy finally spoke up. "His wounds are deep. But he was taken to the *Victorious*, where the ship's surgeon, Dr. Rutledge, is looking after him."

Brittany lapsed into silence, hoping that Achmed would survive. He was such a strong man, and he had been so brave—surely he would not die now.

Brittany's eyes went to the captain. It was still dark, so he was no more than a shadowy outline. "Captain Stoddard, how can I thank you and these men for what they have done for Achmed and myself?"

Thorn frowned, wondering if he had misjudged her. Perhaps there was more to her character than just being the spoiled plaything of the Grand Vizier. She had certainly acted admirably tonight. He spoke to her in a kind voice. "It is all included in the cost of the fare, madame."

"I fear you got the worst of the bargain, Captain. The fare was not near enough to pay for the damages you have incurred because of me."

His laughter was soft. "Have no fear on that point, madame; I shall have a detailed assessment presented to Lord Simijin, your husband . . ." He paused. "No, I don't suppose Lord Simijin is your husband, since you are his concubine."

Brittany did not bother to deny the captain's wrong assumption, but she did so dislike him believing she was a woman of the harem.

"Yes, Simijin will repay you," she said, suddenly feeling very homesick for her mother and stepfather.

Thorn felt cold toward her again. For a few hours he had forgotten that she was little more than a concubine. Remembering was not a pleasant feeling for him.

"Think nothing of it, madame. Your slave was the one who suffered the most."

"Yes," Brittany said. "I fear for him, Captain."

Chapter Twelve

Brittany was seated beside Achmed's bed, holding his hand, as though by the sheer force of will, she could keep him alive. Two days had passed since she and Captain Stoddard had been rescued from the Turkish ship.

Since returning to the *Victorious*, she had helped Dr. Rutledge nurse Achmed. Even though the giant was unconscious and unaware of anything that went on around him, Brittany talked to him soothingly, hoping somewhere in his world between life and death, he would hear her voice and respond.

"Achmed, you just have to get better. I would never forgive myself if anything happened to you. Open your eyes and look at me, please."

The eunuch did not stir.

With heart-wrenching sadness, Brittany stood up to ease her cramped muscles. It was sultry inside the cabin, so she had abandoned her veil, vowing she would never wear it again. She hoped her mother would understand.

She raised the heavy curtain of hair off the back of her neck, wishing the *Victorious* would get underway because it would be cooler at sea.

Brittany had not seen Captain Stoddard since the night he had brought her back to the ship. Of course, she hardly left this room where Achmed lay so near death, and the captain had been occupied with the repairs on the ship.

Brittany could hear sounds of loading and unloading above deck. Apparently they would soon be underway. She would not be sorry to see the last of this island.

She took Achmed's huge hand in hers. What tomorrow would bring, she could not guess, but could anything be worse than what she had lived through? She had been parted from her mother, pursued by the sultan's warships, and, worst of all, Achmed might die—Dr. Rutledge had said so.

As she stared at him, Brittany remembered all the times Achmed had brightened her life. He had always been kind to her, and had gone out of his way to make her life easier. Until lately she had not known how deeply that devotion ran.

"You must live, Achmed, so I can tell you how dear you are to me. You must!"

There was no response, and she moved back, resting her head against the chair, too weary to think. Her eyes fluttered shut and she fell asleep.

The quiet of the early morning was interrupted by the sound of an anchor grinding into place. The sails of the majestic *Victorious* caught the stiff breeze as she put out to sea. Her captain stood at the helm, his sure hands guiding her out of the harbor.

Cappy stood beside Thorn, his eyes watchful, repeating his captain's spoken commands to the crew. Within an hour, the *Victorious* caught the trade wind and moved swiftly out to open water.

The first mate glanced at Thorn. "The port authorities told me that the Turkish ship left yesterday, Captain. But I wonder if she made her homeward journey, or if she is laying in wait for us somewhere."

"We shall assume that she is waiting for us, and act accordingly, Cappy. Post a twenty-four-hour watch."

"Aye, Captain."

"How is the woman?"

"She hasn't left Achmed's bedside. She is very devoted to him."

Thorn was willing to admit that the woman had some human qualities. "Of course she is devoted to him and will nurse him back to health if possible. After all, if anything happens to the eunuch, who would take care of her needs? I have my doubts that she could function if she had to take care of herself."

"I think you misjudge her, Captain. I have seen enough to know she really cares about the eunuch."

"That is certain. As I pointed out, he is that woman's fetch-and-carry boy."

Cappy watched his captain with a speculative eye. Although Thorn Stoddard was often with a pretty woman when they were in port, Cappy knew he did not have a very high opinion of females. But it seemed the captain was unusually harsh toward this one. The first mate knew Thorn's bitterness had something to do with his stepmother, but he did not know the whole story.

"In truth, Captain, our passenger isn't a woman at all, but a very young girl. You see, she no longer wears that veil to cover her face, and I saw her. She sure is a pretty little thing. She has eyes that—"

Thorn's hands gripped the wheel, and the muscle in his jaw tightened into a hard line. For some reason he did not want to hear anything good about that woman. She had been nothing but trouble to him since the beginning. He had little doubt that she would continue to be an annoyance until he was rid of her.

"Spare me, if you are going to sing her praises, Cappy. And, whether she be woman or girl, it's all the same to me. Just see that she follows orders and keeps away from the men. I don't want any more trouble from her."

"Aye," Cappy agreed, wondering why Thorn was being so critical when this girl had proved herself to be bold-hearted. What was there about her that always seemed to provoke the captain?

Thorn paused at the cabin where Achmed lay gravely wounded. Not bothering to knock, he opened the door and stepped inside. The waning light showed the vague outline of the eunuch where he lay on the bunk, so still and lifeless. Thorn's eyes moved from the injured man to search the cabin for the woman, for he had been told she was there.

In the half-light, he saw her in the straight-back chair, her head dropped to the side, obviously asleep. Her midnight-black hair spilled down her shoulders, almost to her waist. Cappy had been right, she was unveiled, and he was about to see her face for the first time.

Excitement throbbed through his body as he stepped closer. He saw the gentle slope of her breasts as they rose and fell with her breathing, and her dainty hands were clasped together and rested in her lap.

Stepping around the bunk, he did not see the table where the medicines had been placed until he had bumped into it and sent the contents crashing to the floor.

Brittany jumped to her feet, instantly coming awake. With large, luminous eyes, she stared at Thorn Stoddard while he stared back at her. Those were the eyes of a seductress, an enchantress, but there was also uncertainty there.

Thorn's eyes moved over the slight figure who came only to his shoulder. She was not dressed in her usual heavy robe. Instead she wore a pale-blue French-style gown with butterflies embroidered along the hem. The high-waisted creation fit snugly above her firm, young breasts. It was what any young lady in a Charleston drawing room could have worn.

Almost reluctantly, he raised his eyes to her face, his attention drawn first to her green eyes with their depth of intelligence far beyond her years.

As if he had no will of his own, Thorn looked upon the face that had so bewitched Sultan Selim that he had sent his warships to capture her. Each of her features was perfectly formed, and, yes, it was a face that men would willingly fight and die for. The dark skin and hair seemed somehow out of place with the green eyes, but they only added to her overall mystique. She was breathtakingly beautiful, there was no denying that.

"I . . . must have fallen asleep, Captain." She glanced at Achmed. "He is still unconscious."

Her words did not penetrate Thorn's consciousness because he was caught up in watching the way her long lashes swept her cheeks.

Brittany was beginning to feel uncomfortable under such intense scrutiny. "Captain, I know Dr. Rutledge has done all he can for Achmed, but I am so fearful of his chance for survival. If only he would awaken."

"Have you rested?" Thorn asked, noting the faint circles under her eyes. "I mean other than sleeping in that chair. You should go to your cabin."

"I will not leave, for I could not rest if I were not with Achmed."

Thorn did not believe that a woman of the harem could be so devoted to a slave. He doubted her motives, and his voice grew hard. "Do you ever think of this man as other than a servant who grants your slightest request?"

Now her gaze was cool. "Of course. Achmed is my friend. I have known him all my life. I have told you this before, but you choose not to believe me."

"Do you really cares what happens to him, or are you concerned that you will be without a servant if he dies?"

Her eyes closed, and her feelings reeled from his bitterness. Until Brittany had met this man, she had never had such angry contempt directed at her, and she did not know how to deal with it. She turned away from him so he would not see the hurt in her eyes.

"Do not concern yourself with my motives, Captain. If I am selfish or not, it is no concern of yours."

"You are right," he answered. "Your motives are no concern to me, but your safety has become my concern, whether I want it to be or not."

She turned back to him. "I have not made you responsible for me."

He stared into the eyes that were so remarkable in depth and color that he could scarcely catch his breath. "Weigh this well: The moment you stepped on this ship, you became my charge, just as everyone else on board the *Victorious* is in my care."

She raised her chin. "As soon as we reach land, I will be glad to remove myself and Achmed from your ship, this releasing you of our tiresome presence."

He smiled, but not with amusement. "You cannot look forward to that event more than I. When next we put ashore, you will step on American soil and out of my life."

"What have I done to make you angry with me? Achmed told me he has paid for our passage. I understand you have been through much because of me, but it was hardly my fault."

He was startled for a moment. "Have I said that I was angry with you?"

"Do you always treat people with such disrespect, or do you reserve your ill temper for women alone?"

Thorn and Brittany stared at each other long and hard. "Perhaps I reserve my ill temper for tempestuous young women who act like queens, when, in truth, they are little more than women of the street." He reached forward and touched the huge emerald at her neck. "Only your price sets you apart from the common harlot."

Brittany gasped at his insult. The eyebrows arched above the green eyes that sparked with anger. "How dare you speak to me thus." She took the several steps that brought her closer to Achmed. "I do not ever wish to talk to you again, Captain Stoddard. You may leave."

He gave her a curt nod. "Just see that you stay out of my way." He turned on his heels and left, closing the door behind him.

Once he was outside, he paused to look out to sea, knowing that he had hurt the girl, and wondering what there was about her that made him so angry. Why should he care that the Grand Vizier was her lover? Why did he resent the fact that she appeared so young and innocent, when he knew she was not?

Thorn stared into the distance where frothy white clouds billowed across the endless sky. He did not even know anything about her. Why did she have to be so damned beautiful, and why could he not cleanse his mind of her?

He turned back with the intention of returning to the cabin and apologizing for his harsh words, but at that moment, Cappy called to him. He would apologize to her later, for he had been too harsh with her. But why?

"Did you see the girl?" Cappy asked, turning the helm over to his captain.

"I saw her," came Thorn's curt reply.

"And?"

"Don't you have duties to perform, Mr. Hamish?"

Brittany bent down to pick up the medicine bottles the captain had knocked over. She righted the table and then moved to sit beside Achmed. When she sank down in the hard chair, she felt as if her heart had been bruised by the captain's unflattering assessment of her character. She hated the lie that stood between them. Most of all, she resented his judging her without knowing her.

What right did he have to accuse her so harshly? Anger still burned within her. What did it matter what this American thought of her? They would soon part company, and she would never have to see him again.

She moved forward, placing a cool hand on Achmed's fevered brow, wishing he would awaken. He would know how to advise her. She had never been allowed to make decisions on her own. She certainly did not know how to deal with men like Captain Thorn Stoddard.

The door opened and Brittany jumped to her feet, thinking it would be the captain returning. She was relieved when the kindly Dr. Rutledge smiled at her from beneath shaggy eyebrows.

"How is our patient this afternoon?"

Brittany shook her head. "There has been no change in his condition, Dr. Rutledge. What can this mean?"

The doctor moved to Achmed's side and raised a limp wrist, placing his thumb down on the pressure point. "It means that he has been gravely injured and his body is resting so it can heal itself."

"Will Achmed live, Doctor?" she asked with hope in her heart.

"I cannot say, little lady. I've done all that I can to help him; now he is in God's hands."

"What are his chances of regaining consciousness?" she pressed, needing an answer.

He shrugged. "I can tell you no more than I have. He was badly injured, and it could go either way with him. Why don't you go to your cabin and get some rest."

"I cannot leave him."

The doctor smiled kindly. "I will sit with him for a while. I'll call you if there is any change."

She nodded reluctantly. "If it will satisfy you, I will go and refresh myself and rest for a short while." She moved across the cabin and paused at the door. "You will let me know right away if he needs me?"

"I will."

Brittany left the cabin, unaware that hostile Turkish eyes watched her from the shadows at the far end of the corridor.

On Admiral Kainardji's orders, the man, Jah, had managed to sneak on board the *Victorious* just before she had put to sea. He had been hiding in the hold so he would not be discovered, for he had a mission to fulfill.

Admiral Kainardji had decided that if he could not take the daughter of the English Rose back to the sultan, perhaps he could redeem himself in the sultan's eyes by reporting that the girl was dead!

Jah had been waiting for the opportunity to present itself to carry out the admiral's order. He watched the girl go into a cabin and close the door behind her. Now he knew where to find her.

Chapter Thirteen

Brittany had stripped down to her thin chemise, trying to find some relief from the oppressive heat. There was not a breath of air stirring. The sails of the *Victorious* hung limp while she drifted upon the calm, silvery ribbon of sea. A poignant silence hung heavy in the air as though a grim prediction of things to come.

Brittany had bathed in cool water, then reapplied the dark stain to her skin. She lay down on her bunk, with the intention of resting for only a moment, because she did not want to stay away from Achmed for very long. He might be concerned if he awakened and she was not beside him.

The lantern flickered low, and she closed her eyes, drifting off into a world of dreams, where there was no hurt and no uncertainty about the future.

Suddenly Brittany was not alone in her dream. She felt a firm hand clasp hers, and she glanced into the angry blue eyes of Captain Thorn Stoddard.

She felt as if the air was trapped in her lungs; she could scarcely draw a deep breath. She pressed forward until her body was touching with full length of the captain's, and she saw his blue eyes swirling with passion. She was overwhelmed by the first stirring of womanhood that sprung to life within her young body.

Brittany was aware that she was dreaming and that the Thorn Stoddard in her dream did not exist. She wanted to hold on to her fantasy world, but even now it was fading. So this was what it felt like to desire a man. The women of the harem had told her about the strong feelings between a man and woman; now she understood the depths of such feelings.

Brittany was jarred awake by a sudden feeling of unrest. Had it been a sound that had awakened her? She raised up on her elbows, her heart beating with some unknown dread. The lantern flickered low and almost went out, casting the far corner of the room in shadow.

Even if she could not see anyone, she felt an ominous presence in the room with her.

Slowly she swung her legs off the bed, wondering if she dared make a dash for the door. She paused. Was she being foolish or was there really someone in here with her? She listened. Was that breathing she heard or was it the beating of her own heart?

"I have found you at last," a strange voice spoke to her in Turkish.

She stood as if frozen, when a dark-skinned man stepped into the ring of light. "You may be in disguise, but I know you are the daughter of the English Rose."

"Who . . . are you?" She cringed in terror. "What are you doing in my cabin?"

"I am the man who has been sent by Admiral Kainardji to end your life. After all the trouble you have caused, did you expect to escape?" He moved closer to her. "Do not scream or make a sound. I am an experienced assassin, and I can slit your throat without you even feeling it."

Brittany made a quick lunge for the door, but the man had anticipated her movement and intercepted her before she reached freedom.

Hard, cruel hands bit into her tender flesh, and she looked into sadistic black eyes that were hardly visible beneath dark, heavy eyebrows.

The assassin's thin lips became even thinner when he smiled. "Would you fly away, little bird, before I discovered what there is about you that makes the sultan desire you so? Some say your mother is the weaver of magic spells. Are you the same as she?"

Brittany drew back in fear, not daring to look again into those pitiless eyes. "What . . . will you do to me?"

His eyes moved down her throat to fasten on her young breasts that were visible through her thin chemise. "Before I carry out my master's orders, I will taste the delights of your body, daughter of the English Rose. Perhaps you will make me as happy as your mother makes the Grand Vizier."

"No," she whispered through trembling lips.

"Yes," he said, running his hand across her breasts. "I die today, too, little rose, because I cannot leave this ship alive, but I die with the taste of you on my mouth."

Unleashed fear gnawed at her insides. This man wanted more than her life, and much more than she was willing to give. She lashed out at him, her flying hand catching hard across his jaw!

For a moment she thought he would release her, but he muttered an oath, and his grip tightened even more. She cringed as the rough hands with black hair on the knuckles moved up her leg, bringing her chemise up to her thigh.

"No," she cried, struggling against his superior strength. "Let me go!"

"We shall be together in death this day," he muttered, his lips traveling down her throat.

Her reaction was swift and accurate. As she struck out at him a second time, the slap she delivered to his face rang across the cabin.

Now the man's anger was out of control. He shoved her down on the floor, his fumbling hands tearing at her clothing. He was so caught up in his anger and passion that he did not hear the door open behind him—he did not see the captain of the *Victorious* with a murderous glint in his eyes.

Brittany stared into Thorn Stoddard's blue eyes, and a whimper escaped her lips. "Help me," she cried piteously. "Please help me."

The Turk suddenly released his hold on Brittany and jumped to his feet. He swiftly turned on Thorn, brandishing an evil-looking, broad-blade scimitar.

With a swift reflex, Thorn gripped the arm that held the blade. For long moments, the two men pitted their raw strength against each other. At times the sharp blade would come close to Thorn's throat, then he would push it away and the Turk would have to hold it away from his own throat.

Brittany watched in horror as the two men struggled for supremacy. She feared for the captain's life because the Turk was a trained killer. The assassin's bulging muscles quivered as he twisted the blade and thrust it toward Thorn's exposed chest. In a swift and lethal motion, Thorn sidestepped the thrust and yanked his foe forward, plunging the blade of the scimitar into the Turk's chest.

For a moment there was a startled expression on the Turk's face, then a look of disbelief twisted his features. With blood streaming down his dark skin, he fell to his knees, the sword still embedded in his chest.

Thorn gripped the ivory handle, and with a quick upward thrust, buried the blade even deeper. The Turk slumped to the floor, his legs twitched, and then he lay still.

When Thorn stepped over the body of the assassin, he glared at Brittany. "What in the hell has been going on here?" he demanded. "How did this man come to be on board the *Victorious*? He is not one of my crew."

Thorn suddenly averted his eyes when he saw that the girl was making a futile attempt to cover her nakedness. "Do you know this man?" Thorn asked.

"I have not seen him before, but he said he was sent by Admiral Kainardji with orders to . . . slay me."

Thorn touched the body with the toe of his black boot. "He will not harm you now. He is dead," he said gently.

By now Cappy and two others had heard the scuffling, and they appeared at the door with startled expressions on their faces.

Thorn nodded toward the body. "Get him out of here and throw him overboard."

"Aye, aye, sir," Cappy replied, taking charge and motioning for the two crew members to lift the body. He smiled encouragingly at Brittany before shoving the man out of the cabin and closing the door behind him.

Thorn saw that the girl had pulled the coverlet from the bed to cover herself. "Are you hurt?" he asked.

"I was more frightened than hurt," she assured him, taking a faltering step and finding her legs would not hold her weight.

When her knees buckled beneath her, Thorn scooped her up and held her in his arms. Brittany laid her head against his broad shoulder, finding comfort there. "I was so frightened. He was going to . . . to—"

Thorn felt the trembling of her body. He wanted to kill the man again for putting his hands on her. He wanted to always be the one to protect her from harm so she would never have to be frightened again.

"Are you certain you were not hurt?" he asked, looking into her wondrous green eyes.

"I was not hurt, but if you had not come when you did, I do not know what would have—" She shivered.

"I was passing your cabin when I heard the scuffle. Try not to think about it. You are safe now."

She could sense his strength, and it filled her whole being. She clung to him, fearful that he would put her down. "Please hold me," she pleaded.

He sat down on the edge of the bunk, cradling her in his arms as if she were a frightened child. "Nothing will hurt you while I am here," he said with assurance. "You know the intruder is dead."

She shivered. "It was horrible. I wish I could get the sight of it out of my mind."

"Think of something pleasant."

"I cannot."

When Thorn shifted Brittany's weight, she cried out in pain. When he gave her an inquiring look, she pushed the strap of her chemise aside, and there was the telltale sign of a bruise—already the skin was discolored. He touched it tenderly. "I thought you said you weren't hurt."

"It is nothing that will not heal with the passing of time," she assured him. "I am just grateful that it was not worse." Her eyes softened. "I have so much to thank you for. It seems every time I am in trouble, you come to my rescue. Once again, I am in your debt."

He smiled. "It seems you are always in trouble."

She returned his smile. "It does seem that way. But that is nothing new in my life."

Thorn found he was watching her lips, wondering what it would feel like to press them to his mouth. He lightly touched her midnight-black hair, unconsciously winding a curl around his finger.

Brittany felt his chest expand with a sharp intake of breath as his eyes traveled from her shoulder to the rise of her breasts where the material had been torn away. She did not move to cover herself, but gazed into his eyes, trying to see if he was feeling the warmth flowing through his body as she did.

"Damn you," he murmured, pulling her close to him and resting his cheek against her sweet-smelling hair. "You know what you're doing to me. You know I have been intrigued with you from the beginning. Everything about you is different from all other women—your eyes, the way you walk, the way you purse your mouth when you are deep in thought."

Emotions he had not even admitted to himself came pouring out of him. His lips brushed across the bridge of her nose. The hand that had wielded the deadly sword now caressed her with a gentleness she had not expected. The lips that had curled in anger now touched hers as softly as butterfly wings. The body that had leaped to battle in her defense was now pressed against hers, and she lost all ability to reason. She wanted to throw off the clothing that kept him from touching his hot flesh to hers.

"Sweet little enchantress." The words seemed to be ripped from his lips. "Have you no mercy for me?"

"I . . . do not know what you—"

"Don't play innocent with me. We both know you are not."

She blinked her eyes. "I have not—"

"Are you certain you did not entice that poor devil into your trap?" he whispered against her ear. "Did you make him mindless with wanting you?"

She shook her head, wondering how he could think such a thing of her. "I did not know the man. He was evil, and he made me afraid."

"How many others have you enticed with your body and your smile—certainly Lord Simijin, apparently the sultan."

"No, I never—"

His hand moved to her chin, and he forced her to look into his eyes. "What is it that draws me to you? Did you set out to make me your conquest?"

"No," she whispered through trembling lips. "I am not that way."

He pulled her closer, his hands running caressingly across her dark skin, absorbing the feel of her into his mind, wanting her—aching to possess her. When his eyes fell on the pool of blood that had seeped into the cracks of the floor, he was brought back to his senses.

Brittany was startled when Thorn pulled her chemise together and placed her on the bed. He rose to his feet and smiled down at her. "So ends this argument," he said in a deep voice. "Henceforth, you might do well to keep your distance from men, me in particular. You see how it is with me. Next time, I may not be so willing to stop. You have already conquered the hearts of two men; you will not add mine to that number."

She wanted to scream and fly at him, for the words he spoke had wounded her more deeply than the knife thrust he had delivered to the luckless Turk. "I will detest you forever, Captain Stoddard."

He smiled. "Good. Hate is an emotion I can deal with. I half feared you might be indifferent to me, and I wouldn't want that."

She turned away, wishing she had never laid eyes on this obstinate man. "Leave me or I shall have Simijin cut your head off."

He laughed and clicked his tongue. "My, my, what a blood-thirsty little temptress you are. Was the life of one man not enough to satisfy you tonight? Must you have my blood on your hands as well?"

She whirled around, her breasts heaving from her anger. "It was you who slew the Turk, when you could have clapped him in irons and tortured him."

Amusement danced in his blue eyes. "Pity that thought never occurred to me while I was wrestling for my life. Had I known that you wanted him tortured, I might have spared him for you."

Her hands went to her hips, and she glared at him. "You are a hateful man."

His eyes raked her softly curved body. "And you, madame, are in a state of undress. Shouldn't you cover yourself—or is it your intention to tempt me?"

She whirled around, picked up the pillow from the bed, and threw it at him. The fluffy missile shot harmlessly past Thorn's head as he agilely ducked out of the way. With amusement dancing in his eyes, he moved out of the cabin, his laughter ringing through the door he closed behind him.

Brittany's face was flushed with anger. Were most men as unendurable as Thorn Stoddard? Perhaps Simijin was more exceptional than she had thought, for she had never seen him torment her mother as the captain tormented her.

Hot tears scalded her eyes, and she slumped down on the bunk, refusing to look at the pool of blood on the floor.

After a while, Brittany washed her face, tied back her hair, and pulled on her gown. She would sit with Achmed tonight, for she knew she would not sleep a wink after all that had happened.

Thorn's expression had sobered by the time he joined Cappy on deck. "I want this ship searched from stem to stern to make certain there are no more intruders on board. It will go hard with you, Cappy, if any more stowaways turn up unexpectedly."

"I will see to it myself, Captain," Cappy agreed. "Is the little lady all right?"

"I believe she is like a cat and will always land on her feet."

"She looked frightened to me."

"Who can say if she was frightened or only pretending. Perhaps she lured the poor man to her cabin and ultimately caused his death."

"I don't think you believe that, Captain. That man intended to do her harm. I suspect he was sent by that man who captured her before."

Thorn stood at the railing. He had not trusted a woman since his stepmother had proved how devious a woman could be. His rule where women were concerned was to make love to them, but never love them. He would certainly never believe one word any woman said, especially the little enchantress who was tugging at his heart and muddling his mind until he could not think past possessing her.

He looked into the inky night, searching for the Eastern Star. Once he located it, he wondered if the girl was like that star, cold and alluring, but with no substance. No, he had felt her warmth. She was alive—soft, and desirable.

"Damn it to hell," he swore, drawing Cappy's startled glance.

"Did you say something, Captain?"

"Nothing important," he mumbled. "After you have searched the ship, go ahead and turn in. I'll stay at the helm tonight and take your watch. I couldn't sleep anyway."

Cappy knew his captain was in a rare mood, and he also knew it was because of the girl. "Aye, Captain. Will you be wanting anything else?"

"No, but post a man you can trust to look after that girl. I don't want another incident that will disrupt the whole ship."

"Aye, Captain," Cappy replied, hiding a grin.

Thorn stood silently for a moment before he took the helm.

The first mate had never before seen the captain so befuddled. If he wasn't careful, this girl would turn him inside out. Cappy chuckled. Perhaps this native girl was just what the captain needed.

Chapter Fourteen

The heat of the tropic sea was at its worst. Brittany sat beside Achmed's bed, fanning him in an attempt to keep him cool. She was desperate because he had not yet regained consciousness. Dr. Rutledge had warned her that if Achmed did not awaken soon and take some nourishment, he would surely die.

She glanced down at Achmed's face, noting how thin he was, and how his cheeks had become hollow. She touched his forehead and found he had no fever.

"Oh, Achmed, my dear friend, why do you linger in that awful darkness when the sun is shining so brightly outside this cabin?"

She heard an unmistakable sound, as if Achmed had just taken a big gulp of air into his lungs. She stared at him with hope in her heart when his eyes fluttered and finally opened.

Brittany's eyes danced with happiness when he turned his head to look directly at her, his dark eyes filled with uncertainty and bewilderment.

"What . . . has happened? Where am I?"

She dropped to her knees, taking his giant hand in hers and pressing it against her cheek. "You have been gravely wounded, and I feared for your life, but you are going to recover." She smiled. "I am glad to have my friend back again."

His eyes glazed over with pain, and he frowned. "I cannot recall what happened to me."

She stood up, feeling great relief wash over her. "It does not matter that you cannot remember. I suspect that with the passing of time, your memory will come back to you."

"You are Brittany?"

"Yes, of course."

He tried to rise up, but the pain made him reconsider, and he fell back against the pillow. "Lord Simijin will be calling for me. I must go to him at once."

Brittany's eyes were now round with concern. "Simijin will not be needing you now. You must rest while I go for the doctor."

She hurried out of the cabin in search of Dr. Rutledge. She was happy that Achmed had awakened, but concerned that he could not recall where he was.

Thorn stood over the eunuch, watching Dr. Rutledge spoon-feed him some dark, foul-smelling broth. "I was glad to hear that you would recover, Achmed. You have been through a great deal, but that is behind you now."

"My memory returns at time, Captain Stoddard. But at other times, I cannot even remember my name. I do remember you, Captain, but later I may not."

"What else do you recall?" the doctor asked.

"I remember what happened the night Brittany was attacked by the sultan's men at the Casa del Oro."

Thorn stared at the eunuch. "I never knew her name until now," he said. "I expected her to have some strange and exotic-sounding name that would be hard to pronounce and that would match her nationality—whatever that is."

"Yes, her name is Brittany, and she is under my protection," Achmed admitted. "Even though I sometimes call her by her name, I mean no disrespect. It is just that I have known her since she was born."

The doctor poked another spoonful of the liquid at Achmed, and the eunuch turned his head away. "I thank you for your care, Dr. Rutledge, but I will not eat more of that concoction. What I need is real food."

The good doctor smiled. "Indeed, I believe you are recovering. But let me caution you that you are not as strong as you might think. You must remain in bed at least until we reach Charleston."

Achmed looked at the captain. "And how long will that be?"

Thorn was thoughtful for a moment. "If the winds hold, within two weeks."

"I have been absent from my post too long now. I must return to my duties." He raised up, but when the room whirled around like a spinning top, he lay back against the pillow, beads of sweat popping out on his forehead.

"As I cautioned you, Achmed, you have not yet regained your strength," Dr. Rutledge said in his professional voice. "You will remain in bed as I said."

Achmed tried to rise again without success. "I cannot. Who will look after my little mistress?"

"She is safe enough," the doctor said. "I suspect there are very few situations she cannot handle by herself."

"My mistress told me about the man who attacked her in her cabin. Can you assure me that there are no others who will try to harm her?"

"The ship has been thoroughly searched, and no one was found. There is no one on board that does not belong," Thorn told him. "You need not be distressed on that account. Your Brittany is safe."

Achmed shook his head, looking most distressed. "You must not call my mistress by her name. Lord Simijin would not permit you to be so familiar with her."

Thorn's jaw set in a stubborn line. "Yes, Lord Simijin would expect to keep her for himself. It is strange that he should care so much about this girl when I have heard he loved only one woman—the one they call the English Rose."

Achmed's eyes became secretive. "Lord Simijin would never allow me to discuss the English Rose with you. Nor should you call my little mistress by her true name. I have been negligent in my duties because I allowed you to know her name."

"How should we address her, if not by her name?" Dr. Rutledge inquired.

"You should not address her at all. I am aware that she no

longer covers her face, but you must not consider approaching her for any reason."

Thorn met the doctor's eyes. Neither of them could understand a society that so jealously guarded their women. Again Thorn felt resentment building up inside him. He did not like the fact that Brittany belonged to a man who had many other women. He wondered how she could love such a man.

"Just rest, Achmed," Thorn commanded. "I have made certain that your charge will come to no harm."

Achmed smiled, feeling reassured. "I trust you, Captain Stoddard. You have proven you are a friend."

Thorn moved out of the cabin, wondering how in the hell he got himself tangled up in Brittany's life. He looked forward to the day when he would set her ashore and see the last of her.

The storm hit just after midnight. Thunder and lightning chased each other across the ebony skies, and a hard rain pelted its fury against the *Victorious*.

Brittany was jarred awake when a jagged bolt of lightning splintered through the night.

With trembling hands, she fumbled around in the dark until she found her hooded burnoose. Not bothering to dress, she slipped the cape over her nightgown, thinking she must look in on Achmed. He had appeared well enough earlier, but perhaps the storm had awakened him. She needed to satisfy herself that he still clung to life.

She left her cabin quietly and padded barefoot down the corridor to Achmed's cabin. Silently, she opened the door to find him sleeping peacefully. For a time she watched the steady rise and fall of his chest, then she closed the door, feeling more relieved about his condition.

On her way back to her cabin, she had an urge to stand in the rain and let it wash all her troubles away. She made no sound as she took the steps that led to the upper deck. Knowing there would be a man at the helm, perhaps the captain, and a man on watch, she moved directly to the railing, hoping no one would detect her presence and send her below.

By now the thunder and lightning had built up in force, but the rain had ceased. She pushed her hood aside, breathing in the clean air. She felt wonderfully revived. She had always loved storms.

"It's late for you to be about, isn't it?" the deep voice of the captain spoke up from beside her.

She backed closer to the railing. "I . . . was awakened by the thunder."

"Yet you were not frightened if you can stand out here in the thunder."

She could have told him she was only frightened of him at the moment. "No, I am not frightened of a little thunder. Why should I be?"

"You would never allow anything as insignificant as a little thunder to frighten you, would you?"

Something in the way he looked at her made her want to flee. His eyes were burning into hers, searching, probing, yet she stayed. Suddenly she felt warm inside, and she clutched at her cape, pulling it about her neck.

"I hope you do not mind that I came on deck, Captain?"

"Why should I mind? If you fall overboard, it will rid me of a nuisance, wouldn't it?"

She drew in her breath at the pain his words caused. Turning to look at the stormy sky overhead, she wished he would just go away and leave her in peace. Her eyes burned, and she could feel tears gathering on her lashes.

"What the hell?" he said, turning her to face him and staring into her face.

Brittany put her hand to her face, fearing the stain had come off her face in the rain. "What is wrong?" she asked, backing away from him.

"I always say the wrong thing with you. Of course, I don't want you to fall overboard. I am not the monster you believe me to be."

"I am aware that I have been trouble for you, Captain. You have certainly called my attention to it often enough." She pulled her cape about her to ward off the rain. "But I fear you are stuck with me until we reach Charleston."

"So it would seem." He saw her shiver and wrongly concluded that she was cold. "You had best go below deck now. The last thing I want is another ill passenger on my hands. You and your eunuch have complicated my life enough as it is."

She could do no more than stare at him. Was this man always angry? she wondered. Did he never laugh and feel lighthearted?

Brittany could not know how appealing she looked with her dark hair blowing with the wind and her beautiful face illuminated by streaks of lightning.

"Go below," Thorn ordered in a stern voice.

Suddenly, she had enough of his highhanded manner, and she decided to fight back. "No, I will not go below. I came out to see the storm, and I intend to stay as long as I like."

With a growl of impatience, and a sudden movement, he scooped her up in his arms and carried her across the deck and down the narrow passageway.

"What are you going to do to me?" she asked through trembling lips, wondering if she had pushed him too far.

"What I should have done when I first had the urge," he ground out in an angry voice.

He held her suspended while he opened the door to his cabin and carried her inside and set her on her feet.

"But I have not—"

Drawing Brittany to him, Thorn lowered his dark head and covered her lips with his, cutting off any protest she might have made.

Thorn had meant only to take his anger out on her with a quick kiss, but when her soft lips trembled beneath his and he heard the sigh escape her throat, all he could think about was possessing her.

All the conversations Brittany had overheard in the harem now came to her mind. How many times had she heard the women discussing the ways to please their lord. She knew where to touch a man to make him mindless with passion. Should she use that knowledge with this man? Brittany had been told that a woman's body had been created to receive a man's. Should she offer her body to this man?

Moving back, her cape fell away, and she realized too late that her nightgown would appear transparent with the lantern behind her. She felt a hot wave of pleasure wash over her when his blue eyes darkened with desire.

Yes, she reminded herself, she had been taught by experts in pleasing a lover. She would now use all she knew to entrap Thorn Stoddard. Too many times he had humiliated her and made her hurt because of his bitter words. Now she would humiliate him.

Her eyes gleamed as she planned how she would humble him. She would take him to the brink of madness and then deny him what he wanted most from her.

Thorn stood tight-lipped, his eyes drawn to the delicate beauty. When he found his voice, it came out in a tortured whisper. "It would be in your best interest to leave now. Stay, and you will suffer the consequences. I am not a man who can withstand temptation."

The air was charged with electricity, and Brittany felt daring. "What if I do not want to leave? I see in your eyes that you do not really want me to leave."

"Perhaps," he agreed with a shrug. "But if you stay, you know what will happen. I doubt that you are willing to take that chance." He advanced a step closer to her. "I would advise you not to."

"What is your pleasure?" She moved closer to him, stood on tiptoes, and purred in his ear, "Tell me, and I will give it to you."

She struggled to retain her cool manner, when in truth she wanted to flee to safety. This man was making her feel emotions she did not know how to handle, no matter how much she had learned in the harem.

"I warn you," he whispered in a meaningful voice, "do not push me too far."

Foolishly, Brittany gave him an alluring smile. She had not been taught that it was unwise for a woman to tease a man like Thorn. She only wanted to toy with him, to make him feel some of the frustrations she had experienced because of him. It was important that she bring this arrogant man to his knees. Only then would she feel appeased.

His breath came out in a hiss, and he gathered her trembling body tightly against his.

"I will be damned for eternity, little concubine, but I will have all of you. No matter that you belong to another man, I will take what the sultan desires, and what Lord Simijin treasures."

"I have been trained to please, Captain Stoddard," she purred. "I know how to make your body find pleasures in a thousand delightful ways. But first you must give me time to prepare."

Thorn stared into green eyes that promised him paradise. "What is to prepare?" he asked hoarsely.

She slipped out of his arms, stooped to retrieve her burnoose, and slipped it over her head. "Give me a few moments, and then come to my cabin. I will give you a night you will never forget."

He stared after her as she moved to the door. "What if I do not want what you offer, Brittany? I have had many such offers." He thought of Wilhelmina. "Some I have accepted, others I have not."

She smiled her most captivating smile. "You will come, I think."

After she had gone, Thorn stood as though in a trance. He would not fall into the trap that was being so cleverly laid for him.

He was beginning to believe she had deliberately come on deck tonight with the express purpose of driving him out of his mind. One other time in his life he had allowed a woman to reach the innermost part of his heart—he had vowed never to do it again.

He closed his eyes as thoughts of how satiny Brittany's skin had felt, and the memory of her beautiful body were burned into his mind.

No, he would not go to her. Instead, he would go on deck and stand in the rain to cool his passion.

He moved to the door, but stood undecided. He would just go to her cabin and tell her that he was not a fool.

He made his way to Brittany's cabin like a man with a mission. This woman would never catch him in her silken web!

Thorn was a man who was not inexperienced in love-making, and she was no novice herself. It would amuse him to flaunt her offer in her face.

His eyes narrowed in contempt. Why had he allowed her to entice him? Had he not already learned this lesson from Wilhelmina?

Chapter Fifteen

Brittany slipped into her dancing costume, glad that one of the women in the harem had placed it in her satchel. She was pleased that the costume was transparent so she could do the dance that Milo, the Egyptian woman, had taught her, for it was the most beguiling of all the dances she had learned.

She dipped her fingers into hyacinth oil, rubbing it through her flowing black hair. Next she applied kohl to her eyes, hoping she would look the part of the seductress.

She ran her hand nervously over her bare midriff, trying to remember all she had been told about the Egyptian dance. Milo had said that the eyes played an important part in this dance, that she should often lower her lashes and look directly into her victim's eyes.

Brittany was now ready for Thorn, although she was nervous. She had never danced for a man before, so she was plagued by doubts. What if he did not come? What if he did not like her dance?

With a suddenness that took her by surprise, Thorn opened the door and stood staring at her. The black transparent costume revealed her soft curves rather than covered them. The short tunic of matching material was trimmed in silver. There were silver bells that jingled whenever she moved. A matching veil covered the lower part of her face. Her dark hair shimmered like an ebony waterfall down her back to her waist.

Thorn had not expected her to look like this. He could not tear his eyes away from the beautiful, dark-skinned girl who stood before him. She indicated that he was to sit on the pillow she had placed on the floor for him. Like a man moving through a dream, he sat down, his eyes never wavering from her gaze.

Brittany slowly began moving her hips, slightly at first, then in a wider circle, seductively, alluringly. The silver bells laced through her fingers made a musical sound when she clicked them together.

Thorn was mesmerized as her bare feet moved gracefully across the room, her transparent gown whirling about her. He could smell the intoxicating scent of hyacinth, and he felt his head reel and his heart pound.

Brittany was becoming bolder in her movements, for she could see she had captivated him. This was her first experience in being a woman, and she was enjoying it. How quiet he was as he watched her every move. How penetrating his eyes were as he stared into hers. Each movement was meant to entice, to intrigue, and to punish. Confident now, she became even more daring, and removed the veil from her shoulder and floated it before Thorn's face, where it touched him like a silken caress.

His eyes were pools of passion as she whirled about him, teasing, tantalizing, and tormenting. She approached him, moving her hips ever so slightly, knowing she had him where she wanted him.

Soon the dance would end, and she would dismiss him. She had no doubt that he would be angered by the trick she was playing on him, but she could handle his wrath—in fact she welcomed it.

As she unfastened the veil that covered her face, her eyes were shining, and her lips were pursed and moist.

Brittany moved closer to Thorn, holding her arms out to him as if inviting him to embrace her. Yes, he was watching her—she would soon have him where she wanted him, groveling at her feet. He was a proud man, but she would conquer him, if only for this one night.

When she made a turn, she felt his hands span her waist, and with gentle pressure he pulled her into his lap.

She laughed up at him tauntingly. "But, Captain," she breathed, "I have not finished the dance."

"You win, Brittany," he said in a voice of agony. "You have accomplished your purpose." He moved his hand up to tangle in her dark hair, and there was no softness in his eyes. "Your body promises—how did you put it—a thousand delights? I am ready to take my pleasure with you."

Her eyes widened with innocence, and she had a ready answer for him. "But you have mistaken me, Captain. I wanted merely to dance for you. Did you not find the dance to your liking?"

His blue eyes seemed to burn into her. "You know I did. You deliberately tormented me. I want you and you know it." His hand moved to cup her face. "Let us be done with games of pretense. I only want what you have given Lord Simijin— and I intend to have you."

Her victory was a short one. He was not supposed to react in this way. She was losing control of the situation and she began to panic. "You are mistaken, Captain. It was a performance, nothing more."

She tried to move away from him, but he held her tight. "You must go now, Captain. My dance was a gift to you. I have nothing more to offer you."

His hands slid up to caress one breast, and she felt a warmth of pleasure spread throughout her whole body. "We both know this is what you want, Brittany. We have known it for a long time." His voice deepened. "I can no longer deny there is desire between us—why should you?"

"No, Captain, you misunderstand me. I only wanted to . . . to—"

He placed his finger over her lips to silence her. "You have given me your gift, now it is time for me to give you mine, little dancer."

He lowered his head, and she knew he was going to kiss her. She did nothing to stop him. She ached for the touch of that mouth on hers. His hot breath fanned her cheek, and he pulled her to him so she was lying across his lap.

"You have asked for this, Brittany, and by God you are going to get it. You have become an obsession with me, and tonight you added fuel to an already hot flame."

There was a tightening in her throat and a throbbing void that cried out to be filled. "This is wrong," she said, though only halfheartedly. "This was not supposed to happen."

"I will steal only a little happiness from Lord Simijin. You don't even have to tell him if you don't want to." His eyes raked her face. "If I know women—and I do—you will not tell him that I made love to you tonight."

She touched his face. "Please do not do this. I truly did not expect you would go this far."

He arched his dark brow skeptically. "Did you not, little concubine? Did you think you could torment a man to the edge of madness and then come away untouched?"

She looked into blue eyes that sparkled with life and deepened with feverish desire. She answered him as honestly as she could. "I am not sure, Captain. Perhaps this is what I wanted all along."

He brushed his mouth across her throat, and her sigh brought a smile to his lips. "That is first truth you have told since I have known you."

Her eyes were seeking. "To my knowledge, I have never told a lie. Why must you always think the worst of me?"

"Right now, Brittany, I am thinking only the best of you."

His fingers played boldly with the material at her neck, while she held her breath. Slowly, he parted the material while his eyes went to her satiny breasts beneath the black material.

Her lashes fluttered while her lips parted in silent invitation.

He lowered his head, and his mouth brushed against the taut nipple. When he heard her gasp, he smiled, knowing he was now in command. His moist tongue rolled around the dusky-colored tip until it swelled against his lips. Then he moved to the other, to deliver the same painful pleasure.

"What are you doing to me?" she whispered through passion-soft lips. "Please stop . . . I do not . . . Ohhh . . ."

He raised his head and stared into swirling green eyes. "I am a man of some experience myself, little dancer. Tell me what you like, and I will do it."

She squirmed, as a flood of untapped feelings rippled through her innocent body. "No, do not do this. I do . . . not know what I want."

His lips moved up her neck, and he whispered against her mouth. "But only a moment ago, you were so sure of what you wanted."

As Thorn's lips closed over Brittany's, she felt the room tilt, and she clung to him, pulling him closer and opening her lips to the probing of his tongue. His hands moved to her waist, and he tugged at the thin costume until he could move it over her hips. All the while he was kissing her until she was mindless.

"Say you want me," he whispered against her ear. "You know you do—admit it."

Brittany knew that if she gave in to his searing demand, she would be lost. She looked at him pleadingly. "Do not force me to do this, Captain."

His laughter was soft, and his magical hands had moved to her thigh. "I have never used force with a woman, Brittany. Why should I with you, when you are so ripe and ready to receive me?" To prove his point, he moved his finger ever so slightly to massage her velvet softness. "Do you deny that you want me?"

Pleasure such as she had never known coursed through her young body. "I want you," she admitted in a strangled voice. "Yes, I want you."

Her hand was resting on his arm, and she felt his muscles bulge when he picked her up and carried her to the bunk. While she watched, he stripped off his white shirt and tossed it aside. When his hand went to his belt, she shyly turned her face to the wall, not knowing what to expect.

His amused laughter filled the room. "Play the coy miss with me, if it pleases you, but we both know better. Before I am finished with you, you will beg for more, and you will know that I am not your Simijin."

When he dropped down on the bed beside her, she could not bring herself to look below his broad shoulders. Suddenly, everything she had been told by the women in the harem went out of her mind. All she could think about was having this man's hands on her body, bringing delight and awakening her to new and deeper sensations.

Thorn lay down beside her and rolled her over so she was facing him. Slowly and deliberately, he pulled her quivering body toward his.

Brittany gasped for breath when their naked bodies touched. She felt his throbbing shaft harden against her, and she went limp with untapped desire. She seemed to have no control over her own body.

Her hand moved over the mat of dark hair on his chest, and she looked into his burning blue eyes, and had the sensation that she was drowning.

"I fear I will displease you," she said in a voice of uncertainty.

His mouth parted as he glanced at her lips. "If I never have more of you than this, you have already pleased me beyond belief."

A whimper escaped her lips, and she buried her face against his chest. Could it be love that she felt for this American? Certainly it was beyond friendship—beyond desire—beyond anything she had ever experienced before.

When he rolled her over on her back and was poised above her, she waited for the moment he would plunge inside her body. Then she would belong to him. The act was accomplished so quickly that she gasped at the stinging pain when he parted her legs and slipped inside her.

Thorn's body trembled as her silkiness closed around his throbbing shaft. He muttered beneath his breath when he came up against the barrier that proclaimed her a virgin.

He tangled his hand in her hair and yanked her forward. "Damn you, what game is this? Why did you allow me to believe Lord Simijin was your lover when your body has never known a man's?"

She touched her lips to his, but he pulled away. "Why in the hell did you deceive me?"

"I never told you I had been with a man. It was your own assumption."

He was still inside her, and she moved her hips, trying to tempt him, so he would satisfy the burning need he had aroused in her.

"It is not too late," he warned. "I have not yet taken your virginity. Tell me what game you play."

As she ran her hand down his stomach and felt the corded muscles, Brittany realized the tight restraint he was keeping on himself.

"I want you to make love to me," she admitted. "I want you to teach me to be a woman."

"No, damn it! This is a mistake." He would have withdrawn from her, but she clasped her arms about him. Thorn felt his resolve slipping when she thrust her hips upward, pushing him past the barrier of skin and taking her deeply within her body.

Perspiration beaded on his upper lip as he fell under her spell once more. She had never been with a man, but her body was fanning a fire within him, and he could no longer control his movements. He plunged forward forcefully, then gently pulled back, setting a rhythmic motion.

Her eyes darkened with passion as she matched her movements to his. He laced his hands in her hair and closed his eyes. She was fulfilling his every fantasy. She *was* the seductress he had accused her of being. He slid deeper inside her, and her satiny softness cradled his throbbing desire.

"Enchantress," he murmured in her ear. "Will you not be satisfied until you have all of me?"

For her answer, she arched her hips, and he gasped with pleasure. "If I did not know better, I would say you were practiced in the ways of pleasing a man."

Her breath fanned his ear and sent a shiver of delight down his spine. "I was born to give pleasure to you," she whispered.

Thorn gathered her to him, wishing he could take her into his body. He never wanted this night to end. He wanted to take her again and again, for he would never grow weary of her.

While the lightning flashed and the thunder rumbled, Thorn introduced Brittany to new and deeper emotions.

The *Victorious* swayed and groaned from the onslaught of the storm, but the two lovers were only aware of each other.

Brittany ran her hands over Thorn's shoulders, while his hot lips covered hers. As their bodies intertwined, they found a meeting of mind and body, and they both knew they would never be the same afterward.

Together they scaled the heights and reached the peak of desire. And when the last shuddering release passed through their bodies like molten lava, it left them breathless and clinging to each other.

Brittany was drifting on a feather-soft cloud of well-being. She clung to Thorn, unwilling to let him go. He had made her his—he had made her a woman. She was suddenly sad that they could never have anything but this night.

He pulled away from her and smiled tenderly, while his eyes moved over her face as if he were memorizing every line and curve. "Are you all right?" he asked, moving his hand over her stomach.

She returned his smile shyly. "Yes. It was . . . it was wonderful."

He touched his lips to her cheek and held her tightly. "Yes, it was beyond belief."

"You were not disappointed with me?"

He drew in a shuddering breath. "Never have I been more

pleased." He pulled back and looked at her for a long silent moment. "Brittany, had I known that you had never been with—"

She placed her hand over his lips. "I know that, Captain."

His blue eyes were laced with humor. "Don't you think that under the circumstances, you could call me Thorn?"

"I cannot. It would not be proper."

He looked at her with a strange expression on his face. "After what has happened between us, you are still concerned about propriety?"

"Captain, I know you will not understand this, but there can never be anything between us after tonight. What happened to us was my fault, and we both know it." She smiled sadly. "I want you to realize that I expect nothing from you, and I never want you to feel remorse for what occurred."

Brittany caught her breath when a flash of lightning made a jagged path across the sky and the illumination of it reflected in the depth of Thorn's blue eyes.

"Remorse is the farthermost thought from my mind at the moment, Brittany. How can I feel anything but joy after what happened between us? Are you feeling remorse?"

"I do not feel sorry in any way, Captain. I shall always treasure what we had together." Her eyes were wide and innocent. "You have had many women before me, but I have had only you, so how can you know how I feel?"

He silently toyed with one of her ebony curls. Then he looked into her eyes, seeking the truth. "I will not deny that I have been with other women, Brittany. But it has nothing to do with what happened between us."

His eyes moved over her perfectly formed body, and a feeling of possessiveness took hold of him. He wanted no other man to touch her, especially not Lord Simijin. He wanted to know about her life with that man and he was determined to find out.

He pulled her head to rest against his chest. "Tell me about your life, Brittany. How did you come to be in Lord Simijin's household?"

Her hair was a curtain of flowing black satin, and when she shook her head, it swirled about her. "I cannot talk about that because I pledged an oath of silence." She felt pain in her heart, knowing he could never understand the promise she had made to her mother.

"Did you? To whom did you make that promise? Lord Simijin?"

"Even though you deserve to know, there is much I cannot tell you."

"If you will not tell me about your life with Lord Simijin, tell me something about yourself."

His body was warm against hers, and she snuggled closer to him. "I had an English governess and a French teacher. I am proficient in mathematics. I speak, read, and write eleven languages. And I know the folk dances of thirteen countries." She looked at him doubtfully. "As you have seen, I also know some of the more daring dances. Is that what you wanted to know?"

"Yes, in part. How did you learn so many dances?"

"In the harem, of course. There are women there from many countries."

He did not like to be reminded that she came from a harem. "You are a very exceptional woman. I know few men who have your background in education."

"I have heard it said that American and English men do not value knowledge in their women. Can this be so?"

"I have known that to be true in some cases," he admitted with a smile. "But now that I have met you, I will no longer subscribe to that antiquated custom."

She sighed. "I am glad Simijin did not share that belief. He enjoyed intelligent conversation. It is because of him that my education is so varied. And of course, I owe much of my education to the women of the harem."

Thorn's eyes darkened, and he felt a stab of jealousy. "Do you love Lord Simijin?"

"Yes, of course. I told you he is a truly wonderful man. If you but knew him you would see that—"

He rolled to a sitting position. "I would rather not hear a glowing tribute to your—" He looked back at her. "What is he to you? Up to this point, he has not been your lover. Was he saving you to take the place of the English Rose?"

"No! No one could ever take the place of . . . the English Rose." Her eyes took on a secretive glow. "I would rather not discuss Simijin with you."

Thorn pulled on his trousers and glared down at her. "I wonder how you can share him with so many other women. I find that repugnant."

She was puzzled for a moment. "I do not share Simijin."

"Not with the woman of the harem?"

"He never goes to the harem."

"I have heard that he loves only the English Rose. It is said that she is a very beautiful woman."

"She is the most beautiful woman I know of—inside and out."

"You are not jealous of her?"

Brittany thought of her mother and was overcome with a feeling of homesickness. "No, never jealous of her. She has always been kind to me."

For a moment he was suspicious that Brittany might be the famous English Rose herself, but he discounted that notion since Brittany would be too young. "The women I have known would never consent to living out their lives in a harem."

Her eyes flashed angrily. "Perhaps not. Why should they, when they could have a stud like you to service them?"

For the first time in Thorn's life, he was stunned into silence. Never had he known a woman who spoke so boldly.

"I can see that I have shocked you, Captain Stoddard. Forgive me," she said with sarcasm. "I forgot you are not accustomed to women who speak their mind. I am sure it takes a lot of courage to be a woman in your world."

Suddenly he saw the humor of it all, and he dropped down on the bed beside her. "I would say it takes much more courage to be a woman in *your* world. Since I have known you, I have only had the Turkish Navy nipping at my heels. You have been kidnapped, and almost ravished by the man who found his way to your cabin to end your life. I can only guess what other adventures await you down the road."

She raised up, pulling the coverlet over her. "I can assure you that I lived a safe enough existence before I met you, Captain Stoddard."

Suddenly he was overcome with tender feelings for her. He took her face between his hands. "Let me be your protector from now on." He was startled by his own words, but he found he meant them. "I will take care of you and keep you from harm." His lips lightly touched hers. "Say yes, Brittany."

"As your wife?" she asked hopefully.

He looked at her through veiled lashes. "No, I would not make a decent husband for you or any woman."

Sadness tugged at her heart. "I cannot be your woman, Captain. I have commitments in my life that must be honored. Besides, I have no wish to be any man's mistress. Apparently I value myself much more than you do."

He came to his feet, pulling her up with him. "You do not have to decide anything now. We have time before we reach port. Perhaps you will change your mind."

"I will not change my mind. Take me at my word on that, Captain."

He pulled her to him, lowered his head, and covered her lips with his. Brittany clung to him, wishing she could accept his offer. Would it not be better to have a little of him than nothing at all?

Thorn raised his head and gave her a warm smile. "It would seem that your only decision is whether you want to be with Lord Simijin, and be a lesser wife, or be with me."

"As no wife at all."

He smiled. "There you have it. Think on my offer. I must leave you for now."

She nodded. "Yes. You must tend to your duties."

He kissed his finger and laid it against her lips. "Until later."

She watched him leave, wondering at the fate that had brought him into her world. She was never destined to belong to him, but she had stolen a little happiness from him—could she be condemned for that?

She lay back on the bed and stared at the ceiling. She had made a promise to her mother, and it was a promise she would keep, but oh, it would be the most difficult promise she had ever made. Thorn was not the kind of man one said no to without giving him a good reason.

She touched her lips, where he had placed passionate kisses. Tonight she would remember until she was a very old woman.

She felt restless, so she got up and paced the floor. She knew what she had to do, although it would be very difficult.

She had to let Thorn know that his offer was unacceptable. Having made her decision, she decided to write him a note rather than face him. It was difficult to put her thoughts down on paper, so she was brief.

The sun was high in the sky when Brittany found Cappy. She gave him the note, asking him to deliver it to his captain. If the first mate thought her request was a strange one, he did not say so.

Thorn took the note Cappy handed him and arched his brow questioningly.

"It is from the young miss. She asked that I deliver it to you."

After Cappy departed, Thorn opened the note, with hope in his heart. Perhaps Brittany was too shy to give him her answer in person.

He stared at the delicate handwriting, unable to grasp her meaning for a moment.

"Captain Stoddard, after giving your offer a great deal of thought, my answer is no."

His eyes were dark swirling storm centers, and he crushed the note in his fists. He had not expected Brittany to say no to him. Would she have said yes if he had offered her marriage? No, probably not. Apparently Lord Simijin still retained his grip on her, even from a distance.

"So be it," he said aloud. "So be it, Brittany."

Chapter Sixteen

Brittany's thoughts always seemed to be centered on Thorn Stoddard. She was not sorry she had written him the note, and she was glad that he had believed her, because if Thorn had come to her, she had little doubt she would have given in to him—and that must not happen.

Now she only saw him from a distance. Even from across the deck of the *Victorious*, she could feel his eyes on her. But she did not go to him, and he did not approach her.

Their parting had been inevitable, for their future lay in different directions. But that did not keep Brittany from reliving the night she had found brief happiness in Thorn's arms and wishing she could be with him again.

She kept busy nursing Achmed, who was growing stronger each day. Now that he was feeling so much better, it was difficult to keep him in bed.

It was almost sundown as Brittany walked along the deck, pausing to stare out at the glorious sunset. She knew the voyage was coming to an end because she could see graceful sea birds floating on the warm currents of wind, indicating they must be getting close to landfall.

She was feeling sad and melancholy as she glanced down at the water breaking against the sides of the *Victorious*. For several weeks, this vessel had been home to her, and soon she would be cast into the unknown. After she went ashore, she would never see Thorn Stoddard again.

If only fate had been a little kinder, if only she had been born just an ordinary girl from America, then perhaps she and Thorn would have had a future together. Perhaps then he would have respected her enough to offer her marriage, rather than asking her to be his mistress.

As if her thinking about him had conjured him up, Thorn's shadow fell across Brittany's face. She raised her head and looked into his eyes, wishing she could tell what he was thinking, but as usual, his eyes gave nothing away.

"We will reach Charleston Harbor in two days," he said, gripping the railing and watching the dying rays of sunlight reflect off Brittany's ebony hair. "I thought you would like to know."

"Yes, I thought as much." Her eyes probed his. "Will I ever see you again?"

He was silent for a moment. Then he took a deep breath and let it out slowly. "That is up to you, Brittany—it always has been."

"You mean if I will consent to be your mistress?"

"Crudely put," he said, avoiding her eyes. "But an apt affirmation."

"How would you word your offer to me without being crude?"

"I would invite you to be my companion, whenever we both felt like it. I would take care of you and see that you wanted for nothing."

Her anger had been tapped by his arrogance. "Would you introduce me to your family and friends as your companion of convenience?"

He swung his gaze around to her. "No," he said flatly. "But not for the reasons you might think. I would never want my family to intrude on my life with you."

She shook her head. "You will have no life with me, Captain Stoddard."

Thorn was not accustomed to being denied anything by a woman, but this was no ordinary woman. The green emerald she wore about her neck would purchase and outfit a ship like the *Victorious*. She had lived in a palace where she had been pampered like a princess. She had been the light of the Grand Vizier's eye, and had been desired by a sultan. What could he offer her that she could not have a hundred times over with Lord Simijin? He had hoped she could come to him because she wanted to be with him, but that had not been the case.

"I can see that you belong to Lord Simijin. I know he can offer you more than I, but you will forgive my foolish pride for wrongly assuming you liked being with me."

Now her anger was foremost in her mind. He had insulted her at every turn: First by offering to make her his mistress, rather than a wife, and now by hinting that she wanted only the material things Simijin could give her.

She fought to control her voice as she spoke to him. "In a way, I shall always belong to Simijin." Pain throbbed in her voice. "He has always been very kind to me, and I owe him that much."

Thorn's eyes moved across her face, and there was tension in his expression, and a clipped edge to his voice. "You will want to have your belongings gathered together so you can be ready to disembark when we come into port, Brittany."

"Yes."

"You may want to put up for a few days in Charleston since Achmed is not well enough to be jostled around on rough roads. Once he is well enough, I will have Cappy make travel arrangements to Philadelphia."

Her eyes fastened on the laces that crisscrossed his snowy-white shirt. Then she lowered her lashes, fearing he would be able to read the hurt and bewilderment in her expression. "Two days is enough time to pack what I brought with me. You need not be concerned that I will inconvenience you in any way."

He gave her a curt nod and moved away, his back straight and his head held high. She wanted to call him back and tell him she would do anything to be with him, but she could not do that. She must go to Philadelphia as she had been instructed.

If only she could tell Thorn that she did not belong to Simijin in the way he thought, but her promise to her mother sealed her lips.

Silence hung heavily in the air as she moved across the deck and down the companionway. Thorn Stoddard would have had many women before her, and she doubted if he would even remember her after she left.

It made it easier to say no to Thorn since he had insultingly offered to make her his mistress. She looked down at her dark hands and wondered if he would have offered her marriage had he known she was white. What did it matter? The insult was there between them, and nothing he could say would change that.

Brittany knew so little about the world since she had lived such a protected life, but she did know that Thorn would never care for her in the way a woman wanted to be cared for.

She reflected on the softness that came into Simijin's eyes when he looked at her mother. That was the way she wanted Thorn to look at her.

Refusing to cry, she packed her meager belongings in the satchel and set it beside the door, her final act in cutting the slender thread that held her to Thorn Stoddard.

Brittany smiled with relief when Achmed took several steps across his cabin. "You are doing wonderful, Achmed, but you are not to overdo," she cautioned.

"We will be leaving the ship very soon, little mistress, and I have to be strong enough to protect you."

"This is America, Achmed. What dangers will I encounter here?"

His white teeth flashed when he gave her a broad grin. "I believe, little mistress, that you can find trouble wherever you go."

She wrinkled her nose. "Yes, I do tend to get into predicaments without even trying. Why do you suppose that is?"

"It is because the breath of life flows through your body.

You are one who has always reached out for life, rather than sitting around waiting for something to happen."

"As you know, Mrs. Potter called that being rebellious."

"What she thinks does not matter. She is one who will one day die without ever having lived."

"Poor woman, she did have her trials with me." She sighed heavily. "It seems a lifetime ago, those carefree days at the palace."

Achmed took another turn across the room and then back again. "Happiness is a fleeting thing, little mistress. You cannot hold it in your hand, you cannot smell it or taste it—you can only take it when it comes along."

She shook her head. "One cannot always reach out for happiness if it will be destructive in the end."

He glanced up at her as though he read her thoughts. "Then it is wise to walk away." He reached the bunk and sat down. "I am almost as strong as ever. I will be able to watch after you and see that neither harm nor unhappiness darken your door."

"For a time, you must be careful and see to your health, Achmed. We shall find rooms when we reach Charleston until you feel up to traveling. That will give us the time we need to send a message to Mama and Simijin, telling them we have arrived safely. Then in a few days, we shall travel to Philadelphia."

Achmed leaned his head back to catch his breath. He knew he had not yet regained his strength. "I see that you have this all worked out in your mind, little mistress."

"No, not all. But we shall make out fine, Achmed." Her eyes clouded. "I wish we did not have to go to Philadelphia to confront relatives who may not welcome us."

"You are not to worry about anything, little miss. Most probably we will not be required to remain in this country for very long. Soon you will be returning home."

Brittany knew Achmed was trying to cheer her up. He did not believe they would be allowed to return to Turkey any more than she did. But she did so want to be with her mother.

The night was dark as Brittany moved across the deck to gaze as the twinkling stars in the eastern sky. High, sparse clouds had drifted in front of the crescent moon, and it seemed that the *Victorious* sailed on an ebony ocean that went on forever. Although she knew they should be close to America, she saw no lights—no indication that they were nearing Charleston.

With a heavy sigh, she moved across the deck and down the narrow passage that led to the captain's quarters. She had decided to tell Thorn good-bye in privacy. It would be remiss of her if she did not thank him for all he had done for her and Achmed.

When she reached Thorn's cabin the door was ajar, and she peeked in to find it empty. Hesitantly, she moved into the cabin and stood near Thorn's rumpled bed, feeling his presence in every fiber of her being. She was surrounded by his maps and charts. His blue jacket was tossed carelessly across a chair, a pair of boots sat beside a bootjack.

Brittany was startled when Thorn came up silently behind her and his hand spanned her tiny waist. "Well, my little beauty, to what do I owe the honor of this visit?"

She glanced up at him and was caught in his warm smile. He must think she had changed her mind. She had to set him straight at once. "I . . . came to say good-bye."

He spun her around, and his eyes darkened with hidden fire. "No, not good-bye. I knew you would come to me." He dipped his head, and his lips nipped at the sensitive hollow in her throat. "I have ached to hold you like this, Brittany."

She pushed him away and stepped back. "This is not what I wanted, Captain Stoddard."

He looked doubtful. "I do not believe that you can walk out of my life like this."

"Believe it," she said, using her anger as a shield against his charm.

"I know I was beastly to you. And if you want an apology from me, then you have it, Brittany." There was tension in his expression. "I do not want to fight with you." His voice was caressing. "I would much rather kiss you."

She felt the gentle touch of his hand on her cheek. Her lips might deny him, but her green eyes revealed the truth—she was deeply affected by his nearness. "I had to see you one more time," she answered with honesty. ". . . to thank you for—"

His hand drifted down to tangle in her hair, and he brought her up on her tiptoes so her mouth was close to his. "If you hadn't come to me, I would have come to you," he said, as if the truth had been torn from his lips. "You have me where you want me, and you know it. All I can think about is the sweetness of your body." He dipped his head and covered her lips with his, and she quivered at his gentleness.

Brittany could feel the lure of his magnetism, but she pulled away from him. "Do not do this. Just because I threw myself at you the other night does not mean it will happen this time."

He stared into her eyes. "Will it not?"

"No-o."

His mouth quirked briefly. "Has anyone ever told you that when you are troubled about something your eyes turn a darker green?"

"I . . . no."

"What secrets do you hide behind those eyes, Brittany? How many hearts have you trampled under your delicate slippers?"

"I . . . have known only a few men in my life."

He looked doubtful. "Surely that cannot be."

"But it is. I know Simijin, Achmed, and several other lesser eunuchs and attendants. And, of course I know you, and some of the men on your ship."

His eyelids flickered, and he brought her body closer to his. "Me, you know intimately. The others cannot make the same claim."

She whirled away from him. "Do you make mock of me, Captain Stoddard?"

"To the contrary. I feel honored that I was the first man to be with you. Have you danced for Lord Simijin as you danced for me?"

"No, of course not!"

His voice deepened. "I would like to think that you dance for me alone."

She wanted to run away from Thorn—to find a safe haven where she could think. With him touching her, she was in danger of falling under his spell again. "No," she whispered as his lips touched the corner of her mouth.

"Yes," he breathed against her satiny lips.

She could feel her objections melting away. She was being drawn to him by a force stronger than her own will.

Brittany turned her face away from his burning lips and looked at him with haughty disdain, her only weapon at the moment. "You have nothing of a lasting nature to offer a woman, Captain. You only want a mistress. That is a position that is totally unacceptable to me."

"So it's marriage you want, is it? Surely you know that's impossible between you and me. We are from different worlds and different cultures. You could not survive in my world . . . as my wife."

Her eyes were cool, and her chin went up just a little higher. "I would not marry you even if you asked me. What makes you think you are such a prize?"

His laughter was soft. "Marriage to you might not be so bad, after all. Certainly you are a woman worthy of consideration. If I were wise, I would probably grab you up and sail away with you so no other man could ever find you." His voice deepened. "I would find some deserted beach and make love to you all day and all night. You would belong to me alone."

"You offend me, Captain. Why is it that men think they honor a woman when they consider her at all?"

His smile faded, his jaw hardened. "No offense was intended. I have never offered any other woman half so much as I have you."

"Well, you can keep your offer. I want never to see you again."

His glance became irritated. "You don't mean that, Brittany. You are only hurt because I will not marry you."

"Do you think you bring me honor by asking me to become your mistress, Captain? The sultan would have given me much more than that."

"Yet you ran away from him."

She placed her hands on her hips, her eyes filled with disbelief. "The more I come to know about men, the less I like them. Women are far more superior in intelligence and understanding than your sex."

"I don't believe that is true of all women, Brittany, but it is so in your case."

She tossed her hair so it became a rippling curtain of black. "I do not want your flattery."

"I don't flatter you, Brittany. I want to be with you. Not just now, but for years to come. I could care for you." His voice softened. "I would make you happy."

She drew in her breath and looked into his blue eyes. Her heart was beating so fast she could scarcely breathe. "We would not be good for one another, Captain."

His voice had edge to it. "Must you call me, 'Captain?' My name is Thorn."

"I . . . will not call you by your name. To do so would be a mistake."

His hand dropped to the front of her gown, and he toyed with the ribbon there. With a quick yank, he untied the ribbon and when she did not try to stop him, he unhooked the top hook.

She could not speak for the lump that had formed in her throat. He pushed her gown aside and softly laid his hand on her breasts. He then moved forward and pressed his lips in the sweet-smelling hollow between them.

"Please, no, Thorn. This must not happen again." Even as she voiced her protest, she knew this was what she really wanted.

Chapter Seventeen

Thorn's eyes flashed with triumph, and he picked Brittany up in his arms and carried her to his bed. "So, at last I am Thorn."

When he lay her down, she sat up quickly and pushed against his chest. "No, Thorn, I will not do this."

Her plea fell on deaf ears. His eyes were swirling with passion, and he gently pushed her backward and followed her down. With tenderness, he kissed and caressed her, all the while pushing her gown to her waist.

Brittany's eyes were no longer pleading for him to stop. Her lips parted under the hot thrusts of his tongue, and she clung to him.

Thorn raised his head and stared at her. He was astounded by her delicate beauty, and he could not look away from her creamy breasts that seemed lighter in color than the rest of her body. His hands moved over her silken skin, and he had a difficult time controlling his need for her.

"Brittany, tell me to let you go, and I will," he challenged.

She drew in a deep breath, and her voice came out in a throaty whisper. "That is unfair, and you know it. I . . . came here to—"

His hand trembled as it traveled down her arm. "Then, if you have no objections, Brittany, I will have you."

All thoughts of objection were gone, and she reached up to touch his ebony hair. She was sad because this would be all they would ever have.

"I will surrender to you, Thorn. This will be my parting gift to you."

"We will give to each other," he whispered. "Each of us

has our own gift. I have given more of myself to you than I have ever given any woman."

Her eyes were shimmering with unshed tears. She turned away quickly so he would not know how much she was affected by his words. She did not like to be reminded that he had been with other women before her.

Thorn tugged her gown over her hips and dropped it onto the floor. With raw impatience, he removed his own clothing and lay down beside her.

Brittany's eyes softened. "I remember the first time I saw you. I thought you quite the most handsome man. I also thought you were arrogant and unbending. I was right on all three assumptions."

He arched his brow at her. "And when was the first time you saw me?"

"The day Simijin invited you to the palace. I watched you behind the latticework at the top of the stairs. Neither you nor Simijin knew I was there."

With a lean finger, he traced her jawline. "Did you now?"

"Yes."

"So you heard me tell Lord Simijin I would not take you to England?"

"I did not know he was making arrangements for me that day. It was not until later that I learned the truth. Then there was no time to think, for I had to flee."

"Had I known then what I have come to know, I would have taken you anywhere you wanted to go."

She looked at him, wondering if he was teasing her. It was hard to tell because his eyes did not always show what he was thinking. "You have said often enough that you will be glad to see the last of me."

"Right now, all I can think of is the green of your eyes and the softness of your skin." He ran his hand down her neck, and he gently cupped her breasts. "If one could hold on to a moment in time, I would choose this one."

Blood ran hot in Brittany's veins, and she gravitated toward him, her lips parted, her eyes shining.

"You do so sorely tempt me," he said, touching his lips softly to hers. Then he moved back and allowed his eyes to take in every curve of her face. "I want to love you, my little dancer."

Raising her arms, she lay back inviting him to her. "I know," she whispered. "It is the same with me."

Thorn shook his head, trying to clear it. She was becoming too important to him, and he had to exorcise her from his mind. He would make love to her, and when it was over, he would put her out of his mind as he had with so many other women before her.

He clasped her satiny body close to him, and with a smooth motion he sunk into her, his body throbbing, his breath coming out in sharp gasps. Never had he been so affected by a woman. Never had he felt so alive as when he held Brittany in his arms.

Thorn had been tormented by the memory of that night he had made love to Brittany. He had tried to put her out of his mind, but it had been useless. With a gentle caress, he conveyed his deepening feelings to her.

Thorn filled Brittany's body while his hot mouth ravished her lips. She closed her eyes and allowed the wonderful feelings to wash over her. This, she thought, was the moment out of time that she would have chosen to hold on to for eternity.

Now Thorn's lovemaking became more intense. Burning passion had fused their bodies together and left them both breathless.

On gossamer wings, they soared the heavens, as sensation after sensation held them together by the thread of desire.

Suddenly, Brittany's whole body seemed to erupt with wave after wave of pleasurable feelings. Was it love that she felt for this man? she wondered. What else could make her want to be with him throughout her lifetime?

When her heartbeat returned to normal, she stared into dancing blue eyes. "It was good between us, just like before, Brittany."

"Yes," she murmured, burying her face against his chest.

"You will be mine alone, Brittany. No other man will ever touch you."

She turned her head away from him. "No, Thorn, I cannot make that promise. I can never belong to you."

His voice had an edge to it. "Is it because of Lord Simijin?"

"In part," she admitted, twisting away from him and moving off the bed. As she pulled her gown over her head, she presented her back to him, hoping he would not ask any more questions. She was startled when he came up to her and hooked her gown.

"I am trying to understand what you feel for Lord Simijin that prevents you from reaching out to take the happiness I offer you."

She turned back to him and stared at him in disbelief. "You do not offer me happiness, Thorn. What you offer is a life where I will be shunned by respectable people. If you love me—"

His eyes were burning, and his voice was scornful. "I said nothing about love, Brittany. Love is for fools and dreamers, who don't know better. What we have between us is preferable to that puny emotion people call love."

Her green eyes were cool. "Are you saying you prefer animal lust?"

He laughed and pulled her into his arms, but she twisted away. He raised his hands in a gesture of surrender. "All right, Brittany. If the only way I can have you is to make you my wife, you win." He caught her hand and pulled her into his arms. His lips touched her ear, sending shivers of delight dancing on her spine. "I will make the ultimate sacrifice and take you as my wife, if that is the only way I can possess you."

Never had Brittany known such anger. Her voice trembled as she shoved him away. "I do not want your sacrifice, Captain Stoddard. After we dock, we will never meet again. Just leave me alone!"

"I wish to hell I could." He shrugged. "Take care Brittany, that you do not tell me to leave you alone once too often and I start to believe you. A man can soon tire of pursuing a woman if she does not know her own mind. You tell me no, while you pull me to you."

All the fight seemed to go out of her. "There is some truth in what you say, Thorn. Sometimes I do not know what I feel," she said in confusion.

She would have moved away, but the look in his eyes held her spellbound. She came to him, and when he held out his hand, she placed hers in his warm clasp.

"You are trembling," he observed. "Is it anger, or are you feeling what I feel inside?"

"I . . . yes."

"You are not afraid of me, are you?"

"No."

"If this is to be our last night together, let us make the most of it."

She looked into his eyes as he unhooked her gown once more and pushed it off her shoulders, where it fell to the floor.

"Come to me," he whispered, pulling her into his arms with a triumphant smile.

His lips were hot and seemed to drain all the resistance from her. He went to his knees and carried her with him. His hands were stroking her into submission, and when he lay her back against the floor, she was only aware of his hard body pressed against her soft curves.

Like a person drowning, Bittany knew that if she didn't save herself, she would be lost forever, but his hands were working magic on her body, and his lips smothered her futile protest.

Gently, he spread her legs apart and stroked her until her breath became trapped in her throat. Her soft groan told him that she had surrendered completely.

"For this moment, you are mine," he murmured in a velvet-smooth voice. "We both know that."

She looked into blue eyes that burned with the flame of passion. "Yes, Thorn, yes."

Brittany heard Thorn's breath come out in a hiss. "I will drive all thoughts of Lord Simijin out of your mind. You will no longer think of him."

Brittany pressed her body tightly against him, not understanding his words. His lips covered her mouth with a burning kiss, and she ached for him to possess her once more.

"You are in my blood, Brittany."

Brittany was tormented, and she ached to feel him inside her, but he seemed to be in no hurry.

"You want me," he murmured, kissing her neck, her eyelids, and then her mouth.

Her mouth opened between his gentle probing. Her body was on fire, and he knew it.

"You were made for a man to love, Brittany," he whispered hotly in her ear. "You get inside my mind, and all I can think about is holding you like this. You know you are torturing me, don't you?"

"No," she breathed, thinking he was the one who was tormenting her.

When his lips moved to her creamy breasts, Brittany groaned with pleasure.

When he moved away, she protested, but he was positioning her hips, and he drove deep inside her with a thrust that left them both breathless. His body trembled as he rested deeply inside her velvet softness.

Brittany clamped her lips together tightly, fearing she would cry out from the beauty of their coming together. It passed through her mind that Thorn had control of her body. With the touch of his hand, he could make her surrender to him.

Opening her eyes, she stared into the blue depths of his eyes. "Damn you, Brittany," he muttered. "What are you doing to me?"

She blinked her eyes. "I do not understand."

But suddenly she did understand. There was no mistaking the naked desire that flamed in his eyes. He was as much affected by her as she was by him.

She smiled at him sadly. "I know," she said in a choked voice. She gently touched his cheek. "There is nothing we can do to stem the passion that flows between us, Thorn."

She moved her hips forward, and he whispered her name just before his hot mouth covered hers. She moved beneath him, and he threw back his head in an ecstasy of delight. She had the power to make him forget everything but her.

Thorn moved deeply inside her, his rhythm building up a tempo in her blood. There was pleasure and there was pain, and there was the feeling that after tonight she would never be alive again.

Brittany was sure her heart would burst from the wonderful feelings that Thorn had awakened in her body. He was the perfect lover. He had gentled his movements so she would feel the full pleasure of his lovemaking. She was overcome with sensuous feelings, and she could not remember why she had ever objected to his touch.

Long after their bodies had cooled down, they lay together as if neither of them was willing to break contact. The *Victorious* swayed gently on the waves, while her captain closed his eyes and pulled his lady tightly into his embrace.

At last, he said, "I don't want to, but I must leave you for a time. It will be my watch. Will you wait here for me, Brittany?"

She pressed her lips against the hollow in his throat. "After tomorrow we will—"

"It is already tomorrow," he said, reminding her of the lateness of the hour.

She placed her hand over his lips. "Two more days, and we will go our separate ways."

"Yes," he said, not really believing she would leave him. "No matter what happens in the future, I will keep the memory of tonight with me for a long time to come."

She raised up on her elbow and looked down at him. "Thorn, I have always felt a great uneasiness in you, but I do not know what it is. Before we are parted, I would like to help you. Can you tell me what it is?"

He rolled to a sitting position. "You ask a question that I am unwilling to answer, but yes—there is something in my life that was left unfinished."

"Does it concern a woman?"

"Yes, in part."

She came to her feet. "We both have secrets to keep, don't we." She smiled regretfully. "It's a pity our lives have been set on separate paths. Let us just say that we were like passing ships that touched, and then sailed away. But I do wish you happiness wherever you go." Her eyes were misty with sadness. "Whatever is driving you I hope is brought to a favorable conclusion for you."

He pulled on his clothing, and she watched as he poked the tail of his shirt into his trousers. He then turned to her and held out his arms and she came to him.

"We will not say good-bye, Brittany, because I have a feeling it is not over between us."

His lips were warm against her trembling mouth. Suddenly, he released her and moved to the door. He smiled slightly. "It could be that I would have made you a good husband, Brittany. But we shall never know, since you refused my suit."

She had a strong desire to tell him that she would be his wife, his mistress, or anything he wanted her to be. But, no, that was never to be.

Brittany watched him leave, knowing there was some force that was controlling his life, just as she had a destiny waiting for her in Philadelphia.

Chapter Eighteen

It was Brittany's last night on board the *Victorious*. Her mind was so filled with agonizing thoughts that she had not been able to sleep. She moved off the bunk and pulled on her cape, thinking she would take a turn about the deck; perhaps that would help her sort out her troubled feelings.

She saw that a light rain had begun to fall. She moved silently up the companionway, hoping she would encounter no one—especially not Thorn.

Now the rain was coming down harder, and she doubted the wisdom of coming on deck, because she was soaked to the skin. As rain ran down her face, she could not help thinking these few hours before dawn would be her last time to stand here like this. She would miss many on this ship, especially the captain.

In the distance, she could see the twinkling lights of Charleston. At daylight she would go ashore. She would be on her own in a strange land, and that thought suddenly terrified her. This vessel had been her safe haven, her shelter from the storm. Soon she would be set adrift, and then what would she do?

Brittany turned her face up to the rain as if it would have some magical powers to wash her cares and troubles away and help her find the answers she sought.

She thought of Thorn Stoddard, and she realized how difficult it would be to just walk away from him. She now had no doubts that she loved Thorn. She must have loved him from the very start.

Brittany was sure her mother would argue that she had not

known Thorn long enough to love him, but she *did* love him, with every fiber of her being.

Hot tears mixed with the cooling rain as she stood there drenched to the skin, her head bowed in misery.

"Have you gone mad, standing out here in the rain?" Thorn's deep voice barked out, and she lifted her face to him. "You will catch your death."

A lantern attached to the masts swayed with the movement of the ship and cast its gentle glow on Brittany's face. "I was saying good-bye to my old friend, the *Victorious*."

His eyes bore into her, reminding her of when she had bid him good-bye the night before. "You have surely completed all your farewells, by now. Should you—" Suddenly his eyes widened, and she saw a look of bewilderment on his face. "What the hell is this!"

"I do not know what you are talking about," she said, wondering at the reason for his sudden outburst. Why was he staring at her so hard?

He tilted her face toward the light and studied it intently. "Damn you, Brittany, do you take me for a complete fool?"

Her eyes were bright with dread when she realized that Thorn must have discovered her secret. It had been foolish of her to stand in the rain, because it must have washed the stain from her skin.

She backed away from him. "I do not know what you are talking—"

Without ceremony, he scooped her into his arms and carried her purposefully down the steps to his cabin. Once inside, he placed her on her feet. His face was a mask of fury as he turned up the wick on the lantern then pulled her into the ring of light so he could see her features.

Brittany raised her hand to her face, wishing she could run and hide from Thorn's probing glance. The anger she saw in his eyes caused her to tremble with fear. She did not know that a stream of hair dye had made a dark rivulet down her face.

She raised troubled eyes to Thorn and found him watching

her with a strange expression on his face. "What trickery is this?" he demanded. "What have you been up to all this time?"

She took a step backward, feeling for the doorknob behind her. "I am sure I do not know what you are talking about, Captain Stoddard."

"Don't you?"

"N-no."

In one swift motion, he unhooked her cape and tossed it to the floor. She stood before him in only her thin nightgown, and he was staring at her white skin. Why had she been so foolish as to go on deck in the rain? She should have foreseen that this could happen.

Brittany felt the water dripping down her face and reached up to wipe it away. Her mouth rounded when she saw the black dye on her hands. "I . . . must go," she said hurriedly. "I want to look in on Achmed."

Thorn blocked her exit. "I think not. Not until I have a few answers."

Brittany was startled when Thorn reached forward and stripped her nightgown away and tossed it on the floor. Her face burned with embarrassment as his eyes moved over her naked body, and there was a light of possessiveness in their blue depths.

With a smothered oath, he scooped her up in his arms and deposited her in the tub of water where he had bathed earlier in the evening. Before she could object, he was lathering her hair and rubbing soap over her shoulders and arms. When her face and shoulders were thoroughly lathered, he reached for a pail of water and poured it over her head.

"I'll be damned," he hissed through clenched teeth. "You and your eunuch must have thought yourselves clever to have duped me for so long. You might have gotten away with it if you had not been so adventuresome tonight."

Brittany sputtered and fought him as he poured more water over her head.

Thorn ground his teeth, and he was not gentle as he

lifted her out of the bath and wrapped her in a towel. His eyes assessed the white skin and the golden hair that spilled down her back.

Plopping her down on his bed, he pulled a chair up, straddled it, and gave her a dark look. "I want some answers, and I want them now!"

Huddled on his bed, without benefit of her clothing, Brittany felt completely at Thorn Stoddard's mercy. She was determined to keep her promise to her mother and not reveal her true identity.

She shook her head in refusal. "I cannot tell you anything about myself. It is a promise I made, that I cannot break. My mother—" She placed her hand over her mouth. "I have said too much already."

"No, not nearly enough, Brittany." His eyes moved over the delicate white skin, and he suddenly knew who she was. "You are the daughter of the English Rose. Simijin is your father."

"No, Simijin is not my father."

"But the English Rose is your mother?"

She looked into his eyes, unable to hide the truth. "Yes, she is my mother."

"And Lord Simijin?"

"Simijin likes to say I am the daughter of his heart."

Thorn's face drained of color, and his eyes were probing. "My God, you are not a woman of the harem, as you allowed me to believe. Why in the hell did Simijin tell me that you were one of his women?"

"Simijin thought he was acting in my best interests. His orders to me were to stay hidden behind the veils. That way, he was confident I would be safe. He had not thought that Sultan Selim would be so persistent in pursuing me. Of course, I had to break my word and I feel terrible about that."

Thorn's eyes darkened with anger at the thought of the carefully planned deception that had been woven about Brittany. "Just who in the hell is your father?"

She pulled the towel up to her neck, hoping her mother would understand that Thorn had guessed her true identity. She knew he would not stop until he knew all about her and perhaps she owed him the truth.

"My father was an American from Philadelphia. I am Brittany Sinclair."

He looked sick for a moment. "Tell me you are not of the Sinclair family, who are silversmiths in Philadelphia?"

Brittany looked befuddled. "Yes, my father's family are silversmiths. Are you acquainted with my grandmother? Is she still alive?"

He pulled her off the bed and retrieved her cape, handing it to her. "I don't know Mrs. Sinclair personally, but I certainly know of her." He shook his head. "There must be some of her in you. I have often heard her referred to as the 'dragon lady.'"

She raised her head haughtily. "I am sure you are laughing at me."

His eyes were dull. "I am sure you have been laughing at *me* all along. Have you enjoyed yourself at my expense?"

"I never laughed at you."

He let out a long breath of exasperation. "What do you know of your grandmother?"

"I have never communicated with my grandmother, and I do not know if she will welcome me. But it was my mother's wish that I go to Philadelphia so Sultan Selim would not find me."

Thorn turned his eyes away as she slipped into her cape. "For that, and other reasons, Brittany, you must go to Philadelphia with all possible haste."

She glanced at him as he turned slowly to face her. "That has always been my intention. Of course, I will have to allow Achmed time to heal from his wounds."

"Yes, of course."

An uneasy silence fell over the cabin, and she started for the door.

"Brittany," he said tonelessly.

She halted, blinking back the tears that threatened to fall. "Yes."

He moved to stand before her. "About what happened between us—"

She proudly raised her head and met his eyes. "It is all but forgotten."

He gripped her shoulders. "Nevertheless, it is my regret that I took advantage of your vulnerability." Remorse was reflected in his blue eyes as they swept her face. "I misjudged you in many ways, Brittany. You were young and innocent, and I, thinking that you were—" He smiled. "Well, what is done cannot be undone. Can you find it within your heart to forgive me?"

She turned away and reached for the door. "There is nothing to forgive, Captain. You were no more guilty than I. Perhaps I am even more at fault than you, because I did lure you to my cabin that first night." She blinked the tears away. "I release you from all feelings of remorse."

He suddenly seemed to withdraw from her. "It will be dawn in less than two hours. Are you ready to go ashore?"

"Yes, I am ready."

"I will see to it that suitable clothing is found for Achmed. He can hardly go ashore wearing his usual attire, since he would attract too much attention. I will also have Cappy accompany you to Charleston and see that you have adequate lodging. He will also help you in any way you deem necessary."

"You are kind as always," she whispered, thinking this was his way of sweeping her from his life.

She heard him call out her name, but she rushed through the door. Her heart was crushed because Thorn could so easily dismiss her from his life. When he had thought she was a woman from Simijin's harem, he had wanted to keep her with him; now, it was obvious he could not wait to rid himself of her.

When she reached her cabin, she threw herself down on the hard bunk, wishing she had never heard the name of Captain Thorn Stoddard.

Although Thorn knew the Charleston harbor well, a pilot ship led the *Victorious* into port, because the sand bars and shoals often shifted with the tide, and with the narrow winding channels and the swift currents, it was a hazardous and complicated entry, even for the most seasoned captain.

The *Victorious*'s sails had been lowered, and she glided majestically into port, past warehouses that jutted out into the water and past ships from many nations, for Charleston was a teeming, bustling port that relied heavily on trade.

On entering the Port of Charleston, the *Victorious* sailed past a merchantman riding low in the water, with her cargo not yet unloaded. Thorn glanced at the Cooper River waterfront with its wharves and shipyards. The dominant structure along the waterfront was the old British Exchange Building, which had been converted to accommodate the seat of government, and was now known as the Great Hall.

Thorn set his gaze on St. Philips steeple, which rose high above her sister churches. Those steeples had guided sailors safely into harbor for almost a hundred years.

His eyes moved in the direction of King Street. Although he could not see it from his vantage point, that was the location of the house that had been left to him by David Stone. Stonehouse was a stately mansion, and even though Thorn considered it too large for his needs, he intended to make it his residence for the time being. He had written his solicitor and informed him to engage servants and have the house and grounds put in order.

At last the weary traveler had come home, but within his heart there was no feeling of homecoming, no jubilation— but rather great dread and uncertainty. He must face the past and try to set things right between his father and himself. His father would be in his seventies now—an old man.

Although Thorn wanted to make peace with him at any cost, his father would have to apologize before they could bury the past.

Thorn had been so young when his mother had died that he did not remember her at all. Perhaps if she had lived, his life would have been different. Because of Wilhelmina's lies and deceitfulness, he was left with little faith in any woman. Even Brittany had deceived him, but then he had expected it of her and her sex.

Against his will, thoughts of Brittany began to weave their way through his mind, and he shook his head to clear it. No, he must not think of her silken skin and the way she had filled him with . . . what? Surely not happiness. Fulfillment of his desires and nothing more. Their paths had crossed briefly, and as she had pointed out to him, there was no place in his life for her. Both he and Brittany would be better off when she was in the protective custody of her grandmother.

The sun shone down on the *Victorious* through a cloudless sky.

Brittany appeared on deck, looking cool and aloof in her blue muslin gown, although she was anything but calm on the inside.

She guessed that Thorn had already alerted the crew to the change in her appearance, because they seemed to be avoiding eye contact with her. She could only imagine their shock to see her so changed.

Dr. Rutledge came forward to stand beside her, but he was not prepared for the golden-haired beauty that seemed such a contrast to the dark-haired girl that he had come to know.

"Take care of yourself, young miss. And for my part, you can sail on the *Victorious* any time you want."

She extended her gloved hand to Dr. Rutledge. "I have you to thank for Achmed's recovery. You will always have my gratitude."

The doctor's face eased into a smile. "I will always be grateful to you, because what would have been an ordinary and routine voyage turned into an adventure." He bowed to her. "I am always at your service," he said earnestly.

She smiled and then swept past him. Achmed walked just behind her, feeling most uncomfortable in the buff-colored trousers and rough linen shirt that were stretched tightly across his broad shoulders. He had exchanged his satin slippers for a pair of scuffed black boots that were several sizes too small for him.

Brittany watched the *Victorious* ease toward the pier, feeling a great sense of loss. She glanced back at the crew members who were busily performing their duties. Most of them she did not know personally, but they had become familiar faces to her, and they had always treated her with respect.

Her eyes moved to the deck of command, where Thorn stood, his dark hair blowing in the wind, his attention riveted on the crew member who brought the gangplank into place. When this was accomplished, he turned his eyes to Brittany and held her gaze for a brief moment. Then with a quick salute at her, he tied off the wheel and seemingly dismissed her from his mind.

Brittany had thought he would at least bid her goodbye, but apparently that was not to be. She turned back to the doctor and smiled at him. "Dr. Rutledge, will you please tell the captain that Achmed and I will be forever in his debt?"

The kindly man nodded. "That I will do, miss."

Cappy now appeared beside Brittany and held his hand out to indicate that she was to move down the gangplank. With one last glance at the ship that had been her home for six weeks of her life, she moved down the gangplank beside Achmed, then across the pier to the waiting carriage.

Cappy politely helped Brittany into the carriage and then climbed in beside her. Achmed, still looking drawn and tired, was made comfortable in the seat opposite Brittany.

So closed a chapter of her life, she thought sadly. Thorn

had brushed her aside as if there had never been anything intimate between the two of them. But then had she not told him that there could be nothing between them?

Life was cruel, she thought, for it had shown Brittany her heart's desire, and had then made it impossible for her to keep it.

With a jingle of the bridle and the clopping of the horses' hooves on the cobblestone street, the carriage pulled away from the pier.

Brittany absently noticed the palm trees that dotted the landscape. She was aware of the bustling seaport, and the city in the distance.

A short time later the carriage stopped before a cheerful-looking inn with tall gables and a sign that creaked in the wind. Cappy got out and helped Brittany onto the boardwalk.

"The captain said you would be comfortable in the Green Gable Inn. The lady who owns it is a widow, and I can attest that she is a good cook."

She followed Cappy through the doorway. He led her up to a counter and spoke to the man there. "This is Mistress Sinclair, who will be staying with you for a few days. She will also require a room for her servant," he said, nodding at Achmed.

Brittany was given a room on the second floor. She insisted that Achmed be given a room where he would be comfortable, so Cappy promised to make arrangement for him to be taken care of in a room near the stables.

Cappy handed her the room key and smiled. "If you require anything, just send Achmed for me. I will be staying on board the *Victorious* until she has been unloaded."

She offered him her hand. "Dear Cappy, you have been a friend to me. I thank you for all your help." She bent forward and kissed his cheek, which brought a glow of delight to his face. "Good-bye, Cappy."

"I know you have troubles, miss. I hope life is good to you and that you find happiness." The first mate moved away, and Brittany watched him until he climbed into the carriage and disappeared.

After she instructed Achmed as to where his quarters were located, she climbed the steps to her room. Everything was so new and frightening here in America. She only hoped she would soon be on her way to her grandmother.

Chapter Nineteen

Thorn reined in the gray gelding he had acquired at the livery stable in Charleston. He dismounted and stood quietly drinking in the beauty of Stoddard Hill.

It was as if time had stood still and he was caught up in a deluge of boyhood memories. Like looking upon a long absent friend, his eyes swept down the wide lawn to the aged redbrick structure that had housed the Stoddard family since the middle part of the seventeenth century.

The manor house had been constructed in the style of an Italian villa, with its main house towering and grand like a sentinel with two indentical flanker buildings on either side. The flanker on the right housed a great library, and the other was where the Stoddard men had gathered for over a hundred years to discuss politics and planting.

Stoddard Hill had spanned the golden years of indigo, rice, and cotton. The magnificent gardens and reflective pools rose above mirror-bright waters of a nearby lake.

But Thorn saw something else, too—there was evidence of neglect. It was summer, and yet he saw no indication that the fields had been tilled. There were no cotton stalks with their unopened cotton balls as there should have been. On closer inspection, he observed that the usually manicured grounds were untended and weeds choked the flowerbeds. What was wrong?

Thorn had come by way of the road, which was considered to be the back of the manor house where all the outbuildings, barns, and stables were located. Here, too, he saw neglect. Slave cabins had fallen into disrepair, and the stable door was hanging on rusted hinges.

He pushed his uneasiness aside. It was a beautiful morning; the mist still clung to the tops of the live oaks that were draped with Spanish moss. The front lawn was terraced and flanked by three reflective pools which sloped down to the Ashley River. Black swans nested near the rice mill pond, and tame deer roamed unafraid in the vast park.

Home. Thorn had come home at last. Until now, he had not fully realized how much he missed the land of his birthright. When he had gone to sea, he had been an angry young man, and the *Victorious* had only been his substitute for Stoddard Hill. Deep inside he had always known that he would one day return, for this land was in his blood, it was his heritage.

For over a hundred years this plantation had gone to the eldest Stoddard son. Now, Wilhelmina must fancy herself as lady of the manor. How she must have gloated in triumph the night his father had ordered him to leave.

Raw anger burned in Thorn's heart. Even now Wilhelmina might try to keep him from seeing his father, but he was prepared to deal with that. No woman, not even the treacherous Wilhelmina, would keep him away.

Of course there was always the possibility that his father might not want to see him. If that was the case, Thorn was prepared to ride away and never again attempt to contact his father.

Thorn looped the horse's reins around his hand and led the animal forward, not knowing what kind of reception he could expect.

Thorn had always thought of himself as a fearless man but the thought of facing his father made him physically sick inside. He had always admired his father, and until Wilhelmina had come along, they had been closer than most fathers and sons, for they had both shared a love for this land.

Now that Thorn was older, he realized what a fool he had

been for allowing Wilhelmina to be rid of him so easily. He should have demanded that his father hear the truth; now perhaps it was too late.

When he approached the stable, a young boy came forward with a smile on his black face. "Does you wants me to stable your horse, suh?"

"No," Thorn answered, looking the boy over to see if he was familiar. He wasn't. "I may not be staying that long. Just keep him in the shade and give him water and oats."

"Yes'suh," the boy agreed, leading the horse into the coolness of the stable.

"Is the master at home?" Thorn inquired, not realizing he was holding his breath, waiting for the answer.

The boy's dark eyes moved over Thorn with open curiosity. "Yes'suh, the master's in, but he's been feeling poorly, and the mistress, she don't let him have visitors no more, and she ain't home right now, so you can't see him."

Thorn's eyes ran the length of the stable, searching for Old Rubin who had been in charge of the horses for as long as Thorn could remember. Rubin had set Thorn on his first horse and had taught him how to ride. With a feeling of dread, at last Thorn asked: "Who tends the horses?"

The boy shook his head. "The mistress done hired a new man when Ole Rubin died. Mr. Turner gives orders now. I's his helper," he said with pride.

"Rubin must have worked in the stables for over sixty years," Thorn said, more to himself than the boy. "I suppose I expected him to live forever."

The young boy's eyes held a puzzled light. "No'suh, he done died of the fever. Ain't none of us live forever, 'cepting maybe ole Esmeralda."

Thorn thought of the slave he had always called Granny. She had to be well over a hundred now. "Is that old woman still alive?"

"Yes'suh. We reckon she'll be here after we're all dead and buried."

With grim determination, Thorn turned his steps toward

the house, not knowing what he would find there, or the extent of his father's illness.

When he stood on the steps, a rush of feelings overwhelmed him, and he placed his hand on the brass doorknob before he reconsidered and raised the lion-head door knocker. He was coming home, not as a son of the house, but as a man seeking his past.

Thorn was not acquainted with the man who opened the door, and stared at him with dark, surly eyes. Franklin had been the butler for as long as Thorn could remember. This man must have replaced him. Was nothing to be the same? he wondered, glancing over the man's shoulder at the shabbiness of the once-grand entryway.

"I want to see Mr. Stoddard," Thorn said in a tone of authority.

"The master does not receive guests, and the mistress is not in. You will have to call another time."

The butler was in the process of closing the door, when Thorn grabbed it and shoved him aside. "I am Thorn Stoddard, and I will see my father. Where is he?"

Now the man looked startled. "You are the son?"

"Have I not just said so? Now show me to my father at once."

"But the mistress left instructions that no one was to see the master," the man persisted. "I was not told to expect you."

Thorn reached out and grabbed the startled butler by the coat front and pulled him forward. "I am not interested in your mistress's orders, or whether or not you were told to expect me. I asked to see my father. Where is he?"

Although Thorn did not raise his voice, the butler knew by the dilation of his pupils that this was not a man to trifle with. "Y-yes, sir. He's in the garden."

Thorn pushed the butler aside and moved down the hall, past the winding stairs and out the back door. He stood for a long moment on the screened-in porch, then moved down the brick walkway while boyhood memories entwined their way through his mind. He thought of the times he and his father had walked in this garden, discussing books they had read, or debating the latest political happening.

He glanced across the reflective pond where the hillside was alive with colorful azaleas. In the distance, he had a view of the flooded rice fields. A sleepy creek glided lazily past stately magnolia trees, while bright sunlight poured its warmth and light onto Stoddard Hill. The land was alive and teeming with life.

Thorn's footsteps quickened across the narrow suspension bridge that spanned the sparkling brook. He knew where to find his father. When he saw the small Honeymoon Cottage nestled among the azaleas, he paused to drink in its beauty. The cottage had been constructed by Vincent Stoddard over a hundred years ago, when he wanted a place of privacy to spend time with his young bride. The cottage had been built of Italian marble, with floor-to-ceiling windows, so it had a magnificent view of Stoddard Hill.

Hesitantly, he moved to the front door to find it slightly ajar. Thorn pushed the door open and came face-to-face with his father.

Time, it seemed, had not been kind to Benjamin Stoddard. His once-proud stance had become stooped; his blue eyes were dull, and his hair was almost completely white.

For a long moment the two men assessed each other, and when Benjamin smiled, his blue eyes held a light of uncertainty. "At last the prodigal comes home to his grieving father. What took you so long, Thorn?"

Thorn did not answer at first; he was too disturbed by the sight of his father's frail appearance. "I was told you have been ill, Father."

The old man shook his head, his eyes bright, his lips trembling. "It's nothing to fret about. Mostly boredom. How have you been, Son?"

"I suppose you know I became owner and captain of the *Victorious* after uncle David's death."

"Yes, I know that. Your mother's brother gave you the

means to see the world. I often tried to picture you in some distant port." Ben's eyes became sad, and his mind seemed to wander. "I wish you had come home sooner. Now I am but a shell of a man. I am old and tired, like this land. Both of us are worn out."

Thorn had never heard his father speak of defeat before, and it cut into his heart. His voice was calm, however, when he spoke. "I wasn't sure of my welcome, Father."

The old man's eyes misted, and he sank down into one of a pair of Queen Anne chairs. "Son . . . Thorn, I have paid handsomely for not trusting you. Can you forgive me for believing the lies?"

"I will put it aside, if you will," Thorn said.

For a moment Ben's eyes burned with conviction. "God, how I have paid. To be torn away from the only person in the world that means anything to me." His eyes became wild. "That woman I married—that woman . . ." His voice trailed off, and when he looked at his son, his eyes were swimming in tears. "I would not have blamed you if you never came back. I am nothing but an old fool, for not trusting you."

Thorn sat down in the matching Queen Anne chair, crossed his long legs, and forced a smile. "If you were an old fool, then I was a young fool. You always said we were too much alike to get along. I should have made you see the truth." He shrugged. "Youth does not always practice good sense."

Happiness illuminated Benjamin's wrinkled face, and his features eased into a smile. "I have prayed for this day for a very long time. I feared I would die before I saw you again. Now that you are here to take over for me, Stoddard Hill will bloom again."

"I am not certain of my plans."

Ben's eyes were eager. "You can see that you are needed. Stoddard Hill is going to seed."

"I would have come sooner, but—"

Benjamin held up his hand. "Don't take the blame, when you know it rests with me. I have been to hell and back, but it was a hell that I created for myself. No one is to blame for what happened but me."

"We don't need accusations and blame-placing between us, Father."

"Let me finish what I have to say, Thorn. It should have been said long ago. I know now what happened the night I drove you away. I know you were innocent of any wrong-doing."

"This isn't necessary, Father."

"It is to me, Thorn. We both know who was responsible for—"

Wilhelmina stood in the doorway, her face livid with anger, her heart pounding with fear and excitement. All those emotions she experienced as she glanced at Thorn Stoddard. That which she had feared had come to pass. So Thorn had returned, and she did not know what might happen.

"Well, well," she said in a voice laced with sarcasm, and putting forth a spirit of bravado that she was far from feeling. "So, the son of the manor has returned."

Thorn's eyes narrowed in on Wilhelmina. She had fared well. Her face was still unlined, and her ebony hair was arranged in curls at the back of her head, showing her features to the best advantage. She was dressed in a green silk traveling gown that fitted her soft curves. Thorn thought she would have been considered pretty by most men—but not by him.

Benjamin struggled to his feet, while Thorn lent him a helping hand. "Yes, my son has returned, Wilhelmina, and now that he's here, everything will be different."

"But, my dear husband, you do so detest change of any kind. How many times have you told me you wanted to keep Stoddard Hill the way it is?" She reminded Thorn of a slinky cat as she moved toward him and then presented her cheek to be kissed. He chose to ignore the gesture and stepped back a pace as if contact with her would contaminate him.

"You look the same, Wilhelmina," he did manage to say.

"Do you think so?" she purred. "How very wonderful of you to say so."

Benjamin's eyes darkened. "Wilhelmina keeps busy with her little charities and other activities," he bit out. "She is happy enough being the social butterfly who flits from party to party."

Brazenly, Wilhelmina moved close to Benjamin and kissed him on the cheek, while her eyes boldly assessed Thorn. "Your father hasn't changed, Thorn. He still imagines that I am not a faithful wife, though I always strive to prove that is untrue."

Benjamin pushed her away. "I care not how you spend your time, madame, as long as you spend it away from me. You can bed every stud in the county, as long as you do it away from Stoddard Hill."

Thorn was astonished by the bitterness he heard in his father's voice, for Benjamin Stoddard had always been a gentle man. Thorn was further puzzled to see the malicious smile on Wilhelmina's face.

The animosity between his father and his stepmother made Thorn feel uncomfortable. He found himself wanting to leave. "Perhaps I have come at a bad time, Father. If you would rather, I can return another day."

Benjamin clutched Thorn's arm. "No, I have waited too long for this day. I will not allow you to leave. You must stay at Stoddard Hill."

"Yes," Wilhelmina agreed. "Stay, and we shall kill the fatted calf."

Somehow the thought of spending an evening with his father and Wilhelmina was distasteful to him. His father had turned into a bitter old man, and it tore at Thorn's heart. He could feel the hatred and distrust between them like a double-edged sword.

Thorn chose to ignore his stepmother and addressed himself to his father. "I cannot stay, since I have to see to the unloading of the *Victorious*."

"Will you be staying at Stonehouse?" Wilhelmina asked.

"No. For now I will be on board the *Victorious*."

His father's eyes were seeking. "Will you be leaving me again?"

"No, Father. This time I have come home to stay. Already I have found a buyer for my cargo. I may even sell the *Victorious*."

Benjamin's eyes sparkled with relief. "Thank God. At last you can take over the running of Stoddard Hill. I am an old man, and I fear everything has fallen into disrepair without you in command."

Thorn saw Wilhelmina's eyes narrow with spite just before she smiled to hide her true feelings. "Yes," she said. "Isn't it good that your son has come home."

Thorn tried to curb his impatience to leave. "We will talk of this later, Father."

"Will you sell Stonehouse, Son?"

"No. I could not bring myself to do that."

"I am glad." Benjamin's eyes softened. "Your mother loved that house. You know she was born there."

"Yes, I had heard you say that."

Wilhelmina turned away to hide her displeasure. She did not like it when her husband discussed Margaret, his saintly first wife. Lately Benjamin's mind had begun to wander more and more to the past. She was often forced to listen to him talk of his first wife, and how wonderful everything had been when she was alive.

"I am sure you gentlemen will excuse me," she said, moving out the door, her eyes on Thorn. "We would be heartbroken if you decided not to come home to live."

Thorn's eyes seemed to burn into her, and she caught her breath at the hatred she saw reflected there. She could not help noticing that he had grown into a self-assured man, and she trembled at the thought of his dark good looks.

She remembered with regret that he once loved her. If only she had not driven him away with her boldness, if only she had not married his father—if only she had been the innocent girl he had once thought her to be.

She looked at his firm mouth, now compressed with anger, remembering a time when those lips had burned into hers. Although he had been young that summer when they had kissed in her cousin's garden, the memory still lingered with her. She had been with many men since, but Thorn had always been in her heart.

She moved out the door, feeling his coldness and knowing she would never win him back. It did not matter, she told herself, because something had to be done about Thorn or she would lose Stoddard Hill.

"Are you all right, Father?" Thorn asked in concern, observing his father's trembling body and pale face.

"Now that I have seen you, I feel better than I have in years. I will recover if you are with me, Thorn," his father said eagerly.

Thorn felt sadness settle on his shoulders. This was not the homecoming he had expected. "Shall I walk you to the house before I leave?"

"No. I spend most of my time here. This is where I brought your mother after we were married. Did I tell you that Thorn?"

"Yes, you have told me that."

The old man moved to the bed and sat back. "I will just rest a bit. Will you come back tomorrow?"

Thorn towered over his father, feeling as if he were being pulling into a web. "If you like."

"Yes, come back." Suddenly Benjamin clasped Thorn's hand. "Everything is going to be all right again, now that you are here."

Thorn extracted his hand and smiled. "I'll see you tomorrow."

Without a backward look, Thorn moved quickly out the door and hurried down the path.

Benjamin Stoddard was an old man whose mind was steeped in the past. Apparently his life with Wilhelmina was so unbearable that he preferred to dwell on the short time he had lived with his first wife. The one thing Thorn could not understand was why his father had neglected Stoddard Hill.

Thorn had suspected that Wilhelmina would be waiting for him in the house, so he took the shortcut across the lawn, hoping to avoid her. The time would come when the two of them would clash, but that time was not now.

The last thing he wanted to do today was to talk to that woman. She had displayed no remorse for what she had done, and he knew not to trust her at all.

He questioned his reasons for coming home. Was this really what he wanted? Was there anything left for him here?

As he mounted his horse he thought of how old and tired his father was, and he knew he could not abandon him.

But did Thorn really want to battle Wilhelmina for Stoddard Hill? Yes, he would fight her, and he would win, he thought. He was determined not to let her defeat him this time.

Suddenly Thorn thought of soft green eyes and golden hair, and he kicked the horse in the flanks. For some reason he wanted to see Brittany.

Brittany was sunshine and a breath of cleansing air. She was what he needed tonight.

Chapter Twenty

Since Achmed was still too ill to be up for long, Brittany insisted on nursing him herself. She had fed him a bowl of thick stew, pleased that he had eaten it all. Achmed had fallen asleep immediately afterward, leaving Brittany to amuse herself.

She walked about his room, examining every object several times. She had been to the stables and looked at the horses. She had taken a turn about the kitchen garden, trying to identify the herbs that grew there. She was bored and restless with so much time on her hands.

Brittany had written a letter to her grandmother in Philadelphia, and it had been posted three days ago. Now all she could do was wait for a reply.

She raised the window so Achmed would benefit from the cool breeze. Since he was sleeping so peacefully, she decided to return to the inn.

As Brittany entered the Green Gables, she thought of the lonely hours that stretched before her. Her foot was on the first step leading to her room when she glanced at the front door that seemed to beckon her. Since coming to Charleston, she had not been outside the inn other than to visit Achmed.

What would be the harm of taking a little stroll? she asked herself. Her heart was beating fast, and her hands were shaking as she moved to the door. She dared not look at the man behind the counter for fear he would try to prevent her from leaving the inn.

She had never been on her own before, and the thought

that she was free to make her own decisions was both exciting and forbidding.

Her hand closed around the doorknob; it turned slowly— she pulled backward and the door swung open. Her first step was the hardest, then she took another and then another. Closing the door behind her, she stood on the front porch, undecided what to do next.

It was a wonderful feeling to breath the air of freedom. There were people walking about, but they did not seem to pay the least attention to her.

Brittany saw a woman with black skin, whom she judged to be about her own age. Since the young woman was also unescorted, it gave Brittany the courage she needed to continue on her own.

She retied her bonnet before moving across the cobblestone street. How different these quiet, tree-lined streets were from the bustling and dirty streets of Constantinople. Here the air was clean, and there were no offensive odors. She paused beneath a tree to listen to the birds singing, and she thought her heart would burst with happiness.

She turned onto Meeting Street, where there were shops on both sides of the street. She smiled at a woman selling flowers and received a smile in return.

Pausing, she glanced in a shop window and saw many wondrous things displayed there. There were lamps, colorful blue-and-white dishes, copper pots and pans. Many of the objects were strange to her, and she could not imagine their use.

Moving on down the street, Brittany stopped before a ladies' apparel shop. Taking her courage in hand, she entered the shop, only to be startled when a bell tinkled over the door. She was staring up at the bell when a woman approached her.

"What can I do for you, miss?"

Brittany smiled at the woman. "I was passing and saw your gowns in the window. They are lovely."

The woman looked at the fashionably dressed girl. Her eyes fastened on the emerald necklace Brittany wore. "You will find nothing as lovely as that gown you are wearing. I have been a seamstress long enough to know a Paris gown when I see one."

"How clever of you to know that," Brittany said, examining a turquoise shawl. "This is lovely."

"Here," the seamstress said, draping the shawl around Brittany's shoulders. "This is a good color on you; it complements your eyes."

Brittany removed the shawl and handed it to the woman. "I have no money."

The woman smiled. "Are you new in Charleston?"

"Yes, I only arrived a week ago."

"I hope you will like it here," the woman said, sitting down to her sewing. "I can imagine that Charleston is going to like you very well."

"Thank you, madame. I must be going now. It was lovely to talk to you."

"Come in again," the seamstress invited.

Brittany left the shop, thinking how wonderful these Americans were. They were friendly and open, and she was accustomed to living in a world of secrets and high walls.

She had made her way up the street, so she crossed and headed down the other side. The afternoon had turned hot, and Brittany stopped before a tea shop, where delicious smells were drifting in the air. She wished she had brought money with her, because her throat was dry and she longed for a cup of tea.

She felt someone behind her, and she turned to find a gentleman towering over her. His blond hair hung carelessly across his forehead, and he had a ready smile. "Pardon me, ma'am, but I have been observing you for some time. Are you lost?"

She smiled at him, thinking how kind he was to be concerned about her when she was a stranger to him. "Not at all. I believe I can retrace my steps with little trouble."

"Allow me to introduce myself to you. I am Robert Devany."

She offered him her hand. "I am a stranger in your city."

Robert Devany could not believe his good fortune that the lovely creature neither turned her back on him nor accused him of being forward. "Well, lovely stranger, would you think it presumptuous on my part if I asked you to have a cup of tea with me?"

Her brow puckered, and she was thoughtful for a moment. "I think I should tell you that I have no money."

He looked dumbfounded for a moment. "I would expect you to be my guest, of course."

She beamed at him. "I like you Americans. You are so kind and generous."

He was reeling from his good fortune. "Then you will have a cup of tea with me?"

Brittany looked over the young gentleman's shoulder and saw Thorn Stoddard striding toward her. "Thorn," she said, smiling, for she was happy to see him. "This is my new friend, Robert Devany, and you cannot guess at his kindness. He has invited me for a cup of tea."

Thorn turned angry eyes on the man. "I just bet he did," Thorn said, grasping Brittany's hand and pulling her to his side. "I am afraid that Mr. Devany has other plans." His eyes challenged the man to deny it. "Am I not right, Mr. Devany?"

"Are you her husband?"

"No. Let's just say that I am the man who means to see that she does not fall into unscrupulous hands."

Poor Robert Devany looked into icy-blue eyes and nodded. "Alas, he speaks the truth, ma'am. I do have a previous engagement." He looked regretfully at Brittany. "I hope you like it here in Charleston."

She watched Mr. Devany walk away quickly before she turned stormy eyes on Thorn. "You were rude to him, Thorn, and don't deny it."

Thorn watched the man until he turned the corner. "Surely you are not so gullible to believe all that man wanted from you was conversation over a cup of tea."

"He was a gentleman, and I liked him. He knew I had no money, so he offered to pay."

Thorn drew in a deep breath. He pulled her forward, his stride so long she had to run to keep up with him. "If you want tea, I will buy it for you."

"I . . . do not want any now. I am angry with you, Thorn."

He paused and looked at her. Innocence shone in her green eyes, and he could see that she was having a hard time trying to comprehend what had happened.

"Brittany, you must understand that a young, unmarried girl should not go about Charleston alone—and you should never speak to a man who has not been presented to you."

She frowned. "Is that an American custom?"

"Yes. It is also the custom in all gently bred ladies in civilized nations."

She shook her head. "I fear I will never learn all the rules."

He spoke to her more kindly now. "You will in time, Brittany."

"How did you find me?" she wanted to know.

"I called on you at the inn, and the clerk told me you had gone out alone. It was easy to find you after that."

"You came to see me?"

"Yes, I wanted to know how you were faring. It is fortunate for you that I took an interest."

He took her arm and led her to a waiting carriage, where Cappy was seated. Thorn helped her in beside Cappy and leaned forward and whispered something to the first mate. Then he spoke to Brittany. "I have decided it is no longer proper for you to stay alone at the Green Gables. Cappy will escort you to more suitable lodgings."

She leaned forward and placed her hand on Thorn's arm. "Aren't you coming with us?"

"No. I have other matters to attend to at the moment."

She leaned back, and to hide her disappointment, pretended to be adjusting the lace on her sleeve. "Good day to you, Captain."

He stood back and motioned for the driver to move on.

Brittany smiled at Cappy. "I fear I have committed a faux

pas, although I am not quite certain how. I am in disgrace with the captain."

Cappy patted Brittany's hand. "Not at all, miss. You just need a bit of looking after."

It was late in the afternoon when the carriage pulled up to the inn. Achmed was made comfortable, propped against pillows, and then Cappy helped Brittany into the carriage and climbed in beside her.

As they pulled away from the Green Gables, she watched out the window as people scurried homeward for the evening meal. She looked at the houses they passed and wondered how the lives of the people who occupied the dwellings differed from hers. She had a strange feeling that she would like to belong here.

When they turned onto King Street, she took notice of the stately mansions they passed, and she blinked in astonishment when the carriage came to a halt before an ornate iron fence.

She turned bewildered eyes on Cappy when the driver leaped down to open the tall gate.

"Cappy, this is not an inn, is it? Where are you taking me?"

"Begging your pardon, miss, but the captain said I was to bring you to his house. I would have mentioned it, but I just figured he'd already told you."

"I . . . no, he did not. Why has he asked you to bring me here?"

"The captain keeps most of his thoughts to himself, miss. But he did tell me to assure you that he would be staying in town at one of the seaside inns and not here at Stonehouse."

"Stonehouse?"

"Yes, miss."

When the carriage moved past the arched gate, Brittany caught sight of the stately European-style redbrick house that was set far back from the road. There were two separate wings to the house, but they were drawn together in harmony by the fig vine that clung to the brick. A green rolling lawn swept down to a brick walkway, and the house had a commanding view of the Cooper River.

"How magnificent," she said, turning shiny eyes to Cappy. "It is only right that Captain Stoddard should live in such a house."

"Oh, this wasn't the house where he grew up," Cappy assured her. "Captain Stoddard inherited Stonehouse from his uncle, who also left him the *Victorious*. He grew up on a Low Country plantation called Stoddard Hill."

Brittany held out her hand so Cappy could help her to the ground, then she watched as he aided Achmed.

She did not want to stay in Thorn's house, but she had become dependent on him.

Here in America she could not find her way alone. And although Achmed had been a commanding figure in Simijin's palace, here he was as lost as she was.

With a feeling of trepidation, she moved up the steps, knowing Thorn had decided to move her to Stonehouse after the incident that afternoon.

She had been afraid that Thorn had gone out of her life forever; now at least she might see him again since she was living under his roof.

Chapter Twenty-one

Brittany moved through Stonehouse, examining each room, trying to find some trace of Thorn, but there was nothing to show that he had ever been here. According to Betty, the housekeeper, she and Daniel, the old caretaker, had looked after the house and grounds, for the house had not been occupied since Thorn's uncle had died.

Brittany had wanted to ask Betty questions about Thorn Stoddard, but she realized her mother would not approve of her questioning a servant.

Stonehouse was an elegant home, and very unlike the huge impersonal palace where Brittany had spent her life. This house, she thought, was a place to raise children, for although the rooms were big, and the furnishings old, she could feel warmth here—yes, and she could imagine the sound of children's laughter echoing down the halls.

She stood before the wide bay window that looked out on the front lawn to the cobblestone road beyond. She watched the carriages, cumbersome landaus, and small buggies move past, on their way to unknown destinations. Where would life take her? she wondered with a feeling of melancholy.

She thought of the tall, blue-eyed American who had been her guardian against danger. As Thorn had proven, he was a man capable of great deeds of valor, and she would always love him.

It was because of him that she spent most of the day watching the road, always with the hope that he could come to see her.

She looked up at the blue of the sky, against a backdrop of fleecy clouds. America was a land of beauty—of life, of new beginnings. This was a young country, and she wanted so desperately to belong. She had always known that Turkey was not her country, and now her former life seemed unreal to her, almost as if it had been lived by another person.

Brittany could not have said what alerted her to the fact that she was not alone. But she turned slowly and found Thorn staring at her from the doorway. Her heart was pounding within her breasts as she saw how intently he was watching her.

"I have taken unfair advantage of you, Brittany," he said, walking toward her. "I have been watching you for some time. What were you thinking about that required such deep concentration?"

She smiled shyly as he took her hand and seated her on the couch. "I was thinking about your country."

"Favorably, I hope."

She clasped her hands in her lap. "Oh, yes. I believe I could feel at home here."

He looked into her green eyes that seemed to have a calming effect on him. When he was with her, nothing else seemed of any importance. "Could you feel at home in this house?"

She shifted her eyes from his disturbing glance. "Well, I did not mean in this house in particular. I have no intention of imposing on your hospitality longer than is necessary. And Achmed assures me we have money to pay you for your trouble, which I will insist on doing."

Her voice trailed away when she heard his amused laughter.

Thorn leaned his head back and looked at her through lowered lashes. "No amount of money could compensate me for the trouble you have put me through, Brittany. And yet, I would not have forgone the pleasure of knowing you for any measure of payment."

She looked at him quizzically. "Sometimes I have a difficult time knowing if you are praising me or insulting me, Thorn Stoddard."

"I was merely stating the obvious. I believe you know I am past insulting you."

Her eyes moved the length of his long legs that disappeared into high-top black riding boots. He wore tan trousers and a whipcord coat. His white shirt was open at the neck, and she could feel the leashed strength in him. When she looked into his eyes, he raised an inquiring brow, and she looked away quickly, knowing he was reminding her of the intimacy they had shared.

She stood up, and in a flurry of silk, moved back to the window to put some distance between them.

Thorn's eyes followed her across the room. Her winecolored gown enhanced her white skin. Her golden hair was devoid of adornment and hung freely down her back to her waist.

Thorn tried to picture her as the dark-haired enchantress he had first come to know. There was the same smile, the same blue eyes, but she was even more beautiful as the golden goddess. He held his breath as she turned to face him.

"Captain, I have written to my grandmother in Philadelphia, but as of yet I have received no word from her. I am hoping for a quick reply, so I will not have to impose on your generosity much longer."

"I would hasten to point out to you that the mail service here in America might not receive the same quick attention as a letter sent by Lord Simijin might receive in Turkey. Be prepared to wait for an answer to your correspondence."

She pursed her lips. "I had not considered that."

"You must feel free to remain here at Stonehouse as long as you wish."

She felt a lump forming in her throat. She owed him so much already. "You are kind as always." She leaned her head against the velvet curtain with a fanciful look on her face. "I have also sent word to my mother and Simijin that we have arrived safely. Cappy said he would see that

the letter is placed on the first available ship sailing for
Constantinople."

"Yes, I know—he told me." Thorn came to his feet and
moved to stand beside her. "Have you thought what you will
do if you don't hear from your grandmother?"

"I . . . no." She raised her head, her green eyes troubled.
"But you have my promise that you shall not be made to feel
responsible for me, no matter what happens."

He glanced down at her, wishing he could take her under his protection, but she had already refused him that
privilege.

"I cannot see you returning to Turkey as long as Sultan
Selim is ruler."

"No. I cannot return to Turkey, no matter what. Even
now, I am frightened that the sultan may have taken his
anger out on my mother or Simijin, although Achmed assures me that will not happen."

Thorn placed his hand on her shoulder and turned her to
face him. "Put all unpleasant thoughts out of your pretty
head. I have a feeling that everything will turn out all right
for you. Meanwhile, consider Stonehouse your home."

"But it is not. It is *your* home, though it could not have
been much of a homecoming for you since you felt compelled to put up at an inn." She looked perplexed. "I have
wondered why you do not stay here with Achmed and myself rather than at an inn. There is plenty of room."

He resisted the urge to take her in his arms. "It would not
be proper for me to stay here, Brittany. Convention dic-
tates certain rules that we must follow. Charleston is a small
town, and there would be gossip if I stayed here with you."

"I am trying to understand your customs, but they are
sometimes perplexing."

Even though she had dazzled him with her sensuous
dance and had given him two glorious nights of passion that
he would never forget—still there was a purity about Brittany, an undeniable innocence.

"This house is much too large for my needs, Brittany.

And it was never my home, although I have fond memories of coming here as a boy, because it was my grandparents' home, and my mother grew up here. Stonehouse came to me on the death of my mother's brother."

"Cappy told me that you grew up on a plantation called Stoddard Hill."

"Yes, that's right."

"Yet you are not living at Stoddard Hill, either. This is very confusing."

His eyes gleamed with mysterious lights. "Let's just say that I need to be near the *Victorious* until her cargo is unloaded."

"After that, will you go to sea again, or will you be living on your plantation?"

"My *father's* plantation," he corrected her with a half-smile. "As I have pointed out to you before, you are an inquisitive young lady."

She nodded. "That is one of my many failings. I always want to know everything about everyone."

"Is this to be a confession about your shortcomings, Brittany?"

Impish lights gleamed in her eyes. "That kind of a confession would take too long, because I have many flaws in my character, not the least of which is that I sometimes lose control of my temper. But you already know that."

Thorn liked the endearing qualities in Brittany that made her honestly assess what she believed to be her shortcomings. He found his troubles melting away, lost in a pair of the greenest eyes he had ever seen.

"Why don't you tell me more about your faults, Brittany," he encouraged.

"Well," she said reflectively, "I am much too stubborn, and I usually end up doing the wrong thing in every situation. My governess always swore that I was incorrigible and unmanageable, and she was right. I sometimes do things when I know they will get me into difficulty." Her eyes glistened. "I believe it is the challenge of the unknown that prompts me."

He had not realized that he had taken her hand. "I hear the wild whisper of your heart, Brittany. There is an excitement about you that stirs my blood."

She pulled her hand away from him. He was standing so near, she could scarcely breathe. "You shouldn't say that to me."

He realized he was being much too serious and lightened his tone. "Do you think you will ever mend your ways, or will you gain more imperfections as you age?"

"Most probably I will only get worse with the passing of time. I fear I am hopeless. My mother always defended me by saying I was only adventuresome, while Simijin once told me that I was like my mother when she was younger." She pursed her lips. "I cannot imagine my mother ever doing some of the things I do." She glanced up at Thorn. "I think my mother is perfect."

His eyes moved over her face, and he smiled again. "Do you look like the English Rose?"

"Simijin and Achmed have said I do, but I believe they were just being kind. My mother is a great beauty."

He turned her face up to the waning light of the setting sun. "You do not think you are beautiful?"

She was thoughtful for a moment, then answered without conceit. "I must be or the sultan would not have wanted me." She shrugged. "Mama says beauty of heart is much more valuable than a pretty face."

Thorn closed his eyes. Dare he believe in Brittany's goodness? Could he learn to trust again? "What else does your mother tell you?" he wanted to know.

"Once when I complained about looking too young for my age, she assured me it would work in my favor in later years. It's hard to feel good about that."

He cupped her face in his hands, needing to feel her body close to his. "And how old are you, Brittany?"

"Seventeen."

"So young," he whispered, aware for the first time of how great an injustice he had done by taking her innocence.

Although every nerve in his body cried out to her, he had sworn he would never touch her again. Even as he reminded himself of his resolve, his hand moved down her back and he laid his cheek against hers. He wanted her, and he would go on wanting her until he could tear her out of his mind.

"I had to see you tonight," he admitted.

Her hand moved to the back of his neck, and she sighed contentedly, answering him with complete honesty. "I have thought of you all day."

He smiled against her sweet-smelling hair. "Have you?"

"Yes, I have."

"Happy thoughts, I hope."

She closed her eyes, loving the feel of his strong arms about her. She loved this man so deeply that she could feel the turmoil within him. "I was wondering if you had found a solution to your troubles."

He stiffened. "And what troubles would those be?"

She moved her head so she could see his face. "I do not know the origin of your difficulties. I only know that there stirs within you a great unrest." She stared into his unflinching eyes, unable to read what he was thinking. "Will you not confide in me so I can help you?"

He roughly pushed her away. "You haven't the slightest notion of the kind of troubles I face, Brittany. Nor would you be able to help me if you did."

She sighed. "As you know, Thorn, my life has not exactly been on an even keel, so I know what it is to suffer. You have done so much for me, and I would like to repay you."

He arched his brow. "Perhaps some would say I had already extracted payment from you." His hand moved down to cup her breast, and she flinched at the anger she heard in his voice. "I would say you have paid the ultimate price, Brittany."

She pushed his hand away, wishing he had not referred to her surrendering of her body to him as payment. "I . . . you make it sound as if I were one of the women who sell themselves to a man for money."

He raised her chin. "And how would you know of such women?"

She tossed her head. "I have heard the women of the harem talking. They have no liking for such creatures." Her eyes were pleading. "Thorn, say you do not think I am that kind of woman. Remember the night you accused me of just that?"

"That was before I knew you. I hoped you had forgotten about that." He frowned suddenly, feeling the weight of his conscience. "I had better go," he said, dropping his hands and stepping away from her.

Suddenly she wanted to cling to him and beg him to stay with her, but pride came to her rescue. "When will I see you again?"

"I'm not certain." He moved to the door and turned to her, leaning against the jamb. "Are you all right? Do you need anything?"

"I need nothing, Thorn."

He stared at her for so long that she began to feel uncomfortable. He was reluctant to leave. At last he said, "Come and walk with me in the garden, Brittany. I have something I want to say to you."

"If you like, Thorn."

Brittany took his offered arm, and together they moved out the door. By now the sun had gone down and dark shadows clung to the far corners of the garden.

Suddenly she glanced up at him. "What did you want to talk to me about?"

His mouth quirked briefly, and his eyelids flickered. "This will be difficult to say."

"Why?"

"Because you turned me down once before. And to tell the truth," he admitted, drawing her close and burying his face in her hair, "I could not bear to leave you tonight."

Her eyes were soft as she pressed her cheek against his. Happiness flowed through her body at his admission. "I did not want you to leave, either."

"You realize what could happen if I stay?" he warned.

"We could just talk," she told him, the longing in her voice betraying how she felt.

Her nearness fired Thorn's blood, and he released a long breath. "You and I are past talking, Brittany. I want to be with you." The moon made a silent path across the garden, while his eyes moved down her throbbing throat. "Yes, we are long past talking, Brittany."

"What do you mean?" she whispered through lips that trembled.

There was a gleam of ownership in his eyes. "I mean that I want you to be my wife."

She pulled back and stared at him in disbelief. "We discussed this before, Thorn. Nothing has happened to make me change my mind."

Tension knotted the muscles in his chest, and his arms tightened around her. "I have never before asked a woman to marry me, you little hellion. And I doubt that I ever shall again."

She was suspicious of his motives. "Why have you asked me?"

"Because you have me caught in your web, and you know it." He hesitated, as if groping for words to express his bewilderment. "I have no choice other than to make you my wife, don't you see that?"

She wanted to hear him admit that he loved her, but he had not. She was wise enough to know that love and desire were two different emotions. "You have not yet said why you should take such a drastic step? Marriage is forever, and I was assured by the women of the harem that desire burns hot and turns quickly to ashes."

"Damn it," he ground out in a thick voice. "A woman is not supposed to know about such things. But if you insist on questioning my motives, I will tell you this: I have wronged you, and there is no way of making it right for you other than marriage."

She shook her head and backed away from him, feeling as

if her heart would break. "I will never marry a man because he feels it is his duty to marry me."

She turned away and ran back to the house. Although she could hear him calling after her, she did not slow her pace until she reached her bedroom and closed the door behind her.

Hot tears she could not control blinded her. She now knew why she sensed turmoil within Thorn. He was feeling guilty because of what had happened between them. He felt obligated to give her the protection of his name.

She moved to the bed and sat on the edge. How tempted she had been to accept Thorn's offer. But she knew that happiness bought at the cost of one's honor was not worth the price—no, she could not do that.

Thorn did not love her at all. He was determined to make her first his mistress, and then when he could not have her that way, his wife.

No, she would never marry him. In fact, she had to get away from him as quickly as possible!

Chapter Twenty-two

Even though rain had fallen during the night, it had done little to ease the heat.

Brittany sat on the lemon-yellow couch in the front parlor, hoping to catch the morning breeze from the open bay window.

She clutched an unopened letter she had just received from Philadelphia. It was not from her grandmother, as she had hoped, but from a solicitor named David Morgan. There was a tightness in her throat as she glanced up at Achmed, her eyes filled with uncertainty.

"Do you not think you should read the words, little mistress?"

Her hands trembled as she opened the letter. She stared at the bold handwriting, then she scanned the page and began reading aloud:

> "Dear Miss Sinclair,
> I am writing in reference to your letter in which you state that you are the granddaughter of Doris Sinclair, and I regret to inform you that she has been deceased for seven years. Her holdings, which included a house, lands, warehouse, and silversmith shop went to her nephew, Stanley Sinclair. If you feel you have a legitimate claim to any part of Doris Sinclair's property, I would advise that you come to Philadelphia post haste and put forth your claim. Until such time as I hear from you again, I remain, your servant."

Brittany placed the letter on the low table in front of her. She tried to feel something for the grandmother that she had never known, but how could she love a faceless woman who had never touched her life in any way, and who had been dead for seven years?

She glanced into Achmed's dark, compassionate eyes. "What shall we do?"

"You do not wish to go to Philadelphia?"

"No. If my grandmother is dead, and I have no reason to doubt that she is, there will be nothing for me in Philadelphia, Achmed."

"But the man who wrote the letter has asked if you want to claim your inheritance."

"My grandmother's nephew is more entitled to her holdings than I. She was nothing to me while she was alive, so I will expect nothing from her in death."

Achmed leaned against the fireplace, his face reflective. "You cannot return to Constantinople," he reminded her. "What can you do?"

"I do not know. One thing is certain, though. We cannot remain here at Stonehouse. I refuse to impose on Captain Stoddard for another day." She met Achmed's eyes. "Do we have the means to live elsewhere?"

He grinned. "Lord Simijin was most generous with you. There is more than ample gold to see to your needs."

"Bless Simijin. I do not know what I would have done without him."

"He is a great man."

"He is to me. I hope he will one day know how much I love him."

"He already does, little mistress." Achmed's dark eyes took on a troubled light. "What shall we do, mistress? I do not know the customs of this country, and we would not want to do the wrong thing and offend anyone."

She knitted her brow in thoughtfulness. "I believe we should leave this house today, but we will remain in Charleston until we hear from my mother. Today you must look for lodgings."

Achmed bowed from the waist. "I must remind you that when we stayed at the inn, it did not work well."

"I know. This time you will see about buying a small house. Do we have enough gold for that?"

"I believe so."

"Then that is what you must do."

"I shall see to it at once, little mistress."

When Achmed lumbered to the door, her voice stopped him. "Achmed, be careful. I have learned just today that the servants in this house are not servants at all, but slaves. It seems that in America, all black-skinned people are slaves, and they are not allowed the freedom of movement to which you are accustomed. I would not want anything to happen to you."

"I will be cautious, mistress," he assured her.

Thorn made his way up the winding stairs to the master bedroom, where the butler had told him he would find his father. When he approached his father's bedroom, the door across the hall opened, and a smiling Wilhelmina stood there, wearing only a thin nightgown.

"Thorn, I am so glad you are here. I am so worried about your father. Since your visit, his condition has worsened."

He paused with his hand on the knob. "Are you saying my father is ill?"

"Last night he could not breathe, and he lost consciousness several times. He seems to be in a deep sleep now. Perhaps you shouldn't awaken him."

Thorn's face became grim. "Can I assume you have sent someone for Dr. Maywood?"

"Haven't you heard—that old man died two years back?" She smiled, all the while moving closer to Thorn, and knowing the light behind her revealed her body through her thin nightgown. "Thorn, you know how stubborn your father can be. He insists he will not tolerate Dr. Cross. What was I to do—go against his wishes?"

"Who in hell is Dr. Cross?"

She toyed with the ribbon at the neck of her nightgown, easing the neck open so the valley between her breasts was visible. "Why, he's very young, and much more capable than that absentminded old fool Dr. Maywood was."

Thorn's eyes were cold. "Perhaps you should get dressed so you can be at the bedside of your sick husband, madame."

The color drained out of Wilhelmina's face. "I can assure you that I do not need you to remind me of my duties, Thorn. Where were *you* all those years when your father needed you to run Stoddard Hill?"

His eyes held a chill. "We both know why I was not here, Wilhelmina, so let there be no pretense between us."

She whirled around and hurried back to her bedroom, slamming the door behind her. Now was not the time to confront Thorn. He was suspicious of her, and she would have to be very careful. But she was not concerned. Everyone had their weaknesses—she had found Thorn's once, she would find it again.

Wilhelmina's eyes gleamed. Thorn was not the inexperienced youth he had been when he had gone away. He was a man of strength, a man who would sweep any woman aside if she got in his way.

She pulled her gown over her head and stared at her naked image in the mirror. Her skin was still white and smooth. She glanced at her black hair; it was still lustrous and soft. Her hips were fuller than they had been, but most men liked a woman with a ripe figure. She parted her full lips and smiled. Men were all fools. Why should Thorn be any different? Of course, she would have to be very clever this time, because it was clear that he did not trust her.

Closing her eyes, she remembered what it had felt like when Thorn had kissed her. Even though he had been a boy, still she could not forget the feel of his hands on her body.

She stared critically at her image. Her eyes had a hard look about them, and tiny wrinkles fanned out about her mouth. She reached for her rouge pot, knowing that with the right lighting, she would appear younger.

"Thorn, I could have had you once," she said aloud. "You desired me then, and I will use that desire to bring you back to me."

Her eyes were bright with passion, and for a moment she forgot about her ambition to be in control of Stoddard Hill. Right now, all she could think about was the blue of Thorn's eyes, and she recalled so vividly how they had looked when they had been fired by passion.

She had been foolish to lose him, but perhaps it was still not too late to get him back. There was no reason she could not have both Thorn and Stoddard Hill.

With trepidation, Thorn approached his father's bedside. In the dim light that filtered through the opening in the curtain, he could see how pale Benjamin was. Thorn pulled the bed covers aside and pressed his hand against his father's chest. There was faint breathing, but it was shallow and labored.

Helplessly, he dropped down in a chair and picked up his father's limp hand, his eyes moving over the frail body. When he had gone away, his father had been a strong and forceful person, now he was only a shell of the man he had once been.

Benjamin mumbled something, and Thorn leaned closer so he could catch the words.

"Margaret . . . beloved wife."

Thorn's eyes burned, and grief settled on his shoulders. His father was calling for his mother.

"I am so cold," Ben whispered.

Thorn reached for the quilt at the foot of the bed and pulled it over his father. How could he be cold when the heat was so oppressive?

With long strides, Thorn moved to the bell pull and gave it a hard yank.

Moments later, a black face peeped around the corner of

the door. This woman was unfamiliar to him. Was no one left at Stoddard Hill whom he had known before? he wondered in irritation.

"Who are you?" he asked, as the woman came shyly into the room.

"I'm Matty's daughter, Livia."

He held out his hand waist-high. "Little Livia, the cook's daughter? The one who used to sleep in a corner of the kitchen with the mother cat and all her kittens?"

She grinned widely, feeling pleased that he would remember her. "Yes'er, Master Thorn, that's me."

He drew in a deep breath. "Well, Livia, I need help, and I don't know who I can trust anymore." His eyes were seeking. "Can I trust you to look after my father?"

She pulled herself up proud. "Yes, sir, you can trust me, Master Thorn."

He gave her a smile. "Then find someone whom *you* trust and send them for the doctor. Then come back here to me as soon as possible."

Her eyes darted to where her old master lay. "There's a new doctor, but Master don't like him none."

"So I have been told, but he will have to do for now. Hurry, girl, we may not have much time."

She moved quickly to the door and paused to glance sorrowfully at the old man on the bed. "He's a good man, Master Thorn. He was always good to me and Mama."

Brittany paced back and forth before the window, her eyes always on the roadway. Panic was rising up inside her with each passing hour. She glanced at the mantel clock in despair. Achmed had been gone since early morning, and the sun was going down. What could be keeping him? she wondered frantically.

She paused, staring at the china face of the clock as it struck seven. Could something have happened to delay Achmed? Of course he could have lost his way, but she doubted it, because he had a good sense of direction.

Moving out of the room and down the hallway, she called to the housekeeper. "Find me transportation, I am going to search for Achmed."

Trained to obey orders, the housekeeper rushed out of the room to find the caretaker.

Brittany was seated in the buggy as it pulled out the iron gate and into the main flow of the evening traffic. Her eyes were ever-searching as the driver moved slowly across town.

They drove up one street and then down another, cross-crossing the town. At last the driver turned to her, his black face etched with concern. "I do not know where to take you, Mistress Sinclair. We been everywhere."

Brittany tried to keep the panic out of her voice. "Could it be that we missed Achmed along the way and he has already gone home?"

"That could be, miss."

"Then let us go back," she said, daring to hope Achmed would be at Stonehouse to greet her when she returned.

Thorn handed his hat to Betty, noting the concern in her dark eyes. "Is Miss Sinclair in?" he asked.

"No, sir, Master Thorn. Daniel took her looking for that Achmed. He left this morning and ain't come back. She was mighty worried when she left here."

Thorn turned back to the door with the intention of searching for Brittany, but by the time he reached the front porch, she was climbing the steps toward him.

When she saw Thorn, Brittany ran to him. "Has Achmed returned?"

"Not yet," Thorn told her, taking her arm and leading her inside the house. "Suppose you tell me what has occurred," he said, seating her in a chair and then sitting down across from her.

Brittany clasped her hands together. "Achmed left this morning to find lodgings for the two of us." She looked up at

Thorn with a frantic light in her eyes. "Something has happened to him. I just know it has."

"Why would he be looking for lodgings? Are you not happy here?"

Her eyes showed her distress. "I just learned this morning that my grandmother has been deceased for several years. Achmed and I were going to vacate your house."

"I see."

She moved off the chair and knelt down before him in a flurry of petticoats. "Thorn, I know you have already done so much for me . . . but will you help me find Achmed? He has not fully recovered from his ordeal, and I should never have allowed him to go out alone."

Thorn stood up and carried her with him. "I will help you if you promise to wait here and do nothing until I return. Don't go off again, thinking you can find Achmed, is that understood?"

"Yes, I understand. But please hurry because I fear for his life."

Thorn read the fear etched on her face. "You really do care for him, don't you?"

"Of course, Thorn. I told you he is my friend."

He smiled down at her. "Try not to worry. I am sure he got lost and couldn't find his way home. Don't forget he has been ill and has not had time to learn his way around."

"Oh, I hope that's all it is, Thorn. I don't know what I would do if anything happened to him. Simijin expected me to keep Achmed safe, but so far, I have failed in that."

Thorn laughed softly, his eyes dancing with mirth. "I had thought Achmed was the one looking after you, rather than the other way around."

"Sometimes Achmed is like a child. He is very strong, but he is too trusting of other people."

Thorn raised his eyebrow. "A trait that is not unknown in you."

"I know, Thorn, but I have learned my lesson. I will never talk to a strange man again."

Thorn touched her cheek. "Between the two of you, you are determined to keep my life in an upheaval. The first day I saw you and Achmed, I should have pitched you both in the sea."

She smiled at him. "You missed your chance; now it is too late."

He moved to the door. "Not all together. Perhaps you are yet in for a good dunking from me."

The troubles of the day seemed to melt away for Brittany. Once more Thorn had come to her aid. If anyone would find Achmed, it would be he.

Chapter Twenty-three

Brittany had not meant to fall asleep, but her eyes were heavy, and she soon dozed off.

When the clock struck twelve, she awoke and looked about her in confusion. Why was she lying on the couch in the parlor?

She sat up, stretching her tired muscles. Suddenly she remembered that Achmed was missing and Thorn had gone out searching for him. She jumped to her feet and raced to the window. The lanterns on the front porch swayed in the wind and it had begun to rain.

She searched the driveway and the road beyond, hoping at any moment to see Thorn returning with Achmed.

She stood there, keeping her vigil until the clock struck one. Time seemed to crawl. Several carriages passed, but none of them pulled beneath the iron gates of Stonehouse.

Too weary to stand, she sank down on the window seat and pressed her forehead to the window.

At last she saw the buggy pull into the driveway. Racing outside, she waited on the porch for Thorn. When he leapt to the ground, his solemn expression told her that he had not yet found Achmed.

Thorn climbed the steps and took Brittany's hand in his. "I will search again tomorrow."

Her eyes looked down the roadway, as if she expected Achmed to appear at any moment.

"Where can he be?" she cried.

"I don't know, Brittany, but several crew members from

the *Victorious* are still searching for him. I am confident they will find him."

"I wish I could do something."

He led her inside before he took her in his arms. "Waiting is the hardest part, Brittany. I would stay with you if I could, but my father is gravely ill, and I have to get back to Stoddard Hill. I will return to you as soon as I am able."

"Oh, Thorn, I am so sorry. Here you are worried about your father, and I place an added burden on you."

His arms tightened about her, and he just held her close for a moment, needing her sweetness to chase the unpleasantness away. "I have some thinking to do about you, Brittany. You cannot stay here alone. We do not want the gossips to make something ugly out of an innocent situation."

She glanced up at his face and saw the weariness etched there. "I will do whatever you think necessary, Thorn. It always seems I am pulling you into my predicaments." She gently touched his cheek. "Now that you have troubles, I wish I could help you."

He raised her hand and kissed it, then realeased it and stepped away. "I may ask something of you tomorrow."

Her eyes were filled with sadness. "Ask what you will of me, and I will do it, Thorn."

"Don't be too hasty," he said teasingly. "You should never obligate yourself until you know what you are committing to, Brittany."

"Thorn?"

"Yes."

"I will pray for your father tonight when I pray for Achmed."

He studied her for a long moment, thinking anyone who looked as angelic as she did must have a deep faith in God.

"I never thought to ask what religion you practice, Brittany."

"Mama told me that my father was a Quaker, but she was raised in the Church of England, and that is also my faith.

Although Simijin was not of our faith, he allowed my mother to have a chapel in the palace."

"Yes," he said, looking at the halo of light adorning her golden head, "say a prayer for my father. He has not had an easy life of late."

"I shall," she assured him.

"Now go to bed and get some rest," he told her. "Everything is being done to find Achmed."

She watched him leave, feeling strangely alone. Moving to the window, she stood there for a long time. She wondered what Thorn wanted to ask of her. Again she had felt in him a great sadness, and it made her sad.

She moved down the hallway and up the stairs. When she reached her room, she dropped to her knees and said a prayer for Thorn, Achmed, and Thorn's father.

Long after her prayer, she remained on her knees, listening to the rain peppering against the windowpane and hoping that wherever he was, Achmed had found shelter from the storm.

Finally, she climbed on the bed and lay down fully clothed. She would not sleep tonight, for her mind was too troubled.

Now she was all alone. What would she do without her faithful Achmed? She thought of Thorn, and how alone he must feel at this time.

Thorn kept the morning vigil beside his father's bed. At times his father would rouse and call out for Thorn's mother, but mostly he drifted in and out of a restless sleep.

Thorn had been told by Livia that Dr. Cross had been with his father earlier, but the doctor had told her nothing of his father's condition.

When the sun came up, Thorn stood up and flexed his stiff muscles. He blew out the lamp on the side table, and dark shadows clung to the corners of the room. Thorn walked to the bell pull and gave it a tug.

Moments later, Livia appeared at the door.

"Livia, I have to go out for a time, but I want you to sit with my father until I return. Is that understood?"

"Yes'er, Master Thorn. But what if the mistress tells me to do something else? She don't like me hanging around. She'll beat me for sure if I don't do what I'm told."

Thorn's eyes hardened. "My stepmother will not ever beat you again, Livia, you have my word on that. And no matter what she says to the contrary, you are to remain with my father. Also, tell the upstairs maid to have a chamber prepared for me. I will be staying at Stoddard Hill."

"Yes'er, Master Thorn." Her eyes brightened with triumph, and she nodded eagerly. None of the slaves liked the mistress because she was cruel and vindictive. Now that the young master had come home, they were all encouraged that there would be a change for the better.

"I am leaving my man, Cappy, downstairs. If my father's condition worsens, tell him, and he will know where to find me."

Again she nodded. "I will, Master Thorn."

When Thorn stepped out into the hall, he found Wilhelmina waiting for him. "I was about to look in on Benjamin. Did he pass a restful night?"

"I would not disturb him just now, if I were you." He blocked her path. "He's sleeping."

Her eyes seemed to spit fire, for she could feel her authority slipping away. Why did Thorn have to return just when she was about to gain control of Stoddard Hill?

"Ben is my husband, and you have no right to keep me from him," she said, pushing against him, but he did not allow her access to the room.

"You should have remembered that you were his wife last night when he needed someone to be with him. When I arrived, he was calling out for a drink of water. Now he has Livia to see to his needs."

"Are you implying that I'm neglecting my husband?"

He took in a long, disgusted breath. "I am not implying

anything. Only *you* can be accountable for the kind of wife you are."

She wet her lips, her eyes running over the breadth of his shoulders. "Accountable to whom?"

His eyes probed hers. "Accountable to me, damn you! I know what kind of woman you are, but make no mistake about it, I will not stand by and watch you destroy my father."

She shrugged. "Your father is a dying man. He has not cared for me since the night you went away. All he talks about is that mother of yours."

Thorn bit back his anger. "I will be back later. I do not want anyone in my father's room but the doctor, Livia, and Cappy." He scowled at her. "You stay away from him, is that understood? And another thing, if I ever hear of you striking Livia or any of the other slaves, you will regret it."

She wanted to lash out at him, but the look he gave her made her reconsider. She moved aside, allowing him to brush past her. What right did he have to keep her from her own husband? And it was no concern of his if she punished a slave.

But she dared not disobey him. Thorn Stoddard was not a man to trifle with. She feared him, and she desired him, but she would find a way to pull him down. She caused him to leave Stoddard Hill once; she would see him leave again.

Wilhelmina slipped into her bedroom and glanced at the naked man lounging on her bed. "He's gone for the day. If you are going to do something, it had better be soon," she told him. "I want that old man out of my life."

Dr. George Cross patted the mattress and motioned for her to join him in bed. "And the son?" he asked. "What about him?"

She shook her head, indicating she did not want to lay with him. "I will deal with the son," she said offhandedly.

He reached out, took her hand, and with a tug, pulled her down beside him. His long fingers trailed across her breast, and he pulled the lace aside and swirled his tongue around the nipple. "You excite me as no other woman ever could," he said, pressing her tightly to him until she felt the bulge of his desire.

"I admit it was exciting to have you here last night," she told him. "Right under Thorn's nose, and him being none the wiser for it. But you had better leave now. The slaves might know you and I are lovers, and they would not hesitate to tell Thorn."

George Cross's eyes ran over Wilhelmina. He had been obsessed with her ever since he had first come to this house a year ago to treat Benjamin Stoddard. He felt no guilt at the slow poison he was prescribing for the old man. He would do anything Wilhelmina asked of him—anything to keep her with him.

"George, are you certain that the poison will work?"

"Of course. You have seen the results. But I am not sure about doubling the dosage as you suggested. You saw what happened when I did."

"Everyone believes he has a bad heart anyway. They will not think it strange when he suddenly dies. Besides, George, you will be the only doctor to attend Ben, so no one will doubt your word when you diagnose his death as heart failure."

"I suppose."

Wilhelmina was reflective. "For the moment, my main worry is keeping Thorn from reading a copy of his father's will."

"You said the old man intended to change his will and cut you out."

"Yes, and he would have done it, too . . . if he hadn't become ill." Her laughter rang out. "The drug has altered his mind. He dwells more and more in the past."

She moved off the bed. "Hurry and dress, George. I want you to leave by the back way."

He pulled on his pants and moved over to her, slipping his arms around her waist. "What does the present will leave you?"

"The day after he ordered Thorn off Stoddard Hill,

Benjamin made a will, leaving everything to me." Her eyes darkened with the challenge. "Even though he has returned, Thorn Stoddard will not stand in my way. I can take care of him."

George looked into her face and saw something raw and unsatisfied there. Her eyes were shining, and her tongue darted out to lick her upper lip. Suddenly jealousy ate at his heart. "I will take care of Thorn Stoddard for you."

Wilhelmina was driven by desperation. She saw suspicion on George's face, and she needed to keep his trust if she was to complete her plan. "No. You take care of Benjamin, and I'll take care of Thorn. It must not appear that you have any interest in him other than as the son of your patient."

Thorn dismounted and rushed up the steps of Stonehouse. He had come by way of the *Victorious*, so he knew Achmed had not yet been found. He dreaded facing Brittany with the news, because he had come to understand how much Achmed meant to her.

Brittany must have seen him ride up, because when he entered the house, she was waiting for him. "Have you word of Achmed?"

"I am sorry, Brittany. No one has seen him. But we are still searching."

"You will not give up, will you?"

"No," he assured her. "The men who searched for him last night are resting while others take their place."

Her brow furrowed with worry. "What is your father's condition?"

"He's not good. I fear for his life, Brittany."

She noticed the tired lines beneath his eyes. "Did you sit with him after you left here?"

"Yes."

"Then you have not been to bed yet?"

"No, not yet. I have too much on my mind to sleep."

"Tell me how can I help you?"

He did not answer immediately, but instead, took her hand and led her into the dining room. From a sideboard, he poured himself and Brittany a cup of coffee and motioned for her to join him at the table.

When she searched his face, she detected something vulnerable about him.

"Do you really want to help me, Brittany?"

She laid her hand on his. "I'll do anything."

His eyes drew hers, and he clasped her hand. "Then marry me, Brittany."

"But we have already discussed this, Thorn, and I told you—"

"Let me finish. Marrying me is the practical solution to both our problems. You are alone, and whether or not you know it, an unmarried woman alone becomes the victim of vicious gossip, and prey for every upstart that comes along."

She was thoughtful for a moment, remembering with an aching heart the love between her mother and Simijin. That was what she wanted in a marriage.

"I can see that you are doing this to help me, but what could I bring to a marriage that would benefit you?"

He lifted her hand and looked at the delicate bone structure, the long, tapered fingers and the half-moon-shaped fingernails. She was so small, yet wiser and far more intelligent than any woman he knew. "You could help me with my father," he said at last.

She shook her head. "You could hire a nurse to perform that duty, and she would not require that you marry her."

His voice came out in an exasperated hiss. "Brittany, for God's sake, I need you, don't you see that?"

She was completely taken aback at the thought that Thorn would need any woman. She touched his face, wishing she could be all things to him. "Marriage is a high price to pay for needing someone, Thorn."

"I am willing to pay it. But first, you must know what you are letting yourself in for. I have talked with my father's solicitor, and I have discovered that my father is deeply in debt. The monies I receive for the sale of the *Victorious* and her cargo will go to pay off that debt. I have very little to offer you in the way of luxury, but I will give you my name, and it's an honorable one."

She came to her feet abruptly. "You are going to sell the *Victorious?*"

"I fear I must."

"Wait right here until I come back. At that time I will give you my answer."

With a quizzical expression on his face, he watched her rush out of the room.

Soon Brittany returned, carrying a large hand-carved wooden chest, which she set before Thorn. "I will accept your offer, Thorn, and this will by my dowry."

He frowned as she flipped the lid open, and there in the black velvet-lined box were gold coins, sparkling diamonds, rubies the size of pigeon eggs, and priceless pearls.

He closed the lid and stood up. "I will not accept the treasures Lord Simijin has given you, Brittany, but I would still be honored if you would be my wife."

"But the jewels are mine to give, and I want you to have them. If you are to be my husband, we will share wealth or poverty. Is that not the way it is in this country between married people?"

He felt a tightening in his throat, and he had the strongest urge to crush her in his arms. "You have never known poverty, Brittany."

Her eyes were shining with earnestness. "Will you fault me for that?"

He pulled her into his arms and laughed with delight. "No, little dancer, I will not fault you for that."

He released her, feeling strangely lighthearted. "Run along upstairs and make yourself look like a bride. I will make you my wife before the sun sets on this day."

She turned tear-bright eyes up to him. "My wedding day. With so much sadness in our lives, I will hold on to this bit of happiness."

He caught her hand and raised it to his lips. "I will try my damnable best to make you happy, Brittany. But I may not always succeed."

She gave him an impish smile. "I'll take my chances with you, Thorn."

Chapter Twenty-four

The night was dark as the well-sprung carriage bounced over the rutted roads. The driver was guided by the lantern carried by the outrider. Brittany had fallen asleep with her head resting against her new husband's shoulder, and she woke when the coach stopped.

Thorn smiled down at her. "Wake up, Mrs. Stoddard, you have come home."

She looked out the window, but it was a dark night and the house was no more than a dark shadow against a pale moon.

Thorn opened the door and jumped down, then swung Brittany to the ground.

"I am sorry I fell asleep," she apologized as he led her up the steps to the front door.

"Think nothing of it," he assured her. "You have had a hard two days and needed the rest."

She felt the gold band that circled her finger. It had been a brief and impersonal ceremony that bound her to this man who had come into her life just when she needed him most. She was determined to make him a good wife, and she hoped she could stay out of trouble.

Thorn led her into the house, and she yawned as she looked around the wide, high ceiling of the entry hall. She could see that it had once been a grand house, but now the carpets were threadbare and the floor was in need of repair.

Thorn helped Brittany upstairs and led her down a long corridor. Stopping before a door, he pushed it open, taking her inside.

He lit a lamp and looked around. "Do you think you will be comfortable here?"

She looked at him, feeling a strange thrill race through her body. "Yes, I believe it will do very nicely." Her eyes moved to the large bed where the covers had been turned back, and she wanted to ask him if they would be sharing that bed.

He gathered her close and touched his lips to her forehead. "Will you forgive me if I desert you on our wedding night? I must see to my father."

She nodded and turned her face away so he would not read her disappointment. She understood that he had many heavy responsibilities weighing on his shoulders. Of course he would want to be with his father since he was so ill.

"Do not concern yourself about me. Go to your father—he needs you."

Thorn looked at her regretfully. "Do you have to be so damned understanding?" His smile took the sting out of his words. "Go to bed, little dancer." His eyes sparkled. "And, dream of me, if you dare."

"I am still worried about Achmed."

He moved to the window and opened it so a slight breeze circulated through the room. "All that it is possible to do is being done to locate him. It is but a matter of time until my men find him, Brittany. Try to be patient until then."

"Yes, I know you are doing everything possible, but I am so anxious for his return." She removed her bonnet and dropped it in a chair. "Go to your father now. I will be here if you need me."

"I need you," he whispered, coming up behind her and pulling her head so it rested against his shoulder. "You are my only sanity in this world of turmoil."

She turned around to him, her eyes large and luminous in the soft light. "I would like to be."

"All I seem to think about for now is my father. Can you understand that?"

"Yes, I can. You have never told me anything about your relationship with your father."

He smiled and put her from him. "Tonight is not the time to bare my soul, Brittany." He gave her a gentle shove. "It's off to bed with you now."

Thorn turned to the door and departed abruptly, leaving Brittany staring after him.

She moved to the window and glanced out, but it was too dark to see anything. How quickly events had happened to shape and change her life. Only a few short weeks ago she had been a young girl with little on her mind other than how best to escape her governess. Now she was in America, and this was her wedding night, which she would spend alone.

With a resigned sigh, she unfastened her gown and pulled it over her head. Struggling into her nightgown, she climbed into the bed and sank into the soft mattress, too weary to think about the events of the day.

She yawned and turned her face to the fluffy pillow. She was Thorn's wife, but there was no sense of belonging, only a deep tranquil feeling of uncertainty. Her eyes closed, and she gave in to the tranquil feeling of sleep. Tomorrow would be soon enough to worry about Achmed and about being a wife.

On entering his father's room, Thorn saw that Matty was sitting at her master's bedside.

She placed her finger to her lips and whispered, "He's doing mighty poorly, Master Thorn—mighty poorly."

Standing over his father, Thorn glanced down at the frail body, thinking he looked ill indeed. "Has he been awake?"

"He keeps on mumbling sometimes, but he ain't opened his eyes."

"Has anyone else been in to see him today?"

"No, sir. Just the doctor."

Thorn ran his fingers through his hair and pulled up a chair. He shook off the feeling of tiredness. "You can go to bed now, Matty. I'll stay with my father."

"You look just 'bout done in, Master Thorn. I just been

here a while. Why don't you go to bed and let me sit with Master Ben."

Thorn shook his head. "No, I want to stay with my father."

Matty had been born on Stoddard Hill Plantation, and she was well aware of the situation between the father and son. She eyed the young master sadly. Things were not good here, and they hadn't been since the old master had taken himself a second wife much younger than himself.

"We're all glad you're back, Master Thorn. We surely have needed you to come home. Now that you are here things are a'gonna get better, I just know it."

He smiled at her. "I have taken the first steps to make things better, Matty. I have taken a wife. I think you will like her."

The woman's dark eyes glowed, and she beamed happily. "Now ain't that a grand thing you've done? I'm happy for you, Master Thorn."

He stretched out his long legs and smiled tiredly. "You might want to inform the others about my new bride. I wouldn't want them to think there is a strange woman sleeping in my bed."

Matty's laughter was muted when she clamped her hand over her mouth. "Yes, sir, I'll do just that." She chuckled to herself as she moved out of the room and into the hallway, wondering how the mistress would take to having another woman in the house, especially one who was younger and probably much prettier. Since Matty had no liking for the mistress, she hoped it would trouble her quite a bit.

Wilhelmina stormed down the hall, her lips pressed together tightly. She encountered the upstairs maid, Livia. Taking the girl by surprise, she grabbed a handful of hair and gave it a hard yank.

"Why was I not informed immediately that Thorn brought a woman into this house?" she demanded. "It's your duty to keep me informed of everything that happens."

Livia squirmed in pain. "I don't know much 'bout no woman. I just know that my mama told me that Master Thorn got himself married."

Wilhelmina flung the frightened girl out of the way. "We'll just see about that!" Her eyes were burning with anger. "I will not have it!"

Brittany was in a deep sleep and did not hear Wilhelmina when she entered the bedroom. She did not know that Thorn's stepmother was watching her with an expression of naked hatred. Innocently, she lingered in her dream world, unaware that she was the object of such intense loathing.

Wilhelmina ground her teeth together as she looked at the golden hair spilled across the snowy-white pillowcase. She looked at the even features and the long silky lashes that curled at the tips.

She balled her fists, resisting an urge to destroy the beautiful girl who was Thorn's wife. This girl represented everything that Wilhelmina was not—young, innocent, beautiful. And she had Thorn.

Brittany's eyes fluttered open slowly, and she found a strange woman staring at her. Her green eyes reflected her discomfort, and she sat up, brushing a tumbled curl away from her face.

"H-ello," Brittany stammered. "Who are you?"

Wilhelmina stabbed the air. "I am mistress of this house, and I demand to know what are you doing in Thorn's bed?"

Brittany realized that the woman had drawn a wrong conclusion. "It is not as bad as it appears, madame. You see, I am Thorn's . . . wife."

"So I have been informed, but I had to clarify it for myself." Wilhelmina's voice held a note of spitefulness as she trailed her finger across the empty side of the bed. "If last night was your wedding night, it must have been a disappointment to you."

Wilhelmina's eyes narrowed. "I have been told that your new bridegroom did not share your marriage bed, since he spent the night with his father. Poor girl, it must have been so frustrating for you, hmm?"

Brittany slid off the bed and pulled on her dressing gown. She was feeling uncomfortable under the woman's close inspection, and she was certain she detected undertones in the woman's voice. "How is your husband this morning, Mrs. Stoddard? I do hope his condition is much improved."

There was something regal about the way Thorn's wife held herself, and that further enraged Wilhelmina. "How should I know? Thorn is the one to ask," she replied in a surly voice. "He has put himself in charge of my husband."

Brittany tried to ignore the woman's biting tone. "What should I call you, Mrs. Stoddard?"

"What!" Wilhelmina's mouth opened in surprise. "Thorn has not told you my name?"

"No. Thorn told me nothing about you. I knew only that his own mother died and that you are his stepmother."

Now Wilhelmina's anger knew no bounds. "So, Thorn thought me such an insignificant part of his life that he did not mention me to his wife."

"I . . . am certain—"

Wilhelmina held up her hand to silence Brittany. Her eyes narrowed, and her lips thinned into a vengeful smile. "Of course Thorn has his reasons for not telling you about me. You will hear why he had to leave Stoddard Hill in the first place." Her laughter sounded evil and high-pitched. "Yes, it is clear to me that Thorn would not want you to know what we have been to one another in the past."

Brittany blinked her eyes in confusion. Then slowly she understood what the woman was inferring, and a sick feeling washed over her. "Are you saying that you and my husband . . . that you and Thorn . . ."

"Were lovers?" Wilhelmina supplied. "Is it so hard for you to say?"

Brittany turned toward the window, needing a breath of fresh air. "Madame, nothing you can say will make me believe anything bad about Thorn. He is a man of honor, and

I know he would never betray his father as you are implying."

Wilhelmina shrugged. "If you do not believe me, then you must ask your husband why his father ordered him to leave Stoddard Hill."

Brittany swung around. "I never will ask such a question of him. If Thorn has something he wants me to know, he will tell me himself." She raised her head, her eyes boring into Wilhelmina. "I would like it if you left now."

Wilhelmina almost slithered across the room. "Of course, my dear. You will want time to settle in and become acquainted with your new home." At the door she turned back to Brittany. "I can assure you that if Thorn were my husband, he would not have spent his wedding night away from my bed." Spiteful laughter rolled off her lips. "Are you certain that Thorn was with his father last night?"

Before Brittany could answer, the woman swept out of the room, slamming the door behind her. Brittany leaned out the window, taking in deep gulps of air. Never had she met such a disgusting creature. Nothing Wilhelmina had said would convince Brittany that she and Thorn had been lovers or that Thorn had spent his wedding night with her, as she implied.

Brittany moved to the side table and splashed water on her face. Thorn would not have asked her to marry him if he loved his stepmother. She shook her head, knowing there was something evil about that woman. Thorn needed her, she could sense it, and she was not going to turn against him now.

She dressed quickly. Then with a determined lift to her head, she walked into the hall where she encountered one of the servants.

"Good morning, ma'am. My name is Livia, and Master Thorn has asked me to look after you. Will you be wanting breakfast in your room?"

Brittany looked into smiling dark eyes. "Where is my husband?"

"He said to tell you he was going into town. Said you would know why." Her brow came together in thoughtfulness. "He said he wouldn't be back until tonight."

"How is my husband's father?"

"He's sickly, mighty sickly."

Brittany stood undecided for a moment. Without Thorn, a long day stretched before her. "I will not be wanting breakfast, thank you. I just want to walk about the grounds and see the plantation."

"Yes, ma'am. If you want something, just ask for me."

"Thank you, Livia. I shall."

Brittany stood on the small bridge and gazed out at the fields. She sensed something was not right at Stoddard Hill. There was too much idleness. Men lounged in front of the stables while the work went undone. The women appeared to be busy enough, but not in doing anything that would benefit Stoddard Hill.

She walked past the slave quarters, nodding to women who stared back at her with interest. Several dark-skinned children who were playing games under the branches of a wide oak tree stopped to stare at her with open curiosity.

When Brittany reached the last cabin, she came upon an old woman sitting in the shade of a wagon, her gnarled hands weaving a delicate basket out of colored straw. She watched the woman with fascination.

"How do you do that?" Brittany inquired, bending down to get a closer look.

The woman's face was stoic. "Been doing it for over eighty years. My mother did it a'fore me, and her mother a'fore her," the woman answered with a feeling of pride.

Brittany glanced at the many baskets that the woman had already completed. They were all in different shapes, and apparently had different uses. "What a wonderful craft. Do you think I could learn to weave the straw?"

The old woman looked at her skeptically. "You wouldn't be wanting to spoil your pretty hands. This here's hard work, and the straw cuts deep into the skin." She held her hands up for Brittany's inspection. "I have calluses on my hands and they are as tough as the back of a mule. This may look like play, but it's hard work."

Brittany nodded her golden head. "I can see that. Would you consider teaching me?"

The woman's proud head raised up, and she stuck out her chin. "You the new missus?"

Brittany smiled. "I am sorry, I did not introduce myself. I am Brittany, Thorn's wife."

"Thought so." The dark eyes softened. "That Master Thorn, he was always a good one. His pa is good, too. The old master always let me sell my baskets and keep the money."

Brittany dropped down on the doorstep, startling the old woman. "What is your name?" she asked.

"My name's Esmeralda," she stated. "Now ain't that a fancy name for such as me?"

"It's a very pretty name."

Esmeralda was beginning to lose some of her suspicion of Brittany. "I've seen many changes in my life. My birthday's in two months, and I'll be a hundred and two. Now ain't that a great amount of time to live?"

"That is splendid, Esmeralda. Your birthday should be worthy of a great celebration."

"Yes'em, it should. If the old master wasn't ailing, he'd plan a gathering and have us all singing and dancing, and I reckon there would be a goodly amount of food."

"I have not yet met my father-in-law," Brittany said sadly, "but I know how ill he is, and how concerned Thorn is about him."

Intelligent old eyes that had seen much in life pierced Brittany. "You ain't from around here, 'cause I'd a'knowed about it iffen you was."

"No, I was not born in this country."

"Thought so. Iffen you was born in the South, you wouldn't be so friendly with the likes of me, and you wouldn't be sitting beside me, neither."

Brittany was startled. "Why ever not? What have you done wrong?"

Esmeralda rolled her eyes. "Don't you know the white folks from the big house don't socialize with the slaves? It just ain't done."

Brittany smiled at the old woman and drew an answering toothless smile. "My husband would tell you that I never do what's expected of me." She ran her finger along the rim of a straw basket. "Now show me how to make this. I want to do something useful today."

Esmeralda chuckled. She was old enough not to fear speaking her mind. "You sure are going to set them on their ear at the big house. I wish I could'a seen the mistress's face when she met you for the first time. Yes'em, that must have been a right nice sight."

Brittany wrinkled her nose. "I do not think Mrs. Stoddard liked me very well."

The old slave's eyes were intense. "You have a care where she is concerned now. It just ain't good to poke a stick at a snake."

Brittany hid a smile. She did not think she should encourage Esmeralda's assessment of Thorn's stepmother, even though she agreed with the old woman.

She picked up the basket Esmeralda had been working on, and attempted to poke the straw through the loose weave. "As you will find out, Esmeralda, I have a habit of finding trouble and always doing the wrong thing."

Esmeralda had never shared the secret of her craft with anyone but her daughter and her granddaughters. But now she took the young mistress's hands and guided them. "You take the long yellow grasses—they're called bulrushes—and just do what I do. Have a care now, they're sharp."

At first Brittany's hands were clumsy, and she cut her fingers several times. But she was determined to learn the craft. Soon she and Esmeralda were laughing and talking like old friends, and she was learning about Stoddard Hill.

As the morning progressed, several of the other women

gathered around, astonished that the young mistress should take the time to be kind to old Esmeralda. But more astonishing still was that old Esmeralda seemed to like Master Thorn's wife.

At last Brittany proudly held the finished basket up for all to inspect, while Esmeralda nodded in approval.

Suddenly Brittany looked at the position of the sun and saw that it was late afternoon. She stood up, dreading the thought of going back to that house and facing Thorn's stepmother.

"Thank you, Esmeralda, for your patience." She held the basket out to the old woman, but Esmeralda pushed her hand away.

"You keep the basket. Show it to Master Thorn." She chuckled. "And tell him old Esmeralda thinks he married well."

Brittany clutched the basket in her hands and smiled at the old woman. "I hope he already knows that, but if he does not, I'll tell him you said so."

As several pairs of black eyes watched Brittany move toward the big house, Esmeralda muttered under her breath, "There's a'gonna be trouble coming—I can feel trouble in these ole bones."

"There's a'gonna be trouble for sure," one of the other woman agreed. "Mistress Wilhelmina ain't gonna like no pretty young woman messing round here."

Esmeralda nodded. "I think I'll just keep an eye on the big house. If any of you see any unusual happenings, report them to me. I don't want nothing to happen to the little mistress."

Chapter Twenty-five

When Brittany entered the house, she carried the basket Esmeralda had helped her weave as if it were a priceless treasure.

Wilhelmina heard Brittany in the hall, and came out of the parlor, her face livid with anger. "Where have you been? I disrupted the whole household to search for you."

Brittany glanced behind Wilhelmina and saw a man staring at her. She held out her treasure for inspection. "I have learned to craft a basket."

Wilhelmina went into peals of uproarious laughter. "How quaint." She turned to the man beside her. "Dr. Cross, this is Thorn's little wife. It seems there is no end to this girl's talents. See, she has made a basket."

Brittany felt the sting of the older woman's ridicule, but she did not know the reason for it. She had never known anyone who would deliberately set out to hurt another. Her head came up, and she faced the slender, bold man who looked her over from head to toe.

"I am pleased to meet you, Dr. Cross. How is my father-in-law?"

Wilhelmina saw George Cross's eyes widen with admiration as he held his hand out to Brittany. When Brittany did not offer him her hand in return, he awkwardly shoved his hands into his pockets.

"I am delighted to meet you, Mrs. Stoddard. I only wish it had been under happier circumstances. I regret to tell you that my patient is not doing well at all."

Brittany's eyes clouded with sadness, and she looked at

Wilhelmina. "I am so sorry. If there is anything I can do to help you, please tell me."

Brittany's genuine concern served to further fuel Wilhelmina's anger. "What can you or any of us do? I fear Ben has not long to live."

"If you will excuse me, I will go to my room," Brittany said.

Wilhelmina blocked her path, and asked in a demanding voice: "When will Thorn be home?"

"Not before dark. Do you feel the need to send for him?"

Wilhelmina considered for a moment, and she smiled to herself. Perhaps it would be better if Thorn was away from Stoddard Hill when his father died. "No, that will not be necessary. Run along to your room and wait for your husband." Wilhelmina sneered. "Perhaps Thorn will be a more attentive lover tonight—but don't count on it."

Brittany pushed past Thorn's stepmother, needing to get away from her vicious tongue. Her heart was heavy as she moved up to the second floor.

She stopped before Mr. Stoddard's door, wishing there was something she could do to help. When she reached Thorn's bedroom, she sank down in a chair, feeling defeated for the first time in her life. Not even when she had been captured by the Turks had she felt this utter devastation. Was it possible that Thorn and Wilhelmina had been lovers? What if they still were?

She refused to dwell on such troubling possibilities, but thought instead of her mother and Simijin—how she missed them. Her thoughts turned to Achmed. Where was he? Was he even alive?

She leaned her head back and closed her eyes. She also was worried about a man she had never met and could not even put a face to. She hoped fervently that Thorn's father would recover, but the doctor had not been encouraging. She pitied the poor man, for apparently his wife was not overly concerned about him. In fact, Wilhelmina seemed only concerned about her own comforts.

* * *

Wilhelmina whirled around and faced George Cross. "I will not have that girl here," she raged. "How dare Thorn do this to me."

The doctor's face was a mirror of amusement. "I don't believe Thorn has done anything against you. I think rather he has made that enchanting creature his wife for reasons of his own. I can't say I blame him."

Wilhelmina's eyes sparked with unleashed anger. "I would expect you to think her kind beautiful. I saw you fawning over her like some sniveling schoolboy."

George Cross wisely changed the subject. "The old man is getting weaker. Considering the amount of poison I am administering to him, he should be out of your way within a week—perhaps sooner."

Wilhelmina paced back and forth. "Can't you get rid of him sooner? I hate the thought of him lingering, day after day, night after night."

George looked sideways at Wilhelmina. "Can it be that you care for the old man?"

She eyed him as if he had lost his senses. "Don't be absurd. I married him to get even—" She shook her head. "Never mind that now. I have never cared for Ben. He has always compared me less favorably to his first wife." An evil smile tugged at her lips. "I will just help him along so he can be with his precious Margaret in death."

George studied her closely. "Why did he marry you?" He smiled suggestively. "Other than the obvious reason."

She licked her lips and moved closer to him. "Let's just say that I set out to get him. It didn't take much persuasion to convince him that I would make him happy. I dazzled him with my . . . smile." Her eyes became wild. "I hated every time he touched me. I will be glad when he's dead!"

George watched as her face became distorted with rage. Where was the beauty in her that had first attracted him? He did not underestimate her seductive powers, though. When she became soft and yielding, he became her slave.

She dropped down in front of him and slid her hand up his arm, pressing her body against his. "Soon we will be together, George. Then I will be your reward, and Stoddard Hill will be mine."

For the first time, there was a note of doubt in his voice. "There are too many people who stand between you and what you want. When we first thought of this plan, there was only the old man. Now that number has increased by two. And if there should be a child . . ."

Wilhelmina scrambled to her feet and whirled around, her breasts heaving, her eyes wild. "I will brush them all out of my way as I would a gnat. Nothing can keep me from what I desire. Stoddard Hill belongs to me!"

George Cross stood up and pulled her into his arms. "When you get that look in your eyes, you are the most exciting woman I have ever known. I have consented to do murder to please you, but will I ever possess you?"

She glanced at his thinning blond hair and a face that was beginning to show the results of his overindulgence of strong spirits. George was more often than not drunk, and she could not see her future linked with his. No, he was not the man to help her run Stoddard Hill once it fell into her hands.

When he dipped his head to kiss her, she looked into small gray eyes, but her thoughts were of eyes as blue as the sky that hung over Stoddard Hill. She knew deep inside that Thorn had always been in her heart, and now that he had returned, he was never out of her thoughts for long.

She felt repulsed when George's hands ran over her hips and he pressed her closer to him. She shuddered at his touch, but she would endure what she must to gain what she wanted. When he covered her mouth with his, she pretended it was Thorn's lips on hers, but she could not delude herself.

She shoved George away and moved a few paces from him. "Are you crazed? Do you want someone to walk in and find us like this?"

He smiled apologetically. "You go to my head and make me forget to be cautious."

She picked up his high-brimmed hat and handed it to him. "It would be best if you leave now."

He looked regretful. "Must I?"

"Yes, we don't want to do anything that will call attention to us or cast suspicion on our actions." She hesitated before she added, "I have decided it will be unwise for you to come to my bedroom at night. From here on out, we will see each other only in the presence of others, and then you must try to restrain yourself."

She saw the disappointment in his eyes. "How will I live if I can't hold you in my arms?"

Wilhelmina pushed down her revulsion. She had always detested a man who behaved like a fawning dog. "It will be difficult for us to be apart," the lie came easily to her lips, "but we will spend the rest of our lives together. Now go, before someone begins to wonder why you stayed so long."

As George moved away from Wilhelmina, she squeezed her eyes shut, wishing she could shut out the image of his face. She wondered how she could bear to have that man make love to her again. Climbing into bed with Dr. George Cross was a high price to pay, she thought, but she would do what she must to gain Stoddard Hill.

Brittany found it difficult to remain in the house because there was so much to discover on the vast and beautiful grounds. Although the gardens were suffering from neglect, they were still extraordinary, and she could see the shadow of their former beauty.

She was walking down a well-worn path toward the river when she heard quickening steps echo along a cobbled lane just behind her. She paused and waited for whomever it was to catch up with her.

When Thorn came into sight, she felt her heart skip a beat. He looked so handsome in his buff trousers and a pale-yellow shirt. His dark hair was windswept, and his eyes were soft as he looked at her.

"So I find you taking a stroll among the flowers." He

glanced down at the weed-choked flower garden. "I see you are enjoying the tulips."

She reached out and touched a crimson bloom that bobbed delicately from the slight breeze that came off the river. "Many people associate the tulip with Holland, but Simijin told me that tulips originated in Turkey and were transplanted in Holland in the sixteenth century—did you know that?"

He smiled. "I do not believe I was aware of that. Is there no end to your knowledge?"

She looked up at him doubtfully. "Does it displease you that I speak of matters that Simijin taught me?"

"Not at all. I will always want you to speak your mind with me. And never hide your knowledge from me. I told you before, I find your intelligence refreshing."

He took her hand and guided her down the wide path until they stood looking out on the curve of the river.

"Have you any news of Achmed?" she asked at last, knowing that he did not or he would have told her right away.

"No. But do not lose heart. He could not have just disappeared without a trace, and there are several people looking for him."

"I try not to think that he might have come to harm."

"I do not believe anyone would want to harm Achmed," Thorn told her.

"The Turkish admiral would."

"I thought of that myself, but on checking with the harbormaster, I found that no Turkish ship has docked in Charleston."

She tried to present a brave face to him. "How is your father?"

His eyes saddened. "Not good. I am sorry that he is not well enough for you to be presented to him. I think you would like him. I know he would like you."

"I am sorry, too, Thorn. Perhaps he will improve in time."

He looked at her doubtfully. "I don't think so, Brittany. It is apparent to me that he is very ill."

She met his eyes. "I met your stepmother today."

His eyes seemed to harden, and Brittany wondered what he was thinking. "Did you?"

"Yes. When I awoke, she was standing over me. I believe I was a shock to her."

"Undoubtedly," Thorn replied dully. His hand seemed to tighten on hers. He quickly changed the subject. "This hasn't been much of a honeymoon for you, has it?"

She smiled impishly. "It has been a honeymoon without a bridegroom."

"I am sorry," he told her regretfully. "I promise to make it up to you." His eyes became suggestive, and she blushed and glanced back out to the river.

"Will you be staying with your father again tonight?"

"Yes. I feel a need to be with him in the event that he might awaken."

"Thorn," she said, looking up at him with innocent eyes. "I have been giving our situation a great deal of thought. Neither of us came into this marriage with glowing hopes for the future."

His lips thinned. "Did we not?"

"No. We were not motivated by any great burning love for one another."

He released her hand. "We both agreed our marriage would be for mutual convenience." He searched her eyes. "Have you changed your mind?"

"No, not at all. I am merely trying to assure you that you do not have to entertain me, and you need not feel guilty for remaining at your father's bedside. I am well aware that you have heavy responsibilities. Please do not worry about me; I can fend for myself."

He smiled and enfolded her in his arms. "I will always worry about you. I fear that if I turn my back on you for even a moment that you will have fallen into some new misfortune."

Although he could not see her face, he felt her stiffen. "Thorn, I do not look for trouble. It is just that I am finding the world outside Simijin's palace is confusing, and I never knew how protected I had been. I don't always know the right thing to do."

He raised her face and brushed a golden curl away from her cheek. "I want to see that you go on being protected. I will never allow anything to harm you."

"I feel safe with you, Thorn." She could see that he was troubled about something.

"You need not be concerned about your safety as long as you are here at Stoddard Hill." His eyes blazed. "I regret to tell you that I have to go away for a few days."

She inhaled sharply. "Where must you go?"

"I have been informed by the United States Government that I must appear before the Senate with a full report on the confrontation between myself and the Turkish ships. It seems a complaint was launched by Sultan Selim himself. He claimed that I attacked and sank his ships without provocation."

Her eyes were sad, knowing it was because of her that he now faced this dilemma. "Will there be problems?"

"Nothing I can't handle," he assured her.

"Oh, Thorn, I am so sorry. I seem to bring you nothing but trouble."

He took her hand and led her back toward the house. "That may be, but at least I have never known a dull moment since you came into my life."

She looked down at her satin-clad feet, hurrying her pace to keep even with him. "Perhaps I can go to Washington with you to explain what happened. It was my fault that you were fired upon and had to retaliate."

He arched his brow at her. "No. You will stay here until I return."

She nodded. He knew best. "When will you leave, Thorn?"

"Tomorrow. It's just that I don't want to leave my father at this time." He shrugged. "I'm certain I can clear everything up."

She looked into his eyes. "You are just saying that to make

me feel better. I know the charges against you are serious. If only Simijin were here, he could help you."

"Put all tiresome thoughts out of your mind for now. It will do no good to worry."

Surely he must know that she was worried about him; she was worried about Achmed; she feared for his father, and she was concerned that the Turkish ship might eventually follow her to Charleston. Not worry—how could she not?

Chapter Twenty-six

Brittany was not certain what had awakened her. She sat up in bed, her eyes searching the darkened corners. Her heart pounded in fear, for she could feel another presence in the room with her.

Her fear turned to excitement when she heard Thorn's muttered oath as he bumped into a chair.

"Thorn, shall I light a lamp?" she asked, swinging her legs off the bed.

"No. I merely came for a change of clothing. I'm sorry I woke you." He stood near her now. "It's almost dawn—go back to sleep, Brittany."

"Your father?" she asked fearfully. "Is he worse?"

"No. Unfortunately there has been no change."

She reached her hand out to him. "Can you not come to bed? You must be exhausted."

He was silent for a moment. "Is that an invitation, Brittany?"

"No, I . . . it's just that you have had so many worries on your shoulders." Her voice was filled with sympathy. "I know how to soothe you and make you relax."

He dropped down beside her, intrigued by her offer. He could smell the sweet scent of her perfume, and he felt anything but relaxed. "How can I turn down such a charming proposition?" he said, stretching out across the bed. "I am now at your mercy, Mrs. Stoddard."

The room was dark, the night was silent, and Brittany could hear only the sound of Thorn's breathing. "You must remove your shirt," she informed him. "The massage will be much more effective if you do."

The bed sagged as he sat up and did as she requested. When he lay down again, she knelt beside him, her fingers kneading the corded muscles on his back and shoulders.

"Ahh, that feels wonderful. Where did you learn this?"

"There was once a Chinese woman in the harem, and she taught me this ancient art."

"Hmm, one of your many talents. Every man should have a wife who was trained in a harem."

"You must think of something pleasant," she instructed.

Thorn was weary, and Brittany's nimble touch was so light and soothing that the tension gradually left his body. "You have magic hands," he said, sinking even further into the soft mattress and allowing the tranquil feelings to take over his mind.

"Are you thinking pleasant thoughts?"

"Um hum. I was thinking about a certain dark haired enchantress who danced for me one night. She tortured me, and then surrendered to me."

Brittany drew in her breath, trying to concentrate on what she was doing, but she was becoming too aware of the muscled body that rested beneath her ministering fingers.

"I am quite certain you were shocked when you found out I was not a native at all, weren't you?"

He turned over and faced her, carrying her hand to his lips. "How could I know that there was a golden angel disguised as an enchantress." He laced his fingers through her hair and yanked her forward until she lay across his chest. "I want you," he whispered, his lips trailing down her cheek. "I have thought of little else but you for days. I have been tortured by the thought that you are my wife and I could not touch you."

"I have thought of you also," she admitted as thrills of delight moved through her veins.

He nipped at her ear. "Have you?"

"Yes."

"Do you mean I was torturing myself for no reason? If I had come to you, would you have taken me into your bed?"

Her hand trailed up his arm, and she lightly touched his dark hair. "I am your wife."

He pulled back. "There are things in my life that need to be resolved, Brittany. Things that make it impossible for me to have a life with you until they are settled."

"I do not understand."

He let out a long breath. "Some day I will tell you everything. But for now," his hand trailed down her neck, and he pushed her gown aside, circling one rose-crested breast and then the other, "for now, I want to bury myself in you, and forget that another world exists outside this room."

By now the first streaks of sunrise painted the room with a soft glow. Brittany looked into eyes that were like liquid blue fire. "I will give you whatever it takes to help forget your sorrow," she said, taking his hand and placing it on her breast. "Anything."

His cupped her breast, feeling the essence of her flowing through his body. She was as important to him as the air he breathed. He needed her goodness to survive in a world filled with deceptions and untruths.

With practiced accuracy, he raised her nightgown over her head and dropped it onto the floor. In a short time, he also disposed of his own clothing. He pulled her to him so every soft curve nestled against his hard, muscled body.

By now the room was streaked with a glow that fell across Brittany's body, and her skin took on a golden tint.

"My golden enchantress," he murmured as he nuzzled her neck. "I have waited all my life for you."

Brittany felt tears sting her eyes because of his beautiful words. She was not certain that Thorn was even aware of his admission. His hand moved over her hips, and he held her to him tightly.

She ached for him to possess her, and he must have read

desire in her eyes, because he positioned her beneath him and slowly moved forward until he rested inside her. His body trembled with emotions, and she felt the ache inside her being appeased by his swollen shaft.

Thorn's hands moved smoothly over her back, and he was pulling her even closer to him. He moved against her, slowly at first, then when they were both caught up in a turmoil of hot passion, his movements became deeper and more penetrating.

His voice was intense with emotion. "Sweet, sweet Brittany, your body was created to bring a man joy. To bring *me* joy," he corrected.

She felt a burning need building up inside her. He made her tremble with desire by his masterful knowledge of her body. Caught in his all-consuming touch, she was in a world where a whispered command brought an immediate response from her.

In a white-hot joining of their bodies, she arched her back as he reached to the very depths of her being. Frantically, she turned her head, while a groan escaped her lips.

"Thorn," she called out to him. "Oh, Thorn."

He cradled her in his arms, until her body stopped trembling. "I know," he said, touching his lips to her eyelids. "I know what you are feeling, sweet Brittany."

She seemed to float beneath his gliding motions. She clutched at his shoulders, throwing her head back as he drove deeper, pulling at her emotions, asking more of her and giving more at the same time.

She was tossed about like a ship that had lost its rudder, with only Thorn to guide her safely to port as he had with the *Victorious*. She was aware of his every touch, his every movement. She could hear his ragged breathing, and she was aware that he called her name over and over.

Like liquid fire, his body erupted inside her, and her body gave an answering capitulation.

His body relaxed and he rolled over, clasping her to him. "You are very good, little dancer," he told her.

She was content to close her eyes and listen to the steady beating of his heart. "I am glad I please you."

He smiled and tilted her chin up so he could look into those beautiful green eyes. "Brittany, I like the way you relaxed me."

Her smile was bright. "My aim is to please my lord and master."

He shook with laughter. "The thought of anyone being your lord and master is most unlikely. I have been at your mercy ever since we met."

She frowned, troubled by his words. "Are you saying I am—"

He placed his finger over her lips. "I am saying that I am your slave."

Now her eyes danced with humor. "I like having control over you, but I doubt that any woman would exercise power over you for long."

He kissed her lips and rolled to a sitting position. "Alas, I cannot remain to test that theory," he said regretfully. "Unfortunately, I must leave as soon as possible."

She could not mask the look of disappointment. "Must you?"

"Yes, I fear so."

She stood up and pulled on her dressing gown. "I will have a bath drawn for you." She moved to the bell pull and tugged sharply.

He came to her, his arms sliding around her waist. "It has been a long time since I have had anyone look after me. I may grow to like it."

She tossed her head, her hair swirling around like shimmering gold. "I have told you that I have been trained to please a man."

He laid his cheek against hers. "You have been trained to please *this* man," he corrected.

"Yes, only you." She threw her arms around him, aching inside at the thought of his leaving. "Come back as quickly as you can."

His eyes held a serious expression as he looked down at her. "I have a lot to come home to, Brittany. I never have before."

There was a knock on the door, and Brittany moved away to admit Livia. "Have a bath prepared for Captain Stoddard," she said with the authority of one born to give orders, but her smile softened her words. "See that the water is hot and that there is plenty of it."

When Livia had gone, Brittany turned to Thorn and found him staring at her with a strange expression on his face.

"Have I displeased you in any way?" she asked.

"No, to the contrary. I was just wondering how you will take to being mistress of Stoddard Hill."

"Do not say it!" she cautioned, rushing toward him and clamping her hand over his mouth. "Do not wish anything ill on your father."

He was puzzled, and then his laughter rang out. "So you are also superstitious?"

She looked uncomfortable, as if she did not want to be accused of believing in wives' tales. "No, but as Simijin always cautions, it does no harm to be cautious just on the chance that superstitions have some basis of truth."

"You are the delight of my heart," he said, gathering her close once more and wishing he did not have to leave her. His eyes fell on the rumpled bed, and the idea of taking her to bed again was tempting indeed.

The decision was taken from his hands when Livia entered, flanked by three young boys carrying a tub and buckets of hot water. In no time at all, Thorn was submerged in the tub while Brittany folded his clothes and packed them in a satchel.

Thorn lathered his chest while watching Brittany. She seemed to know just what he would need. "You have proven most useful to me. I believe you could take the place of a valet."

She neatly folded a white shirt. "You do not have a valet."

"Come here," he said, curling his finger. "I want to see if you are good at scrubbing my back."

Obediently, she came to him. But when she would have reached for the soap, he gave her a tug and she fell into the tub with him. She sputtered and wiped the soap from her eyes while he shook with laughter.

"Now you have me wet," she said, trying to get out of the tub.

His unhooked her dressing gown and pushed it over her hips. "So I have. I'll just remove this wet garment." He tossed it on the floor and pulled her on top of him. "Now isn't that much better?"

She was incapable of answering him because his hands were moving over her hips and his mouth closed over hers. Her body became soft and pliable under his manipulation. Raising her up, he brought her down and slipped inside her.

He groaned with pleasure as she sat up, driving him deeper into her.

"You do please me, little enchantress." His breath came out in a short gasp. "I like having you nearby. I never thought I would say that about any woman. What would I do without you?"

"Nothing I have been taught has prepared me for you," she said, laying her head against his chest and listening to the thumping of his heart.

His eyes glazed with desire as she demonstrated just how well she had been trained. Her hands slid over his soapy body, and her lips parted beneath his. "Oh, yes, you have been well trained," he breathed. "I will have to be careful or you will steal my heart."

Brittany rode across the meadow toward the stable, the wind whipping at her hair and the sun warm on her face. For the first time in days, she felt almost lighthearted; she was a good horsewoman, and she loved to ride.

She had been restless with so much idle time on her hands,

and it was pleasant to get away from the house, where the very air she breathed was oppressive.

Brittany waited daily for some word from her mother, and she waited to hear from Cappy, knowing he was continuing the search for Achmed. She had begun to despair of ever finding her dear friend. She also waited for some word from her absent husband—but none came.

Brittany dismounted at the mounting block, and a stable-hand led the horse away. With hesitant steps, she made her way toward the house, dreading the thought of encountering Thorn's stepmother. Fortunately, she managed to evade the woman most of the time because Wilhelmina was a late sleeper and took most of her meals in her room.

Brittany was halfway up the stairs when Wilhelmina's voice stopped her. "Brittany, will you come into the morning room? I would like to talk to you."

Reluctantly, Brittany came back down the stairs. She did not trust the woman's motives, and she did not want to talk to her. "I have but a moment," Brittany informed her, stripping off her gloves and clutching them in her hand.

Wilhelmina walked around Brittany, looking at her red riding habit. "Your gown is well tailored but somewhat antiquated. Wherever did you come by such a creation?"

Brittany sat down on the edge of the sofa. "Thorn had told Matty that I might find useful clothing in his mother's trunks in the attic. These were his mother's gown and gloves." She pulled up her skirt to display the knee-high riding boots. "Is it not amazing that Thorn's mother and I appear to be the same size?"

Wilhelmina bristled, her anger visible in her sparkling eyes. "I was just wondering how you spend your days. I hardly see you."

"I ride, and walk by the river. I have no particular routine."

"I am told by the servants that you have a peculiar habit of bathing each day, Brittany. Can that be true?"

"Is it a peculiar habit? Where I come from, one is expected to bathe daily."

Wilhelmina shook her head. "Needless to say, the people of your family must not live to a ripe old age. Too much bathing is not good for one." Her smile was cruel. "Have a care, or you may succumb to some malady."

Brittany had an uneasy feeling because Wilhelmina kept staring at her. "I have always been healthy. If you have nothing more to say to me, I shall go to my room," Brittany said, coming to her feet.

"Not just yet. I would like to ask you a few questions." Wilhelmina made an attempt at a smile. "I know so little about you, and, after all, you are my stepson's wife."

Brittany sat down again, although she was impatient to leave. "What would you like to know?"

"I understand you were born in Turkey."

"Yes, I was."

"But your father was an American. I believe he was from the eminent Sinclair family of Philadelphia."

"That is right," Brittany answered woodenly. "You are well informed. I cannot think how you would know so much about me."

Wilhelmina's expression became harsh. "I have my sources. I believe you know that Thorn and I . . ." She shrugged. "I am certain you are not interested in how Thorn and I feel about each other." She sat down beside Brittany. "I have heard that you lost a slave and are most anxious to get him back."

Brittany tried not to show her distress at Wilhelmina's innuendo about Thorn and herself. "Achmed is not a slave—he is my friend."

"Another oddity," Wilhelmina muttered. "I assume there has been no word of your . . . friend?"

Brittany nodded. "No, none."

"Pity. You seem to suffer from this Achmed's absence. If you have no objections, I will enlist Dr. Cross's help in finding your man. The doctor visits most of the plantations in the county, and I will tell him to keep a look out for Achmed. Can you describe him for me?"

Brittany's eyes rounded with hope. She could not believe that Wilhelmina would want to help her find Achmed. She was thoughtful as she decided how to describe him. "He is very tall and strong, and very black. He is intelligent, can read and write, and speaks several languages."

Wilhelmina stared into Brittany's eyes. "I will tell the doctor to look for just such a man. With Achmed's special aptitudes, he should be easy to locate."

Brittany came to her feet. "You are most kind."

Wilhelmina seemed to forget that Brittany was there. She stood up and moved to the window. "I would not be at all surprised if Dr. Cross were to find your man."

Chapter Twenty-seven

After lying awake for most of the night, Brittany finally fell asleep near morning. Her sleep was restless, and when she awoke there was no morning sunlight to greet her, for the room was gloomy and dark.

Slipping off the bed, she padded across the floor to the window and looked out on the storm clouds that now shrouded the sun. The dark, ominous clouds appeared to roll and boil violently. Her brow knotted with concern. The storm was coming from the direction of Charleston.

It was so dark that she was forced to light a lamp so she could dress. She quickly fastened her gown and left the room. She had wanted to ride today, but that would not be possible with the approaching storm. The air was heavy, and a feeling of foreboding that she tried to shake off enveloped Brittany.

George Cross trailed his hand across Wilhelmina's breasts and down her stomach. "If this plan works, you will be one step closer to your heart's desire."

She curled up in his arms, soft and yielding, bestowing her favors on him because she needed his help. "Yes, when Thorn's wife is dead, I will not be concerned about her having his child." Her voice was laced with spite. "I detest that girl with her superior manners."

"She is beautiful. It is a shame to end her life," he said regretfully.

Wilhelmina twisted her head and looked at him. "More beautiful than I?"

He shook his head. "No one can compare with you."

"When we are rid of the girl, there will only be the old man and Thorn to contend with."

"Yes, only Thorn and Ben."

George fumbled with her heavy breast. He bent forward and sucked on the nipple, and she closed her eyes, hating the feel of his mouth.

Her hand trailed down his back. "Are you certain the man you engaged will know what to do?"

"Yes. I have given him careful instructions."

George pushed Wilhelmina over and mounted her while she forced a smile. When he drove into her body, she wanted to scream out at the unwanted invasion, but she could not. She had to pretend that she enjoyed his clumsy lovemaking. He slid in and out of her, his breath coming out in short pants. His hands moved over her breasts, and his wet mouth closed over hers, making her feel nauseated. Waves of revulsion churned in her stomach until she thought she would scream.

She tried to imagine that it was Thorn who was in command of her body. She pretended it was his hands that caressed and teased her breasts—his lips kissing her into a heated surrender. Her breath was trapped in her throat, and she heard George grunt with a shuddering release. The fantasy could not last. George was a poor substitute for Thorn.

When George attempted to pull her into his arms, she pushed him away. "Can you trust this man not to talk after Brittany meets her . . . untimely death?"

"Yes. He is loyal to me."

She got out of bed and moved to the window. Arching her body, she looked out the window as rain peppered against it. "George, this storm could work in our favor. If Brittany puts up a struggle, the rain will wash away the evidence."

It was after lunch, and Brittany was resting in her room when the knock came on the door and Livia entered.

"Dr. Cross wants to see you, Miz Brittany," she said. "He's in the morning room with the mistress."

Brittany quickly moved off the bed, fearing the doctor had grave news about Thorn's father. She rushed downstairs and into the morning room, where she found Dr. Cross and Wilhelmina waiting for her.

Wilhelmina came across the room to her, smiling all the while. "You will never believe it," the woman gushed. "I told you the doctor could help you."

Brittany looked puzzled for a moment. "This is not about Thorn's father?"

Dr. Cross come forward. "I fear your father-in-law's condition has not changed. My reason for asking to see you is about another matter entirely. I have found your Achmed!"

Brittany could hardly believe it. To see her friend again would be wonderful. Suddenly her eyes darkened. "Is he well? Has he suffered?"

"I believe that he is now in perfect health. When he went into town for you, I am told he became ill. A kindly woman and her husband took him in to nurse him back to health. He did not know how to contact you since you had left Stonehouse."

"When can I see him?"

The doctor glanced at Wilhelmina. "Well, the weather is bad today. It's too muddy to take a carriage."

"I can ride," Brittany said excitedly. "I have to see Achmed for myself and know that he is well."

"Well," he said, pretending doubtfulness. "I have my man at the stables and he knows the way." He shook his head. "No, it is unthinkable in this weather."

Wilhelmina shook her head. "It is much too foul a day to be about. But if you do not go today, perhaps the roads will flood and you will be unable to go for days. That happens sometimes when the rain is heavy like it is now."

"I am going to see Achmed today," Brittany said with conviction. "I would appreciate it if your man would show me the way, but if he does not, Cappy will be here later in the day and he will accompany me."

Wilhelmina's face drained of color at the mention of the first mate. "I forgot about him," she said, knowing that Cappy could ruin her plans. She looked at George Cross with a pretense of pleading. "Can you please convince your man to take Brittany into Charleston?"

George pretended to capitulate. "I suppose it will do no harm. Yes, I will have him lead you."

Already Brittany was racing out of the room. "It will take but a moment for me to change into my riding habit."

Wilhelmina's face was etched with a satisfied smile. "Run, little bird," she said maliciously so only George Cross could hear. "Run to meet your death!"

Brittany glanced at the doctor when he introduced her to Mr. Deavers, who would be leading her to Achmed. She then turned her attention to Wilhelmina. "If Cappy should come, tell him I will return as quickly as possible. If I find that Achmed is too ill to be moved, I may remain in Charleston."

"Are you sure you want to go in this weather?" George Cross asked. "It will probably rain again."

Brittany adjusted her hat at an angle so the rain would not settle on the brim. "Yes, I am going."

Wilhelmina stood beneath the protection of the porch, a half-smile on her lips. "Deavers, take care of your charge. See that she comes to no harm."

A secret look passed between Deavers and the mistress of Stoddard Hill. "I will see to her," he said with assurance. "You can depend on me."

When Brittany would have ridden away, Deavers reached out and grabbed her reins, forestalling her. "Know this from the beginning—you will do exactly what I say at all times, is that understood? Or else I won't go with you."

She was startled by his forwardness. "I will do as you say, if it is in Achmed's best interest," she concurred, not liking the man's high-handed attitude. "Can we go now?"

"Just so you remember that I am in charge."

Brittany jerked her reins free and moved ahead of the man. She did not like him in the least, but she could endure him because he was taking her to Achmed.

As they rode away from Stoddard Hill, the storm clouds seemed to darken, and it began to rain once more. Brittany, unmindful of the discomfort, set her chin. It might be raining, but it was a glorious day. Achmed had been found!

They had been riding but a short time when the rain grew heavier, and still Brittany rode on, her great horse splashing through the puddles of water that stood in the roadway. She knew Mr. Deavers was beside her, but she refused to look in his direction.

It was late afternoon when Mr. Deavers motioned for Brittany to halt her horse. "You are pushing your horse much too hard, Mrs. Stoddard," he shouted, shifting his gaze away from her. "We must not tire the poor beasts, who have to labor twice as hard in the mud."

She whirled her horse away from him, resenting his attitude more than ever. When he caught up with her, she shouted to him. "I do not need instructions from you on how to care for a horse. I was taught by a man called Simijin, and he was a master with horses. This horse is not even winded."

He regarded her with a cold stare. "Slow your pace or I'll turn back."

She did not know why Mr. Deavers was behaving so rudely. Her horse was still fresh. "I intend to push on. Since we have to go all the way into Charleston, we should hurry. If that is not satisfactory with you, then tell me where I can find Achmed, and I will go without you."

A surly expression hardened the man's features, and suddenly Brittany felt uneasy. "Ride on, Mrs. Stoddard." His voice was almost like a warning. "Surely you have noticed that the roadway is becoming flooded."

The rain was coming down in heavy torrents, and Brittany's hair hung lankly down her face. She was drenched and miserable, but still she pushed forward. Her burning desire was to find Achmed, and she also intended to show this man that he had no control over her.

Mr. Deavers glanced ahead for a satisfactory place to stop. He had been promised a great deal of money if he made certain that this girl did not return to Stoddard Hill. He was not a particularly sentimental man, and he had no aversion to seeing that she met with a fatal accident.

Just ahead, he saw a place where the roadway had washed away. If he could hurl her off the road there, it would look like an accident. He drew even with her, and, reaching out, jerked the reins from her hands and pulled her horse to a halt.

"We had best slow down now, ma'am."

She bit her lip in vexation, knowing he was being unreasonable. "I will not stop here. Why are you doing this?"

There were dark forces at work within the mind of Mr. Deavers, and his eyes burned into hers. "I believe we should get off and walk here, ma'am."

"How much farther is it to our destination?"

"In this rain, an hour, maybe less."

Here the land was flat, but there was a green valley just ahead. "I do not mind the rain. Let us ride past the valley. After we are there, I will do whatever you think is best. If you insist on walking the horses then, I will agree."

He saw that she was not going to comply with his plan. It would make it harder, but the end would be the same—she would still be dead. He was almost glad to end this one's life. She had superior airs, she was stubborn and proud—but he would show her that he was superior, in the end.

"Very well, Mrs. Stoddard. We will ride on past the valley."

Brittany urged her horse forward, but soon had to pull him up short when she saw that a whole section of the roadway had been washed away by gushing floodwaters. She was faced with a sheer drop on either side of the road, and the middle had become like a raging river.

Mr. Deavers appeared to be having trouble maneuvering his horse up the slope. With a gleam of determination in her eyes, Brittany resolved to go forward, with or without him. She was mounted on a stalwart gelding, and she was certain that with its powerful legs, the animal could clear the swift current.

Without pausing to weigh the consequences, she prodded her mount forward. The gelding did not hesitate. Like a bird taking flight, he leaped the distance between the cliffs, landing safely on the other side.

Brittany's heart was beating with excitement as she looked back at Mr. Deavers, who stared at her in anger. She shrugged her shoulders and smiled. "It is but a short jump," she taunted. "Surely you are not going to allow a little danger to stop you."

The man's eyes held a chill as he glanced across at her. With a quick kick to his horse's flanks, he, too, sailed over the newly formed ravine to land safely on the other side.

His lips curled in a snarl. "Surely you did not think my horsemanship would be inferior to yours, Mrs. Stoddard?"

Her head went up and her shoulders back, for he was making her feel like an impulsive child. "Shall we ride on?" she asked coldly.

"No, now we stop."

She dismounted and looked back across the wide gap. Her brow knitted with a perplexed expression. Up ahead, she saw where the roadway had disappeared, completely covered by the raging flood.

"We cannot go on," she said with a heavy heart. "We shall have to turn back."

Mr. Deavers dismounted and moved closer to Brittany. "Yes, it's swift." His eyes gleamed. "Anyone caught in the current would be swept all the way to the river and would surely drown."

With a suddenness that startled her, he reached out and grabbed her arm. "Hold on there, Mrs. Stoddard. You are a mite too close to the edge."

Fear ate at her mind. "Let me go," she stated in anger, jerking her arm out of his grip. "I resent your manner. I want to go back now."

He smiled, showing a row of blackened teeth. "I would be less than responsible if I allowed you to rush headlong into danger."

Her eyes sparkled with anger. "I do not need you to accompany me any farther. I can find my way back to Stoddard Hill on my own."

His eyes narrowed. "Perhaps I have overestimated the danger. Why don't you cross here?" He advanced toward her, and she backed away from him.

Brittany reached for her horse's reins with the intention of mounting when she felt the man's hand on her back. She spun away from him, and her sudden movement spooked her horse, causing it to bump against her. She cried out as she felt the ground give way beneath her and she fell forward.

Caught in the current, Brittany was being swept along by the floodwaters.

In desperation, she looked back at Mr. Deavers for assistance, but she saw that he made no effort to save her. Instead there was a satisfied smile on his lips.

She made a desperate attempt to save herself by grabbing on to a protruding tree root. Her hand slipped, and she went plummeting over a cliff.

It seemed as though Brittany was suspended in the air for an eternity. She closed her eyes, not wanting to see her death. When she hit the water, she felt stunned from the force of the fall.

She plunged deeper and deeper into the swirling waters, and her lungs felt as though they would burst from want of air. She fought and struggled to reach upward so she could breathe, but her boots and heavy clothing were dragging her down. She was caught in the current and it pushed her forward.

It flashed through her mind that she would never see Thorn again, and with that thought came a heavy feeling of loss. She had lived with danger for so long now that she found she had little dread of death, only a strong sense of sadness that her passing would cause grief for those she loved.

All the struggle went out of her, and she went limp. With her acceptance of death came a feeling of passiveness, as if she were floating on a lethargic sea of well-being.

Deavers watched Brittany go under with a smile on his face. Hearing a rider in the distance, he quickly mounted his horse. His laughter ran out as he took to the woods. It was raining so hard that his tracks would be washed away, leaving no evidence of his part in the woman's death.

Already Deavers was counting on his reward for a task completed.

Cappy's horse thundered through the rain. He had been on his way to Stoddard Hill when he saw Brittany and a stranger riding in the opposite direction. He would have been able to stop Brittany if he had not stopped alongside the road to scrape mud from his horse's hooves. Because of the heavy rain, they had not seen him, and when he had called to Brittany, his voice had been drowned out by the storm.

Cappy let his horse run full out in hopes of catching her. Thorn had asked him to keep an eye on his wife, and Cappy intended to do just that.

Suddenly, just ahead, he saw Brittany's riderless horse. Looking around, he saw no sign of Brittany or the man who had accompanied her. Dismounting, he noticed where the cliff had broken off, and he knew immediately that Brittany had fallen over the side.

Without pausing to consider the consequences, Cappy dove into the water below. He did not consider that he might drown, because if he allowed anything to happen to Brittany, the captain would probably murder him anyway, so his only concern was for her safety.

When the mud-colored water closed in around Cappy, he felt a consuming blackness and fought to reach the surface.

At last he came up for air. Dragging air into his lungs, he frantically searched for Brittany.

At last he saw her surface just ahead of him. He could tell she was unconscious because she was facedown in the water. He swam toward her with powerful strokes, only to see her sink into the murky depths before he could reach her.

Diving under the water, Cappy searched for her without success. In desperation, he dove lower, the muddy water shrouding his vision. He held his breath until he thought his lungs would burst from want of air. Lower he dove, feeling around for Brittany.

Just when he thought he could not hold his breath for a moment longer, he found her! Pulling her into his arms, he kicked his feet and floated upward.

At last Cappy broke through the surface and filled his lungs with precious air. The current had swept them a long way downstream, and he could not see his horse.

With his last bit of strength, he swam toward the bank where he stumbled ashore, the unconscious Brittany in his arms.

He put her limp body down and stared at her in disbelief. His heart was heavy with dread. How still she was. He raised her hand and it was limp. Deep despair settled on his shoulders as he realized she might be dead. Sadness tore at his heart, because the captain loved this woman.

Cappy quickly dropped down beside Brittany and turned her onto her stomach. He then began pressing against the small of her back with heavy pressure. This process was repeated several times, and when she did not respond, he pressed harder.

At last relief washed over him when he felt her move ever so slightly.

A shout went up, and he raised her up and held her while she expelled the river water. He then cradled her in his arms while she caught her first cleansing breath.

Brittany was breathing easy, and yet her eyes were still

closed. Cappy realized that she was just too exhausted to open them.

Seeing a road in the distance, he gently lifted her in his arms and carried her in that direction. Surely someone would come along to give them a ride back to Stoddard Hill so he could get her out of this rain.

Cappy wasn't certain what had happened to Brittany or how she had ended up in the river. It was apparent that her companion had either drowned or had left without rendering aid to her.

With Brittany in his arms, Cappy sat down beside the road and waited, feeling grateful that the rain had stopped.

At last he felt Brittany stir, and her eyes fluttered open. He knew she was going to recover.

Brittany smiled weakly at Cappy. He had pulled her back from the jaws of death. "You saved my life," she whispered.

"I had to," he replied. "If anything had happened to you, the captain would have blamed me." He glanced down the road thinking he heard a wagon in the distance. "Can you tell me what happened?"

She turned troubled eyes to the river. She could not accuse Mr. Deavers of trying to kill her without knowing for certain. It could have been that he was trying to save her. "I do not know, Cappy. I suppose I fell."

He nodded. "Don't fret. I'll have you back home in no time."

Chapter Twenty-eight

When Cappy carried Brittany into the house, Wilhelmina appeared shocked by what had occurred. She insisted that Brittany be put to bed at once and bestowed constant attention on her, remaining with her and seeing to Brittany's slightest need.

Brittany thought she would despair from all the attention.

"Didn't Mr. Deavers attempt to save you when you fell into the river?" Wilhelmina asked, her eyes searching.

"I cannot say for certain, since I was unconscious soon after I hit the water. It could be that he tried to help me and was drowned himself. I hope not, but I just do not know."

"Sadly, I fear that might be the case," Wilhelmina said, glad to pass off Brittany's assumption as the truth. "Mr. Deavers has not contacted the doctor, so he probably drowned. Poor man, such a tragic end."

"I still wish to find Achmed. Will the doctor know where I can find him?"

"Alas, no. Mr. Deavers never told Dr. Cross where he had located Achmed. We shall just have to keep looking."

Brittany turned her face to the wall. "I will never give up searching for him."

Brittany had been in bed for three days, but now she was feeling well and was not content to remain there any longer. She dressed, and slipped out of her room, fearing Wilhelmina would be lurking about and try to be solicitous.

Thorn had been away for so long, and there had been

no word from him. Brittany stood on the front porch and searched for some sign of him. She was not quite so lonely because Cappy was her almost constant companion, and she had come to rely on him for company.

Sometimes when Cappy was occupied elsewhere on the plantation, Brittany would wander down to the slave cabins to visit with Esmeralda.

One thing she was thankful about was now that she was out of bed, Wilhelmina no longer troubled her.

Indeed, it seemed that Thorn's stepmother was most always away from Stoddard Hill, and everyone was more content with her gone.

Each day, Brittany would pass by the bedroom of Thorn's gravely ill father. She often had an urge to go in and see him—but of course she did not.

It was a bright day with the sun high in the sky. As Brittany entered the small sun room, she sat down and gazed at the view of the river. She preferred this bright, cheerful room, with its yellow and green decorations, to the other rooms in the house. She had been told that Thorn's mother had decorated this room, and Thorn's father would allow no changes. Brittany was aware that she could always come here to avoid Wilhelmina, who avoided the sun room.

Today, she was feeling alone and abandoned. Brittany was a wife, but her husband was not with her. She was lonesome for her mother, and wished for her wise counsel.

Hearing heavy footsteps in the hall, she glanced at the door, hoping Thorn had returned. When Cappy stuck his head around the corner, she rushed to him.

Since he had saved her life, they had formed a special bond. "I am so glad you came, Cappy, I had just about given up on you today. Would you like a cup of tea?"

His eyes were troubled. "No, not just now."

She sat down on the yellow sofa and indicated that he should sit beside her. "Is something wrong, Cappy? Have you news for me?"

"Of a sort. I hate to be the bearer of ill tidings, but it looks like more trouble's coming."

She held her breath. "Of what nature? Thorn is all right, isn't he?"

"He's fine, as far as I know. This concerns the *Victorious*. I have heard through a reliable source that the Turks are planning to have her impounded as recompense for the ships they lost."

"Can they do that?"

Cappy took a deep breath. "Anything's possible. Unless we can find a buyer, and he could have the ship at sea before the Turks get their hands on her, the captain may lose her."

"Have you a buyer?"

"No. And, with the captain away, I fear he won't be back in time to save the *Victorious*."

"If the Turks can take the ship, can they also take Thorn's other properties?" she wanted to know.

"They might. Of course, I suspect Stoddard Hill still belongs to the captain's pa, so they can't touch that."

"Could they take Stonehouse?"

"Yes, ma'am, they might. Let us hope they will not find out about that property."

Brittany tapped her foot while her mind whirled. At last she looked at the first mate, her eyes shining. "Cappy, I believe I have a solution to our dilemma. Will you go along with me on this?"

His eyes held an earnest light. "I would do anything you asked of me, Mrs. Stoddard. You are my captain's lady."

"Can you authorize the sale of the *Victorious*?"

"I can't, but the captain gave his solicitor the power to sell in his absence—just on the chance that someone wanted to buy the ship before he returned."

"What about Stonehouse? Does the solicitor have the power to sell that?"

He looked puzzled. "I don't believe so. The captain would not consent to sell his mother's home. But I don't see what you—"

"Wait here, Cappy. I'll only be a moment." She nodded to the side table. "Make yourself a drink if you like, I shan't be long."

Cappy watched her disappear through the door, wondering what was on her mind. It wasn't likely that she had the funds to help the captain. He poured a fair amount of whiskey into a glass, and downed it in one gulp. He hated to see Captain Stoddard lose everything, but the situation looked grim.

A short time later, Brittany rejoined him, carrying a small chest, which she held out to Cappy. "You will take these and do whatever you must to buy the *Victorious*."

He was shocked into silence when she raised the lid to reveal the magnificent jewels, silver, and gold within the velvet-lined box.

She unclasped the large emerald from her neck and dropped it in the chest.

"Do you think this will be enough to buy the *Victorious*, Cappy?"

"I am certain that when the value of the jewels are assessed, there will be more than enough," he replied, bewildered and awed by her sacrifice. Most women would not give up their jewels so willingly. "Are you quite certain you want to do this, Mrs. Stoddard?"

"Yes. Go at once to Thorn's solicitor and tell him what I want to do. I am certain he will find a way to save Thorn's property from Sultan Selim."

"I don't think a wife can legally buy property from her husband."

Brittany's brow creased in thoughtfulness. "I had not thought of that." Her face slowly brightened. "We will not use my name, but my mother's maiden name. No one, not even Thorn, knows my mother's family name." Now her eyes were bright with excitement. "Yes, you will have the solicitor use the name Lady Jillianna Maridon."

Cappy chuckled. "So that is the name of the English Rose? Many people would give much to know that."

"You know of my mother?" she asked in surprise.

"I know nothing about her personally, but I have heard of her, as has everyone who ever sailed the Turkish waters. She is something of a legend."

"My mother is wonderful, and very beautiful, but I do not think of her as a legend."

Cappy thought the daughter also had legendary beauty, but he did not say so. "I should leave immediately, Mrs. Stoddard, if I am to reach the solicitor before he goes home for the day." He frowned, not wanting to leave her alone since the accident—if it had been an accident. "You stay close to the house, and don't go riding off with strangers."

"I won't," she readily agreed. "Next time you might not be there to rescue me."

"If anyone ever tried to harm you, I would damned sure . . ." He lowered his eyes and looked shamefaced. "Begging your pardon, ma'am—what I mean to say is I will try never to fail you."

She offered him her hand and he squeezed it lightly.

"I know you won't, Cappy. But promise me that no one, not even Thorn, will know that I am the one who purchases the *Victorious*. In any event, do not tell the solicitor, since he may feel compelled to tell Thorn."

Cappy did not like the thought of going behind Captain Stoddard's back. "But why not tell the captain, Mrs. Stoddard? Surely he would approve of your actions."

She smiled. "You know him better than anyone, Cappy. You know that Thorn is a proud man. It is my belief that he would lose everything before he would allow me to help him."

Cappy was reflective for a moment. "I suppose you are right."

"Then you will keep my secret?"

He grinned broadly, thinking the captain was a most fortunate man. "To the death, madame—to the death."

"Hurry along, Cappy," she said, feeling the urgency. "It is a long ride into town, and we want this to be done as quickly as possible."

Cappy took the chest and moved to the door. "I will do as you say," he told her as he left the room and headed toward the stables.

Brittany moved down the hallway and into the front parlor, where she went to the window and watched Cappy mount his horse. When he glanced in her direction, she waved to him and watched until he rode out of sight.

He was on his way to save the *Victorious*.

As Brittany moved toward the slave quarters, the cobblestone steps glistened from the rain that had fallen earlier in the day. The shadows were lengthening into evening, and the garden was filled with the vibrant throbbing song of the whippoorwill.

Since she had become a frequent visitor at old Esmeralda's cabin, the other slaves no longer stared at her when she came among them.

Esmeralda was rocking in a hard-back chair, and her dark eyes lit up with pleasure when she saw Brittany. "Pull yourself up that cane-bottom chair and sit a spell," she said, pointing a knobby finger at Brittany.

Brittany sat down wearily. "The rain cooled things down," she observed.

"That it did." Esmeralda leaned back and studied the swaying branches over her head. "I heard 'bout your dunking in the river the other day. It don't seem you are any the worse for it."

"How did you hear about it?"

"I have my ways." She looked into Brittany's eyes. "You'll want to be more careful, you know."

Brittany did not want to remember that awful day; it was still not clear in her mind what had happened. "Have you finished weaving your baskets for the day?"

The wise, dark eyes saw past the polite chatter. "You have more on your mind than baskets and the weather. You want to tell me what's bothering you?"

"No, not until I sort past my confusion. Instead, will you tell me about Thorn? What was he like as a boy?"

The old woman's eyes became reflective. "He was always a bright boy. Since his ma died when he wasn't much more than a babe, he was always at his pa's heels. The two of them was close . . . until that woman came."

"You do not like Wilhelmina, do you?"

"Did I say so?"

"No, but—"

"Then don't put words in my mouth."

To Brittany's surprise, Esmeralda pulled a corncob pipe out of her pocket and popped it into her mouth. Since it was unlit, she merely chewed on the stem.

"Master Thorn was always a good-looking devil. You can bet the girls hung around Stoddard Hill just wishing for a look from him. He was always one who loved the ladies." Esmeralda chuckled. "My, my, but the ladies loved him." Suddenly her eyes dulled, and she poked the pipe back in her pocket. "Young ladies weren't the only ones who cast their eyes Master Thorn's way. There was those who were bound to make trouble for him—and they did."

"Esmeralda, when I first arrived at Stoddard Hill, Wilhelmina hinted at something between herself and Thorn. I did not believe her."

A mask seemed to descend on the wrinkled face. "I don't fuel gossip by adding to it. If you want to know 'bout that, you best ask your husband."

Brittany shook her head, knowing Esmeralda would say no more. She shrugged her slight shoulders. "Everything is so confusing. I live in a world that I cannot comprehend. I have learned that there is dishonor and deceit in this world. I am beginning to think my mother did not prepare me for life. She was trusting, and she instilled that trust in me. I have since learned to be suspicious."

"Maybe your ma hoped you wouldn't have to know that good don't always win, and evil can sometimes be stronger."

Brittany's eyes widened. "What do you mean?"

"I mean that your husband is a good man, but there are forces around him that will try to pull him down. You're the only one who can help him."

Brittany's heart skipped a beat. "What forces?"

"I think you already know."

"There are those who have sailed halfway across the world to see Thorn fall. I wonder if I alone can hold them all at bay?"

Esmeralda settled back against the chair and rocked furiously. "If I was you, I'd worry more about them that was closer to home that mean him harm. And while you're about it, you might want to be careful yourself."

"I sometimes don't know friend from foe, Esmeralda."

The old woman's eyes narrowed. "Trust no one in the house except Matty and her daughter, Livia. And, of course, Master Thorn's man Cappy."

"Why are you telling me this?"

Esmeralda looked about to make certain no one was near. She then leaned closer to Brittany. "I will say no more. Just heed my warning. Don't let anyone lure you away from here with any pretense."

Thorn was seated across the table from the two men empowered by the Senate to question him. The interrogation had been going on for hours, and Thorn felt his patience slipping.

One man, a Mr. Balsome, looked at his companion, Mr. Whitting, with a grave expression. It was apparent to Thorn that neither of them believed him.

"Let's go over this again, Captain Stoddard," Mr. Balsome said wearily. "You said you were attacked by four Turkish warships and only returned their fire to protect yourself?"

"That is correct."

"Are you asking us to believe that your ship took on four Turkish ships and you came out the winner?"

"Yes, sir. That is exactly what happened."

Thorn could read disbelief in each man's eyes. "Are you also asking us to believe that you had a woman on board your ship and you were not aware of it?"

"That is correct also, Mr. Balsome. She was a stowaway at that time."

Mr. Whitting, who wore thick bifocals that made his eyes appear twice their size, leaned into the table. "Are you aware that the Turkish government has lodged serious charges against you?" He shuffled some papers in front of him. "First of all, you stand accused of kidnapping the girl whom they claim is a Turkish citizen. They demand her release at once."

"I did not kidnap her, and as I have told you over and over, she was a stowaway on my ship."

Mr. Balsome spoke up. "Tell us what you know of the woman's situation."

"The lady's name is Brittany Sinclair. Her father was an American, and her mother was British. Although she was born in Turkey, it is arguable as to whether or not she is a citizen of that country."

"Do you know the girl's whereabouts?"

"I do."

"We may call upon you to produce her since the Turkish government demands her return."

Thorn crossed his long legs and looked at each man in turn. "I am not prepared to tell you her whereabouts, and she will not be returning to Turkey under any circumstances."

"Will you defy a direct order, Captain Stoddard?" Mr. Balsome challenged.

Thorn nodded. "You're damn right I will in this case. You see, the lady in question has since become my wife, and I have no intentions of giving her up to my government or the Turkish government."

Shock registered on Mr. Balsome's face, while Mr. Whitting blustered, "This is preposterous."

"Nevertheless, the lady is my wife. I foresaw that this might happen, and wanting to keep her out of Turkish hands, I gave her the protection of my name. And I believe by law that gives her the protection of the American government."

Mr. Balsome folded his hands and suddenly smiled. "By God, to think that you took on the Turkish Navy and won! Now you've outsmarted them again. I always said our ships were worth two of those from any other nation. But to sink four ships! My boy, I am amazed."

Thorn came to his feet wearily. "Gentlemen, I believe I have answered all your questions to the best of my ability. My father is ill, and I have been away from my wife for three weeks, and I'm going home."

Mr. Whitting stared down at a paper before him. "I am not at all convinced that you will not have to produce your wife, if she is indeed your wife."

"She is. I can easily prove that—"

"Like my colleague, I, too, am impressed by your fighting ability," Mr. Whitting interjected. "However, just between the three of us, we are dealing with a madman in Selim, and as a representative of our government, I may be forced to make a gesture of reparation in the sultan's direction."

Thorn stood unbending. "I don't feel that I owe the Turkish government anything. Not the *Victorious*, and certainly not my wife."

"Nevertheless," Mr. Balsome stated, "it is my judgment that you will soon be ordered to hand over to a representative of the Turkish government your ship, the *Victorious*. We will decide later about your wife."

Thorn stared at the man in disbelief, but he said nothing.

Mr. Whitting spoke with conviction. "And may the damned ship sink before the Turks have use of it."

Chapter Twenty-nine

When Brittany entered the dining room, she was surprised to find Wilhelmina seated at the table. The older woman's eyes were spiteful and knowing; there was no sign of her earlier display of friendship toward Brittany.

"Good morning, Brittany. So, your wayward husband still has not returned. Did you pass a peaceful night, hmm?"

Brittany picked up the porcelain teapot and poured a cup of reviving liquid. "I slept very well, thank you." She moved to a chair and sat down.

"I suppose it is easy to sleep when one's husband is not in one's bed to disturb one's rest."

Brittany attempted to mask her anger. She detested this woman's common insinuations. "What a considerate hostess you are, Wilhelmina, that you should concern yourself so much with my comfort."

Wilhelmina's eyes blazed with vindictiveness. "I am told that there are men still searching for your man, Achmed."

"Yes. I have come to realize that Mr. Deavers only pretended to know where to find Achmed. I do not know his reasons for such a pretense, but I am certain Thorn will discover the truth when he gets home."

Wilhelmina suddenly paled. "I hope you are not blaming me for your mishap. Dr. Cross and I were as shocked by what happened as you were. We trusted Mr. Deavers, but he misrepresented himself."

Brittany looked directly into Wilhelmina's eyes. "I have come to the same conclusion."

"Do you really think it is necessary to tell Thorn what happened?"

"Why should I not?"

Wilhelmina leaned toward Brittany. "Thorn does not seem overly interested in your welfare. He has been away an uncommonly long time."

Brittany would not give this woman the satisfaction of knowing the barb had wounded her. "I will not tell Thorn about the incident, but I feel certain Cappy will."

Wilhelmina shoved her plate aside and studied Brittany with a practiced eye. "That man, Cappy, annoys me. Every time I turn around, he's underfoot. I want you to tell him to leave immediately."

"No," Brittany said flatly. "I would never presume to tell Thorn's first mate what to do." She smiled. "I would not advise you to, either. Thorn might not take it kindly."

Wilhelmina tried to hold on to her temper. "I have observed Thorn when he looks at you, and I am puzzled."

"About what?"

"There is no light of possession there, no warmth. Why do you suppose that is?"

"Perhaps if you spent more time worrying about your own husband and less worrying about mine, you would be far better off."

Wilhelmina tossed her napkin on the table and stood up. "I have always thought that those who soar the highest, fall the hardest. Watch out that you don't take a tumble."

Brittany stared at Thorn's stepmother, for her words had sounded very like a threat. She looked into eyes so cold that it sent shivers down her back.

"As you will recall, I already fell. But you can be assured that I will step carefully next time, Wilhelmina." Brittany took a sip of her tea. "Thank you for worrying about my welfare. I am sure Thorn will express his gratitude for your solicitude upon his return."

Wilhelmina rose to her feet. "You think you have Thorn, but you don't. You will never understand the needs of a man like him." Her eyes narrowed. "God, he must be bored with an innocent like you."

Brittany was saved from replying when Wilhelmina rushed out of the room.

Brittany's hand trembled as she raised the teacup to her lips. Never had she been subjected to such ruthless behavior. She neither knew how to react to it nor the reason for it.

She stood up and moved quickly out of the dining room, with the intention of going outside for a breath of fresh air. When Brittany moved past the parlor, she noticed the door was slightly open, and she heard the mumbled voices of Wilhelmina and Dr. Cross.

Brittany stood as if rooted to the spot when she saw them locked in an embrace. She took a quick step toward the front door, hoping she could escape before they discovered her presence.

Suddenly the parlor door was flung open, and Wilhelmina gave Brittany a haughty look.

"Are you in the habit of skulking around corners to listen to others' conversations?"

"I was just passing by on my way outside." Brittany turned to the doctor, choosing to ignore Wilhelmina's rudeness. "How is my husband's father today, Doctor?"

He cleared his throat and jammed his hands into his pocket. "I fear Mr. Stoddard has had a turn for the worse. He is very weak. I do not expect him to live through the week."

Brittany saw the look that passed between the doctor and Wilhelmina, and she wondered at the reason for it.

"Thorn should be notified at once. Can we send word to him in Washington?"

Wilhelmina's expression was hard and spiteful. "The doctor was just telling me that your husband returned during the night." Laughter rolled off her lips. "Poor little wife, your husband seems to go to great lengths to avoid you, does he not?" she taunted.

Before Brittany could answer, Thorn himself entered the room his eyes going directly to his wife. Brittany wanted to run into his arms, but she dared not, because there was no sign that she would be welcomed. She was hurt that he had not let her know he had returned, but she would not allow Wilhelmina to see that hurt.

"Thorn, thank God you have returned," Brittany exclaimed. "The doctor has just told me that your father is worse."

There was a look of desperation in Thorn's eyes as he faced the doctor. "Is there nothing you can do to make my father more comfortable? He is in a great deal of pain."

"I have given him all the medication I dare. I regret to tell you that your father's situation is desperate. There is nothing more I can do for him."

Thorn's expression hardened. "Are you telling me there is no hope?"

"I would be less than compassionate if I allowed you to hope needlessly."

Brittany wanted to rush to Thorn and give him what small comfort she could. But instead, she stood with her hands clasped together, wishing he would at least acknowledge her presence.

Without another word, Thorn moved out of the room, and Brittany rushed after him. Her heart was breaking for him, and she wanted to be with him at this dark time in his life.

Quietly, she followed him up the stairs. When they came to his father's bedroom, he opened the door and nodded for her to enter. When she lingered near the door, he motioned for her to join him at his father's bedside. Slowly she moved forward, dreading the thought of watching Thorn's father suffer.

The odor of medicine hung heavy in the air. The man on the bed was pale and listless, and she saw nothing about him that looked like Thorn.

Benjamin groaned and tossed his head back and forth, flinging his arms wide, while his eyes glazed in pain.

Thorn caught his father's wrists and talked to him soothingly. "You will feel better if you don't fight, Father."

"Margaret," Benjamin murmured. "Margaret . . . the pain . . ."

Brittany stepped to the water basin and wet a cloth, which she applied to the old man's head. "Who is Margaret?" she whispered to Thorn.

"My mother."

She touched Benjamin's head and found it clammy. She could see that he was in agony, and his condition reminded her of one of the women in the harem who had eaten some tainted food and had almost died from the poisoning.

Always quick to make a decision, she caught Thorn's arm and motioned him to the corner of the room, noticing that he looked haggard and needed a rest. "Thorn, I know you are going to think I have completely lost my senses, but would you turn your father's care over to me?"

"It's useless, Brittany. I can see that the doctor was right. He cannot live, and it would not be fair to make you share his agony."

"I want to try something. I promise you I will make you father as comfortable as possible and not allow him to suffer unduly. I can do it, Thorn," she insisted. "I know I can."

He drew in a deep breath, knowing Brittany could do nothing, because the doctor had said there was no hope. "Yes, try anything you wish, but I fear nothing will help."

"Leave me now, but send Esmeralda to me. Have the servants bring in a tub of water." She rolled up her sleeves and moved to the window, giving a tug on the heavy velvet curtains that sent them crashing to the floor in a stream of dust. She then flung the window wide to let fresh air into the room.

Brittany turned back to find Thorn watching her. "Hurry. Send Esmeralda to me."

"Is that old woman still alive?"

"More alive than most people I know. Hurry, Thorn!" She moved to his father's side. "Do not allow anyone but Esmeralda into this room."

An uneasy silence had settled over the house. It was as if everyone were holding their breath, waiting to hear that the master of Stoddard Hill had died. Servants went about their tasks talking in whispers.

Thorn had been banished from his father's room by Esmeralda, who claimed he was just in her way. He had not seen either the doctor or his stepmother since he had told them to stay away from his father. When the doctor protested, Thorn had reminded him that he had said he could do nothing more for his father.

Brittany watched Esmeralda mix a powdered substance with water until it became a white paste. "You hold his head while I spoon the theriac down his throat."

Benjamin meekly took the liquid into his mouth because he was too weak to protest. Brittany felt pity for him as Esmeralda spooned more of the horrid-smelling liquid into his mouth. His skin was as white as the pillow he lay upon, and he looked more dead than alive.

"Now what?" Brittany asked.

"We will wait a bit. He will become ill, and vomit. If there is poison in him, I hope he will get it all up."

Brittany watched Ben's face for any reaction, but he lay still and lifeless. Then he began to stir and moan. In a short time, Benjamin became violently ill and begin to retch. Esmeralda held a pan for him while Brittany held a damp cloth to his forehead.

"Leave me alone," he mumbled. "Let me die in peace, old woman."

"If I leave you alone, you *will* die, Master Benjamin. We have to get the poison out of your system."

Brittany met the old woman's eyes. "I was right then; he ate something that made him ill?"

Esmeralda's eyes became black slits. "Yes, he ate something that set ill with him. Come, let's dose him up again. We got to get it all out of him."

For over two hours, Brittany and Esmeralda worked over Thorn's father. At last he lay quietly, and it seemed his pain had eased. Brittany had changed the bedding while Esmeralda dressed him in a clean nightshirt. Now Brittany stood beside him, wiping his face with a cool cloth.

Ben licked his lips and glanced at her. "When I look at you, I think I am in heaven, but when I see Esmeralda, I know it must be hell." He turned his eyes to the slave. "You and me aren't going to heaven are we, old woman?"

Crackling laughter came from her lips. "That's right, Master Ben. You and me's too ornery to go to the good place, and most likely they won't have room for us in the other place. I always thought I'd get there first and then have the place made ready for you, but now I ain't so sure."

He smiled slightly. "If I'm not in heaven, then who is this beautiful angel?"

"Why, Master Ben, don't you know your own son's wife?"

Ben's eyes widened, and he raised a weak hand. "I always knew that boy had a head on his shoulders." His eyelids fluttered. "I'm going to sleep now. There's no more pain."

Brittany picked up a fan and circulated the air around him so he would sleep more peacefully. "Thank you, Esmeralda. He would have died if not for you," she whispered.

"Yes, he would have—and he still might. It would be wise if you saw to his food from now on."

Brittany's mouth rounded in shock. "Do you mean that you think . . . that someone . . . No, that is not possible."

"I know when someone's been poisoned, be it by good means, or foul. I'll say it again—the master needs looking after by those you can trust."

Brittany nodded. "I see that now."

"I'm too old for such goings-on. I'm going home. Want me to send Master Thorn up?"

"Yes, please. And, Esmeralda, let's keep this between ourselves for the time being. If someone means Thorn's father harm, we can catch them better if they do not know they are suspect."

The old woman moved agilely to the door. "Please yourself. But make sure he don't eat nothing you haven't seen to first."

Brittany's eyes softened when they rested on her father-in-law. "I'll watch him as if he were my own father."

"If you need me, send someone for me."

Brittany smiled at the dear old woman who had been a true friend. "I will. But get some rest now."

Esmeralda padded out of the room, feeling useful for the first time in years. Master Ben had been right, the young mistress was an angel sent from heaven. It was certain she was too good for this house.

Thorn watched Esmeralda make her way toward him. She gave him a wide grin and wrung his hand. "You came back just in time. You should stay where you belong."

He smiled. "The choice was not mine. I had to go, Esmeralda."

"Go on up to your pa now."

"Is he . . . is he . . ."

"He's sleeping peaceful. Iffen God's willing, he'll be up and about in a few days."

"Are you saying that—"

"I'm saying that he's alive, Master Thorn, and if I'm any judge, he'll make it. Now, why don't you go on up and sit with that pretty wife of yours."

Thorn felt a shock wave of relief. "How is it possible that my father could improve so quickly when the doctor had given up hope?"

"How should I know? Am I a doctor?"

Thorn started toward the stairs, almost afraid to hope. He paused on the landing and looked back to Esmeralda. "You like Brittany, don't you?"

The old woman chuckled and moved to the door, her homespun gown flapping against her bony legs. "She's a keeper, Master Thorn—a real keeper. She taught this ole woman that there is still goodness in the world. Iffen you don't look to her, someone will run off with her."

Thorn took the steps at a run. When he stood before his father's door, he felt nervous and unsure.

He opened the door softly, so Brittany was unaware of his presence. He stood in the shadows, watching her for a moment. She was fanning his father, a soft and loving expression on her face.

He rubbed his hand over the dark bristle on his chin. He hadn't taken the time to shave—would she mind?

He moved to stand beside Brittany, who gave him a tremulous smile. He was lost for a moment in a pair of deep green eyes.

"Did Esmeralda tell you that your father is better?" she whispered.

"Yes, but I can hardly credit the remarkable change in him," he answered in a low voice. "His color is better, and he is breathing easier." Thorn looked around the room and found it smelled fresh and no longer like a sickroom. In fact, the whole atmosphere of the house seemed to have changed since Brittany's arrival—or was it just his imagination?

"I like your father, Thorn."

He drew her to him. "What about the son?"

Ben opened his eyes, and his voice boomed out. "What are you two whispering for? Do you think this is a sickroom? For God's sake, Thorn, if you are going to make love to the girl, take her out of here." Ben winked up at Brittany. "I don't think my old heart could take much more of this."

A blush tinged Brittany's face, and she moved away from Thorn. "I have decided I will sit with you tonight, Mr. Stoddard, since Thorn stayed with you most of last night."

"Where did you find this beauty, Son, and why didn't you tell me you had a wife? What's your name, young lady?"

"Brittany."

"Well, Brittany, I like to be called Ben by pretty girls, especially when they're young enough to be my daughter."

She smiled brightly, liking Thorn's father more by the minute. "All right, Ben."

Thorn slid his arm about Brittany's waist. "So, you like my wife."

The old man grinned weakly, tired from his ordeal. "I always gave you credit for being clever, Thorn, but if that's true, then what are you doing here? Both of you go on, I don't need a nursemaid hovering over me."

Brittany knew that until they found out if someone had tried to poison Ben, he could not be left alone. "You must not fret, Ben. I am going to stay with you," she insisted.

Ben saw the determined light in her eyes, and was too weak to argue with her. "Can you read?"

Thorn laughed. "In what language would you like her to read to you, Father? She knows eleven of them."

Ben looked disbelieving. "Can't no man read in eleven languages. That's quite a feat for a tiny slip of a girl." He glanced at his son. "Bet she has you running to keep pace with her."

Thorn glanced at the ceiling in a gesture of helplessness. "You cannot imagine." He took Brittany's hand. "You don't mind if I tell my wife good night?"

The old man waved them away. "Don't keep her too long. I want her back."

Thorn pulled Brittany to the door, and she looked up at him coyly and asked, "Did everything go well for you in Washington, Thorn?"

He had decided not to worry her with details. "About like you would expect."

"That is no answer."

"It is not worthy of your concern, but I have news of Achmed."

Her eyes shone with hope. "You have found him?"

"Not yet, but one of the men I hired to look for him reports that Achmed has been seen. It seems a slaver came upon him the day he went into Charleston, and finding him without papers, took him to the auction. But not, I might add, before Achmed sent a dozen men clamoring for a doctor to tend their cuts and bruises."

"Is he all right?"

"That we don't know. But we *do* know that he was sold to

a plantation; we just don't know which one yet. Tomorrow I'll go into Charleston and see what I can discover."

"I don't understand why anyone would take Achmed. He is not a slave."

Thorn could not control the smile on his lips. "I was told he was bought with the understanding that he would be a good breeder."

"But Achmed, cannot . . . He is a . . . eunuch."

Thorn laughed, and his blue eyes danced with humor. "You know it and I know it, Brittany. But the man who bought him didn't know it. Can you imagine how surprised he will be when he learns the truth?"

Brittany failed to see the humor of the situation. "I just hope the man doesn't punish Achmed for what he cannot do. I want Achmed back, and I want him tomorrow!"

Thorn pulled her to him, holding her so tightly the buttons on his coat pressed against her. It was glorious to be held in his arms. He bent his dark head and touched his lips against hers.

"How will I sleep without you beside me, Brittany?" he whispered.

Her face was flushed, and she melted against him. Suddenly she remembered they were not alone, and she twisted out of Thorn's arms.

"You have managed very well until now. You look weary, Thorn. Please go to your room and get some rest."

He nuzzled her ear. "I suppose I'll have to be content to dream about you."

She gave him a warning look and pushed him toward the door. "Go to bed."

"Brittany, are you going to read to me, or not?" Ben called out.

She turned to her father-in-law, while Thorn watched her move gracefully across the room. With a feeling of regret, Thorn went to his bedroom alone.

He thought of soft green eyes, and fell asleep with a smile on his face.

Chapter Thirty

The sun had just made its appearance above the pine trees when Brittany tiptoed out of her father-in-law's bedroom and walked the few paces to Thorn's room. It was a glorious day, and she hoped there would be more word on Achmed's whereabouts.

When she opened the door, disappointment crushed in on her. It was apparent that Thorn had slept in the bed because the sheets were rumpled, but the room was empty.

She hurried out into the hallway and down the stairs, hoping she would find him having breakfast. To her dismay, he was not in the dining room, either, but Wilhelmina was.

Wilhelmina's hard gaze settled on Brittany. "If you are looking for your husband, you missed him. He said he had pressing business in town." Her eyes became narrow slits, and her voice was sarcastic. "Thorn does seem to keep his distance from you, does he not? You must have lost your confidence, since your husband seems to prefer to be where you aren't."

Brittany moved toward the door, unwilling to match wits with Wilhelmina today, but the honey-sweet voice stopped her.

"So, you and Esmeralda are feeling proud of yourselves this morning. Perhaps you should hang out a shingle and practice medicine."

Brittany turned back to Thorn's stepmother. "I cannot take any credit for helping your husband, madame. Esmeralda was the one who discovered what his trouble was. She has exceptional knowledge of herbs and potions. I would think you would be glad that he is improved."

Wilhelmina's eyes were stabbing. "And what *was* my husband's trouble?"

Brittany watched Wilhelmina's face. "As I am not a doctor, I cannot say. Esmeralda believes he ate something that disagreed with him. It does not appear it was his heart at all. I am certain that if you were to visit with Ben, he would tell you how much better he feels."

Wilhelmina shoved her plate aside and came to her feet. "You would do well to remember not to meddle in other people's affairs."

Wilhelmina sailed out of the room, leaving Brittany to ponder her actions. Wilhelmina did not even try to hide the fact that she cared nothing about her husband's recovery.

Esmeralda was right. Strange things were happening in this house. Brittany intended to look after Ben and see that his health continued to improve.

Brittany had lunch in Ben's room so she could cajole him into eating the food Matty had prepared for him. Afterward, she read him a few pages from a farm journal until he fell asleep.

She closed the book and laid it aside. She then tiptoed out of the room, whispering to Livia, "Stay with him, and do not leave him until Esmeralda comes to relieve you for dinner."

The girl nodded and took up her vigil beside her old master.

Brittany had discovered the little cottage some time ago, but she had never gone inside, since the door was always locked. Today, however, the door stood open because one of the servants was cleaning it. Brittany stepped inside, immediately aware of the peace and serenity that surrounded the cottage.

The servant had dusted and scrubbed and waxed the three rooms until they sparkled and smelled of beeswax.

Approaching the bed, Brittany sank down into the soft

mattress and felt the breeze from the open window cool her cheeks. She imagined the faceless Stoddard women who must have come here before her. She tried to imagine herself and Thorn here, but then she sighed and turned to glance out the window.

A shadow fell across Brittany's face, and she turned to see Thorn standing over her.

"I did not hear you come in," she said, sitting up. "I hope you do not mind that I am here."

He sat down beside her, although he kept his distance. "Why should I mind?"

"Did you find out about Achmed?" she asked hopefully.

Thorn nodded. "Yes, I have located him." He smiled at her. "How would you like to take a carriage ride tomorrow and bring him home?"

Before Brittany had time to consider her actions, she threw herself into Thorn's arms and hugged him. "You are truly wonderful. I can never thank you enough for your persistent search for Achmed. You are the kindest man I know."

He glanced down at her, feeling her nearness in the depths of his heart. "Have a care, little dancer, it might be that I did this just to get you in my arms."

She drew back, embarrassed by her actions. "I am sorry. I was carried away with gratitude."

Instilled in Thorn was the strength and dignity of the Stoddard men who had come before him. Hot blood ran in his veins, and he wanted to dominate this woman who belonged to him. "What if I came to claim you as my wife, Brittany?"

She looked at him with uncertainty, then dropped her eyes to his brooding lips and a ripple of pleasure washed over her. "But I *am* your wife. And . . . you have already claimed me," she reminded him.

His laughter went through her like a warming tide. "I love your honesty and your straightforwardness. Don't ever change, little dancer."

While Thorn had been talking, he was expertly unfastening her gown. He had not meant to make love to her, but when his fingers trailed across the silkiness of her slender body, he could not help himself.

He sank back on the bed, surrounded by a shimmering cloud of soft gold. In no time at all, Brittany's gown was in a heap on the floor, quickly followed by his clothing.

Outside in the garden, a bird sang sweetly, and was answered by the warble of its mate.

Brittany eagerly came into her husband's arms, stirred by the flame she saw in his eyes. His caress heated her blood, and his lips were hot against hers. She groaned as he rolled her over and clasped her to him.

The thrill she felt at his entrance into her body made her cry out. Wave after wave of sweetness engulfed her while her body answered his strong forward thrusts.

Her heart was hammering, and her breath quickening as he mastered her body.

Thorn lost all reasoning. He could not think past the pleasure he found in Brittany. His fluid movements swept them both away in a torrent of passion.

At the moment of surrender, Thorn quaked with the power of gratification, while Brittany's body answered his burning desire. A soft groan was torn from Brittany's throat as Thorn fired her desire and then satisfied her needs.

Their bodies cooled and their heartbeats slowed as the shadows of night crept across the cottage.

A cool breeze stirred the curtains at the window while the two lovers nestled together.

After wandering for so long and living in fear, Brittany was afraid to trust Thorn. With him she felt safe, and for the moment cherished, but was this all an illusion that would disappear with the morning sun?

"This wasn't supposed to happen," Thorn told her, still clasping her to him. "But when I am near you, all I can think of is the pleasure I find with you."

She raised her head to look at him, feeling warmed by his admission. "Thorn, I will always want you to find pleasure with me."

With a disturbed expression, he looked into her eyes. "I want to take care of you and make you feel safe. I thought I owed you that much. My intentions were good"—he smiled—"but my flesh is weak."

"Why do I detect a note of apology in you, Thorn?"

"Because I *am* apologizing. This should never have happened between us at this time. So many things stand in our way. I owe you—"

Her breath came out in a hiss, and she moved away from him. "You owe me nothing, Thorn. It was I who thrust myself upon you when I came on board your ship. If anyone is indebted, it has to be me."

His expression was sorrowful. "I have hurt you again, and that was not my intention, Brittany. I have problems in my life, and I do not want to make you a part of them. Although I am not certain I can keep you from being pulled in to them, I am sure as hell going to try."

"I do not understand."

"I prefer not to go into what occurred in Washington. But suffice it to say that you might still be in danger from the Turks. I feel it is best if few people know you are at Stoddard Hill."

"Thorn, it would not surprise me if your government wants to turn me over to the Turkish government—which is, of course, Sultan Selim. Is that what happened?"

He was amazed at her quick mind, but he thought it best not to alarm her. "The Turkish government does not dictate to Washington."

She sat up with a perplexed expression on her face. "Why do you speak in riddles and tell me nothing, Thorn? I should think you know by now that I will not swoon at the first sight of danger."

He ran a frustrated hand through his hair. "If you insist on knowing, I was asked to send you back to Turkey."

"Yet you have decided not to?"

"Of course I won't. You are my wife. I anticipated that something just like this might happen, which is one of the reasons I married you. Even the United States government cannot make a man give up his own wife to another government."

She moved off the bed and pulled her gown over her head. "So that is the real reason you married me?"

"That and others."

"It seems that once again you are caught up in the intrigue that surrounds me, Thorn. You have troubles of your own, and did not need the added burden of my difficulties."

He smiled at her. "Even before we met, I was drawn into your difficulties. If you will recall, I had not laid eyes on you when the Turkish Navy let loose their volley."

Her eyes held a haunted expression. "So you married me to keep me from falling into the hands of the sultan. Is that why, Thorn?"

He sat on the side of the bed and pulled on his trousers. "Why did you accept me as your husband?" he said, answering her question with a question of his own.

She shook her head, her eyes sad. "Perhaps we were both a bit hasty in deciding to be married. If I had asked my father's family, I feel certain they would have intervened with the government, and I could have remained in this country under their protection."

"Perhaps," he agreed. "But if I were faced with the same choice, I would act no differently. There was no time to do otherwise."

"I have given you nothing, Thorn, while you have sacrificed your bachelorhood for me."

The blue of his eyes deepened. "It has been my pleasure to know you, Brittany Stoddard. Whatever the reason, and whatever the outcome, your life and mine have become intertwined."

Proudly, she raised her head and forced a smile. "I am certain it has been no pleasure for you to be at odds with your government because of me."

His eyes swept across her face. "There have been compensations."

Sadness weighed heavily on her heart. Thorn had married her for all the wrong reasons. Each day, she depended on him more and more. If this was love, why did it have to hurt so much? she wondered. Why did his casual manner tear at her heart?

She turned away from him, fearing he would read the hurt in her eyes. "Being your wife is one of the hardest things I have been called upon to do. Given the choice, I am not sure I would agree to marry you again."

He came up behind her, but did not touch her. "I know that life here at Stoddard Hill cannot be pleasant for you. I am aware of Wilhelmina's vindictiveness toward you. And, since my father's illness, the plantation has fallen on hard times. The kitchens are unorganized, and the fields have not been cultivated. Was it a mistake for me to drag you into my troubles?"

She turned around, glancing up at him with rounded eyes. "I know that Stoddard Hill will one day bloom again, and I do not really mind your stepmother's viciousness, but I have been troubled by some of her insinuations."

His eyes became veiled. "Such as?"

"I . . . she has implied that she was the cause of your leaving Stoddard Hill in the first place."

He glanced past her, to the garden beyond the window. "In that, she spoke the truth."

Brittany lowered her eyes, unwilling to believe that Thorn would covet his father's wife. "She also hinted that you and she had been . . . lovers." She raised her eyes to his, feeling sick inside that she should question Thorn's honor.

"If Wilhelmina were speaking the truth, Brittany, what would be your feelings be toward me?"

"If it is true, I will be very disappointed in you, Thorn, and you will not be the man I thought you were."

His nostrils flared. "What did Wilhelmina say to you?"

She lowered her head. "It is of no importance."

Seeing the doubt in her eyes, he gripped her chin and forced her to look at him. "I say it is important to you."

Her gaze flickered. "I do not want to talk about Wilhelmina."

He sighed wearily and took her hand, leading her to the bed. When he sat her down, he pulled up a chair and sat opposite her.

"What I am about to tell you, I have never told anyone else. I find the whole incident distasteful, but I can see I owe you the truth."

She shook her head vigorously, ashamed that she had lowered herself to pry into matters that had happened to Thorn before she came into his life. "You do not owe me anything, Thorn. Keep your counsel, and I will keep mine."

He gave her a half-smile. "Are you keeping secrets from me?"

She met his eyes without flinching. "Yes, I suppose I am."

He stared at her long and hard before he spoke. "Nonetheless, I will tell you this: The reason I left Stoddard Hill was because my father thought I had seduced his wife."

Brittany's face whitened as she waited for Thorn to deny that he had been a party to such an atrocity. "Surely you would never betray your father," she cried out.

He took her hand and studied it. "What matters is that my father believed it, so he ordered me to leave Stoddard Hill."

She hated herself for asking, but she had to know. "You were never her lover, were you?"

He took a steady breath. "You asked for the truth, and it is not easy to tell." He griped Brittany's shoulders, wishing he knew the words that would make her understand. "Yes, I was once her lover."

Brittany's heart shattered, and an unwelcome tear trailed down her cheek. "I would not have thought she was . . . that Wilhelmina was the kind of woman who would attract you." She pushed his hands away, not wanting him to touch her. "I am not a very good judge of character, am I?"

He chest felt tight, and he had a hard time taking a deep breath. "It's not what you imagine, Brittany. All I ask is that you trust me."

He stood up and held out his hand, and she reluctantly placed her hand in his. "I will walk you to the house, and you can make yourself ready to go into Charleston." His smile did not reach his eyes. "I do have one bit of good news. Cappy has found a buyer for my ship."

"A buyer?"

"Yes. Some woman wants to buy the *Victorious*. So you see, all is not lost."

Brittany could not meet his eyes, fearing he would guess that she was the woman behind the sale of the *Victorious*.

"We have many good things in our lives, Thorn. Your father is much improved, and I will soon have Achmed back. The sun always shines after a storm."

He took her arm and led her out into the garden. "And who armed you with that bit of wisdom?"

"My mother."

"Ah, yes, the English Rose."

Chapter Thirty-one

The driver guided the carriage beneath a vine-covered archway and up the winding road that led to Johnson Plantation house. The horses clopped along the hard-packed road beneath a canopy of blue.

Brittany sat beside Thorn, every nerve in her body tense with apprehension.

"Are you certain Achmed is here?" she asked.

"I am told that he is indeed here."

She worked her fingers into her lace gloves. "I never realized how much he had meant in my life until he was taken away. I am not happy with this man who took him."

"You will have to understand, Brittany, that Mr. Johnson may not be the villian in this. He must have purchased Achmed, thinking it was a legitimate sale. It is the slavers who are to blame."

"I find them all equally guilty. To me, no man, woman, or child should ever have to suffer the indignity of being bought and sold like cattle. I know about your slave auctions. My own mother was once placed on a slave block, and she has told me of that indignity."

Thorn studied Brittany's face. "I wonder how your mother came to be the wife of the Grand Vizier. Did Lord Simijin take her away from the auction?"

"Yes, and we can be grateful that Simijin was the one who bought my mother that day. Later, after my mother became Simijin's only wife, she asked him to release all his slaves, and because he loved her, he complied with her wishes immediately. Of course, many of them, like Achmed, remained because they loved my mother. I never thought Achmed would have to suffer such an atrocity."

Thorn looked past Brittany to the ivy-covered plantation house. "In the South, slavery is a way of life. As vile as it is, it will probably take years to be abolished."

The carriage came to a halt, and Thorn stepped down and then swung Brittany to the ground while Mr. and Mrs. Johnson walked slowly down the wide steps to greet them.

Ina Johnson was a shy little woman, with black hair and equally black eyes. She hung on to her heavyset, boisterous husband as if she needed his protection.

Theodore Johnson was the first to speak. He introduced himself and his wife, looking apologetic. "I was sorry to hear that I was a party to a blatant deception, Mrs. Stoddard. Had I known the slave belonged to you, I would have notified you immediately."

Brittany was in no mood to appease Mr. Johnson's conscience. She was disturbed that she did not see Achmed. "Where is he?" she demanded. "If you have harmed him in any way, it will go hard with you."

Ina Johnson's eyes took on a nervous twitch. "Just because you are from Stoddard Hill, there is no need to talk down to us, or to threaten us. We . . . made an honest mistake and cannot be . . ."

Brittany glanced past the woman to her husband. "Bring Achmed to me at once."

The man shifted his eyes away from her piercing glance. "I regret to tell you that I had to have him . . . whipped."

Thorn moved forward, and Johnson quickly stepped back. "You *what!*" Thorn hissed between clenched teeth. "You informed my first mate that Achmed had not been harmed."

Theodore Johnson shifted his stance. "Well, you see it's like this. We knew you was coming after Achmed today, so we decided, since we had lost money on him, we might at least have the use of . . . We put him in with three of our strongest breeders. When he refused to . . . well you know, I had him stripped and beaten. We never tolerate disobedience on this plantation."

Brittany whirled on the man. "You fool! Achmed could not do what you asked. He is a eunuch. Surely he must have told you that."

Johnson's face paled beneath his tan. "He is a stubborn one. I can assure you, he told us nothing of the sort. I had no idea . . ."

"Of course he would not admit the truth to you," Brittany said angrily. "Achmed is a private man, and a proud one. Why should he admit anything to you?" Tears glistened in her eyes. "Take me to him at once."

Thorn gave Theodore Johnson a warning glance. "You had better do as she says."

Johnson cleared his throat. "I had thought that I might offer you seventeen hundred dollars for Achmed."

Brittany became further enraged. "You insult me, sir. Achmed is a free man, and no one is going to buy and sell him. I want to see him at once."

Thorn stepped toward Theodore Johnson, his eyes blazing. "If I were you, I would do what my wife says without delay."

The man pushed his wife up the steps, urging her to go into the house. "Follow me," he said to Thorn. "I have him at the slave quarters."

Thorn took Brittany's arm, and they walked beside Mr. Johnson. Brittany was so angry she did not trust herself to speak. When they came to a building set apart from the others, Johnson motioned them inside.

"This is the infirmary. Achmed is being treated here. As you will observe, he has received the best of care."

"He would not need to be treated at all if it were not for you," Brittany said with feeling. She pushed Mr. Johnson aside and entered the long, narrow building with its dirt floors. When her eyes adjusted to the darkness, she saw three straw mattresses on the floor.

She rushed forward, examining each face and finding Achmed on the last mattress. He was lying on his stomach, and she cried out in anguish when she saw the angry red welts cut deeply into his back.

She dropped down beside the gentle giant, tears blinding her. "Oh, Achmed, Achmed, they have hurt you."

Achmed's eyes opened, and he tried to rise. "Little mistress, is that you, or am I dreaming again?"

She gripped his hand. "You are not dreaming; I have come to take you away from here."

"Do not let them hit me again, mistress. And forgive me because the money Lord Simijin gave me was stolen by the slaver."

A deep sob escaped her throat, and she turned to Theodore Johnson. "You have done sorry work here, sir. You have hurt the gentlest soul I know."

The man had no answer for her, but turned his eyes away from her accusing glance.

Thorn pulled Brittany to her feet and then motioned for Johnson to assist him. "Take it easy, Achmed," Thorn said as he helped the man to his feet. "We are going to take you home. No one will ever hit you again."

Achmed had been made comfortable on the third floor at Stoddard Hill. While Esmeralda had refused to climb the stairs to Achmed's room, she had agreed to mix one of her healing potions for his wounds, and his pain had lessened.

Ben no longer required constant care, and was able to get out of bed for long periods, and Brittany spent much of her time going up the stairs between Ben and Achmed's rooms.

Thorn had left for Charleston the night he had brought Achmed home, and Brittany had not heard from him since. An uneasy quiet hung over Stoddard Hill, as if everyone was waiting for something to happen.

Brittany had just peeked into Achmed's room to find him sleeping. When she applied more salve to his wounds, he hardly stirred. She was glad to see that his back was healing nicely, and she expected him to be up and about within a week.

Poor Achmed had paid dearly for accompanying her to America.

Brittany moved down the stairs to the second floor, thinking she would go to Ben's room to read to him before lunch. When she heard whispered voices in the hallway, she pressed her back against the wall. Wilhelmina and Dr. Cross were engaged in what appeared to be a struggle.

"You have lost all reason, Wilhelmina. What you ask is impossible," George Cross was saying.

Wilhelmina glared at him. "You will do as I say, George. You are in too deep to think you can walk away now."

Brittany turned her face away when Dr. Cross pulled Wilhelmina into his arms and boldly fondled her breasts. "You know I will do anything for you," he said in a husky voice. "All it takes for me to be happy is to get between your legs."

Brittany felt her stomach churn. She had come to suspect that Wilhelmina and the doctor were lovers; now she was certain. It made her sick to watch the disgusting display. Had Wilhelmina no shame? How could she carry on so right before her husband's bedroom?

Brittany did not look again until she heard a door open and close. When she glanced up, the hallway was empty. Apparently Wilhelmina had taken her lover into her bedroom.

Brittany hurried through the hallway and down to the first level, not wanting to encounter Wilhelmina. How would she ever face that woman now that she knew the truth about her and George Cross?

Brittany wanted to breathe in fresh air and to get away from the oppressive feeling that hung over the house. She ran out the door and down the long stretch of lawn that led to the Ashley River.

Standing in the cleansing air, she watched the muddy water wash against the shore. For several days, Brittany had managed to keep from thinking that Wilhelmina and Thorn had once been lovers. Now she shuddered when she thought of Thorn standing in the doctor's place.

She found it difficult to believe a man like Thorn would

betray his own father to be with a woman as unworthy as Wilhelmina. She wiped the tears from her eyes, feeling strangely detached from the people who lived at Stoddard Hill. Everyone here was steeped in deceit. Did she really belong here? One thing was certain, she was no longer an innocent. She had witnessed the sordid side of life, and she did not like what she had seen.

Brittany was not aware that Thorn had come up behind her until he dangled her emerald necklace before her face. Since she had given the emerald to Cappy to buy the *Victorious*, she was shocked to see that it had fallen into Thorn's hands.

She turned to see his jaw tighten and his eyes burn with anger. "If I had wanted your help, I would have asked for it, Brittany. You must have thought you were very clever using an assumed name to buy the *Victorious*."

She felt as cold inside as the green stone in her hand. "I only meant to help."

"And you might have gotten away with it, if my solicitor had not been so honest. He saw you once when you were in Charleston, and he paid particular attention to this emerald. When it was given to him as payment for the *Victorious*, he recognized it immediately. You will find the rest of your jewels in your bedroom."

She held the necklace out to him. "Thorn, please take this. I want you to have it."

He jammed his hands into his pocket. "You don't know anything about a man's pride, Brittany. I want to be the one to give you jewels, not take them away from you."

She nodded in understanding. "I once told you that I do not understand many things about your country. I now realize that is even more true today."

"I am interested to know how you decided on the name Lady Jillianna Maridon?"

"That is my mother's maiden name." She reached out to him, but he igonored the gesture. "I meant only to help, Thorn. If I did wrong, I am sorry."

She turned and moved away, and he caught up with her. "I do not mean to appear ungrateful, Brittany, but never attempt to go behind my back like this again."

She turned furious green eyes on him. "*Me* go behind *your* back! How can you accuse me of such a thing, when you are the one who went behind Ben's back to bed his wife." She saw his face whiten, but still she continued. "I am sick of deception. I wish . . . I wish I had never come here."

He was silent for a long time. "I can see how you might believe the worst of me. I wish you had trusted me, Brittany."

"I do not know who to trust, or who is my friend. All I know is that when I saw Wilhelmina take Dr. Cross into her bedroom, all I could think of was you and her together."

He grabbed her arm and spun her around. "When did this happen?"

"Just a short while ago. It is possible that he is still there." She angrily brushed a tear from her cheek. "Are you jealous of the doctor?"

The look he gave her was chilling. "Think what you will, Brittany."

Brittany watched him move toward the house, wondering if she had told Thorn about Wilhelmina and the doctor out of spitefulness. She hoped that had not been her motive.

Wilhelmina trailed her finger down George Cross's stomach. "I think a fire would be the best way of getting rid of all three of them, George."

He grabbed and held her hand. "Are you crazed? We can't kill all three of them—someone would suspect!"

She looked at him ponderously. "Of course a fire would mean I would lose the house, but that can't be helped. Houses can be rebuilt."

"I won't do it, Wilhelmina."

She rubbed her naked body against him. "You will do it for me, won't you?"

George Cross never got a chance to answer, for at that

moment, the door was thrust open, and there stood Thorn and Cappy, looking like avenging angels.

Wilhelmina froze, her eyes wild with apprehension. "How dare you burst into my room like this, Thorn. Your father will have you . . ." Her voice trailed off, and she pulled the bed covers up over her nakedness.

"You have one hour to get your belongings together and get out, Wilhelmina! As you can see, I have Cappy here as a witness to your little indiscretion."

Thorn walked over to a cringing George Cross, reached down and yanked him out of bed. "And take your lover with you," he said, shoving the man with such force that he slammed into the wall and landed on the floor, gasping for breath.

Wilhelmina tossed her head defiantly. "You cannot make me leave."

"Oh, can't I? What if I told you that Cappy located a certain Mr. Deavers who is willing to tell the authorities how you and this man tried to poison my father, and how you hired Deavers to kill Brittany?"

Wilhelmina lowered her eyes. "I have no place to go," she said, knowing she would get no sympathy from Thorn Stoddard.

Thorn's eyes were cold, and there was a look of distaste on his face. "Perhaps you can persuade your lover to take care of you."

Thorn turned his gaze on Dr. Cross, who had managed to scramble to his feet and pull on his trousers. "For the good of your practice, Doctor, I suggest you might find another state more to your liking." Thorn's expression hardened. "If it were not for my father, I would see you both hanged. But, make no mistake about it, if I ever find either of you in South Carolina again, I will turn you over to the authorities."

Cappy watched the color drain from Wilhelmina's face, for she knew she was beaten. Finally she had been caught at her bold game. There was no pity in Cappy's heart either for her or the doctor, for they had conspired to do murder.

After Thorn and Cappy left the room, Wilhelmina slipped out of bed, her face a mask of rage. "I will not have it," she cried out. "Thorn cannot put me out."

A chastened George Cross tucked his shirt into his trousers. "You have no choice, Wilhelmina. It's either leave, or be arrested. Thorn Stoddard meant what he said."

She made a wide sweep with her hand. "I cannot give all this up."

"You will have me," he reminded her. "I will take care of you."

Hysterical laughter bubbled out of her mouth. "I have you! Good Lord, man, do you know what I will be losing?"

"But you *have* lost, Wilhelmina," he reminded her.

Her shoulders slumped, and she dropped down on the bed. Yes, she had lost everything. She tried not to think about that night so long ago, when she had stood in a moonlit garden with Thorn, and he had pledged her his love. That was the night she had lost. That night she had the world at her fingertips, and she had thrown it all away.

A short time later, a buggy pulled away from the house and rattled down the dusty road. No one had come forward to wish Wilhelmina good-bye, and no one would grieve at her leaving.

As the buggy pulled out of the gate, she turned back to look for the last time upon Stoddard Hill.

Chapter Thirty-two

Cappy was raising the new sails over the *Victorious*, because Thorn had insisted that she be shipshape when she was handed over to the Turks.

Out of the corner of his eye, Cappy watched the Turkish ship approach Charleston Harbor. It was close enough for him to see that the name of the ship was the *Marmora*. With a feeling of dread, he sent Francisco to keep an eye on the Turks while he finished the last task he would perform aboard the *Victorious*.

The United States government had ordered Captain Stoddard to turn his vessel over to the Turkish government. More than likely, the crew aboard the *Marmora* was here to take command of the *Victorious*.

After the sails were in place, Cappy instructed the crew that the decks were to be swabbed until they gleamed. This was a grand old ship, and she would be clean from fore to aft when she was relinquished.

"Cappy," Francisco called out, hurrying up the gangplank, his eyes darting back behind him. "There is a Turk and a woman coming on board. I don't know who they are."

Cappy looked first at the tall, distinguished man, who was dressed in long, flowing robes. He appeared to be someone of importance.

His eyes went next to the woman at the man's side, and Cappy was taken by surprise with her delicate beauty. She was like a golden angel in the white gown that flowed with each graceful motion. If Cappy had ever seen a more beautiful woman, he could not remember when. As she drew closer, he saw her green eyes, and he knew immediately who she was.

"The English Rose," he whispered to himself.

"May I come aboard?" the man called out.

Cappy also knew who the man was. "Yes, Lord Simijin, come aboard; but have a care, for the deck is wet."

"You know who I am?" Simijin asked in surprise.

"I figured it out."

"I fear I do not know who you are," Simijin said apologetically.

Cappy came to full attention. "I am first mate of the *Victorious*. Name's Cappy Hamish."

Simijin glanced around. "Is your captain on board?"

"No, sir. He's at his house in town. Can I be of assistance to you?"

Simijin saw that the crew swabbing the deck had paused in their work to stare at them with interest. "Can we go somewhere where we can talk?"

"Of course, Lord Simijin. The captain won't mind if we use his cabin." Cappy dared to steal another look at the beautiful English Rose, and he saw worry reflected in her green eyes. "Come with me," he said kindly, knowing she was worried about her daughter. He wanted to assure her that Brittany was safe.

Jillianna looked around the captain's cabin without really seeing it. When she and Simijin were alone with the first mate, she could no longer contain her questions. "Do you know my daughter, Mr. Hamish?"

"Yes, Lady Jillianna. I know her quite well."

She reached out to him, her green eyes swimming with tears. "Is she here? Is she unharmed?"

"Yes, madame. But you will want to talk to my captain about her."

Jillianna sank down in a chair, her eyes pleading. "I have come a long way, Mr. Hamish, and I cannot tell you of the concern I have for my daughter. Please do not make me wait another moment for word of her. I beseech you to tell me everything you know."

Cappy knew he could not deny her desperate plea. As he looked into luminous green eyes so like Brittany's, he wondered if any man living could deny the English Rose her slightest request.

Thorn rushed up the stairs, calling Brittany's name. When he got no response, he looked inside his bedroom, but she was not there. Anger tugged at his mind as he retraced his steps. He had in his pocket a bill of sale for the *Victorious* that proved Brittany had been meddling in his affairs once again.

Standing on the back porch, his eyes made a wide sweep of the lawn, and he located Brittany by the river. Still angry, he made his way down to her.

When he drew even with her, he waved a paper in her face. "Even after I told you not to, you still interfered."

She shook her head in bewilderment. "I do not know what you are accusing me of."

"Don't you?"

"No."

"I have here a paper signed by Lady Jillianna Maridon. Who would have done such a thing but you?"

She glanced at the paper he shoved at her. "I do not know unless . . . unless . . ." Her heart pounded with joy as she recognized the handwriting. She glanced up toward the house, and mouthed the words: "Mama."

Thorn turned to see a woman walking slowly toward them. The setting sun was behind her, and it shone brilliantly upon her golden head.

Brittany ran toward the lovely vision, with her arms outstretched. "Mama," she cried. "Mama!"

Brittany was enfolded in her mother's arms, and they both wept tears of happiness. Simijin joined the happy reunion, and Brittany went readily into his arms.

"This is the happiest day of my life," Brittany cried, hugging Simijin, then going back to her mother. "I cannot believe you are here!"

Jillianna held her daughter at arm's length and looked her over with a mother's eyes. "You have grown into a beautiful woman, my dearest. I have been so worried about you, but it seems my worries were unfounded." She glanced over Brittany's shoulder and saw the dark, handsome man walking toward them.

Jillianna smiled brightly at Thorn. She approached him and surprised him by putting her arms about him. "I know who you are, Thorn Stoddard. Lord Simijin and I have much to thank you for."

Thorn looked into the green eyes of the English Rose, and he knew why she was a legend. She had the same striking beauty as her daughter. "I assume you also know I am your daughter's husband?" he asked.

Jillianna laughed, and the sound of her laughter was magical. "Of course, I know—Cappy told me." She looked at Brittany and saw uncertainty in her eyes. "Come, my children, I have had a long, hot ride, and I want something cool to drink."

Jillianna placed her hand on her son-in-law's arm. "I really am grateful to you, Thorn Stoddard. Without you, my daughter would not be here today."

Simijin was walking with Brittany, and Jillianna saw pain in Thorn's eyes when he looked at her daughter.

"Your daughter is exceptional," he said.

"Of course she is," Jillianna readily agreed. "She always has been."

Thorn held out the paper with Jillianna's name on it. "Can I assume that you are responsible for this?"

"Cappy told me about your ship and how Brittany tried to help you. This was my little jest, and my way of telling you that the *Victorious* still belongs to you. The Turkish government no longer has a claim on the vessel. Simijin saw to that."

He threw his head back and laughed, charmed by the

mother, almost as much as he had been by the daughter. "I can only imagine the jolly chase you must lead Lord Simijin, madame."

She nodded her head. "Alas, it is true. You cannot imagine how much trouble I have cost my Simijin."

"If you are like your daughter, I can, madame." Thorn's eyes moved to Brittany, who was just ahead of them. She walked with her head leaning on Simijin's arm. "Indeed, I can well imagine."

"I was surprised to find my daughter married to you, Captain Stoddard."

He let out his breath. "Not half as surprised as I was."

She studied him closely. "I can see that you love her," she said softly.

He gazed down at the beauty on his arm. "If you can see it, why can't your daughter?"

"Have you told her?"

"Not in so many words."

Jillianna paused and glanced back down the slope at the Ashley River, with its meandering twists and turns. "A woman likes to be told that she's loved and cherished. We have already agreed that Brittany is special. Tell her how you feel. I see sadness in her eyes that should not be there."

Thorn followed Jillianna's eyes to the river. "I will never know a contented day until she is happy."

Jillianna felt her throat throb as she looked into blue eyes soft with love for her daughter. She smiled and tugged at his arm, leading him forward. "Then you have it in your hands to create happiness for you and Brittany both."

"I am not certain how she feels about me. She believes me guilty of a great wrong."

Jillianna lifted a delicate eyebrow. "*Are* you guilty?"

He answered without hesitating. "Not in this instance." His eyes were seeking. "Do you believe me?"

"Of course, Captain, but I am not the one you must convince."

Thorn was thoughtful for a moment. "At least I do not

have to fear that Brittany will leave me and return to Turkey with you."

"Do not be too sure, Captain. You see, Sultan Selim has relinquished the throne, and Sultan Mustafa now sits in his place. My husband and I have received a formal apology from Mustafa, and all charges have been dropped against you. There is nothing to prevent Brittany from returning to Constantinople."

Thorn's jaw tightened. "Nothing but me, madame," he challenged. "I will not easily let her go."

Jillianna's eyes searched his. "Good. That's what I wanted to hear. I can see that my daughter will have a good life with you, Captain. It's up to you to see that she stays. I can tell you for a certainty that if Simijin thinks she is unhappy, he will want to take her home with us." She looked at him, a faint smile tugging her lips. "You may have defeated the Turkish Navy, but you have not yet come up against my Simijin."

Thorn returned her smile. "You are wrong, madame. I came up against him when he was determined that I would transport your daughter to safety."

Dinner went well. Ben had been well enough to come downstairs and join in the reunion. Simijin and Jillianna were the perfect guests, listening to their host's plans to make Stoddard Hill a productive plantation once more.

Brittany and Thorn were strangely silent, leaving Jillianna to observe them more closely. It was apparent to her that her daughter was most unhappy, and she intended to find out why.

After dinner, the gentleman moved into the parlor, and Jillianna drew her daughter aside. "Walk with me. I want to hear all about your life here in America."

It was a brilliant night, with stars twinkling in the ebony sky. A cool breeze was blowing from the direction of the Ashley River.

"This is a lovely place to live and raise children, Brittany. I like Mr. Stoddard, and," she smiled, "I adore that handsome husband of yours."

"Mama, Thorn is wonderful. I want to be his wife, but there are certain events that stand between us."

"If you love him, you should do everything you can to remove any obstacles that hinder that love."

"I want to, but I do not know how."

Jillianna took Brittany's face between her hands. "My dearest love, I wish I could take you home with me and wrap the high walls of the palace around you to keep you safe forever—but that cannot be. In my heart, I realize that your happiness lies with Thorn Stoddard."

"I love him, Mama, but I do not think he loves me."

Jillianna knew that she could not help Brittany in this, because if her daughter was to learn to cherish love, she must find it for herself. "You must talk to Thorn and find out how he feels."

"And if he does not love me?"

"You made a commitment to him, and you are his wife. But if you are going to be unhappy with him, then you might want to consider coming home."

"I do not think I could ever leave him, Mama."

"Therein lies your answer, Brittany."

A servant had helped Ben upstairs to bed, and Thorn and Simijin were deep in conversation.

"I am glad that Achmed is recovering from his wounds," Simijin said. "He has not had an easy time of it, has he?"

"Not at all," Thorn agreed. "He is to be commended for his loyalty. He stood by Brittany at great risk to himself."

"Yes, that is why he was chosen to be her protector." Simijin stared at Thorn. "It seems I chose well when I placed her in your care, as well."

Thorn raised his brandy glass to study the contents. "There were times when I did not thank you for having her smuggled on board the *Victorious*."

"And now? What do you feel now?"

"Humble, uncertain, frightened for the first time in my

life that a little slip of a girl does not love me as much as I love her."

Simijin nodded. "I know that feeling. I am certain you will reach the same conclusion with her that I once reached with her mother."

"Which is?"

"There is no meaning to life unless there is commitment and love."

"The world envies you your good fortune, Lord Simijin, because you have the English Rose."

Simijin leaned back and observed Thorn. "And you have the daughter of the English Rose. Treasure her well, and be good to her, because if you do not, I will come and take her from you, for she is like my own daughter."

Brittany walked with her mother to the room that had been prepared for her and Simijin. After a warm embrace, Brittany's footsteps lagged as she approached her own bedroom.

She opened the door to find a lamp glowing and the bed turned down, but with disappointment she saw that there was no sign of Thorn.

She undressed, blew out the lamp, and slipped into bed, hoping Thorn would come to her. She lay there for over an hour, listening to the settling of the house. But there were no familiar footsteps in the hallway, and Thorn did not come.

Brittany was tortured by unanswered questions. Where was Wilhelmina, and how deep were Thorn's feelings for his stepmother?

At last she knew Thorn was not coming to her bed. Unable to sleep, she got up and moved to the window. Pulling aside the curtain, she gazed out to the river that looked like a winding silvery ribbon.

Suddenly she knew where she would find Thorn. He would be in the cottage.

She pulled her nightgown over her head and tossed it across a chair. She quickly dressed and ran out of the room and down the stairs. If Thorn would not come to her, she would go to him!

As Brittany moved down the path to the cottage, she came to a sudden halt. Suppose Thorn was in the cottage with Wilhelmina?

Bravely, she put one foot in front of the other. She had to know if Thorn preferred Wilhelmina to her.

As she approached the cottage, she found it was in darkness, and she almost decided to return to the house. What was she so frightened of? Thorn was a man of fine character, and yet he had admitted that there had been something between him and Wilhelmina.

She paused on the doorstep. No, Thorn would not touch that woman—he could not have. He had asked her to believe him, and she was trying awfully hard to do just that.

She glanced down the grassy slope where the Ashley River touched upon Stoddard land. Tonight she would find out if there was a future between herself and Thorn.

Her hand was on the doorknob when she saw the lone figure standing at the river's edge. It was Thorn, and he was alone.

Chapter Thirty-three

The moon hung in the sky like a great ball of fire, illuminating the river and giving the countryside a soft golden glow.

Noiselessly, Brittany approached Thorn, who had not moved from the spot where she had first observed him. Although she could not see his face, she could sense the restlessness in him, and she felt like an intruder in his world.

Thorn turned slowly toward her, and when she saw his tortured expression, she almost cried out.

"It's late for you to be about, Brittany."

"Yes, I . . . when you did not come to . . . I knew you would be here."

"Did you?"

"Thorn," she moved closer to him, "will you talk to me?"

"Yes, if you like," he said without looking at her. "You want to know about Wilhelmina?"

"You said you would tell me about her, but if you would rather not . . ."

"I owe you an explanation. I assume you know she is gone and will not be coming back."

"I was not certain what had happened to her, since you did not tell me and I did not want to ask Ben."

"My father knows only that she left. I did not think it was prudent to tell him I forced Wilhelmina to leave. As I had long suspected, but could not prove, she and Dr. Cross were lovers and had conspired to harm both you and my father."

"I had come to that conclusion on my own. Are you sorry she has gone?"

He spun around to look at her. "Good God, no. How

could you believe that? Do you have so little faith in me that you think I would—" He shuddered, unable to go on. "No, I am not sorry she is gone."

He was quiet for a long time, and both of them watched the restless movement of the river. At last Thorn spoke. "I was very young when I first met Wilhelmina. She was older than I, and more worldly. I thought that I loved her, but now I know what love . . . I know what I felt for her was not love. You once pointed out to me the difference between desire and love."

"You desired her?"

"Yes. But, that was a very long time ago. I quickly became disillusioned with her, when I discovered she had been with many men before me. I might not have minded so much had she not represented herself as an innocent. When I decided not to see her again, she said she would get even with me— and she did." ———

He gazed up at the moon, as if he were remembering. "I never guessed at the extent of her hatred, until a year later when she came to Stoddard Hill as my father's wife. In that year, I had forgotten all about her."

"You no longer wanted her?"

"No, and I can say in all honesty that she never crossed my mind."

"You do not have to say anymore if you would rather not, Thorn."

"Let me tell you what happened so there will never be any doubt in your mind that you have heard the truth." He drew in a ragged breath. "One night, when my father was away from home, Wilhelmina came to my room. I tried to send her away, but she was determined to remain."

He paused as if it was difficult to continue. At last his voice came out in a whisper. "When she embraced me, I tried to push her away. Unknown to either of us, my father had returned, and when he saw us together, he drew the wrong conclusion. Wilhelmina made it appear as though I were seducing her."

Brittany could hear the anger in Thorn's voice. "What did you do?"

"Before I could explain, my father ordered me to leave Stoddard Hill. I left without taking anything with me. I did not come back until now. The rest you can guess."

"I cannot believe your father thought you guilty of betrayal."

"Why not, Brittany? *You* believed it."

Her eyes were swimming with tears. "Yes, I did, and I am so sorry. Will you forgive me for a very human failing?"

He touched her hair ever so softly, and then withdrew his hand. "What human failing would that be, Brittany?"

"Jealousy," she admitted. "I was jealous of Wilhelmina when I thought you loved her, and I wanted to scratch her eyes out."

His expression was cynical. "You have no reason to be jealous of anyone. Since you came into my life, I have not even thought about another woman."

"Are you saying you l-like me, Thorn?"

He suddenly gripped her by the shoulders and stared into her face. "Look at me, Brittany. I am a man who stands on the brink of uncertainty. I have married you, without courting or wooing you. I brought you to my family home, unknowingly placing you in danger. I have left you to your own devices, seldom coming to your bed. How can I expect you to know how I feel about you?"

She was trying to understand what he was telling her. "Why did you try to avoid my bed?"

"Because," he blurted out, "I was afraid that if I made demands on you, you would want to leave me. And that is the last thing I wanted you to do. You cannot guess at the nights I stood outside your room, wanting to go in to you."

"Oh, Thorn, I wish you had. Where did you spend those nights, if not with me?"

He nodded to the cottage. "Here—alone."

She glanced down at the ever-restless river that rippled in

the moonlight. "Mother and Simijin will be leaving in three weeks' time. Achmed will be going with them."

He closed his eyes, dreading to hear that she had sought him out to tell him she would be going with them. "I thought Achmed would never leave you. Does this mean you will be going, too?"

"Do you want me to go, Thorn?"

"I have been standing here thinking that since you no longer need me to protect you, I might lose you, Brittany. I know you can return to Turkey with your mother and Lord Simijin now that Sultan Selim is no longer a threat."

Thorn still had his grip on her, and he pulled her slowly toward him until her head rested against his shoulder. "I cannot bear to think what my life would be without you. I can never go back to the way it was before I met you. If I thought it would do any good, I would beg you not to leave me."

She looked up at him, catching her breath at the love that was shining in his eyes. She saw his throat working convulsively, and she buried her face against his chest as happiness rippled through her body.

"Oh, Thorn, I doubt I could leave you if you threw me out. I love you so desperately. I have from the beginning."

She heard his quick intake of breath, and he slowly raised her chin. He saw tears swimming in her eyes, and he knew that she spoke the truth. His arms tightened about her like bands of iron. "Oh, God, if you knew how I have agonized over you leaving me."

She reached up and gently touched his face. "You once told me that love was for fools and dreamers."

"Yes, and I am guilty of being both a fool and a dreamer. If only I could have your love, I would be a most fortunate man."

"Oh, Thorn, how can you not know how I feel about you? I have loved you for a very long time."

His look of uncertainty was suddenly replaced by one of triumph. He gave a loud whoop and picked her up in his arms. "Little dancer, you had better mean that, because no power on earth will make me give you up now."

She felt joy sing through her heart. "You have not said you love me," she reminded him. "At least not in words."

His voice trembled with emotion. "I love you with every beat of my heart," he whispered. "My life has been an upheaval since you came into it, and still I love you." He smiled. "You danced your way into my heart one night, and there you have remained."

At last he released her and set her on her feet. He turned her toward the river, while his hand slid about her waist and he brought her body against his.

"Will you be contented to be a planter's wife, little dancer?"

"Yes, oh, Thorn, yes."

His lips rested against her velvety-soft hair, and she knew that later he would take her into the cottage, and they would make love. But for now, they were both content to stand beneath the bright moon and watch the ageless Ashley River meander on its way to the sea.

With the wine-dark river as the backdrop and the scent of the climbing rose filling the air, Thorn held Brittany in his arms.

"Here my love, between the ebbing and the flowing of the river, I will make love to you through the years again and again. Here, before God, and on this land of my ancestors, I pledge you my heart for all eternity—and if God be willing, even beyond that."

CONSTANCE O'BANYON

The Blue Norther swept across the Texas plains with a fury that would alter lives and change destinies. It killed Shiloh's father, leaving her to run their struggling ranch and raise her little brother alone. It also stranded a feverish young Indian girl in their barn. Shiloh knew the Comanche would come for Moon Song sooner or later, but nothing could have prepared her for the fierce war chief who appeared at her door.

Shadowhawk was full of restless energy, like a wild animal that couldn't be tamed. And now he owed the blue-eyed beauty a debt of honor for saving his sister's life. Shiloh was *his* to protect, his to shield from the dangers of the frontier. He would spirit her away to his village, woo her in the way of his people and make her a woman beneath the magical light of a

Comanche Moon Rising

ISBN 13: 978-0-8439-6265-9

LISA COOKE

"Mega fun, fast-paced and with a sexy to-die-for hero—
my favorite kind of historical romance."

—Lori Foster on *Texas Hold Him*

A Midwife Crisis

THREE MEN AND A LADY

Katie's family has decided she needs a husband. And
when Katie's family puts their mind to something, it's as
good as done. In fact, they're so good, they've arranged
three fiancés for her in less than a week! What's a midwife
to do? Katie figures the best course is exactly what she
tells her patients: bear down and push through it.

Dr. John Keffer is used to helping people. It's why he
came back to the Appalachian Mountains—to build a
new practice and leave behind painful memories in the
big city. But usually his help is of a medical nature, not
advising the most captivating woman he's ever met which
man to wed. Especially when he's not even on the short
list. With a good dose of wooing, he hopes to convince
Katie that marrying *him* is just what the doctor ordered.

ISBN 13: 978-0-8439-6362-5

☐ **YES!**

Sign me up for the Historical Romance Book Club and send my FREE BOOKS! If I choose to stay in the club, I will pay only $8.50* each month, a savings of $6.48!

NAME: _____

ADDRESS: _____

TELEPHONE: _____

EMAIL: _____

☐ I want to pay by credit card.

☐ **VISA**   ☐ **MasterCard.**   ☐ **DISCOVER**

ACCOUNT #: _____

EXPIRATION DATE: _____

SIGNATURE: _____

Mail this page along with $2.00 shipping and handling to:
Historical Romance Book Club
PO Box 6640
Wayne, PA 19087
Or fax (must include credit card information) to:
610-995-9274
You can also sign up online at www.dorchesterpub.com.
*Plus $2.00 for shipping. Offer open to residents of the U.S. and Canada only.
Canadian residents please call 1-800-481-9191 for pricing information.
If under 18, a parent or guardian must sign. Terms, prices and conditions subject to change. Subscription subject to acceptance. Dorchester Publishing reserves the right to reject any order or cancel any subscription.